CHEROKEE WOMAN

Meet the Author

Elsa Leopold Watters was born in Cleveland, Ohio. While growing up, she lived in Lakewood, Ohio in the winters and on South Bass Island (Put-In-Bay) in Lake Erie during the summers.

Her interests in Indian culture began as a child when she used to hunt for arrowheads in the grape vineyards on South Bass Island, and read of the Ottawas who came to the Islands to hunt in the 1700s.

She also had a great-uncle who had fought with the Western Cavalry under General George Crook. This uncle was a great story teller, and left a lasting impression on Elsa.

Mrs. Watters has a bachelor's degree from Oberlin College, and has written two other stories about the Osage and Shawnee Indians in *Land Fever* and the Comanche and Apache Indians in *Hank*. She resides in Lakewood, Ohio.

CHEROKEE WOMAN

A Cry in the Wilderness

By

ELSA L. WATTERS

Library of Congress Catalog Card Number: 91-51234

ISBN: 0-923568-24-7

Typesetting / The Boufford Typesetters

Cover art / Nanci Grzesiak

Library of Congress Cataloging-in-Publication Data

Watters, Elsa L., 1906 —
    Cherokee woman : a cry in the wilderness / by Elsa L. Watters.
      p.   cm.
    Includes bibliographical references.
    ISBN 0-923568-24-7 : $13.95
    1. Cherokee Indians--History--Fiction.   I. Title.
PS3573.A863C47 1991
813'.54--dc20   91-51234
                                                CIP

PUBLISHED BY WILDERNESS ADVENTURE BOOKS
Fowlerville, Michigan 48864

Manufactured in the United States of America

In memory of my husband, Andy,
for his encouragement

And to my best critics, my daughters
Sally Burson and Nancy Russell

"THERE ARE TWO WORLDS: THE WORLD THAT WE CAN MEASURE BY LINE AND RULE, AND THE WORLD WE FEEL WITH OUR HEARTS AND IMAGINATION."

—LEIGH HUNT

And the Cherokee Indians experienced the utmost pain of both worlds. They were harassed and driven from their lands.

Contents

Preface

Before the Louisiana Purchase in 1803, the United States government was turning its eyes upon the West for expansion. Northeastern Indian tribes had felt the impact of this and now efforts were being made to push the Southeastern tribes westward. Routed from their homeland to make room for settlers who were interested in the cotton belt and purchasing low-priced land, the five civilized tribes were suffering.

The Cherokees, Creeks, Chickasaws, Chocktaws and Seminoles found themselves gradually moved farther west into Georgia, Tennessee and to lands beyond the Mississippi River.

It was during Andrew Jackson's presidency that the full effect of the effort to move the tribes was felt and the most desperate attempts to remain on their land occurred. Cherokees were the best educated and most easily adaptable to the white man's standards of living, and thus found it harder to consider a move.

The removal came about in three ways. First, treaties dealing with land cessions between the tribe and the United States government were broken; second, land was taken by Georgia illegally and the act condoned by the Federal government; third, methods of harassment were used, even theft of property and murder.

Finally, what was called the Jackson–Georgia machine (the alignment of Georgia state officials and the President), plus what became known as the Treaty Party (those who were disloyal to the Cherokee Nation and Chief John Ross) were joined together to fight the Ross Party. Ross and his loyal supporters formed three-fourths of the Cherokee Nation and fought through the media and legal processes from 1814 to 1838 for a means to remain on their land. The act of Congress, when the removal bill was passed by one vote, forced the Cherokees to move west of the Mississippi River by March, 1838. The disgraceful decision was the final blow to an exceptional people.

Some had large plantations and owned slaves. Some were wealthy farmers and merchants. They had adopted the white man's form of government and had a good judicial system. They learned English while attending Missionary School. They published a newspaper and had a Syllabary invented by George Gist (Sequoyah), writing and reading in Cherokee as well as in English. They were more advanced in some ways than their white brothers.

Thus the battle between Andrew Jackson, the Georgia state officials and a disloyal band (John Ridge's Treaty Party) went on against John Ross and his loyal Cherokees until the tragic ultimatum of removal when the long trek of 8,000 people began. Of that number, 4,000 died en route or upon arrival.

Acknowledgements

I wish to give credit to Grace Steele Woodward in her book, *Cherokees*, and to John Ehle in the book, *Trail of Tears*, for quotes by historical characters. Also credit to another author, Gloria Jahoda, for the information in *her* book, *Trail of Tears*.

I want to thank the personnel at the Lakewood Library for their help in furnishing me with material for the historical background for my novel.

And many thanks to my daughters, Sally and Nancy, for their encouragement and helpful criticism.

I

1814 - 1819

At dawn on a morning during The Moon of Falling Leaves piercing screams came from the cabins in a Cherokee village on Hiwassee River and there was a sound of fading hoofbeats. Only a few hours earlier, preparations had been made for the warriors, who were returning from a victorious battle against the Creeks under General Andrew Jackson.

Coughing and choking, the children tumbled from Great Wolf's cabin. Only eight-year-old Tsika lagged behind.

Niamhi shouted, "Go, Tsika. We can save nothing but our lives." The matriarch pulled at her daughter. "Star, hurry."

Star Flower ran from the cabin clutching a colorful shirt and holding a cradleboard that carried tiny papoose Micha.

Crying, they hovered together with their neighbors as they watched their homes burn.

Suddenly Tsika dashed toward the burning cabin and Star turned to her eldest son. "Arapho, stop her, she's going back."

Arapho caught her by the arm, but she pulled away.

"I'm going back. My kitten's in there."

Aiku saw his stubborn friend running toward the burning cabin and joined Arapho in a rush to stop her.

Just as she reached the threshold, he threw himself at her,

grasped her legs and they both fell. As the flames licked over them, Tsika's skirt caught fire.

"Roll, roll over." He pushed her from the doorway. "Look at you," he grumbled. "You try to look like the whites and see what it's got you. A burned leg."

"I know, and it hurts," she cried.

"Of course it hurts, but you're lucky I came along."

"Oh, boys! I'm crying because my kitten's died."

Arapho and Aiku helped her to stand, then her brother said, "Now go to Mama, Tsika. Aiku and I must help put out the fires," and Tsika was left to limp to the large council hall where the families had congregated.

On their way Aiku said to her brother, "Tsika is like a woodland creature, fun to chase. She's stubborn, but someday when I marry her, I will tame her."

Arapho laughed. "No one will ever tame Tsika, Aiku. Best you not try. Hurry. The runner said our braves would be here soon and we must then join the ball play to celebrate."

Aiku was anxious to see his father, White Fox, but also was afraid to see him, for while the warriors were away, his mother died giving birth to a papoose. He wished with all his heart someone else would convey this sad news.

"I'll help put out the fires, Arapho, but I don't feel like ball play for I must tell my father about Soft Wings."

"Don't be cowardly, my friend. Your father will take this like a true chief, calmly and bravely."

"He is brave about war and wild animals, but this is very different."

Tsika sobbed, "Father will scold me, Aiku said so."

"Perhaps. He will certainly want to know why you are burned when the rest of us are unharmed," Star said as she gently rubbed grease on the burned skin.

"Why did they do this? I thought we would be safe here."

"Tribes will always be raiding one another."

"But it wasn't another tribe, Mama. No moccasin prints. Only boot footprints outside our cabin."

"Oh no, the Unaka threaten us again. They want us to leave this land." Star wrapped Tsika's leg with a strip of her petticoat, then turned to speak to Niamhi.

"The same thing happened when we were driven from our homes in the North Carolina mountains and probably our warriors did the same thing to the Creeks under Jackson. Oh why is there so much fighting?" Star wiped her tears away. "It is so sad."

"You cry for us, Mama?"

"I cry for all of us—for our land—for our children."

"Don't cry, Mama. I won't let them take it away from us."

Star rocked the gangling child in her arms. "No, little one. Your papa and your brothers will take care of everything. You are going to be a pretty Indian maiden, not a warrior. You will dress in fine full skirts, do women's work and have many fine papooses."

"Aiku makes fun of my long skirts, because he and his father still wear moccasins, and doeskin tunics and blankets."

"Yes, I know and they wear guns and knives in their belts."

"Ha!" grunted Niamhi. "Soon squaws wear knives and guns.

"Don't give her ideas, my mother. Already she carries bows and arrows, like the boys."

"And you! You wear dress like whites. Wear long skirts. They laugh at us."

"You're wrong, my mother. There are good and bad whites, just like there are good and bad Cherokees. Admire what the Cherokee Nation is doing to get along with them. Have we not adopted their form of government? The missionaries gave us plows to cultivate the land and some of the Cherokee landowners have even married white women."

Niamhi's dark eyes shot daggers at her daughter-in-law. "You even grab that colored skirt out of burning cabin, you love whites so. Whites burn our homes?"

Star smiled, "I had to save something."

Star turned to speak to Tsika, but she was gone.

"Juni," Star called to her second son. "Go bring Tsika."

"Again Mama? She's like a trout in the stream. You reach for her and she slips out of your hands. Ask Arapho to find her."

"Arapho is helping the old men at the fires. Go!"

Juni was always slow to respond and even slower to act. Star doubted he would find her. Even with a sore leg, Tsika could outdistance him.

Even now, she was out of sight.

While her mother and grandmother discussed the whites, Tsika had recovered from the fright of awakening in a smoky room and the sorrow of her kitten's demise. She tested walking on her bandaged leg. It felt better, so she decided to find Aiku and urge him to help her track the whites who torched their cabins.

She hobbled to the Fox cabin and together they followed the tracks to the woods.

They tethered their horses there and crept in on foot. "See. Horse droppings. Satisfied?" Aiku asked.

"I know that, dummy. I want to go after them, and see where they live so we can torch their houses some dark night."

"Follow on foot? Some mounted men? You're daft."

"You're afraid." she taunted.

"Is any Cherokee boy afraid? We're trained to be brave, but also to be sensible. Look at you, with your burnt skirt halfway off, and a guimpy leg. How far could you go in the forest?"

"I'm going."

"And if you meet them, what could you do? You have no gun. You couldn't run. Look Tsika, I'm strong, yet I will not be foolish." He took her by the arm, "Come on home."

She pulled away. "I'm going and you can't stop me."

Smiling to himself, Aiku shrugged. "Girls! Very well, go."

He started back to the village knowing she couldn't make it through the brush and fallen logs and would soon follow him.

At the bend of the river, he met Juni.

Aiku hailed him. "Are you searching for Tsika?"

"Aye, have you seen her?"

Aiku pointed to the forest. "Looking for the torchers."

"She's loco. No one goes into the forest unarmed."

"That's what I told her."

"Come with me. I must find her and take her home."

They called her name and their voices echoed against the nearby cliffs.

Tsika stirred. Dazed she thought she heard hollow voices. Was she in a cave? She moved her legs. Oh! It hurt so. What had happed to her? Then she heard it again. "Tsika-a-a-a."

She'd move somehow. Suddenly she looked up to see the boys standing over her. "Go away," she shouted. "I'll get home by myself." She tried to sit up and fell back in pain.

"Stubborn, as usual," said Juni, as they made a latticed seat with their arms and hands to carry her home.

On their arrival, they found the camp in a turmoil. The victorious warriors had returned; the celebration had begun. While there was sadness over the loss of their homes, it was soon forgotten in the dancing, singing and games that followed.

Tsika saw her father stride forward. He looked so dashing in his war paint and belt of scalps. White Fox, Aiku's father walked beside him, and as they approached the Council House, Star came out to greet them. Would she tell Fox about Swift Wing's death and relieve him of that unpleasant duty? Ah, they were walking together toward Laura's cabin.

Aiku sighed, "Juni, I am spared the task. Thank your mother for me. Now I must greet my father, then we can play the ball game."

Tsika groaned, "I can't play.," and her tears fell.

"It will be a long time before you can play any games with us," Juni laughed.

"Brothers!" she spat. But perhaps she had been too stubborn.

White Fox nodded as Star and Great Wolf talked to him,

then after grasping Aiku's arm with a manly wrist-arm greeting, he knocked on Laura's door.

"Coming," a high voice called, and when the door swung open the widow appeared carrying a papoose. "Here's your son. Soft Wings named him after Missionary Father Ard Hoyt."

Fox scowled, "I will call him Attakulaculla, 'The Little Carpenter,' for that one went to England and saw the King. Atta shall travel with me wherever I go, Spring Day."

"So be it, then." Spring Day bowed, "but call me Laura."

She had accepted the white man's ways and given herself an English name when she learned to read and write in English. Now her three little daughters, dressed in long skirts, also bowed.

Stoically, Laura served him a draught of Indian brewed corn whiskey. Stoically he drank it. Talk could come later.

Laura finally recounted Atta's birth, Soft Wing's death, Aiku's help on the farm and how they kept his cabin clean. Then she handed him the papoose.

White Fox felt his heart turn to stone. He would never forget this moment when his strength deserted him. Tears came to his eyes and for a time, he even forgot his sons, Aiku and Attu, thinking only of Swift Song and her beauty.

Laura said, "Stay here, Fox."

"No, I must go to my cabin."

She gave him the child's clothing and a supply of food.

He strapped Atta to the cradleboard muttering, "Thank you, 'til I can repay you. I bring some game soon."

Laura turned away from the door smiling and whispered, "I do not want game, my friend. I want you, and in time I will have my way. You will live here."

It became a familiar sight to the Cherokees working in the fields to see White Fox headed for the mountains on his horse, with a cradleboard strapped to his broad back. From its opening peered a pair of bright black eyes. As a rule Aiku followed.

The timing of these hunting-trapping excursions was carefully observed by the widow, Laura, and on this particular spring day when he left at dawn, she noted Aiku was not along. He'd been hired to work on Great Wolf's land to plant the crops, and would stay there for two days.

Laura sighed. Would Fox ever take notice of her comeliness, her desire to please him with gifts of food and blankets? It had been over a year since his squaw had died. Perhaps he objected to a ready-made family, her three small daughters.

She shrugged and turned to her morning's work. She would watch for his return and make him aware of her.

White Fox felt her eyes on his back and smiled. She was out to catch him. He thought she was a beauty even after bearing three papooses, but she was bossy. It might be good, for she owned much land, but would she expect him to use her new plow, her hoe and grinder from the agency? Would she expect him to plant her corn, flax, cotton and indigo? Would he have to give up his beloved hunting and trapping?

Fox followed the river to the northeast, savoring the leafy, moldy odors of spring in the forest. It was cold. This morning in the high country there was still frost on the ground. Spring blooms this year would be late.

By noon Fox had reached the dense growth of juniper and pine trees. He tethered his horse, then fed Atta some goat's milk. He anticipated checking his traps where he hoped to find a white fox, as he had in his early youth. That one had given him his name. He had always felt guilty about that for he'd never been quite sure whether he'd dreamed it as he fasted or had actually trapped it. But there had been that tuft of white fur in the trap. So many years ago! Well, today he hoped to prove positively there were white foxes. He had set the usual number of traps in the usual places.

As he swung along over the pine needles, he sang, "Papa catch a white fox skin to wrap my little Atta in."

Atta cooed happily in his cocoon.

"Then I'll hang it on a branch and you'll watch me skin it."

He climbed over a log on the path.

Snap! Crack!

White Fox groaned as he fell. His right foot was caught, broken and bleeding. The cradleboard flew from his shoulders. Atta howled.

"God damn," he shouted the only English words he knew. His voice echoed against the nearby rocky cliffs. Pain contorted his bronzed features as he freed his mangled foot from the trap. He crept to Atta and fainted.

When he opened his eyes, it was dark. Atta was crying. He felt over the child's body for breaks. There were none. Thank the Great Spirit for that!

"There, there little one, all's well."

He was rewarded with happy gurgles. Hitching himself along on a hip and elbow and holding the cradleboard in his hands, he inched slowly and painfully toward a small tree. The night creatures of the woods rustled in the brush. A wolf howled, reminding him of the immediate night dangers. With his last ounce of strength, he swung the straps of the cradleboard onto a low branch, then promptly fainted again.

This time the screech of a mountain lion roused him. There was a whinny, a scuffling noise and a frantic scream as the cat dealt the final death blow to his faithful horse.

"Oh, Great Spirit, let him ignore us. Let him have no mate nearby."

The papoose slept. Alternately, Fox was feverishly and painfully conscious or unconscious during the night.

The following day passed in much the same manner except for the frequent wailing of the infant. Fox's next conscious thought was of food. Gone was any hope of getting to his saddle bags; gone was any hope of survival for him and his little son—unless—he had some parched corn in a paraflech tied to his belt. Perhaps he could chew the corn kernels to a mulch and place it in the child's mouth, for there was no milk. He'd try it. It took a long time, but worked for awhile. The infant's crying stopped.

The next important thing was to build a fire to protect them from prowling wild animals. He felt for the flint he always carried. It was gone. Jarred loose by the fall? He searched through the pine needles in vain. He used the age-old method of rubbing two sticks together. There were plenty of dry pine needles for a start and enough firewood about to keep the fire going if he could stay conscious to feed it from time to time. Painfully he pushed into a mound enough to last the night. Atta was crying again. Fox chewed more kernels for the peculiar feeding, then struggled to replace the cradleboard in the branch of the tree.

Fortunately, when the child cried out and he was awakened, it was a time when the fire needed more fuel. Then he again succumbed immediately to the thumping swollen foot pain and blissfully sank into a stupor. Where was Aiku? Why didn't he help? That's right, Aiku wouldn't come. He didn't even know of the trapping trip. Laura perhaps? She'd watched him leave—Great Spirit, let Laura search for me.

Laura anxiously watched for the travois that would be returning with skins and meat. When Fox failed to appear by dusk on the second day, she hurried to Big Elk's cabin.

"Elk," she shouted, pounding on his door. "Let me in!"

"Ah, my pretty," he greeted her. "So, you have finally come to me." He pulled her to him in a bear hug.

"Stop it! I want you to go find White Fox and Atta."

Elk laughed. "That one! He can take care of himself. He is like the leaves on the trees, the rocks on the hillside, so much a part of the wilderness. He'd never get lost. Let Aiku go. Come now be nice to Big Elk. Be my squaw."

She pushed him away. "I'll go after him myself."

He called after her, "I'll go for him tomorrow."

She whirled around, "Tomorrow will be too late. Please go now, Elk. You have that fast horse you stole from the whites."

"Aye, and what you give me in return?"

She smiled. "I bring you some soup."

"To get started soon, I need help gathering things to take."

"You'll take two blankets, whiskey, dried corn, milk for Atta, bandages and herbal salve," Laura told him. "Come on, move!"

"Think he'd been gone for a week," he grumbled. "If it wasn't for Atta, I'd not go. That wildcat could live for a month in the wilderness."

The next evening he returned pulling Fox on the travois, and carrying Atta in the cradleboard on his back. Laura rushed out to meet them.

"Ah," Elk boomed, "now I collect."

"Yes, you get soup, but now go get the white doctor."

"No, I get witch doctor."

"Get Fox inside, watch the children and I'll get Dr. Adam."

"*No, No,* I go. I no watch those."

It was a long time before Fox could limp around Laura's cabin. Impatient at the enforced inactivity, he scowled and bellowed. "I'll never be able to hunt and trap again."

"Aiku will do your hunting. Dr. Adams said you will be riding soon. Meanwhile I'll teach you to read and write English."

"No!" Then he mellowed. "I can't complain. You take good care of me and my boys."

Laura had welcomed the opportunity to care for him. Now finally he had seen what a good housekeeper she was and would want her for his squaw. She comforted him, "The doctor said you were lucky to be able to keep that mangled foot. He stitched you up pretty good. You'll walk soon."

"Hmph!"

"You will be able to help me farm."

"You expect me to plant and plow with those new things the missionary got from the agency?"

"Of course, and I expect you to marry me Christian style."

He grinned. "I didn't know I asked you. You're converted?"

"Yes, and you will be too now your nose is out of that

wilderness long enough to see what the missionaries are doing to educate the Cherokees.

Fox turned his head to hide a smile. "I not farm or marry you Christian style in Moon of Budding Trees, but marry Indian style; when I shoot venison for meat, give you. You give ear corn, show you be good squaw."

Laura patted him on the shoulder and kissed him on the cheek. She had won half the battle.

Tsika sat beside her small brother and rocked the cradle the missionary Father Chamberlain had given them. Arapho and Juni hunted; her mother and grandmother gardened and her father discussed the Cherokee's problems with White Fox at the far end of the cabin. She pouted. It was not fair to be a girl and have to stay inside with the papoose when she would rather be hunting with her brothers.

Suddenly what the men were saying caught her interest.

Her father said, "After we came back in '14 we found our cabins burned by the very white men we were fighting for in the Creek war beside General Jackson. That's the kind of reward we get? There was no praise for our bravery. Instead, Jackson, in his puffed-up conceit over the government's recognition of him for his victory at New Orleans, forgot all about us and our peace terms. He demanded twenty million acres from the Creeks knowing that four million acres of that land belonged to us."

"And President Madison agreed."

"Yes, and it's time we did something about it!"

"I'm interested in getting paid for that land, Wolf, but not in other Governmental affairs."

"Well, you'd better be interested, Fox, because you're going with us to Washington to straighten out our problems with Jackson and the President."

"I can't do you any good."

"You know what the Cherokees have been trying to do ever since the 'Old Ones' were warriors in 1750."

"Yes. Trying to hang onto our land, and some of you believe if you dress like the whites and learn to do everything their way, you'll win. Well, you won't. Once we were their good source of pelts, bear oil and beeswax. Now we've learned we're just in the way of the settlers."

"Through with your speech? You're wrong, Fox. In learning to farm, raise livestock, and become educated, we can fight them their way—with their own weapons—diplomacy. You'll see."

"If I go."

"You'll go. It's important. Even back in Washington's day, Jackson wanted him impeached because he introduced the Holston Act that gave the Cherokees training in blacksmithing, iron working, and carpentering. That's how unfair he's always been to the Indians. Now Colonel John Lowrey, Major Ridge, Captains Walker and Taylor, chiefs and Adjutant John Ross will go to Washington to make a fair treaty."

"Ha! You know what our treaties mean to the whites. Right now, Jackson threatens us with the rules of the 1802 Georgia Compact that says, 'Georgia is given the right to obtain, on reasonable terms, ownership of Indian lands in that state.' It's that simple and that devastating."

There was a knock at the cabin door. Good, thought Tsika, who was tiring of the talk about Jackson. She was interested in Cherokee affairs and would take him on herself when she was older, but a knock always meant a surprise visitor and diversion from everyday chores.

She laid aside her weaving and hurried across the colorful hand-woven hemp rug that covered the dirt floor. When she opened the door, a hearty greeting of "Hello" boomed out as the American landowner, Chuck Bronson, entered.

"I heard a delegation of Cherokee chiefs is going to Washington."

"Yes, John Ross, The Ridge, Chief Painkiller, his son Charlie Hicks and some lesser chiefs like me," said Wolf. We're hoping to get the government to agree on a three point treaty. Also, we'll make some demands."

"Do you have a chance without giving up some more land as a concession for those demands?"

"Wolf shook his head. He wore the colorful turban of the Cherokee, but otherwise was dressed in the clothing usually worn by white planters like Chuck—heavy pants, homespun shirt and leather boots.

Chuck jerked his thumb in Fox's direction. "I see our friend still likes his comfortable clothing."

Wolf laughed, "He's going to have to climb into something civilized when he goes to Washington with us.

Fox shrugged, "Tell Chuck about the demands of the wounded Cherokee, who fought in the Creek War."

"I know about those. What about the others?"

"There are three. I quote, first: 'We require payment in the amount of $26,000 for the damage done to our land when U.S. troops passed through on their way to the Creek War.' "

"And?"

"Second: 'We want the U.S. Government to designate a clear boundary line that will recognize Cherokee land claims south of the Tennessee River.' "

"And?"

"Third: 'We want more iron works and smith shops and will make a request, the arrest of intruders who want to take our land before a boundary has been established.' "

"That's four."

"Didn't I tell you, Fox. This man's a demon for precise amounts. It's his white man's book training."

Chuck smiled. "Those are legitimate requests. What will you have to give the government in return?"

"We should give nothing, but we'll end up with a cession of a triangular wedge, our last hold in South Carolina."

"Ah, I thought so. Well, my friends, don't let them take advantage of your generosity. I believe President Madison is on your side. Possibly he can convince Andrew Jackson to back off."

Tsika wondered, did Aiku know about this? She ran to ask her grandmother to watch over Micha while she told him and also she wanted to see Fox's reaction to this news.

Laura had long ago given up the doeskin tunic and leggings for voluminous calico skirts and petticoats. She had bought Fox white man's pants, shirt and coat.

When Fox came in, Tsika, Aiku and Laura's girls were lined against a far wall waiting to see sparks fly.

Laura said, "Fox, since you're going to Washington tomorrow with the chiefs, this is what you will wear."

"Ah, my sweet bossy squaw." He hugged her. "You changed me from a trapper-hunter to a rancher-farmer; from an ignorant Cherokee to one who can read white man's papers and write in white man's talk. Now you insist that I be a voice in the affairs of our people. I am proud of you, but I won't wear those damn foolish clothes." He stalked from the cabin.

Laura laughed and called after him, "You will."

The Cherokee Nation had changed also. It had strengthened since the days when the tribe was divided into clans named for nature's wonders that surrounded them. Since the white man had penetrated their Allegheny mountain stronghold, the people had become, with the Missionaries aid, a nation of traders, farmers animal husbandrymen and builders. They were educated, interested in national affairs and willing to fight by other means than by bow and arrow, gun and hatchet. Because of intermarriage, there was a better understanding of the existing problems, so demands could be made and intelligent decisions reached.

On March 22, 1816, the Cherokee boundary settlement, known as The Treaty of 1816 was signed by the Cherokee delegation and twelve delegates of the United States Government of whom Jackson was one. The chiefs were led to believe the National Cherokee Council would ratify it before it became final. The Cherokee representatives ceded the South Carolina triangle as planned and felt that that part of the treaty was agreeable because it allowed the whites to travel the Federal

Highway through their lands and enabled them to place inns and shops along the way.

While the several headmen of the tribe, who lived on the Hiwassee were away from the village, the daily routine for the rest of the residents went on as usual; the women wove baskets and cloth, made clay cooking pots, and cared for the animals; the men plowed and planted and the youths hunted. The children helped when urged then followed their usual playful pursuits.

On the day before the chiefs' expected return, as Aiku helped Laura on the farmland in front of the orchard, he saw Tsika skip toward the village. He wished he was free to go with her. Then he saw her turn toward Big Elk's Trading Post.

As she reached the wooded path on her way to buy thread for Niamhi, the spring songsters flitted from one budding dogwood branch to another, chirping their objection to her presence. She went the long way because she loved the sweet damp spring smell of the woods, and to enter the rear door of Big Elk's Post she could see his horses before she climbed the hill. He'd built "high-up," he said, so he could see who was coming "At him." It was where Big Elk chose to spend his days after he was wounded stealing horses.

It was a wondrous bright haven for it held a myriad of interesting items from the white man's world; magical bright calico, dishes, and jewelry. There were also beads, rawhide articles, feathered headdresses, tunics, moccasins and headbands. There was a collection of herbs. She loved the odor of pungent spices, the smell of tanned skins and even, although sometimes overpowering, the smell of the bear grease. But best of all were the stories Big Elk told, particularly the one about saving Atta and White Fox from the wild animals in the northern woods.

On this day, Big Elk was in the back room distilling Indian whiskey. He didn't see the two white men, who were coming "At him."

"Here it is, Shorty. See ahead, them's our horses."

They rode to the front of the Post, dismounted and tethered their horses to the hitching post. The taller one swaggered through the entrance. Beneath the wide-brimmed hat
his florid features showed pleasure for the task at hand. The
other broader shorter man followed, looking over his shoulder
like a groundhog ready to dive into his hole.

"Better put our horses out in back," he suggested.

"Naw, nobody's around. We kin do this job quick-like."

Below on the village square, were a blacksmith shop, an
iron works, a grist mill, a public granary and community gardens where several women were digging in the red earth. They
looked up, momentarily, then continued with their task.

As the tall man entered the Post, he took a gun from its
holster, then quietly moved to the back room and, shoving his
gun into Elk's ribs, sneered, "We know ya stole 'em. Now yer
gonna pay."

Big Elk, who was considered the bravest of Cherokees, was
shaking. "I already paid. Now what?"

"Ha, Shorty, he don't know what we want. Should we show
him now or test him first?"

"Butch," Shorty whispered, "I hear someone coming in."

Elk reached for his knife and received a blow to the head,
and as he slumped to the floor the gun went off.

Shelves were overturned and bottles crashed. Shorty flailed
a board at the still smashing the equipment, then shouted,
"Damn it, let's get out of here."

Tsika entered through the back door.

An hour had passed and Tsika had not returned. Star was
worried. As she gazed from the window of her cabin, she saw
Aiku plowing next door. Her boys were hunting, so she called
to him.

"Go after Tsika, Aiku. She went to Big Elk's."

He dropped the plow handles and ran to the village.

And when Wolf came into the cabin, Star lamented, "My

husband, Tsika is too long away. What can we do?"

"And where is the little adventurer this time?"

"At Big Elk's on an errand for Niamhi."

"Why do you worry? No harm can come to her there."

At that moment Aiku rushed through the door shouting, "Big Elk is on the floor all bloody. The Post is torn up and Tsika isn't there."

Screaming, kicking and biting, Tsika had been bound and gagged, then flung over the saddle in front of the red-bearded man. She heard a crack, felt extreme pain at impact, then fainted.

Later a muffled hum of words drifted down to her, "Did ya have ta take the girl, Butch? Thought we went after Elk. They'll sure get us fer kidnappin'."

"We did an' we got him just like they told us to do. We'll dump the girl up ahead in the hills."

Tsika told herself to be brave. Somehow, she'd get away.

The riders went upgrade into the forest. At dusk, they stopped, untied Tsika's hands then removed the gag, tossed her beside the path, and headed for Atlanta.

As she rolled down the hill, her head hit a rock, and, bleeding and unconscious, she lay there as darkness fell over the valley.

She awakened to see a half moon between the overhanging branches. She heard the scampering of small woods creatures, then the sharp screech of a wild cat. When she tried to rise, a sharp pain pierced her side. She was dizzy and her head ached. Why was she here in the woods? Did she fall on the way to Big Elk's and hit her head? She felt of her forehead. It was sticky.

Then she remembered Elk's bloody shirt and the white men. The wildcat screamed again, and in spite of her pain, she pulled herself up thinking of Elk's story about Fox caught in the trap. She couldn't build a fire, but she could climb a tree for safety. At least they hadn't taken her with them. But what had they done to Big Elk? Was he killed? Her climb into a spruce tree sleep-place was prickly and her ribs hurt, but she gritted her teeth and grasped a higher branch. Here was a triangular area where two limbs met. It would be a secure perch.

However on reaching it, she couldn't sleep. Above her an owl hooted, then wolves howled. Would daylight never come? She knew when it did she could find her way home doing what her brothers had taught her of woodland signs: the bark on the trees told one which way was north. Animal tracks, if followed, showed one where a stream flowed, or could lead one to danger, a den. Finally with legs that ached from the strain of remaining in one position all night, Tsika carefully climbed from her perch and started to walk down grade. Which way was home? Where were the tracks she could follow to find water? She was growing thirsty and hungry, and now her head pain had become worse.

Travel west away from the rising sun, she told herself.

By high sun, she felt faint, and staggering from tree to tree, willed herself to keep moving. She should search for edible roots as Grandma Niamhi had taught her to do, for there was no stream. They would be moist and help for a time. Had she forgotten the kind to look for? There were some broad-leafed weeds. Frantically she dug with her fingers until she unearthed the roots. She crawled beneath a low, thorny bush and chewed root and dirt as well, then succumbed to pain and dizziness.

This time when she awakened, she was on a cot in a small cabin and a white man was leaning over her.

"Ah, you wake up, little one."

He looked like a grizzly bear; brown hair all over his face, head and chest, but he was smiling. She smiled at him.

"And you shall have a feast, my woodland princess."

He was funny. She laughed, "You're a nice white man."

"And are not all of us nice?"

Tsika scowled. "No, two white men took me away on a horse."

He went to an open pit fire and stirred something in a pot. "And where from they took you?"

Tsika felt a tight band where the pain had been and knew it had been bandaged.

"Thank you for fixing my hurt ribs. I am from Hiwassee village. I am Chief Great Wolf's daughter."

"Ah, I knew you were a princess. I know where it is. I'll take you home tomorrow, but first I have something to do."

After a meal of rabbit stew and hard bread he left saying, "I'll be back later. Now don't run away, little one."

Why would he think she'd run away, when he'd promised to take her home tomorrow?

Wasn't this a gift from heaven; to find a girl from a Cherokee village when he was on his way to spy for the Georgia officials. Hiwassee would do as well as any other. After his parents were murdered by the damned Indians he'd vowed to help chase them clear to the Pacific Ocean. Johnson would pay him well. All he needed now was to get into his Indian garb. What an opportunity; he'd be gratefully accepted because he'd saved the young one's life.

On his return, he tethered his horse a few yards away from the cabin and saw her waiting at the door. She ran out arms outstretched, thinking it was someone from her village come to get her, then stopped short.

"Oh, I thought you were a—a Cherokee friend."

"Good! I want to look like a Cherokee. You see I'm hiding from an enemy. Will you help to keep my secret?"

She clapped her hands together, "Oh, I'd like that. It will be an adventure."

"Yes," he smiled, "quite an adventure, little one. Now I need a Cherokee name."

"You could be called Tahchee. He was a brave chief."

"Make it Cochee. I wouldn't want to steal Tahchee's name."

"That's nice. It sounds like Tahchee."

Now he would have the opportunity to brief Johnson and Jeremy Cole on how the harassment tactics were affecting the

Cherokees and to report to them on the Cherokee's reaction
to Jackson's policies concerning all the eastern Indians.
Shortly he'd travel to the capital of Georgia and help to abrogate the Boundary Treaty of 1816.

When they reached the village, Tsika was greeted with hugs,
tears and kisses by her mother, grandmother and friends.

She laughed through her tears, "The whites say we show
no emotion. But where is Papa?"

"Out hunting for you with half the warriors of the village."
Star turned to say, "Arapho, Juni, go tell them she's home, and
Tsika, who is this Cherokee?"

"This is Owi Cochee, my friend who rescued me."

"Welcome to Hiwassee, Cochee," Laura said. "You may
stay with us until you wish to travel on."

"I accept," he bowed.

When questions he could not answer were asked, Tsika
aided him in his deception. She believed no one suspected he
was a white man, but wait until Great Wolf and White Fox returned.

However on their return, Cochee was welcomed into Fox's
home and Tsika was taken to the Missionary doctor.

Once inside the cabin, Fox said, "Indian from no tribe, with
no knowledge of origin—a white man in hiding, eh?"

Cochee nodded and looked guilty. "Aye for a time."

Fox smiled, "You a friend of Cherokee. That enough for
me. Come I fix you a sleep-place."

Aiku welcomed the visitor from the white world. He could
now learn how life was in the cities and be shown modern
farming methods.

Cochee worked beside Fox and Aiku and even though
none of the Cherokees doubted he was white, they accepted
him as long as he tilled the earth and stayed out of trouble.

And Cochee bided his time. Soon he would contact Johnson, receive instructions and report on how the harassment
tactics were affecting the Cherokees. Also hear their reactions

to Jackson's policies.

One morning Fox saw him return to the village from the direction where the Calhoun Agency was located. When questioned Cochee responded, he had gone to the agency to meet an Indian friend, who was on the way to Washington.

Shortly after this, Fox learned that several chiefs were bribed to turn more land over to the Georgians. He kept silent, but decided to follow the man sometime, to prove what action was afoot. However, it was more than a year later, after the Cherokees were pressured by President Monroe to cede their North Carolina lands to the government in 1819, and refused, that he had the proof.

John Ross had called a council meeting at Rossville to determine what the Cherokee Nation's response should be.

People came from miles around, arriving on foot, by wagon and on horseback, to hear what Ross had to say.

Although Chief Painkiller and second Chief Charles Hicks were in control of governing the tribe, John Ross attended to all of the Cherokee affairs. He sought to right this constant wrong of bribing chiefs for more land.

John Ross was one-eighth Cherokee Indian. He had brown hair, blue eyes and was of slight stature. He looked like a white man but his heart was with the Cherokees. He owned a vast plantation on the Georgia side of the Tennessee River, where he ran a ferry boat service. Periodically he went to Washington to settle the differences that constantly arose between the Cherokee nation, the Georgia State and the U.S. Government.

Tutored by whites, he completed his education at Kingsport, Tennessee, then was called to join the Army to fight the Creeks under Andrew Jackson. Many mixed bloods had served their white neighbors and come to be leaders in the Cherokee community. Ross who was diplomatic and had good rapport with the whites was the logical choice.

Now in view of the latest development the chiefs would go to Washington for an audience with President Monroe and the Secretary of War, John Calhoun. Major Ridge, who also had a

powerful voice in Cherokee National affairs, agreed with Ross
that no more land should be ceded. Their views expressed,
Monroe tired of the whole affair and turned the matter over to
the new commissioners, Andrew Jackson, John Coffee and
Joseph McMinn.

"This is the worst possible turn of events, Chuck," Wolf
told his white friend on their next encounter. "Andrew Jackson has been given a most powerful position, and that can
mean trouble for the Cherokees. John Ross said that the subject of Removal was even brought up at the last meeting of the
delegates in Washington: a suggestion that our land be traded
for land across the Mississippi in Arkansas, where there's good
hunting."

Several townspeople had congregated. One said sadly,
"Our people don't understand their father in Washington. A
few years ago he sent us plows and hoes and said it was not
good for his red children to hunt—they must cultivate the
earth. Now he tells them there is good hunting across the river
in Arkansas. If they will go there, he will give them rifles."

Many turned away in sadness.

"Chuck, we have no answers. Ross says, no violence, we
must do business white man's way, but they pay no attention to
our talking-papers. They act as though we cannot govern our
own."

"Wait, we will show them. Sequoyah has invented a syllabary for the Cherokees. If it is a success, we will be a well-
educated nation soon."

"I must investigate this writing." Wolf grinned, "Fox may
be able to learn this reading before Laura can teach him."

"Sequoyah left for Western Cherokee country. After he,
Chief Jolly and some lesser chiefs unlawfully sold Cherokee
land they were threatened with renewed enforcement of the
Blood Law. Only Battling Gourd praised him for his inven-
tion."

By spring, Fox had become a model farmer. When cultivating or planting the cotton, corn, indigo or flax, he wore his

calico turban, his buckskin tunic and leggings, his blanket draped over one shoulder and tucked under the other, glad to be out of the white man's waist coat and pantaloons.

On this day after a lunch of pork crisps on corn bread he and Aiku sat beneath a maple tree overlooking the acres they had planted. Happy but weary, Fox dozed as bees buzzed overhead. Cochee had left to get the new cultivator and Aiku stole from his post to climb the rocky cliff beyond the fields. To the left, 100 acres of tilled land spread out before him and on the right, fourteen horses grazed contentedly.

Aiku carried a quiver of arrows and his trusty gun. He hoped to see a deer at the salt lick below beyond the next bend in the path, but in the distance he saw three horsemen approaching the lick. He scowled. That for certain, would frighten any wild life away.

But they passed the lick and, with lariats ready, made for the pasture. The animals whinnied. One man on a red saddle roped a horse. Aiku reached for an arrow. No, it wouldn't go far enough. He took his gun from the holster, aimed and fired. One man fell from his mount. The others stopped, picked up the wounded man and left.

Fox came quickly. He placed an arm around Aiku's shoulder.

"They'll be back, Papa."

"I know, but don't worry. We'll be ready for them."

In late summer, the delegates returned from Washington, in time for the Green Corn Festival. It was a time for celebrating prosperity and optimism, but Chief Painkiller's news dampened the people's spirits. The music and dancing ceased.

"You know what will happen when Jackson goes into action," said Chuck Bronson.

Black braids swinging, Fox nodded in agreement, "And some will even move across the river into Arkansas."

"We will go to Georgia to Springplace, where John Ross lives," Wolf asserted with a firmness of purpose.

Suddenly Cochee rushed into the central cabin, shouting,

"They're coming. Lots of whites on horseback."

By the time the braves had hurried to the door there were three men and a militiaman with weapons aimed, blocking their way, and flames were shooting skyward from the cabins that surrounded the main building.

"Where in hell were you from that time until now," Fox demanded. "You saw them torch our cabins and did nothing?"

"I saw them coming, so I thought I could stop them. Then one knocked me out. I just now came to—I guess too late."

"You're damned right, it's too late."

A gravelly voice boomed, "I want this man," and he pointed his revolver at Fox. "Let this be a warning to the rest of you red Devils, never mess with whites."

Aiku pulled on Fox's tunic, "Papa, that's the man I shot. See he has a red saddle."

Two men grabbed Fox, pulled his arms behind his back and attempted to bind them as he struggled. Wolf and Charles Hicks rushed at them with knives poised for a hand battle as four gun shots exploded in rapid succession. Three Indian braves fell and Laura dropped to the ground. The women screamed as they ran to her aid. The front of her dress was bloody.

As the whites pulled Fox along, Aiku clung to his father's tunic and received a sharp rap on the head that threw him aside.

By this time several Cherokees had found guns in the large lodge and finally the whites were routed, dropping Fox and Gourd to the ground on the way to their horses.

As soon as he was free, Fox rushed to Laura's side. He had become very fond of this woman who had helped him to accept the white's ways and had been so loving with his boys.

He called to Aiku. "Go for the white doctor! Hurry!" He cradled her head in his lap.

"No need, my husband," she whispered. "I know when the Great Spirit calls, I must go. My oldest girl will care for you all."

Fox bowed his head in grief, but knew she spoke the truth. No one could lose so much of life's blood and live long.

Many were returning to the remains of their burned cabins to see what could be salvaged.

Tsika was screaming, "Grandmother, where are you?"

"Oh, no, Niahmi," Star wept, "not in a burning cabin."

Because her aches would not allow her to walk the distance to the central log house, she'd remained behind. Frantic now, Tsika, Star and the boys ran toward the burning building.

"Mama, she'll be in the hen coop. She told me—" Tsika rushed ahead out of ear shot.

"Why, would she do that? You're daft." The others ran to the henhouse. Now a spark had ignited its thatched roof.

"Grandma," Tsika called, wiping her tears on the back of her hand. "You there?" She crawled inside.

"Sure, and so's the chickens."

Doubled up in a crouch, she unfolded herself, and smiled. "Told you I'd hide in the chicken house if whites came again, didn't I?" The rest had congregated.

"My little Tsika knew where to find me."

Arapho and Juni, part of a water brigade, poured water on the coop dousing Tsika, Grandmother and the chickens.

Amidst tears and hugs, Niamhi was welcomed, and in wonder Juni asked, "How did you know to get out of the cabin?"

"I saw them torching Big Elk's house. I knew we'd be next."

"Grandma, weren't you afraid the fire'd reach you there?"

"Yes, but I knew you'd come and pull me out."

"The silence has a certain ominous quality. Like the calm before the storm," Wolf remarked. "I believe we'd better plan to leave Hiwassee immediately. Come let's warn the others."

"We can't leave until we honor the brave ones who helped us, my husband."

In the large lodge, preparations were already underway for a fitting ceremony for the three braves and Laura. Wolf hesitated at the door, then motioned to Gourd and Elk to meet him outside.

"We are left with only our crops and a few barn animals. We must share our belongings for the trip to Springplace."

"As soon as there has been a decent time for grieving, Wolf. You know the people's feelings for custom." Elk advised.

"I know, but we must move soon. I have a feeling they'll be back."

"Very well, we'll take what crops we can, buy horses and carts from the Cherokees who chose to remain, pack our saddle bags and leave by the end of the week."

That night the soldiers came back and at gun point routed eleven braves from their straw pallets with threats to rape their squaws and take the children captive. Then they were bound and lead to the Hiwassee jail. One brave who raised his knife was hit on the head with the butt of a gun. Done with the least amount of disturbance, neighbors in nearby cabins were unaware of the capture.

As soon as the pounding of the horse's hooves receded, the terrified women whose cabins had been entered rushed to warn others and immediately plans were made for Wolf, Gourd, Elk, Chuck and Sixty Stones, a strong giant of a man to go after them.

Wolf decided to send a spy to town to be informed of the soldier's departure to Atlanta.

"I'll go," Chuck volunteered. "No one in the town will be surprised to see a white man doing a bit of trading."

All agreed, and on his return the following noon, he gave a full account of the situation at the prison.

"Six soldiers were left to guard the makeshift prison. We can easily surround it when the jailer is off duty at midnight and the soldiers are asleep or relaxed."

"I get first chance at them to avenge my squaw's death," Fox told them. "Then you can all take turns."

Clouds covered the half-moon when the Indians arrived at the jail. They tethered their horses and the extra four mounts at the edge of the woods behind the prison.

Two soldiers were stationed at the entrance. One was at the rear and three were asleep inside. Wolf nodded.

Before the front guards saw Fox, he crept to within two feet of them, stabbed one and hit the other a hard fist-blow at the back of the neck. Wolf used his knife to attack the soldier at the rear of the building. At the sound of scuffling the soldiers from inside rushed out to face the Indians. Flailing clubs and knives reduced two to flight and one to a bloody death from Sixty's knife.

Only one of the attacking party suffered injury. Chuck fell against a metal hasp on the prison door as they entered to free the prisoners. He bound the flesh wound with a strip of his shirt. Of the Indian friends they'd freed, those four who had families decided to return with their rescuers to Hiwassee to prepare for the journey to Springplace.

The others, young and venturesome, chose to escape into the wooded hills and take their chances.

"May the Great Spirit grant you protection, my friends," Wolf grasped each in the customary arm hold. "Before the news reaches Atlanta, you will be far into the hills."

"And hopefully we will also be on our way," Fox contributed.

Immediately upon their return, they prepared to awaken the camp, but found wagons being packed and squaws collecting food and clothing for the journey. Generous Cherokees, who planned to escape into the surrounding forest by foot had sold carts and livestock to the would-be travelers.

Wolf urged, "Come with us. It is fine in the spring and summer in the forest, but in the winter . . ."

Sixty interrupted, speaking for the group that had decided to remain in the area. "Tsali did it, and managed to keep his group together in the North Carolina mountains for three years."

"That's true, Sixty, but remember, the whites finally found

them and urged Tsali to confess to the murder of the soldier, then he was hung. Is that what you want?"

"We'll manage, and we won't get hung."

Wolf nodded. They grasped wrists in a farewell they knew would be their last.

Star and the children were weeping. "They want to go, little ones. Our paths separate here as we leave for Springplace and they go into the hills to live."

"I'm crying because, I don't want to go," Star complained.

"We must. Get into the wagon, Star. I'll attend to the livestock."

"But Little Turtle says their language isn't like ours."

"Then we learn. Come, tears are unbecoming. Help Red Branch into her wagon. Help Niamhi."

"But I'm leaving my vegetable garden I planted, and I . . ."

"Hush," said Niamhi. "We can plant more. Push that crate of hens over here. I must be able to feed them on the way."

Everyone seemed to be glad to leave Hiwassee except her. She looked back longingly at the charred ruins silhouetted in the faint moonlight. Why couldn't she believe this move was for the best? She sighed, shed a few more tears then decided to talk to Cochee before leaving. His advice was always good. "What do you think of this move, Cochee?"

"Perhaps it is wise."

"Then why are you not going?"

"I will come to Springplace later."

She thought it was strange. Should she tell Wolf?"

Then Wolf called to her, "Hurry, Star, we're ready."

Cochee smiled. Harassment had worked. Now to expedite some of the same in Springplace. There he would be closer to John Ross and know immediately of Cherokee plans to be reported to the Georgia officials.

The procession from the Hiwassee River camp began at three o'clock on the morning of March, 23, 1819. Great Wolf and Fox led the way. Muttering, Fox often looked over his shoulder.

"What you mumbling about? We're not being followed—yet."

Fox shrugged, "I know, but aside from our immediate problem there are also the new Government Factories. If we could trade in the old way, life would be simple. We have to buy supplies from them and the last food was spoiled. Now we must buy more and can't pay for it, so what does the government say? Our debts will be cancelled if we give them more land. It's a losing battle, Wolf. And it may not be any better at Springplace."

"Things *will* be better at Springplace. Of all the forty-five Cherokee villages, it is the best location, because Ross lives there." Also there is Brainard Missionary School, best in the Cherokee Nation, Our Valley Town School of Posy's and the Overhill School were too far away for us at Hiwassee camp to send our children. They can stay nights at Brainard if they live too far away. I'll send the boys and Tsika there."

"Schooling for our children will show the whites we are educated, will become citizens and can vote. Also it is the headquarters for government." Fox had forgotten the troubles.

"You are always interested in government. Do you have a desire to be an official, Wolf?"

"Perhaps."

"That's good. You make a fine delegate and would be able to help the Cherokee Nation in any way. I'll vote for you."

After leaving the pine-strewn forest paths, the travelers came to a lush valley, where a stream beckoned them to camp for the night. The women set up the tepees while the men dressed the game they'd shot along the way. The children gathered wood for the cooking fires and soon the worries of the past hours were forgotten.

Surprisingly they were not followed by the militia and the families reached their destination late on the fourth day of travel at a point northwest of Springplace on the Canasauga River. Each established ownership of 100 acres of fertile farmland and began to chop down trees for their cabins and barns.

It was a country of clean air where during the spring season the hilly crevices in the distance were abloom with laurel, flaming azaleas and rhododendrons and where white magnolias grew on the slopes.

Several Cherokee farmers came to each new neighbor with palms outstretched in welcome, a gift of corn and game and an offer to help build. In this manner of easy acceptance, staunch friendships were formed.

Missionaries Samuel Chamberlain and Elizur Butler offered their services of religion and education to the children. Second Chief Hicks guaranteed his support and protection.

A Cherokee called Chaim Owi, when he heard of Laura's death, offered to have Fox and his children stay with them until Fox's own cabin was built. The man's features were round, more Caucasian then Indian, although he professed to be a full-blood Cherokee. Chaim's squaw welcomed them and delighted the girls with her stories of forest animals. Roper and Aiku immediately became close friends, partly in defense against a household of girls, for along with Laura's three daughters Chaim had two girls younger than Roper.

Chaim was happy to have new neighbors. "We will be good friends, I feel it, here." He pounded his chest. "You will find living here not much different from Hiwassee. We came from the south, after our livestock was stolen and our cabins and barns burned. So far, we have had no trouble here and people are very friendly, the land productive and the school good."

Fox was surprised at Chaim's enthusiasm. What about the news of Cherokees who moved across the Mississippi because the chiefs took bribes. Altogether the Cherokees have lost some 40,000 square miles because of treaties and cessions to the whites using their land stealers."

"You mean the white man's compass, or Andrew Jackson?" he smiled. "True he's one of those speculators who have robbed us, but we will beat him yet. Ross says if we band together, we'll succeed."

"Chaim, you are an optimist. I hope you're right. I believe we have a real fight on our hands. Jackson tried to ignore the Holston Treaty and have Washington impeached at one time, and just because it started the Cherokees in farming, animal husbandry and mechanical skills. He resented our being trained as iron workers, wheelwrights, carpenters, smiths, weavers and millers. He won't be satisfied until we're all across ol' Miss. Now he's a commissioner, he's using the Georgia Treaty to force us to give up more land."

"Well, for the present you will find the land productive. Summers are cool, winters are mild and your children will grow strong and healthy. What more could you want?"

Fox insisted, "Peace, and to be able to *keep* this land."

"Then you must go up to hear John Ross speak next week at Red Clay. It is for chiefs and council members only, but I will take you with me."

The following week Wolf called for Fox at his unfinished cabin. "Come. We have a long way to go where White Bird speaks."

Fox ambled out. "You are always in a hurry, Wolf—to go —to do important things. My friend, you will be killed some-day with your hurrying."

"So! Do you know Jackson is again stirring up trouble?"

"Yes, ever since the whites came," Fox sighed. He counted the times off on his fingers. "First there were overdue debts, that caused cessions in spite of the Holston Treaty of 1802. Next, some of our chiefs were bribed into selling or giving some thirty million acres away, then because of the Georgia Compact with the U.S., we sold ten million acres of land for $1,250,000."

"Aye," Wolf smiled. "You have learned your Cherokee his-tory well, and speak English very well. This Federal Highway we will travel is government owned because Chief Joseph Vann took bribes for some of his land on the Conesauga River. It's the road between Augusta and Nashville."

Immediately upon rounding a bend in the road, they saw

Chaim. He greeted them, as usual, with information.

"Next time we will go to Rossville, the vast acreage on the river where there is a two story white house overlooking Ross's slave-tended property and the ferry station."

"Do many own slaves?" Fox asked in shocked surprise.

"A fair number. There are several wealthy mixed-bloods like Ross who went to school in the East and married white girls. They adopted the white man's way of living. Ross, however, married an Indian Princess, Quati, who is as nice as she is beautiful. You will meet her soon for she attends the meetings."

The speech that Ross gave was not as moving and powerful as the one Major Ridge gave later, but in his delivery his love for the people gave them assurance that he would do anything in his power to thwart the Georgia officials and the U.S. Government in order to keep their lands.

He told them, "There is good news. Some cessions have been discontinued after the War Department conferred with the Department of Indian affairs about the U.S. Government's demand for peripheral lands. It was to pay for supplies needed for past and future migrations to the West. However at the same time Georgia is demanding land for settlers and removal from all the land the Cherokees inhabit (by adhering to the Georgia Compact). It is a confusing situation. In view of these facts and in fear of Georgia's enforcement of the Compact, we must *unify* for our protection against removal."

1819 - 1824

Another meeting was held within a month, and *unity* was again the theme. Progress also was emphasized as a plan for survival. The request went out for all Cherokees to attend.

People came from great distances, bearing tents and cooking pans. They came on horseback, by foot and in carts. Some who came from the hills wore Indian garb; the beaded headband, moccasins, deerskin tunic and leggings; townsmen wore a mixture, wearing white man's shirts and heavy cord pants and the Indian calico turban and moccasins. And many planter's wives were dressed in voluminous skirts, indicating the latest white styles. The colorful gathering camped on the vast acres, beside fences and beneath trees. It was a noisy gala picnic, but when Ross arose to speak, there was a respectful hushed silence.

Missionaries Elizur Butler, Elias Boudinot, Chiefs Ridge, Painkiller, Charlie Hicks and several lesser chiefs, were there as well as Quati, and wives of three of the missionaries.

Plans were made to reorganize the Cherokee Nation's government, to increase the number of Cherokee managed businesses, such as millers, wheelwrights, iron workers and carpenters, and to insist that there be an increase of missionary schools, so that by the end of 1821, all Cherokee children would be in schools, their youths would be in training as apprentices for those businesses, and each farm would be productive. All left the meeting feeling inspired.

Great Wolf's two older sons, Arapho and Juni, and daughter, Tsika, were enrolled at Brainard as boarding students, as were Alda and Ulah, two of Fox's step-daughters and his son Aiku. It was on the Tennessee River a short distance from John Ross's homestead, several miles from Springplace making it necessary for the boys and girls to board and room at their respective cabins. There were also houses for the missionary families, a meetinghouse and the usual washhouses, kitchens and mealtime areas. There were garden plots for vegetables and fields for grazing animals. Students were expected, as part of their training, to help with both gardening and the tending of the animals.

Father Hoyt, the first missionary manager, often wrote to Boston headquarters for drafts to keep the school going. Fathers Butrick, Chamberlain and Butler were hard at work there and starting other schools.

Sixty to eighty students attended Brainard: whites, mixed-bloods, full-blooded Indians and a few negroes. School hours were devoted to religious pursuits. The work was introduced as much to help pay for maintenance of the mission as for training the children.

Juni often complained, "The worst thing is getting up early."

"Come on, Juni. You've got to get up." Each morning Arapho prodded his younger brother. "We'll be late for tending the stock and then won't get any breakfast."

"I don't care. I don't want to get up."

Arapho gave a final tug and Juni lay sprawled on the hard wooden floor.

He continued to grumble, but obeying the sudden assault of hunger pains, he jumped up, saying, "Oh, well, I can sleep in Butrick's schoolroom."

"So? Not in Chamberlain's. We have drills and are supposed to study aloud while he walks up and down the room. There's no chance for sleeping there, but after class we can go out, tear off these white boy's clothes and play ball, swim or hunt blackberries. I sure like the blackberry part."

A month earlier he had gone to swim, and hearing girl's voices around the bend in the river, approached with caution. He peeked through the tree branches as two girls were walking away from the area. Becky McAllister remained, splashing water toward the banks. He'd been interested in this daughter of a white planter and speculator for some time; now was his chance to make her notice him.

He held her clothes high in the air, teasing, "A kiss for these, Becky," and she had complied without any objections.

After several such experiences, an intimacy so sweet resulted, he was loath to leave Springplace when the term ended in late June.

The boys were preparing to leave.

"I wish we could stay all summer," Arapho said, "but this last year I will have to stay home and help on the farm or take an apprenticeship in town."

"I don't want to come back alone."

Arapho laughed, "You won't be alone. The rest will come."

"But I don't like it here. I don't like to get up early, or eat at a table, and I don't like that smarty John Ridge."

"He'll be gone. He's going to Cornwall to college with Jones and Boudinot. Lots of the children would rather be home, Juni, hunting and chewing on parched corn and jerky, but the girls like it, and soon you'll like the girls."

"I will? They do?"

"Ask 'em. Here comes Unah and Alda."

And Arapho escaped to be with Becky this one last time before he left; to kiss her and to rub her soft white skin.

"Ask us what, Juni?"

"Why you like it here."

"Because. I like to sing and dance and learn my letters, and make patch-work quilts," Alda said. "Now I have to leave you. I must work in the kitchen."

Juni asked Ulah, "Don't you hate to work in the kitchen and washhouse?"

"Yes, but I hurry so I can get out early and can go down by the river." Her eyes grew wide. "Guess what I saw yesterday! Your brother and Becky, in the bushes without any clothes on."

"You what?"

She clamped her hands over her mouth, mumbling, "Guess they were hunting blackberries," and skipped away.

Would he dare to confront his brother and accuse him of that? Of what? Maybe that was why Arapho didn't want to leave Brainard. Juni fled to his cabin, chatted nervously about inconsequential things with his friends as he frantically finished packing his bundle to take home.

In late November of 1820, Juni and Tsika came home for a holiday the whites called Thanksgiving. They were pouring over the new alphabet invented by George Gist known as Sequoyah, their slates and markers ready for forming the letters. Arapho whistled as he washed in the lean-to behind the kitchen. Micha and the papoose, Greta, played by the fireside as Star and Niamhi went from the kitchen to an adjoining room setting the table. Great Wolf reposed in a large chair next to the fire, his turbaned head bobbing occasionally in exhausted semi-slumber, the long pipe like Sequoyah's unsmoked in his hand. A loud knock brought Star to the door and Wolf to his feet.

A tall dark-bearded white man burst into the room almost knocking Star down.

He raised his fist and shouted, "I'll run you out of town and string your bastard son up by the thumbs, you damn redskin."

"With clenched fists, Great Wolf calmly requested,

"Explain please."

"You have a son—Arapho."

"I do."

Arapho heard the commotion and, about to enter, hesitated when he heard his name. Then he dashed for the barn, mounted his pony and raced down the path to the road.

"What has my son done to cause this intrusion?"

"He's ruined my daughter, that's what he's done."

Star Flower gasped, motioning Tsika from the room.

"Let's get my son in here. Let him defend himself." He called, "Arapho." There was no response.

Again there was a knock at the door, and another white man similar in appearance but smaller in stature than his brother, pushed Arapho before him. "Caught 'im leavin', Al."

The boy stood with head bowed.

"I'd like to hear your name, sir," Wolf asked containing his fury, "and state your complaint to my son."

"It's McAllister, and he doesn't take this lightly," the brother spouted. "Property owner and he's influential in Georgia politics."

"I'll speak for myself, Jason." He stood with feet astride, hands on hips, glaring from angry eyes beneath frowning black brows. "I want 100 acres, twelve horses and *he's* got to marry my daughter."

"Where is your daughter?"

"Out in the carriage."

"I'd like to speak with her."

McAllister considered for a moment. "Jason, get Becky."

Shortly the girl entered: her flaxen hair floated almost to her waist; her blue eyes were rimmed with tears. "I didn't . . ."

Wolf demanded, "Is this true, Arapho?"

Arapho nodded and, through her tears, Becky smiled at him. As always his heart thumped with desire.

"I want to marry her, Father."

McAllister looked surprised, then scowled at Wolf. "See that you're off this land by next week." They started to leave.

"Wait," Great Wolf also scowled. Now was the time to fight. "It is enough to have the United States and Georgia after more of our land. I'll not surrender my land and livestock to you, do what you will to me. I will give it as a marriage gift to our children."

"I'll take you to court, you damned red."

"Oh, Papa, can't we do this peacefully?"

"Quiet! You've disgraced the family. Marry your damned Cherokee. I disown you. I told you that's what I'd do."

Again tears showed in her wide blue eyes. "I didn't think you meant it."

"And I never want to see that damn bastard you'll call my grandchild."

She ran to him. He flung her back and the brothers left.

Awkwardly Great Wolf patted her slim shoulders; Star put her arms around the sobbing girl and crooned, "There, there, dear. We will take good care of you."

Shyly Arapho placed a kiss on her cheek, assuring her, "I'm happy, Becky."

She sniffed, looked up into his dusky face and whispered, "I too."

Great Wolf shook his head in disbelief. "He was not even willing for me to give the land to his daughter. I cannot understand such a hard man. *I* will be the one to go to court.

"My husband, the court will not hear testimony of an Indian against a white man. You don't have a chance."

Becky came to him, "I am so sorry, Chief Wolf, I have caused you so much pain."

"Not you, my dear, your father and the State of Georgia are at fault. I will see Sam Kellog. He'll help me out."

Tsika spoke from her banished location, "You will have to wait until you return from Rossville, Father. You promised Fox you would go up to hear White Bird speak."

Wolf smiled, "So I did. Weren't you supposed to be out of hearing? Is this what education does to our young? Makes them our advisors?"

"Aiku said his father is anxious to go." She ignored the admonition.

Wolf sighed, "All right, I'll wait until we return from the meeting to see Sam."

At sunup the next morning, Wolf cut through the woods behind his cabin and took the river path to Fox's land, entering it at the rear. The barn door was open and the horse gone. He hurried to the front of the cabin. There was no sign of Fox. Then he knocked on the door.

"I'll catch up with him," and he galloped away.

Six horsemen awaited Wolf's departure from his home and coming from the south road, rounded up Wolf's horses in the far pasture. One man crept beneath the house.

Niamhi awakened Star, "I smell smoke, my daughter. We must flee again. I told you we wouldn't be safe here."

"Arapho, Juni," Star shouted, "get water, hurry!"

As Tsika and Becky handed buckets to the boys, and they worked furiously, pouring and chopping, the flames subsided.

"Run, Arapho, get your father. He's at Fox's by now."

"He's left for Rossville so long ago, Ma."

She nodded, "I suppose it's too late. He will be greeted with this bad news when he gets home."

Then cleaning and washing began in the shell that was left: Tsika and Betsy laundered scorched and smoky clothing and Star and Niamhi scoured. Micha and Greta, tied to the apple tree in the yard played contentedly, unaware of the confusion within the cabin and within its occupants.

When Wolf and Chuck arrived at Rossville, and no one had seen Fox, Wolf suddenly realized that perhaps there was a reason he had not been at the farm. Suspicious of Cochee for some time, Fox had said, "I aim to find out what he's up to."

"I'll not wait for the end of this meeting, Chuck. I must get back to town."

"What's so pressing? I thought you were anxious to come."
"I am now anxious about Fox, and I must see Sam Kellog."
"About some business?"
"Aye."
"I understand. I'll leave with you."
"No. Stay and tell me all about what was said later."
Chuck nodded, knowing his friend had something more serious on his mind than Fox.

At dawn as Fox prepared to leave for Rossville, Aiku called, "Pa, come here, there's a horseman going full speed from the direction of Wolf's house."

"Ah," he smiled. "Always looking for Tsika, eh?"

Aiku colored and was glad it was still faint daylight so his father couldn't see his embarrassment, but Fox was at the window.

"Look at him go!" Then Fox saw the barn door was open. "I'll be—get Pinto out of the stable, Aiku. I'm going after him."

As he drew close to the rider, and the morning sun shone, he determined, yes, it was Cochee. Just as he suspected, the man was up to no good. He'd follow at a safe distance. He could catch up to Wolf later and still get to Rossville in time.

For so long it had seemed impossible to think ill of a man who worked on his farm, tended his stock, and generally was helpful and cheerful, but ever since he'd been assaulted at Hiwassee, when Cochee was absent, he'd been suspicious.

He stayed well behind the man for several miles, then turned into a tree-lined driveway. Well back from the road was a white-pillared home that fronted vast acres of planted land.

Fox dismounted at the edge of the property and crept forward just as Cochee went to the side door and walked in.

Fox carefully climbed onto a log at a side window and saw Cochee shake hands with McAllister. So this was where the aide to Johnson lived. Drinks were served to them by a negro slave, they smiled and nodded. Fox couldn't determine what was said, but remained posted watching their lips move.

As they started for the front door, the log slipped and banged against the house, alerting the men, McAllister was saying, "Good Work. Keep it up. Soon they'll all be driven out."

Cochee ran to his horse, but Fox had escaped through the woods at the side of the property where he lay in wait to follow still further.

Two miles beyond on the same road was another mansion. This was the home of Jeffrey Johnson, serving under Governor Gilmore of Georgia. Fox tethered his mount at the rear of the property next to Cochee's horse.

This time Cochee was admitted at the front door. When he left, Fox was waiting for him.

"You deceive Indian friend." Excited, Fox reverted to his hesitant English.

"What in hell are you doing here?"

"I follow you to see why you dress like Indian and are white friend to McAllister and Johnson."

"It's none of your damn business."

"Yes, it is much my business—Cherokee business. You lied, you betrayed Cherokees who liked you." He grabbed Cochee by the arms pinning them back. "Now tell!"

In the struggle that ensued, Cochee broke loose, shouting, "Damn you, you'll suffer for your snooping," and landed a sharp blow to Fox's head.

"Grunts and groans indicated more punches, and Fox was losing. Not trained in boxing, he resorted to the rough ball game sport where mayhem was popular. He broke Cochee's arm.

As Cochee fell he got off two shots. One was wild; the other caught Fox in the chest. As the Indian fell to the ground, Johnson's slave ran to them.

But the help was not for him. He was dragged to the edge of the woods and hidden in the underbrush.

After Wolf returned home and talked to Aiku, he started

out within the hour, carefully tracking the horse's hooves on the road, and in the fields and woods.

After two days of following impressions of the peculiar pattern of the horse's hooves, Wolf came to the Johnson barnyard. Here someone had bled profusely and there were signs that a body had been dragged over the bloodsoaked ground. He heard a low whistle and saw a black man motioning him into the woods. He was led to a log and straw hut where a large black woman tended Fox.

"She fix him up with herbs like Indian do," he grinned.

To see again the destruction of his house and find he must buy more horses (for he would not use Big Elk's method to procure them), he felt the need to compensate for it by making Cochee pay. Forgetting his constant urging to settle differences peacefully when talking to his hot-tempered friends, he set out for the informal meeting place, Big Elk's.

In his fury and frustration, he forgot the many dealings with the Indian Bureau, the government representatives in Washington, the Georgia officials and thought only of McAllister's threats and the injury to Fox.

He began with a tirade, "We can't live with this kind of harassment any longer. Law or no law, and in spite of Ross's advice against violence, I must act to avenge Cochee's attack on me and my family, on Fox's injury and on the unjustified faith we all had in that fake Cherokee. Do you blame me?"

"No," Chuck agreed, "but Cochee is but one cog in the Georgia officials' wheel of harassment. They will send many Cochees in retaliation if you do something desperate. We must use diplomacy and have patience; you've said that yourself, Wolf. Ross will work out a plan with his idea for Unity."

"And while he's working out his plan, I am going into action. The hunt is on. Who's coming with me?"

"I'll join you," Chaim offered.

Battling Gourd and Big Elk murmured their assent.

"Chuck? Are you game?"

"If Rena says it's all right with her."

"We leave next sun-up. Pack supplies." There was no sign of emotion on his chiseled features. Then he smiled, "We'll do as the whites do, toast our venture with spirits. Let's have some of that good home-brewed corn whiskey, Elk."

"Some of their customs appeal to me," Fox admitted.

Wolf departed feeling more encouraged by his friend's support than by the task to which he was now committed.

Seven Georgians met in Governor Gilmore's office to hear Cochee's report, and to welcome three new recruits who were ready to help them accomplish the program of harassment.

Johnson said, "We are becoming alarmed at the speedy progress the Cherokee Indians have made of late in all their endeavors: milling, farming, merchandising and most of all in the field of education, since Sequoyah's alphabet has been introduced. The Cherokees now regard themselves as a well-functioning nation with a governing body. Spies have informed me that soon they will have a judicial department.

"If the U.S. Government doesn't do something to stop this nonsense, we must, or the area will never be open to settlers."

Heads nodded in agreement, and, at that moment, Governor Gilmore and his staff were committed to a method of unlawful acts that shunned ethics and dropped them to a new level. Governor Gilmore gave his permission for concentrated harassment in all Cherokee towns and the officers agreed that McAllister's recommendations be followed: (1) that Chief Great Wolf's 100 acres of property be seized, (2) that Big Elk's Trading Post on Federal Highway be closed, (3) that White Fox be charged and arrested for attacking Cochee, and (4) that there begin vicious attacks through press, state government and courts to promote Cherokee removal to the West in 1821.

There must have been some feeling of guilt among the officials, for they bided their time and none of the orders were carried out immediately.

Wolf and his volunteers hunted for Cochee in villages, towns and cities to no avail, and they came home to a village where there seemed to be no serious thoughts about Cherokee removal or anything beyond parties, balls and feasts.

John Ridge, Elias Boudinot, David Brown and others had returned from Cornwall in Connecticut where they had enjoyed the gaiety of social affairs in New England. The mix-blood owners of the large mansions entertained them lavishly.

It took Tsika's breath away. She and Aiku were invited to all of the parties at Rosses, Ridges, Vanns, and Browns. The halls of marble held lovely tapestries and paintings from Europe. Satin draperies and highly polished dark furniture, glassware and silver glistened in the candle light from crystal chandeliers. It would be easy to become accustomed to this kind of living. Tsika, Aiku and their friends spent the late spring and early summer in this state of pseudo well-being, and they talked of marriage and having homes like these.

Wolf was disturbed. Cherokee people, old and young, rich and poor were disregarding caution. Business in Springplace went on as usual. Even the people from the more primitive villages and those in the hills seemed to feel the need to celebrate the hiatus from harassment.

The colorful wooden water drums throbbed out their rhythm to dancing feet. Ankles were bedecked with tortoise shells that jangled with every step made to the sound of the cane flute, and with the shaking of gourd rattles in hand and shouts of joy. The noise was deafening. The Ball Game played with vim and its usual competitiveness later was cause for betting and occasional mayhem. Wolf finally decided he would also use this time of respite and started to rebuild his two-story home. It was finished in time for the Corn Dance Celebration in late August.

In the fall of 1821, a Georgia official decreed that their property would be taken from them. Wolf, Big Elk, Gourd, Chuck Benson and Al Wheaton were approached and told to warn others.

Ross told them, "This is just some State official. We will appeal to the Federal Government. It will see that our rights are considered."

"We'll do as you say," said Wolf. "We'll fight them with words, laws and intelligent diplomacy as benefits a nation whose citizens are learning to read and write in both English and Cherokee, but we've been promised help by the government before and it didn't come."

"We will deal with the U.S. commissioners instead of with the Georgia officials."

Wolf turned to the others. "Ross is so determined to keep us from violence that he tends to lose track of the times we have appealed to the U.S. Government for help."

So by the new year, there was another trip to Washington, and an audience with President Monroe had convinced the Cherokee leaders, John Ross and Major Ridge, that it was hopeless to get a clear answer to their problems with the Georgia officials.

U.S. officials, the Agent of Indian Affairs, Secretary of War and the President stated that the Cherokees did not have to abide by the Georgia Treaty of 1802, and Georgia insisted that the Cherokees had to trade their property for Western lands. And Georgia officials, if it served their purpose, would ignore any ultimatum by the U.S. government, as they had done in the past. The delegates came home feeling discouraged.

By June, 1822, John Ridge and Elias Boudinot had graduated from Cornwall and John was ready to step into the role his father, Major Ridge, had planned for him. However at the moment, both young men were more interested in enjoying life.

So there were more parties, balls and teas at the beautiful homes in Springplace.

As they danced eastern style, Tsika told Aiku, "It would be

easy to drift into this kind of life. So carefree and pleasant."

"You're a farmer's daughter. We must just regard this as a whirlwind of ease that belongs to the wealthy mixed-bloods. We really don't belong here."

"Then we'll enjoy it while it lasts. From what my father says, I think John Ridge and Boudinot will soon become involved in the politics of the Nation, and be through with these frills. He said he heard they were leaning toward removal and were upset about that."

The next day Wolf spoke to his friends who sat before the fireplace in his newly renovated home.

"How serious is it that John Ridge and some of the youths in the Nation are leaning toward removal?" asked Fox.

"They have no authority to sign Treaty papers. I wouldn't worry about them," said Gourd. "It's when the lesser chiefs start to plan to leave for Arkansas and trade land that I begin to wonder."

"I can't believe any of them would take the chance since the Blood Law has been reinstated. They'd face death."

"How do you think the young men will react to our plans for a Cherokee Supreme Court?" asked Fox.

"They should approve mightily, if Major has trained his son in the ways of the loyal Cherokee," asserted Wolf.

Tsika, who always listened with interest to discussions about Cherokee affairs, made a decision. She would work with the missionaries, Chamberlain, Butrick and Butler teaching at the school. She had always admired the reading and writing teacher, Sophia Sawyer, in spite of her stern-faced, strict manner, but she would teach about the government so the children would know how to deal with the Georgians.

She interrupted the men, expressing her wishes.

"My daughter tells me what she will do? No, Tsika," said Wolf, "you will go to a girl's school in North Carolina to learn your manners."

"But I won't know anyone there."

"All the better, then you will study hard and learn much."

Tsika scowled. She would go to please her father, but she wouldn't stay. She'd travel to Washington, and talk to the President about Cherokee problems. She didn't know how she'd gain admittance to the President, but something would turn up.

"If I have to go away to school, I will write for the newspaper there. I can tell about our people, and what they have accomplished in reading, writing, religion and farming."

Wolf shrugged and turned his head, a smile on his lips.

"Where do you get such ideas?"

"From Quati. Mrs. Ross has many good ideas about how to help our people. She goes to some of the council meetings. She can't vote or speak there but she listens and tells John Ross what she thinks."

"Granted, and no doubt he listens to her and follows some of her suggestions. We Cherokees value our women, and that's why I am sending you to college, Tsika."

Quickly she looked up at her father. Was he joking or did he mean it? He was on his way out of the door with the men to attend a meeting to discuss plans for the creation of a National Supreme Court. But she knew he meant it.

The remodeled house was furnished like an eastern home, except perhaps for her mother's new spinning wheel and a loom where Niamhi worked beside the stone fireplace on bright colored yarn. At her feet, the small children played with a kitten.

Tsika sighed. How could she leave all this? Home was where the heart beat faster and the direction in which the weary traveler's footsteps hastened. The leaving would not come for over a year, but it would come too soon.

Many times during the following winter and spring she spent pleasant hours at the Ross mansion where Quati inspired her and the children delighted her. The Indian Princess was very fond of her and Quati's black eyes sparkled with pleasure at her arrival.

The Ross family home was as large and lovely as any of
those in which she'd been entertained, but its atmosphere was
different. Quati's personality showed through. Walls and floors
were embellished with her handiwork: clay pots, colorful woven rugs and wallhangings added warmth and charm to the
otherwise large cold marble-floored, marble-mantled rooms.

Bright sunshine came through the real glass windows and
gleamed on the dark furniture the slaves polished so carefully.
Tsika loved to gaze from the windows to the green lawns
where proud peacocks strutted.

It was during the summer of 1822 that she saw Aiku most
frequently. He worked on the farm, but found many moments
to escape to the wooded hills behind the Ross estate to meet
Tsika.

They talked, rode horseback and practiced for a game the
Cherokees played during the ceremonial dances. The subject
of Tsika's going to college came up and Aiku responded in a
sulky manner. "I thought we were supposed to get married and
have a farm."

She laughed. "And I thought we were supposed to get
married and have a papoose."

Aiku blushed, then announced, "Guess my father needs
me," and without so much as a goodbye, he jumped on his
horse and rode away.

Tsika was puzzled. Why was he so shy about marriage and
papooses? She must remember to ask Quati. Then she too
rode home.

On her return the household was upset concerning the latest demands from the Georgia officials.

Her father was saying, "They've heard of our plans for the
Supreme Court, and along with the news of the extensive effect Sequoyah's alphabet is having on the illiterate, they're
fearful we will demand citizenship.

"Their representatives in U.S. Congress have demanded
action, so to appease them, the National Cherokee Council
heard from the Secretary of War that U.S Commissioner

McIntosh will come to negotiate a treaty for land cession."

"They can't do that, Papa."

"They can try, but we will call a Legislative Council meeting in New Town, to pass a resolution that the Cherokee Nation will cede no more land to Georgia or the U.S."

Arapho asked, "Do you think that will hold in Washington?"

"It takes two to make a treaty binding and unless some very foolish lesser chiefs or some uninformed Cherokee unlawfully signs the 'talking papers' we should have enough reprieve to talk again to President Monroe."

"But papa, he didn't help you before."

"I know, but I believe he doesn't like to exert authority concerning the Indian affairs. At least he might postpone it."

At the end of the church service at Brainard Missionary chapel on a Sunday in September 1822 that Father Butrick held up his hand, saying, "And it came to pass that the Georgians let matters rest after the Legislative Council passed the resolution that no more lands be ceded."

His parishioners sighed with relief and the Cherokee villagers again forgot their worries of cessions and removal rumors, and went about their daily farming chores and town activities as usual.

It was almost a year later when full realization that Tsika would be leaving for the East came to her and Aiku. These days when they were together their conversation began and ended in the same manner. He had ceased to treat her like just another boy with whom to ride through the wooded hills, or to rough and tumble for possession of a ball or a much desired object, when, after one of their wrestling matches, he had kissed her, and a world of new emotions had charged down upon them both.

Each time when he greeted her that late summer of 1823, he would kiss her and say, "Tsika, you're going to stay here and marry me. You're not going to go away to school."

And her answer was always the same, "My father says I am going and that must be. We can marry later."

"We could run away, maybe go across to Arkansas."

"With the disloyal Cherokees? Never!"

"Then we'll go down to New Town. Have Butler marry us and live there."

"Well, maybe . . ." He was so dear. How could she ever leave him?

He kissed her. "Will you, Tsika, please?"

"I . . . I . . . guess so."

"Tonight. We'll elope. Get your things packed. Roper will help us get away."

"But, perhaps we'd better wait a few days. I must think more about it."

"Why? I love you. You love me. Our parents have always known we'd be married. I think after a while your father will not mind—too much."

"I know, and my mother has always said she would be pleased when we marry, but she would be disappointed if we ran away."

"Please?" Again he kissed her. They hugged and she clung to him. He was so dear—and persuasive.

"All right. Tomorrow night."

But the following day was the beginning of the Corn Dance Festival, one of the most important celebrations of the year, and there was no opportunity to do anything except join their respective families in preparation for the festivities. Tsika was roused before dawn.

"Tsika, come," her mother called. "I have your doeskin tunic laid out for you. The children are ready for breakfast and then you must take them down town to the central council house. The festivities begin at six."

Aiku was told to take his brother Atta and his step-sisters to the council house also for the activities that were planned.

At the end of the third day, when feasting, praying, games and dancing were over, the eve of partying came on fast wings.

There was only one hour before bedtime to plan an elopement. Aiku went to the Wolf home. He would make an attempt to urge Tsika to leave tonight.

But it seemed that misfortune plagued him. Wolf met him
at the door and asked if he came to wish his daughter God-
speed. It seemed almost as though Wolf had read his mind.
Wolf stayed in the room while Aiku shuffled from one foot to
the other. Finally he decided to be meek and plead his case in-
telligently, but instead, his voice came out harshly and an un-
bidden surly demand issued from his lips.

"Tsika and I want to marry. She can't go away to school."

"I do the telling in this house, Aiku. There will be time for
marrying after Tsika finishes her education." Wolf sat down.

1824 - 1828

In spite of all his entreaties, Tsika had left for the East after all. No hugs and kisses, no proper goodbye. No elopement. Springplace was not the same without her.

Aiku farmed, he studied, but he could think of nothing but Tsika—so far away.

"The Moon of Falling Leaves" was Nature's way of telling what was to come, but it seemed as though the trees and flowers were dying for good, just as he was dying inside. Everything in nature rests throughout the "Cold Moons" and is renewed in the "Moon of Blooms," but he couldn't rest—and he couldn't go after her—and he couldn't wait for spring.

The root vegetables had been dug and stored in the cellar. Now he had to pick the damned apples. He climbed to a high crotch in the tree, grabbed an apple and viciously bit into its crunchy flesh. There was a rustling of dry leaves below and Alda's sing-song voice came through to him.

"Papa says to pick 'em, not eat 'em."

"All right, smarty, suppose you climb up and help me then."

"Can't, I have to wash dishes."

"What ho, who's up-a-tree now?" Roper called.

"Calling on Alda again! What do you see in that sassy half-sister of mine?"

Roper winked at Alda. "This time I came to see *you.*"

"Ha!"

"I want you to go down to New Town with me. I have to deliver a message to my father. He's with the members of the new Supreme Court."

"Why did he go down there?"

"Will you go or not? I'm in a hurry."

"If I can get away from this job and get a substitute."

"Alda will take your place, won't you, my sweet?" He smiled at her.

"Of course, Roper."

"See, Aiku, honey does a better job than vinegar."

"Oh, you two, go on." She waved them off.

Aiku jumped down and they raced to their ponies.

"So, what's the important message?"

"My Pa's to come home, that's all."

"There's got to be something more to it than that."

Roper hesitated. "Guess it's all right to tell you. Ever since he introduced the bill to create a Cherokee National Supreme Court and bragged the Georgians don't have one, they've threatened to burn our house, but now his life is on the line. My ma got a note in the door this morning. It was scary. It said they'd send someone to scalp him alive, if the court wasn't disbanded and he didn't stop teaching Cherokees to read."

"Do you know who threatened him?"

"No, but I have a pretty good idea. It could be Cochee or that once-upon-a-time Creek Chief, McIntosh, who promised he'd come back into Cherokee country in October."

"I'll never forgive Cochee. Look what he did to my father after we took him into our house. But why is there a meeting in New Town today?"

"You remember when Chief Jolly, Sequoyah, and several lesser chiefs were bribed to exchange Cherokee lands for land in Arkansas without approval of the National Council?"

"Yes. After that the Blood Law was reinstated in 1819. If it wasn't obeyed, the death penalty followed."

"The committee decided to appoint a body of thirteen men to set up a check on chiefs to be sure the ruling isn't disobeyed, to let them know the Blood Law is still in effect. Pa believes they're sending McIntosh here to get more chiefs to cede land."

New Town was new. It was still sparsely populated: the few cabins and farms were scattered, and cabins near the council house were occupied only when council was in session. The main building was at the edge of a wood and surrounded by brush.

The boys tethered their ponies. As Aiku followed Roper up the path, he felt movement in the brush beside him. It was so slight, he knew no twig moved, nor did he hear anything. It was rather a sensation. He stooped to pick up an imaginary pebble, and, throwing himself into the brush, reached for pair of boots that retreated over cracked twigs. A white man's boots, not Indian moccasins. He told Roper to alert his father.

An hour later, eight men left the council house, hands on their gun belts in readiness for an attack. There was silence.

After mounting their horses, each man went his own way. Roper, his father, Chaim and Aiku took the route through the woods behind the council house. New Town was situated at the confluence of the Oostanaula and the Conastauga Rivers, a fertile area of farms and fields. Traveling northwest they came to the narrow trail beside the Conastauga River where they would go through a dense forest. From that point on it became necessary to travel single file.

Just one mile outside of Springplace, the land dipped into a valley, and suddenly there was a rustling, a shot rang out and receding hoof beats pounded the earth. Chaim groaned and fell to the ground. Roper jumped from his horse.

His father's face was contorted with pain for a moment, then relaxed into a mask of acceptance as his body went limp in his son's arms.

"Oh, Papa, I thought we were so careful." He rocked the frail form in his embrace, unashamed tears falling on Chaim's face.

Then he jumped up suddenly. "I'll get that damned bastard."

He mounted his horse and rode as though possessed, branches whipping his face.

Aiku took off after him. The assailant was easily followed for ahead, broken branches revealed his passage as he left the main trail. Abruptly they came to the edge of a small canyon and far ahead a man galloped along the ledge.

"Look it's Cochee!" Roper shouted. "I'd know him on foot or on horseback." He pulled out his gun.

"He's too far away to hit, Roper." Aiku placed his arm around Roper's shoulder. "Come. We must take your father home."

Grieving and dejected, the boy bowed his head. "How will I tell my mother? How can we live without him?"

"We'll seek revenge. The Sioux say *'Tapke.'* It's good. It cleanses the soul and eases the mind."

After Father Butler performed the funeral services for Chaim, Aiku looked for Roper. His friend was nowhere to be seen. Aiku thought, where would I go? To Big Elk's, of course. The friend of all the people, the gathering place for the weary, the troubled, and, most of all for those searching for news or information about anyone or anything. He should have been named Big Heart.

Aiku hurried to the post. "Hello Rope. I thought I'd find you here."

"I'm asking Big Elk about Cochee."

"And I'm telling him. Go to the next meeting at Rossville."

"He wouldn't dare."

"That one would dare anything. He knows an Indian can't testify against him in court. He's hard as nails. The only way to get at that rat is to *be* a rat."

"I know," scowled Roper. "Give him some of his own treatment. Shoot him."

"I guess I shouldn't do this, but here's where he lives now." Elk gave Roper a piece of paper. "Be mighty careful. He's dangerous."

"Tomorrow at sunup, Aiku, are you with me?"

"Of course. Why else would I come looking for you?"

They thanked the big man and left arm in arm.

"I don't want my mother to know until I've left."

"My Pa wouldn't like it either, because Ross said not to meet violence with violence."

"Then what do we do?"

"Go anyway. We can sneak out before dawn."

When Aiku bridled his horse in the pre-dawn darkness, he felt a hand clamp down on his shoulder. "Where you off to so early this morning, son?"

A chill went through his body. He felt such love for his father he couldn't lie to him. "Roper and I—we thought—" he expelled it in one breath, "were going after Cochee."

"And what? Kill the man? You can't do it. I won't allow—"

"But he killed Chaim. We can get away with it."

"And if you don't it's life imprisonment or be hanged. Are you prepared for either?"

"We won't get caught," he stated more bravely than he felt.

Fox sighed. "Very well, you have my prayers and good wishes.

Aiku was taken by surprise. "You mean it?"

Fox hugged his son and patted him on the shoulder. "Yes, but be careful. He almost killed me when I went after him. Remember, he's full of tricks."

Aiku nodded. "I'll be careful," and rode away.

On the third day they rode into the enemy's camp.

"We will stand out like Niamhi's red dye on white cotton."

Aiku frowned.

"We don't have to go into town. He's at the edge near the woods, and we brought provisions," Roper said, biting into a piece of jerky. "So it's good Elk sold us the parched corn and this jerky. It'll last a long time."

Aiku began to feel better about the plan. "We'll tether our horses in the woods behind the property and creep up to the barn."

"We're early enough that he should be coming to the barn for his horse—if he's home."

"What do you mean, *if* he's home. He's got to be home. Elk is never wrong."

Shielded behind brush and grasses, they waited for two hours on a rise behind the barn. Finally they heard whistling, and soon Cochee limped toward the barn door. Now was their chance. They crept forward. Roper reached for his gun and looked at Aiku.

"Now?"

Aiku pushed the gun down. "No, we can't do this. Shooting from cover reduces us to his level. Let's face him for an honest fight."

"Well I'll be damned. If we approach him, he'll kill us. We won't have a chance."

"Yes we will. We'll use knives. A shot would cause people to come running, and we couldn't get to our horses to get away."

"All right, you sneak up behind him when he saddles his horse, drop a pebble and when he turns around I'll jump him."

"Sh."

As Aiku crept into the barn, a pebble in one hand and his knife in the other, Cochee suddenly shouted, "Get up you lazy bastard. No nigger on my place is going to loaf on the job."

A negro boy jumped from a stall and as he saw Roper, he shouted, "Watch out, boss," and no one heard the pebble fall.

Gun in hand, Cochee turned around and aimed at Roper who was coming at him. Aiku rolled under a carriage as Roper screamed once and fell headfirst into the negro.

The boy pushed Roper aside and scrambled to his feet.

Kicking Roper in the ribs, Cochee bellowed, "Get the damned Indian bastard out of here! Throw him in the ditch!"

As Cochee turned to mount the horse, Aiku rolled from under the carriage, pushed himself up and stabbed Cochee in the thigh.

Groaning, Cochee grasped his leg, fell and mumbled, "Get help." Then he fainted.

The boy's eyes widened in terror. "I'se goin'."

Fearfully Aiku felt of Roper's pulse. His pulse was beating but the shirt front was bloody and he lay limp and unresponsive to Aiku's pleas.

"Roper can you hear me? I've got to get you out of here before they come."

Roper groaned, "I can't. Go—can't stand—pain."

Aiku wrapped a strip of his shirt around Roper's chest. Roper groaned and fainted. Aiku lost hope. How could he get his friend to his horse, much less on it and away before help came for Cochee? He tried again. He slapped Roper's face.

"Come on Rope. You've got to help me. Help yourself. Grasp this rag. Cross your arms in front of you and I'll pull you up."

Roper fainted again as Aiku dragged the limp form to the back of the barn and struggled to prop it upright against the stone foundation. Somehow he wedged Roper between two large protruding stones, grabbed a saddle from the barn and ran for the horses.

When he returned, he roused Roper, who was now bleeding profusely. "Come on, Rope. You've got to get up on this horse. Aiku scooped up some chicken feathers from the yard and stuffed them into the wound, mumbling, "Damn it, Rope. I can't do this all by myself."

"Can't make it. Can't." Tears rolled down the pale cheeks.

"If you can cry, you can do what I tell you. Come on now, dammit we've got to survive." Now Aiku was also crying.

"Water."

"I'll get you some water, soon. Now hang on to me, and I'll boost you up on Pango."

For what seemed like an eternity, he struggled with Roper's limp form. He finally managed to get him on the horse, tied his feet to the stirrups and tied Roper's shoulders to Pango's neck. For the first time he saw the advantage in having a white man's saddle.

In the distance, dogs were barking, and Aiku mumbled, "God, how I wish you could hang on. We've got to travel fast."

He held Pango's reins in his left hand and his own mount's reins in his right. Somehow it had to be done, for now he heard the pounding of horse's hoofs. He mumbled, "Please Great Spirit, let me get into the woods. Let the dogs follow the negro's scent, not ours.

He moved as fast as his burden allowed. Finally the barking and pounding receded and the silence of the forest gave him a feeling of safety. He sighed. His prayers were answered.

By nightfall they came to a stream and Aiku gently slid the limp form to the ground. The shirt strips were bloody. He roused Roper with cold water, and carefully examined the wound. He discovered that the bullet had gone through the boy's body in the fleshy part of the chest, and come out the back. So! There were two wounds, but at least there was no bullet to be removed.

Now to search for the herbs Tsika's grandmother found in the forest for wounds. Buzzard feathers or moss would staunch the flow of blood and willow bark bring the fever down, but what herb did she use for infection and healing? It was one that would withdraw poisons from the flesh when leaves were steeped.

As he pushed aside some brush, there was a rustle in the undergrowth beside the stream, and suddenly he was looking into the eyes of a ragged Indian brave. He reached for his knife.

"Don't! I friend," a voice squeaked. Then the boy turned

and fled. He shouted, but couldn't leave Roper to give chase.

As he stooped to dig up a root, the boy returned.

"Here, I find for—hurt one," and he pointed in Roper's direction. He handed Aiku a herb, then turned to flee again.

"Wait." Aiku grasped thin air, then taking a few steps felt fabric and pulled. The boy's head turban came off in his hands and long black hair fell in a cascade around pinched features.

"My God, a girl!" He held the healing root in his hand, its juices spreading over his fingers. "Let's help our friend."

"Aye. I help. I know herbs. I know sick people."

She spoke the Cherokee tongue, but in a different accent from his people. As they worked over Roper she talked on.

"You are Cherokee."

"Maybe. My people die in North Carolina mountain. I live on roots and berries, many moons."

"I bet, like one hundred. How old are you?"

"I don't know. Maybe fifteen summers."

"From the land of mountain laurel and rhododendrons. I know it well. We came from there twelve years ago. Come back to my village with me. My step-sisters will take you in."

She smiled. Her black eyes were luminous. "I like that." Then she laughed aloud. It was like a merry trickling stream going over a waterfall. "I tired of roots and berries."

"What is your name?"

"Is Tani. What are you called?"

I am Aiku and my friend is Roper. I hope he lives."

"He will live. I take care of him."

Aiku thought, dirty, but pretty. Almost as pretty as Tsika.

When Aiku brought game or fish, she cooked in pots she had made of clay from the stream banks. She wove baskets from the reeds for carrying herbs and fruits she found on forays into the woods and thickets, and daily, Roper improved.

When he was ready to travel, both boys had accepted Tani as a good friend.

"They will sure wonder what happened to us, Rope."

Tani's eyes became large. "Why, what you do?"

"We found a white man who killed Roper's father and once attacked my father, so we went after him. Roper had his knife out, but the man shot first. Someday we'll get him."

"You go home first, yes?"

"Yes, to Springplace."

"It sounds nice. A pretty name. Will your sisters like me?"

"If they don't, Tani," Roper announced, "you can come live at my house."

The contest was on. Roper looked into his friend's eyes and saw a challenge. Maybe Aiku would try to forget Tsika, and how about Alda, his own girl if he liked Tani too well?"

"I guess, Tani, you will be welcome at either place," he grinned. "But I think Roper's sister will have you studying the Sequoya syllabary."

"That is good?"

"Yes. It will teach you how to read and write."

She nodded. "I will do, if you say I should do."

Sarah Ridge and Katherine Brown, both young Springplace girls who were sophomores at the Moravian Seminary in North Carolina, introduced Tsika to their classmates and showed her around the college grounds and buildings. They assured her that she would like it when she became accustomed to the new lifestyle. Then, thinking they had done their duty, they became involved with their own pursuits and Tsika was left alone after classes started.

She hoped she would like it, but after the first week she began to doubt. The girls in her class ignored her. Perhaps they thought her strange because she wore her hair flying loose and wore a headband. She would dress hers as they did. Or maybe they thought her accent of the English language differed and disliked her color. They stopped talking when she entered the room. Not only did all this make her feel uncomfortable, but her shoes hurt. She was accustomed to the full ruffled skirts, but hard slippers were no match for moccasins when it came to freedom.

She decided she'd stay awhile and study hard, but if, after ten weeks she still didn't like it here, she would go to Washington and see the President about the Cherokee problems.

Late in October a letter from her father told about a bribe of $12,000 offered to Ross for land cessions, and of the land McAllister had taken. Her father still had the house and Arapho and Becky could keep the plot he'd given them. Generous!

She scuffed through the dry leaves on campus in early November, her thoughts were as dark as the clouds overhead. They promised snow which she disliked as much as the cold. At home winters were mild and usually the Moon of the Fallen Leaves had barely left when the Blossoming Moon began. Sometimes the weather was so mild that the roses at their doorstep bloomed all winter. Was she homesick? Come now, Tsika, where's your stoicism?

"Tsika," a voice called, "just a moment. I'll walk with you."

She turned to face a tall, blond man, handsome except for his prominent nose. However, it seemed to be a good feature, giving his face the strength of a sturdy bridge as it separated melting blue eyes.

She stammered, "I—I—I'm just going over there," and pointed to a nearby building. "How did you know my name?"

"I told Katherine Brown I wanted to meet you when school started, but I got busy with my own studies, and this is my first opportunity to welcome you. I thought why wait for Katherine to introduce us. I'm Sean Dolan, law student in the men's college nearby." He extended his hand.

Surprised, shocked, yet pleased, she felt this was meant to happen. He was her knight in shining armor. She smiled. "Thank you, I am happy to meet you."

At Brainard, after Miss Sophia Sawyer had read about King Arthur and his Round Table, Tsika had dreamed that someday she would meet a knight like Lancelot. Maybe she'd like it here after all.

He was telling her, "I went to college at Yale."

"Oh, some of our Cherokees went to Cornwall, not far from there. Katherine's brother David, Elias Boudinot, John Ridge and some of our white missionaries. Will you practice law here?"

"No, my father wants me to follow in his footsteps, be a Washington lawyer."

"John Ross, our chief goes there often on behalf of our people. Perhaps someday you will meet him there."

"What problems do the Cherokees have? Your brow is surely unfurrowed." He looked into her eyes with an expression that was at the same time teasing and loving.

She blinked, swallowed and went on, "They are constantly being harassed by Georgia officials to cede more lands."

"The U.S. Government should prevent such action."

"Jackson is an influential commissioner, and he has agreed to aid the Georgians in their efforts to make life so miserable for us, we will want to move West. Also there's the white man McAllister, who uses every possible excuse to take Cherokee property, steal livestock and burn homes. We've been fighting him for years. Somehow he always manages to send orders from his large plantation to others to do his bidding. My oldest brother is married to his daughter, so that has made us personal enemies as well, and he has taken some of my father's land and livestock.

"I never realized your people were so troubled. You're well educated and have formed a good government."

"I know, that's what worries Governor Gilmore and his staff. They're afraid we'll demand citizenship because we've just established a National Supreme Court, before their state of Georgia initiated theirs.

"I'm interested in government, and this amazes me. To think that our government would put up with such unfair treatment."

"There was a treaty made in 1801 and the Georgia officials think they can use it against us by taking land for settlers. I am going home soon. I cannot stay when I know of trouble. A let-

ter from my father yesterday said a bribe of $12,000 was of-
fered John Ross for more land, and I am deeply concerned
about my father's loss."

"You must stay. I want to see you again."

Her dark eyes widened. "You do?"

"Yes. I wish you would reconsider. There's a dance a week
before Christmas vacation. Will you go with me?"

"I will disgrace you. I cannot dance, except Indian dances."

"That dance is six weeks away. Come, I'll teach you."

"Here? Now?" Her dark eyes sparkled.

"Of course." He placed her books on a stone bench, then
showed her something called a waltz. "It's just like drawing a
pattern for a box with your feet. Come try it."

"I'll be late for my class."

"It won't take long. I think you'll be an apt pupil."

He had a crinkly grin. She liked his frank pleasant manner.

On the next day, when Sean met her at the same place, he
said, "Now it's your turn to show me how to do an Indian
dance."

"You really want to know how?"

"Of course."

"The War Dance, Eagle Dance, Green Corn Dance or—
what?" She blushed—she'd almost said, 'or the Fertility
Dance.'

"Whichever you prefer," he bowed. "I'm ready."

After she showed him a few gestures that went with the
steps of the Green Corn Dance, and he'd followed hers, they
laughed, holding one another closely. A group of students,
who watched nearby, began to applaud.

Tsika blushed again, "That's the lesson for today," and she
broke from his embrace. "Now I'll tell you about the other
lessons I learned at the Brainard Missionary School." She sat
on the stone bench, patting the place next to her. "Sit here."

It was so natural to talk to him, she seemed to lose all shy-
ness. He didn't seem to mind that she was Indian.

He reached for her hand. Chills ran down her spine. It was

never like this with Aiku.

"Lessons like this?" he teased, leaning over to kiss her.

"No," but she didn't withdraw her hand. "We were taught by white missionaries to believe in Christianity, hard work and how to read and write."

"Didn't you resent whites coming in to teach you?"

"Oh, no, we were pleased. They are wonderful people, and they prepared us for college. Chamberlain and Reverend Butler are good teachers. There's Doctor Butrick, who is also our physician."

"Did those, who were educated in the East, stay there?"

"No. They married white girls from Cornwall and went back to Cherokee country."

"Cherokees wish to plan for a government modeled after your country's and John Ross our chief is in Washington right now, speaking with the Secretary of War and President Monroe."

"That's admirable. And you're admirable. It's a pleasure to meet a girl for a change who can discuss things of importance."

"Thank you, kind sir, but I guess I get too serious at times," she grinned. "Is the dance formal?"

"Yes, but wear what you're wearing today. You look lovely."

"Like an Indian."

"Like an Indian princess, Tsika."

It seemed so long ago since Aiku had called her that. How far away he seemed at this moment. She looked up and Sean was smiling his teasing smile.

"What's going through that pretty little head of yours? You're miles away. Come back, Tsika."

She laughed, "I'm worried about the dance."

"Don't. Everything will be fine." He twirled her around in a waltz step. "See, you know how to do it."

But she was worried. When the evening arrived, she arranged her hair four times and danced the waltz step around the room as she dressed. She thought she looked like a white

girl now that her hair was done in a coronet style and the net-
ting atop her dress was cut out to reveal her shoulders. But did
she want to look like a white girl? Sean loved her as she was.
Oh, it would be a disastrous evening.

And it was. When Sean introduced her to his friends, the
women smiled at her with their lips only. Their eyes held contempt. The men ogled her with undisguised desire. It was dis-
gusting. Stoically she accepted their snubs and even one de-
grading remark by a beautiful white girl, "Don't worry, Madge,
she's just an Indian bitch."

She tried to show no emotion, but felt her muscles tighten.
Sean must have felt it, for he guided her from the dance floor.

"We're leaving, Tsika. If that remark had been made by a
man, I'd have slugged him."

"I'm sorry, Sean. I've spoiled your evening."

"Never. Your attitude tonight makes me admire you even
more. They don't know what they're missing in not knowing
you. Come, we'll go over to the Carriage House for coffee and
cakes."

Sean couldn't help but blame her for a rotten evening. As
soon as she arrived back at the dormitory, she decided to pack.
She looked in the mirror. She took the pins from her hair and
it cascaded down her back. There, that was better. Now her
large brown eyes told her the dusky, finely chiseled features
were her own and they smiled back at her.

After a restless night, she started to write Sean a note. As
she sat at her desk, her bell rang.

Sean greeted her at the foot of the stairs. "Tsika, I have a
splendid idea. Come home with me for the Christmas holiday."

Tears came to her eyes. "You—you really want me to meet
your parents?"

"I want *them* to meet *you.*" He hugged her. "Don't you
know, my little Indian princess, I love you?" He picked her up
and whirled her around.

"Oh, Sean, put me down, I—"

"You can't be too surprised, Tsika. We've been together as much as possible for two months."

"Well—no—but—"

"No buts. Say you'll come."

"All right, I'll come. When?"

"I'll pick you up tomorrow morning at seven. We'll take the early stage."

Again her heart was singing. It was strange how she could be in the depths of despair one moment and when Sean appeared, become almost forgetful of plans to return home.

But as she packed, she decided she would go to Washington first to see the President, then home so she packed both straw cases. Perhaps it would not be long before Sean would come to Springplace.

As Lotta and Gerald Colan prepared to entertain Sean's young lady for the Christmas holidays, they exchanged doubtful thoughts about their son's choice.

"A Cherokee, Gerald! I cannot believe Sean would choose to become involved with an Indian. She must have heard of his background, your wealth and position, and tricked him into this. What *can* we do?"

"Just because he says he wants to marry the girl doesn't mean he's gotten her into trouble, Lotta."

"Why otherwise?"

Her husband shrugged, "Maybe he really loves her."

"Don't you believe it!"

But when the dainty, vivacious, dusky beauty was introduced to them and, in her direct gracious manner, acknowledged the meeting, they were almost convinced to reverse their opinion.

Lotta drew herself up to her full five-foot eight height, looked down at Tsika, and said as graciously as she could, "We welcome you, my dear." But, as the white girls at the dance, she smiled only with her lips.

Tsika recognized it for what it was, a polite rejection.

Gerald Dolan masked his initial surprise not at all, but she felt drawn to him immediately when he said frankly, "I thought you'd look like an Indian, but—you don't look like those I've seen."

She liked an honest man. She laughed. "I *do* look like an Indian, Mr. Dolan. There are lots of girls like me back in the Cherokee Nation in Georgia, educated and mannerly. Some day you must come out to visit us and see for yourself."

They were even more surprised when she told about the many Indians who had married whites and had luxurious homes, and of the many trips John Ross had taken to Washington to talk to the presidents and secretaries of governmental departments about the every increasing Cherokee-Georgia State problems.

Tsika felt she was doing fairly well and that Sean would be proud of her. She was describing John Ross, "He is only one-eighth Cherokee and seven-eighths white, yet his heart is all Cherokee," when Lotta interrupted her.

"You must want to freshen up, Tsika. The maid will show you to your room, and help you unpack."

The maid treated her with contempt, but that in itself was not of concern. It was later, when she was in the dressing-room off the bedroom, and she heard Mrs. Dolan say, "She won't know the difference whether you press them or not," that she decided to leave for home early.

On the second day, Sean went into town with his father. Mrs. Dolan said, "Come, my dear, we'll have coffee together in the morning room. The maid will bring the service."

Here it comes, thought Tsika.

"Well now, how did you happen to go to the college?"

"To be well-educated has become desired and necessary to the Cherokees if they want to have recognition in Washington as a force to be reckoned with when the removal bill is brought before Congress."

"You sound well-informed on governmental procedures."

"I have learned much from my father, who is an educated

chief."

Lotta nodded. "And is your mother educated also?"

"No, but she has the strength and courage needed to face all adversity."

"I see."

"She survived a miserable trek from North Carolina to Hiwassee, Tennessee and another from Hiwassee to Springplace, Georgia, after we were burned out by whites both times."

"I didn't know you valued land. I thought all Indians liked to wander and hunt."

Good, Tsika thought, stay away from my family. "That's true of some of the Western tribes and was true of us years ago, but now the Cherokees prefer to be progressive. We even have a Supreme Court and plan to have a government modeled after the U.S. Government. At the present time we have a National Council and a head chief, John Ross, who will be our President soon."

She felt herself growing too defensive. Might as well get it over with. "Why do you ask about my parents?"

"I am bound to be interested in the background of the girl my son wishes to marry."

Tsika blushed. She was pleased, and although she was angry Sean had not asked her before he'd told his parents, she reacted in a direct and forthright manner. "Oh, I didn't know that."

"Well, I wouldn't count on his asking you now."

Now her anger surmounted her pleasure at the news. "I am going back to Springplace soon, and I shall not worry you about your son." She rose and hurried to her room to pack. She'd not tell Sean what his mother had said, for how could she marry a man against his parent's wishes. She'd just go home.

When Sean returned he'd find her gone. No. She couldn't do that to him. Quietly she replaced her clothes, chose a becoming flounced blue dress that was not too wrinkled to wear to dinner, and prepared to be charming and diplomatic.

The Grandfather hall clock chimed six times. No one was in the parlor. Was she too early? She heard papers rustling in the room beside her and peeked in. Darell, Sean's younger brother sat at a large mahogany desk furiously creating a windstorm as papers flew around him.

"What's causing this upheaval?" she asked, daring to pry.

"It's this damned Latin. I can't get languages, and exams are coming up soon. My father will boot me clear out of the house if I don't pass it."

She laughed. "You should take Cherokee. Sequoyah makes it easy for even the most ignorant woodland Indian. Maybe you could learn Latin by the same method."

"I'll try anything. Show me!"

"It may not apply to a dead language, one you wouldn't use now to converse, but this is what he did."

She explained Sequoyah's method, and Darell was more interested in the man than the procedure.

"Tell me all about him and how he arrived at the idea of creating a written language and transposed it into English for the Cherokees."

"He had a Cherokee mother and an English father who left them when George (as he was called) was very young. He wanted to be able to read and write as his father had done, but all the interesting papers had been taken from the log house.

"One day he stole a letter from the body of a white man who'd been killed in a hunting accident, and poured over the strange symbols. George was too old for school, but he came into our school room and looked over the teacher's shoulder as she read to us. We heard he'd formed a Syllabary or alphabet, but had unlawfully accepted money from some whites for land, so he hurriedly left for Arkansas. Battling Gourd was the only friend who'd encouraged and not ridiculed him about his letters.

"One day Sequoyah returned and initiated his alphabet. Now even while plowing or sawing wood, or during any work men do, they can say these letters over to themselves and learn. They didn't even have to go to school to learn to read and write. Sequoyah'd sit there, dressed like a white except for his turban of many colors and smoke his long stemmed pipe, looking very studious and professor-like. He's quite a character."

"I'd like to meet that man. Could I come to Cherokee land and visit you sometime?"

Tsika was taken aback. "Why—why of course. If your parents think it wise."

He laughed. "I'll just come. From college. They won't know the difference."

"I hear footsteps, Darell. Perhaps we'd better go into dinner."

"You'll make a mighty fine sister-in-law," he grinned.

The men had news to report and dinner went well. Neither of them, nor Darell, noticed that Tsika and Lotta were very quiet.

During the evening, Mr. Dolan discussed the Cherokee Removal issue with her and he promised to aid her people in their quest for their freedom from Georgia laws.

"I have several friends who are influential in government circles. It is a good time to approach them, for newspapers in the East recounted some of the horrible experiences your people have endured at the hands of the Georgia state officials, and public opinion seems to be in your favor."

"That's good to hear, sir. The spoken and written word have much power, and to approach this problem through the press and legal channels will give us more success with the U.S. officials than resorting to violence. I hope to write for a newspaper someday."

Lotta was surprised. The girl was not only beautiful, charming and mannerly, but she was bright. Granted she was remarkable for an Indian, but she was not for her son.

When it was time for Tsika to leave, she thanked the Dolans politely for their hospitality, but she knew Mrs. Dolan, and she knew they could never be mother and daughter.

Mr. Dolan waited with his coachman in the brougham to take the couple to the station where Tsika would get a stage back to school.

As soon as the conveyance left, Tsika announced, "I'm not going back on this coach, Sean. I'm going to see the President."

"To Washington? You can't be serious, Tsika. You can't go that far alone. Do you expect to just walk up to the door and say you want to see the President?"

"I can try."

"You must have an appointment. Talk to someone who could get you in to the inner sanctum."

"John Ross is there. He could help me."

"How would you get in touch? You don't even know where he's staying."

"At his brother's." She was short with him. She still resented the fact that he had spoken to his parents of marriage before he'd asked her.

Sean shook his head. "I can see I will have a stubborn little wife, and one who doesn't look before she leaps."

"And who says I'm going to be your wife?"

"*I* say. I thought you knew."

"How could I know, when I haven't been asked," she snapped. "And you don't even know if I'll accept."

He looked hurt. She said, "This is a strange state of affairs, Sean. I've known you for only two months, yet we're in love. You told your parents you'd marry me before you asked me and I don't like that. They think I'm not right for you, and I don't like that, so I'm going home. If you really love me, you'll come out sometime and I'll be waiting for you. Goodbye."

"Goodbye?" He turned her around in the middle of the path and kissed her soundly. "You're not going anywhere without me."

"Do you mean it?"

"Of course, I'll go to Springplace with you—now. We'll be married as soon as we arrive."

She gasped. "Sean, you must finish your law studies, get your degree. Your father will be disappointed if you don't stay."

"All right, I'll finish, take my bar exam, if you will promise to wait for me, but I'm not obligated to stay here. I love you, Tsika. I'm coming West in the spring after graduation and we will be married in Cherokee style. Meanwhile we will see one another regularly."

"You take my breath away, Sean. Are you sure, even if your parents object?"

"How sure is sure. Does the sun rise every morning? Come, we'll have no interview with the President. I'll put you on the stage to Springplace today; the sooner you go the sooner you'll come back to me."

"But I'm going to stay there. I'm not coming back."

"If that's your wish." He shrugged. He was beginning to find this girl he couldn't do without, was maddening as well as lovable. "I'll go as far as Johnson City with you, then return."

When the coach reached Johnson City, they jumped to the platform. John Ross was waiting there and came over to them.

"So, my little friend, you have finished your first term. The stage I was on broke down; I had to take this detour and now I'm glad it did. It affords me the pleasure of your company."

He looked imposing, just as though he was about to make one of his moving speeches. In spite of his slight form and his five-foot, six-inch height, he looked impressive in his waist coat, high hat, white shirt and cords. His sparkling blue eyes held ones own in a mesmerized fashion and belied his claim to being even one-eighth Cherokee.

Always entranced by his gaze, she forgot for a moment to introduce Sean.

"Oh, I'm sorry—ah—this is my good friend Sean Dolan, who is a law student. He may someday help us in Washington."

Ross turned to Sean; the men shook hands.

Sean said, "My heart is with the Cherokees. I will soon settle in Springplace." He grinned at Tsika.

She blushed, John Ross smiled at them both. "I think your heart is with a *certain* Cherokee, but we will welcome you with open arms, for we surely will need all the help we can find.

"Was your trip successful, sir?"

"It's always hard to say. Our talks seemed to go well, but we won't know until we see the actual results. The U.S. Government promises to protect our property, but so far we have not enjoyed that protection."

"Ready," called the driver.

Tsika kissed Sean goodbye, climbed back on the coach, the passengers settled in their seats and the stage rattled toward to its destination.

"This leaves much to be desired, but it's better than traveling by horseback, right, Tsika?"

John Ross proceeded to tell her of his trip from Washington to Johnson City, while they swerved and rocked on the rough roads through the remainder of North Carolina and Tennessee.

After the coach crossed the Potomac River, it followed a good road to the winding, hilly one through the Blue Ridge Mountains. For almost four hundred miles the scenery was breathtaking, but the climb on some mountain roads necessitated hairpin curves and a sickening up-and-down motion that defied description. The passengers were anxious for a respite at the end of each day to rest their aching bones. The way-stations left much to be desired, but they offered some comfort."

Tsika felt for them. She looked at the other six passengers and thought they appeared pale and uncomfortable, as though their bones were poking through their clothing.

What a ride! She was glad she hadn't gone to Washington.

They reached the Federal Highway, then the road leading to Springplace, and finally the stage arrived at the station.

They were greeted by a noisy crowd, but it was not a cheerful sound. There was crying and moaning and a few shouts of "You said you'd get us protection."

Ross was led by the people to an area where Cherokees

were driven from their homes, and livestock was stolen.

Great Wolf greeted Tsika. He kept her by his side. "Some of the Cherokees are growing violent. Tom Dorchester came in from Atlanta with news that since Georgia official's threats hadn't sent people to the West, action would be taken. This is action."

The crowd dispersed, Tsika and Wolf climbed into their carriage and began a more normal conversation.

"You wrote of trouble, Papa, so I wanted to come home. But first I wanted to plead our case to President Monroe, so I considered going to Washington."

"You what?"

"I wanted to talk to him myself."

Wolf shook his head, smiling at her daring. "And did you?"

"No."

"Did Ross influence you otherwise?"

"No, a student lawyer prevailed upon me to forget it. He's coming here to help us."

"A student—is coming here? Pray what is this gallant student's name."

"Sean Dolan. He is concerned about our problems."

"But not as concerned as he is about you?" Wolf smiled.

She blushed a burnished copper, and looked up at him. She decided to get it over with. "I—we—we want to get married in the spring after he gets his law degree."

"I thought Aiku and you—"

She nodded. "I know. He thought so too. I wrote him."

"And I already knew for he told me. He is heart-broken."

"I knew he would be, but—but—I love Sean. Where is Aiku? He didn't come to Springplace."

"You could hardly expect him to, could you? He is at Big Elk's on Federal Highway. Big Elk's rebuilding since the fire."

"You will go back to school—or you will stay home—in either case you will wish to marry this lawyer?"

"Oh, yes, Papa. You will like Sean and he is willing to marry me Cherokee style, and settle here after his graduation."

"So? Then let's go to report this astounding news to your mother, grandmother and the boys. You know he must ask me for your hand in marriage, white man's style. I must approve of him.

"Of course, he will be here for his spring holidays."

Wolf agreed that would be fine, and thought, let her stay home and perhaps she'd forget him. Go back and she'd see him frequently at college. Maybe college hadn't been such a good idea after all.

He remarked, "Aiku and Roper had a little trouble while you were gone."

"Oh, tell me about it!"

Ah, there was still a spark of interest in Aiku. As Wolf recounted Aiku's and Roper's experience with Cochee, he watched her reaction. "They brought a beautiful child back with them. Presumably she came from North Carolina, had been living in the woods on berries and roots. She tended Roper's wounds. It seems he's quite taken with her."

"Oh, poor Alda. I must meet the beauty who could take Roper away from her."

"He claims Aiku is a rival." Wolf saw Tsika quickly mask an obvious reaction of shock at that news.

Did she still love Aiku? Was she doing the right thing?

When Aiku received Tsika's letter a few weeks earlier, he'd opened it with great anticipation, but when he read the first line, he knew, and his heart turned over.

Dear Aiku,

I hope you will forgive me for what I must tell you. I am going to marry Sean Dolan, a white Washington lawyer in the spring. I will always have a special kind of love for you, and hope we will always be friends. I will be home in January to get ready and will teach at the mission.

Regretfully,

Tsika

But he had the advantage of nearness, so he still had hopes. He would see her every day. Her suitor-lawyer could not. He'd make her change her mind. Sean was just a fancy. She really loved him. He'd prove it. If she was teaching at the mission, he'd get a job there. Always optimistic, he bounced back.

The next day he appeared at the Springplace Mission, asking, "Reverend, I would like a job here at the mission. I could help Jeremy in the herb garden; it needs weeding. Or maybe I could help you in the office."

"Whoa there, Aiku. Not so fast. I would have to get permission from my superiors in Boston. We do need extra help, but—" Reverend Chamberlain hesitated.

"How long does it take to get this permission?"

"Sometimes as long as two months. It's hard to tell."

"Meantime, could I just help Jeremy and draw no pay?"

Chamberlain raised his brows. "Oh—in that case, I guess you may start any time."

"I'll have to finish my work with Big Elk first. Is next Monday all right with you?"

"Of course. And you can have your lunch here."

Tsika was hired to aid Miss Sophia Sawyer at Brainard Missionary School at the beginning of the new term. As she left on the first day, Aiku dropped his spade and ran after her.

"Hello, Tsika. It's good to see you. I'm going your way."

"So I see." Tsika smiled. "I hear you and Roper had quite an experience."

Aiku frowned. No greeting reminiscent of their closeness. Well, maybe in time.

"Yes, both bad and good. It was a foolish thing to do. Roper could have died, but Cochee was wounded also."

"I understand you saved Roper."

"No. I just got him away from danger. Tani saved his life."

"Tani?" Tsika teased.

"Didn't you hear about the little wood nymph, our savior,

who came to us with herbs in her hands?"

"Yes, and I heard she is very attractive."

Quickly he glanced at her. "I will never love anyone but you, Tsika. You know that." He reached out to take her in his arms.

She stepped back. "No. Put your hands in your pockets, Aiku! I'm not your girl now."

He scowled. "I can try to win you back."

"No. As I said in my letter, I love you as a very special friend, but I am not *in* love with you. There's the difference."

"You don't know your own feelings," he sulked.

"I believe I do. Now look, Aiku. We can be friends only if you will stop bringing up how you feel about me."

"All right," he grumbled, then smiled and shook hands. "I agree, if you see me often."

She laughed, "I can't help it, can I, if you're going to be working at the Mission."

There was that appealing bell-like laugh that had kept ringing in his ears. Now it was real. Her beauty and her wonderful sense of humor endeared her to him. She was part of his existence. He couldn't lose her.

He nodded. Pleased he'd won his point. Propinquity would help to cast Sean from her thoughts.

"Ah, there she is, Aiku. She's come looking for you."

Tani crossed the road. "I am so pleased to see you," she greeted Tsika. "Welcome to our village."

Here was no pretty child, but a beautiful woman: tiny, dusky, shapely and charming. Her dark eyes shone with a special love for Aiku. Her blue-black hair swung freely, the front locks cupping a determined chin, and when she smiled, her lips parted over even white teeth. Yes, she was beautiful. Didn't Aiku see?

Tsika resented it that the girl had welcomed *her* as a visitor and there was a small twinge of jealousy. Didn't she want Aiku to love again? Of course she did. She'd always been of a generous nature and really wanted everyone to be happy.

"Aiku, you haven't introduced us."

"Oh yes. Tani, this is Tsika. She is Chief Wolf's daughter, just come from college in the East."

Was he saying that to impress Tani, or to tease *her?*

"But I am not returning to the Seminary, Tani. I am staying here to teach at the Mission while I plan my wedding."

Tani's eyes filled with tears. "You marry Aiku?"

They laughed in unison, nervously at first, then whole-heartedly. "No, Tani, to someone else."

"Ah," Tani sighed, taking Aiku's arm.

He looked embarrassed. "Roper is very fond of Tani," he said patting her hand. "I believe she has given him second thoughts about Alda."

What complications, thought Tsika. *Roper loves her, she loves Aiku, he loves me and I love Sean. Oh, Sean, come soon!*

Someone called to them, "Ho, look who's here." Roper bounded across the road. "Welcome home, Tsika. We've missed you." He cast a knowing glance in Aiku's direction.

"Thank you, I'll be here for awhile."

They had reached her home. Micha ran to meet her and she swooped him up in a bear hug.

"Can I go to school with you, Tsika?"

"In two months when you're six."

Aiku called after her, "I'll bring Attu. He can go too."

January and February were mild months. Tsika was delighted to be where there was warmth from the sun and glad that Aiku was as mild as the weather. There had been no more efforts to hug her or declare his love for her.

Roper visited the Fox home frequently to see Tani now on a pretext of seeing Alda, and neither girl was happy. Alda was devastated by Roper's change of affection while Tani tried more and more to avoid Roper and attract Aiku.

Alda determined Tani had to get out of the house. She prompted Ulah to make a suggestion.

"Tani, Miss Sawyer would like to see you today. She wishes to have help at her house and for that help she will give lessons in Sequoyah's Syllabary. I told her you wish to read and write. I hope I was not presuming too much."

Tani was delighted. And now Aiku was pleased. That would take Tani away at dinner time and he could invite Tsika over and convince "his girl" that her eastern lawyer was forgetting her.

When his invitation came in March, Tsika explained, "I can't come, Aiku. Sean is arriving today for his Easter holiday."

Suddenly Aiku was faced with the fact that he hadn't a chance. Love was in the air all around him, but it wasn't for him. Roper did a turnabout. He and Alda were planning a June first wedding and Tsika and Sean would be married on the fifth.

Aiku complained to Roper, "You're a lucky one. You got the girl you wanted. I'm going into the hills and live on nuts and berries." The thatch of black hair that always struggled to escape from his headband bobbed as he nodded, "I've lost to him."

"You're not really going to the hills, are you Aiku?"

"You know me better than that, Rope. I'm going to New Town, buy some land to farm, and perhaps do some harassing of my own."

"All that? I'll believe it when I see it. I'd more believe you'd marry Tani and settle down to the good life."

"I'll go it alone, friend. Thoughts of getting married make you soft in the head."

As Tsika walked home from work she thought of what she'd heard about Aiku's plans. What a waste. He could study to become a diplomat and be an important force in the Cherokee Nation's politics. She cared! Was it nostalgia for the years of their close friendship, and for the first romantic thrills? Yes, but now there'd be a new chapter in her life, a truly wonderful one. She might have to give up some of her Cherokee customs, but Sean was worth it all. Wasn't she sure? What was wrong with her today?

Rain clouds pushed over the valley. Lightning flashed and the predicted storm swept into the town. The wind howled, whipping branches from the trees, and Tsika was struck a sharp blow on the head. Sleet slanted tingling ice pellets against her face. The thunder sounded as though the mountains were caving in on her. When she finally arrived home, and poured out her fears of marrying, she felt physically as well as emotionally weary.

Star advised, "You're having prenuptial jumps, Tsika. Come, I'll put a poultice of comfrey on your head. You'll feel better."

The Wolf farmhouse buzzed with excitement. Sean more than met with the family's approval. He went hunting with the boys and his excellent marksmanship astounded them. His acceptance was assured. He complimented Niahmi's and Star's cooking prowess which endeared him to them. He even felt at ease with her gruff father as they discussed Cherokee customs, the chief's dealings with the government and an acceptance of the white man's way of living.

Possibly one reason he felt at home was because the Wolfs' house was like any home in the East. There were fine furniture, lovely dishes and silverware, and a kitchen full of pots and pans that produced delicious foods. Yes, he liked this place and knew he could live and work here.

After their first meal together, when Sean and Tsika rose to depart, Arapho remarked, "He fits us comfortably, like our moccasins."

"Yea," Micha chimed in, "and his nose is like the eagle's beak. Let's give him a Cherokee name, 'Eagle Dolan.' "

Wolf scolded, but Sean laughed, "Both boys say the truth, now I will really fit into the Cherokee community."

"We welcome you, Eagle Dolan," they chorused.

"Thank you, and I am fortunate to have such a good new family." Then he raised his eyebrows and firmed his lips in an expression they would often see when he objected to what he had to do. "Now Tsika and I are leaving to visit some friends."

"Tsika," he asked her on their round of visits, "take me to an area where you'd like to live when we're married."

"There aren't any houses like ours available, Sean, but perhaps we could find a cabin."

"I plan to build a house, my sweet. Pick out a good location where there is enough land to farm."

"You want to build?"

"Of course, we will have a beautiful home like the Ross's we've just visited."

This was a delightful surprise, and Tsika immediately thought of the hill beside the river where she went to think, or to—meet Aiku. No. That wouldn't be advisable.

"There are acres of unclaimed land near New Town, just off the Federal Highway, beautiful hilly land that flattens as it rolls down to the river and that has excellent fields for planting. Come, I know just the place."

However, when they arrived at the site, they found a small cabin occupied by a wizened Indian squatter.

"What in hell do you want?" he questioned the couple.

"We thought we'd like to buy some land around here," Sean answered.

"Hmph, how much'll you give me?"

"Come, Sean, we'll—" Suddenly she jumped down from the carriage. "It's Rattling Gourd! I'm Tsika. You old rascal, what are you doing here?" She hugged the ragged figure.

He grinned. "I'm McAllister's watch dog. After I got burned out, McAllister threatened he'd see to it I was attacked again, unless I just holed up in here and guarded this place."

"Then we'll have to see him. Don't tell him, Gourd. If he knew I wanted his property, he'd never sell. You know ever since Arpho married his daughter, Becky, he's never forgiven the Wolfs. Sean will approach him. Oh, this is my husband-to-be."

"We shake hands white man's fashion," said Gourd proudly. "I am native American and now new American, learning new ways. I help Sequoyah promote his Syllabary."

"Did you ever learn it as you promised me you would?"

He shrugged sheepishly. "Little bit. Speak well, yes?"

"Yes. Now we must go."

"Will I stay if you buy?"

"Of course, and you will be our watch dog. But remember Gourd, tell no one that you saw us here."

He nodded and waved them off.

"I'll take you home, Tsika, and go to see McAllister immediately."

"A man of action. I like that, Sean." Then she laughed, "But you are too impetuous. First you must ask my father for my hand in marriage."

"Oh yes, that little formality." He kissed her. "Do you think he will say no?"

"Yes, and then what will you do?"

"Just carry you off."

"We'll have a wedding you'll long remember, Sean. It will draw Cherokees and whites closer together. The ceremony will be a combination of both marriage customs."

"You plan it, my sweet. I'll be there."

Tsika wondered about Aiku. He would be invited, but was he too hurt to appear?

When the great day arrived she was too excited to think of anything but Sean. On June fourth, 1825, on the eve of her wedding day, a grand banquet was held at the large council hall in the center of town. Quarters of venison turned on spits and wild turkeys and ducks roasted in hot ashes; all kinds of sauces and vegetables were cooked; wild spring berries were served with thick cream, and any number of sweet cakes graced the long table.

Tsika, resplendent in her white fringed deerskin tunic and leggings that were decorated with colored quills, floated from one group to another on moccasined feet. Her gem-trimmed headband glittered in the candlelight. Sean also wore the leather tunic, leggings, moccasins and headdress of the tribe. The tall blond man looked incongruous among the dark-skinned Cherokees, but he was completely unaware of his difference as his adoring eyes followed Tsika.

The guest list was long. It included White Fox, Battling Gourd, Big Elk, Al Weatherby, Chuck Bronson, Charles Weaver, Dorchester, John Ridge, Major Ridge, Chiefs, Ross, Vann, Lowrey, Hicks and their families, and many other townspeople and hill folk. The couple was greeted with raised palms or an arm grasp in true Cherokee manner.

Then came the dancing, and Sean was good-naturedly ridiculed as he attempted Indian dance steps to the beat of the skin drum, the flute and rattling gourds. The shells on dancing ankles jingled to the rhythm of the music, and, forming an enclosed circle for the dancers, young and old alike swayed to the tempo.

Finally Wolf clapped his hands for silence. Speeches by the attending chiefs and toasts went on while tantalizing cooking odors permeated the council house and children began to get restless.

"What do you think of our Cherokee part of the ceremony, Sean?" Tsika questioned him.

"It's very impressive, but I'm damned hungry."

Tsika's black eyes sparkled. "You danced well for a white man; you only stepped on my toes twice."

"I felt awkward, but I didn't mind the ridicule as long as you were there to protect me. I have only one worry. Are the young braves going to prevent me from attending my own wedding?"

"Don't worry, they won't do anything before the banquet."

"And after?"

"I'll protect you," she giggled.

"I'm looking forward to tomorrow and the official ceremony."

"Don't think the full blood Cherokees are through now. They'll continue celebrating all through the night."

She rose, and the guests cheered.

"Tomorrow I will present my husband with an ear of corn to say I will be a good squaw." She nudged him, and whispered, "It's your turn."

"And I will present my wife with game to show I will be a good mate." He turned to her and whispered, "Time for dinner?"

"Sh. Not yet."

"Have a heart. How much do you think I can take?"

She laughed, "Don't worry, I've omitted this next part, and tomorrow you'll be able to dress formally and I'll appear in my white gown like a white bride, except—"

"Except for what?"

"More speeches and dancing by the medicine man." She watched for his reaction.

"No! Absolutely no! I'll go back to Washington."

"I'm teasing. We'll say our vows for Reverend Chamberlain."

"Thank God. Now we have our wedding feast?"

Dancing continued after the festive meal. Tsika and Sean waltzed to the beat of the tom-toms.

"No small feat, this," Sean said as they danced toward the door and outside into the soft cool air of the spring night.

Other couples were in close embrace and Sean gathered Tsika into his arms. "It seems to be the style."

Star and Rena Bronson descended upon them. "Come, Tsika," her mother said. "From now until tomorrow's service, your bridegroom must not see you: white man's way. Meanwhile you will go to the marriage hut: Cherokee way."

"Mama, that's old-fashioned. I refuse to go into that putrid hut. You can't make me!"

Star shook her head. "Rena, what can I do with her? She will not observe our customs anymore."

Rena laughed. "Come, Star, we are all taking on the white's manners and customs. You will, whether you like it or not. You're progressive in your home and its furnishings and in your dress. Why not customs?"

"Very well then. You don't have to go to the hut, but you can't see Sean until tomorrow. We'll go home."

Tsika gave Sean a look of resigned submission, took her mother's arm and left for their home.

This night Sean was to stay with the Bronsons. Chuck approached them. "Ready, son?"

"No, but I will call it a night."

"Damn right, you will!" shouted John Ridge. "And it'll be a busy one. You belong to us for a few hours," and the youths, who were bent on some form of devilment, hurried him away.

As Tsika heard the war whoops, drums and music in the night, she worried about his capture. What were they going to do to him? Would he be able to find his way back for the wedding if they abandoned him in the woods?

Sean was better equipped to handle the situation than John Ridge or any of the captors knew. It was training in college wrestling versus inebriation. Several would-be pranksters fell by the wayside; the others were bested by some holds that begged for release. So his escape at five o'clock in the morning was well-earned. He appeared at the Bronson breakfast table on time.

Other than a special Cherokee dance to the goddess of marriage and fertility, The Corn Mother, a purely English ceremony was performed.

Tsika's dusky beauty was enhanced by the ivory lace bridal gown; Alda and Ulah, bridesmaids, were dressed in pale blue and Quati, matron of honor, wore pink. Tsika was ecstatic; the only sad note was that Sean's parents were not there.

As soon as the dancing started after the ritual of cake-cutting and bouquet-tossing, Sean and Tsika disappeared.

By the time the couple returned from their honeymoon in the east, their new home was completed. Rattling Gourd proved to be more than a watchdog. He had taken on the responsibility of watching over the contractor, driving the workmen hard, and had managed to get the new furniture uncrated and in place before their arrival. Except for a few pieces to be shipped from Europe, the Dolans were settled.

Sean was welcomed as a lawyer in Sam Kellog's office and Tsika spent the remainder of the summer becoming accustomed to the duties of Mistress of Riverview Acres. Several field hands and three house servants were hired. All had won their freedom when they stepped on Sean's land. They blended into the large holdings as though they had worked there forever. At first Tsika objected to Manda and Nilla, the cook and maid, but finally realized she couldn't handle the housekeeping of the mansion alone. The largest, most beautiful mansion in New Town in 1824 needed good care.

Battling Gourd was doing famously as manager of the farm until a white stranger appeared at the barns one fall morning. A minor disagreement started among three new stable hands, Gourd stepped in to settle their differences and suffered a knife wound that ultimately caused his death. The white stranger, Ron Bullock, had also intervened, and Sean had hired him to take Gourd's place on Sam's recommendation.

The story that reached town was pure fabrication, or so Sean thought. It was impossible that Ron could have planned to get this job in so bizarre a manner: by provoking a quarrel, pretending to come to Gourd's rescue, then stabbing the man. The idea was so preposterous that Sean cast the entire incident from his mind.

Bullock was a gaunt man with a perpetual frown on his ferret-like features. Also reminding one of the little animal were his green eyes, hard as marbles, and his russet hair.

He had never forgotten the sadness and anger that consumed him when he had crouched behind a stone wall, at eight and saw his father killed and his mother and small brother burned to death in their cottage in Ireland. He'd pounded his fists on the bare earth in frustration and swore he would get even with the man Dolan.

It had taken 20 years and many hardships, even a term in jail, but finally he was here where he could get at the father through the son. He still felt nauseated when he visioned the glazed look in his father's eyes as the front of his shirt bloodied. And then the British murderer left for America.

Tsika had never dreamed of living in a home such as this, the kind only a few mixed-bloods and white folks owned. It was a pillared mansion with a veranda. It had large parlors, library and dining room. The kitchen and storage rooms were enormous. On the second floor were six bedrooms and a cubby closet and the third floor housed the servants. As she looked out over the property from the second story window at the rear of the house the stables and supply sheds were bright against the green hills and mountains and from the front she could see the river and the rows of fall plantings. She sighed. It fairly took one's breath.

It was impossible, yet here she was, an Indian maid, the mistress of a vast plantation. The missionaries had changed her people, bringing them Christianity and education. The changes had given her an opportunity to meet Sean and have all this. She would be thankful and help her people in any way she could. She would entertain the Vanns, Rosses, Ridges, but she would cling to her Cherokee traditions. Enjoy it with her beloved husband and always be caring and loyal. But she was restless. Accustomed to working with people, she felt uncomfortable sitting by while the servants did the housework. She had to do something worthwhile.

That evening with some trepidation, she approached Sean, as he worked on the plantation ledgers. "Sean, I have an idea. Now that the house is running smoothly, I believe I will go back to teaching at the Mission."

"Taking care of me and the house isn't enough?"

"Well, no," she pled with those liquid brown eyes that always changed a no to a yes.

"Of course, but how will you get to Springplace everyday? Or will you go to the new missionary school here, where there are only five children?"

She defended the new location. "I know there aren't many pupils, but New Town will grow."

"What will Butler say about that? He doesn't need help with so few children."

"I will teach weaving and pottery making. They must know the old crafts as well as learn reading and writing."

Sean smiled.

"If he won't take me on, I'll write for an eastern paper."

"Where do you get those remarkable ideas?"

"Now you're laughing at me."

"No, my love. Admiring your spirit and your ambition, but let's have a family first."

"I want a family too. I can do both, raise children and—"

"And ride and keep house. My dear, your energy is wearing me out. I'm tired just listening to all you want to do."

"When do I start?"

"Having a family? Right now." He picked her up and headed for the stairs, nuzzling her neck.

"Oh, Sean, in the middle of the morning?"

There was a knock at the front door.

"Sean, put me down," she laughed. "I'm the lady of the house. I must look presentable when Jeremy opens that door."

"Must I?" he frowned.

"Come now—"

The knocking became insistent, and since Jeremy hadn't appeared, Sean went to the door.

"Oh, hello Ron, come in."

"Mr. Dolan, there's trouble with the hands. They are determined to leave the farm to go up to Rossville to hear White Bird speak. They can't go. We must get the hay in. It's going to rain tonight."

Ron Bullock was a conscientious and demanding manager. "Come talk to them, sir." Then as though he was making fun of Tsika, he bowed and said, "Ah, the lovely mistress. Good morning, my lady."

My lady, indeed! During the entire conversation with Sean he had stared at her. She hated him and his green eyes. Ever since he'd helped her down from her horse at the stable one day, and held her longer than necessary, she'd avoided him. His appraising look seemed to be undressing her. She shivered.

"Excuse me. I'll tend to dinner preparations."

As she departed she felt his piercing green eyes drilling into her back. She imagined that half-smirk. How could Sean hire such a man?

Ron felt his goal slipping. He'd made a vow to pay the father back by killing the son, but now he became obsessed with the Indian wench. He wanted her and by God, he'd have her. For accomplishing either, he'd have to bide his time. And the right time wasn't now. He and Sean left the house.

He'd been right in first applying for a harassment job from the Georgia officials; it would be a good cover-up for his real purpose. Anything he did would appear in the line of duty. His friend Cochee would help him.

When Sean returned from the fields, Tsika asked him, "Where did you find that awful man?"

"I told you, the day Gourd was stabbed, I hired him on Sam's recommendation."

"I don't like him. I don't trust him."

"He's a good manager, Tsika."

"I wish you could find someone else."

"Good managers are hard to come by." And as far as Sean was concerned, the matter was closed.

"Sometimes, I don't trust Sam Kellog either," she muttered.

"Sam? Why?"

"Just a feeling." Then she asked, "What did Ron say White

Bird would speak about?"

"You know after the Cherokees formed a Supreme Court, and the Georgia officials were worried that you'd demand citizenship, the Secretary of War notified the Cherokees that soon commissioners would be coming to the Nation to negotiate a treaty of land cessions, so the council meeting is called today to determine what to do about it."

"I'm going up there."

"Only council members are allowed at the meeting, Tsika. You'd have to stand outside."

"I know that, but if the farm workers can go, I can go."

"I can't see why you want to go if you can't attend the meeting," Sean said stubbornly.

"Clearly you don't want me to go. Why Sean?"

"Removal harassment has begun again and anyone can be a target."

"Quati will be there. We'll be together. No harm can come to me when I'm with John Ross's wife."

"Don't be too sure. All right, go, but do be careful. I'd go too, but the ledgers call and I must prepare for a case that goes to trial next week."

She grinned, "I may get some information about that case for you." She kissed him. "I'll be careful. You are a darling."

"Yes, I am," he laughed. "Don't forget that dinner you started."

"Men and their food!" She hurried out.

Tsika hurried to Boudinot as he came from the building. Her black hair streaming over her face in the wind, she called, "What did they say, Mr. Boudinot?"

"Oh, hello Tsika. A resolution was passed that there would be no more land cessions with the United States, and the thirteen men set up to check on the chiefs reported that none had disobeyed the rules like they did at Calhoun Agency in 1819, when Sequoyah and Chief Jolly unlawfully sold some land."

"Thank you. I'll tell my husband. Now I want to ask a favor of you. I want to teach the children of New Town. How do I go about it, contact Father Chamberlain or go to Reverend Butler?"

Elias scratched his beard. "That's admirable, Tsika. I'll talk to Chamberlain myself."

She returned in jubilant spirits, anxious to tell Sean about her conversation with Boudinot. She jumped from her horse calling to the stable boy, "Benny come, take my horse."

"Whoa, little one," Ron called. He took the lines from Benny's hands. "You'll want to walk the horse a bit. I'll join you." He grasped her arm and pulled her to him.

"Stop it, Ron!"

"Come on. A little hug won't hurt you."

She jerked away. "I'll tell Sean and he'll fire you."

"Ha! He can't or you'll find something out about him you don't want to hear." He strode importantly back to his cabin.

She raced up the path to the house. She was breathless from the exercise, but more from the anger and revulsion she felt when that man touched her. She'd tell Sean, but—maybe she'd better not if—was there something she wouldn't want to know?

She was crying when she entered the house. She hated Bullock's smug sneering smile, his green eyes, his thick reddish hair and mustache. A hairy man was repulsive. Indians were clean looking and clear-skinned, like Sean. Why couldn't Sean fire him?

If she locked the study door, he'd be out of her mind. At first it didn't work, but soon she was immersed in a study plan for pupils from six to sixteen. And she began to write an article for the Boston paper about what Boudinot had told her. She'd send it off in the next mail. In the process, she forgot Bullock's pawing, and suddenly, she realized there was another distraction from his unwanted attention. She was pregnant.

During the first week at New Town Missionary School, where Mr. Butler taught, the children were restless to be gone from their wooden benches even before recess time. A summer of outdoors in the fields and at play had brought with it a desire that did not include writing Sequoyah's syllabary on a slate.

But teaching was Butler's forte and Tsika was expected to keep order. Perhaps after the first fall days had passed, the children would accept the curtailment of their freedom. She sighed. She certainly hoped so.

At dinner she told Sean, "I said I wasn't hired to be a disciplinarian but to teach, and Butler said, 'I have managed to get along for quite some years without advise, Tsika, and I will do so now.'"

Sean hid a smile behind his napkin. "There are always problems when you work for someone."

"I suppose so. Only it will be hard to get used to. I'd rather write. Be my own boss."

"You are writing. The *Boston Herald* editor said you could free-lance, and the article you wrote is good. I'll send it in."

"When I become a full-time writer, I'll give up teaching."

"You talk about giving up teaching? You've just begun."

"Oh, I enjoy the children. I wouldn't give it up soon."

"If what you say is true, my love, you'll be giving it up before June."

"It's true as true, Sean," and she jumped up to kiss him. He rose, and hugging her to him they danced together as he hummed the tune they'd danced to on their wedding trip.

Butler banged into the school room one October morning. "I don't know where it's all going to end. '24's a bad year."

Her back to the door, Tsika jumped. "What's the trouble, Reverend?"

"A Creek Chief, William McIntosh, an emissary of the commissioners, attempted to bribe Chief Ross, Charles Hicks second chief, Alexander McCoy, clerk of the Council and several minor chiefs. He offered $12,000 for Georgia lands."

"Of course John Ross refused."

"Yes, he was contemptuous and so the Indian agent reacted. McMinn, Meigs successor, has continued to harass the members of the Legislative Council, taking their livestock, and burning their homes and barns."

"This has been going on far too long. I will write about it for the *Boston Herald*. The U.S. Government will do something."

"Don't be too sure, Tsika. The Georgia State officials have a friend in Washington by the name of Andrew Jackson."

"How well I know that, but I'll write anyway. We have friends in Washington too, Reverend Butler."

"Maybe so, but I doubt it will do any good. If Georgia officials feel so inclined, they'll harass us continually."

"Sean thinks they will leave us alone for awhile now, but I doubt it. The thieving and burning have gone on for years. Something's *got* to be done."

"Boudinot said the council will send John Ross, George Lowrey, Elijah Hicks and Major Ridge to Washington in January to ask President Monroe to abrogate the Georgia treaty of 1802, and kick McMann off Cherokee land."

"They've tried to abrogate that treaty before. Will they be any more successful this time?"

"I believe they might. Monroe leans to our direction."

When Chief Ross and his delegation returned from the capitol, the Dolans were invited to dinner at the Ross mansion. They were anxious to hear about the proof Ross had presented to the president about the Holston Treaty and if it had been accepted. Would they win that round or be disappointed again? What would Ross say about the Georgia Treaty of 1802?

Quati and Tsika had been good friends since her Brainard school days. She looked forward to the trip as they would also visit her family at Springplace.

Sean advised, "You'd better not ride, Tsika. We'll take the carriage."

"But I'd much rather ride, Sean. It may be my last for ever so long. You're much too protective."

"Six months is too far along to ride, so we go in the carriage, my little rebel."

Tsika sighed. "I suppose you're right. It's good the school is close. I can walk these last three months."

"So you're planning to teach right up to the last minute?"

"Of course."

"For shame, girl. Have you no modesty?" he teased.

She swatted at his shoulder.

He dodged. "Don't, I'm just saying what my mother would say."

Tsika tired on the trip, and realized for the first time since her pregnancy had begun that she had no control over the responses of her body. She wouldn't be able to travel over these rough roads much longer. How could she ever have thought she could ride horseback? Maybe she was a bit too stubborn. She was glad when they arrived at the Ross home.

Quati the former Indian princess, diminutive and beautiful, had a truly regal posture. Her head held high and with graceful step, she seemed to glide into the room as she welcomed them.

The home's furnishings reflected her training at an Eastern college and the meals she served were a combination of Indian foods and those served in white homes. The pheasant and yams were accompanied by delicate asparagus and apple dessert with a delicious sauce.

There was polite conversation about the weather, but that must be before serious questions could be asked about the trip.

"It's become quite cold for February," John began. "Some years there are magnolias budding."

"I know," said Quati. "Sometimes spring comes before the leaves on the trees whisper their farewell."

"Yes, my father says the climate here is more mild than where we lived in the North Carolina mountain land of pine."

"I'm glad you moved here," said Quati.

Tsika laughed. "Now I can smile about it. We had no

choice. It was move or be burned out and chased into the forest."

"I too am glad you're here," John agreed. "I rely on you to keep the Easterners posted on our progress."

Sean could bear this trivial chatter no longer. "We are anxious to hear your views on the meeting with President Monroe."

"Ah, yes, to get down to Cherokee business. Delegates from both sides were present and of course the issues were first discussed by the Georgia contingent. When we had our chance, President Monroe was impressed with the educated way in which our requests were made, but the War Department refused them so Monroe suggested a waiting period."

"Does that mean you must return?"

"Yes, perhaps in April."

"Then Governor Troupe of Georgia, who is as pro-removal as his predecessor Gilmore was, took up the tirade against the Cherokees and accused Monroe of not keeping his word to the Georgia Delegation."

"Didn't Monroe disagree with him?"

"Yes, he stated to Congress that Georgia's Compact did not entitle them to remove the Cherokees by force. So it was a stalemate. Removal proceedings were postponed."

"That's encouraging, isn't it?" Tsika asked.

"Yes, any postponement is encouraging. We also had other business with the government. We brought up the old request for payment long overdue the Cherokee Nation for a land deal in northeast Georgia, called the Wafford Settlement; a change in location of a Cherokee agency and a request that the Federal Government collect taxes from the white traders using the Federal Highway through our property."

"Now what do we do?"

"Wait, and make some rules for our people, so they will have some procedure to follow. We know, but do they?"

"You will call a meeting of all the people to tell them?"

"Yes. Here are the rules:

"One: Fight the Georgians with the press; tell about the harassment, the cruelties, the injustices. Their sympathies for us are evident in eastern newspapers now.

"Two: Send delegates to Washington regularly to hound the President.

"Three: Take the slurs and the harassments quietly, bear with them, do not fight. Any violence would make Washington authorities side with the Georgians against us, saying we are savages.

"Tsika, you might write a short summary soon about the plans to establish a new capitol in your New Town. I'll keep you informed. Samuel Worchester will be here shortly to work with the Cherokees on a translation of the Bible and Hymns. Later he will help Boudinot to publish a newspaper."

"A newspaper!" breathed Tsika.

Ross smiled. "Yes, we plan a building for printing in New Echota."

Tsika could hardly contain herself. "How soon?"

"The Council will probably determine details by November '25, and hopefully the newspaper will be printed by October '27."

"Over two years away?"

He smiled. "These things take time, Tsika."

She turned to Sean. "We could have two children by then."

Quati watched them in admiration: *Sean, so enthused and dear Tsika, so dedicated to her people. Together they would go far. Sean was a true Cherokee these days.* She hoped it would last and he would continue to work for their cause.

Quati took Tsika aside as the men walked to the door. "You have a good life with Sean, Tsika. During your baby-raising years, don't work too hard on Cherokee causes."

"Oh, writing at home won't keep me too busy, because I have decided to give up my teaching when I'm hired to write for the *Phoenix.*"

"Have you written to ask Worchester?"

Tsika grinned. "No, but I don't see how he could refuse me

when I've had articles published in the eastern papers, do you?"

Quati laughed. "No, I don't, and I love your spirit, dear, but do be careful. Words can sometimes cause trouble. John doesn't want you to write anything too controversial, anything that might put your life in danger."

"You're just like Sean, Quati. You worry too much. But, if it pleases you, I will promise to be careful and be aware of any danger."

"Good. Now no more traveling until after your child is born." Quati called to John, "They must stay with us tonight."

"No thank you, Quati," Tsika was quick to refuse. "We don't have far to go. We're staying with my folks tonight."

One half-hour later, Wolf greeted them at the door with a hearty "Welcome children," then turned to his youngest son. "Micha, take the horse to the barn. These relatives of ours need food and rest from their travels."

"Thanks Wolf. Tsika's ready. We've had a full day."

"Speak for yourself, Sean. I'm fine. I'm not going to bed immediately," she scowled. "I aim to hear what my father says about the Washington meeting."

Wolf shook his head. "Better let her do as she wants, Sean. Wolf women are stubborn." He winked at Star.

"Of course," said Star. "We're all anxious to hear about it. I'll get some tea and biscuits for us and some of that good strong corn brew your father makes for the men."

"You heard all about it from Ross," Sean objected.

"I know, but I want to hear Papa's views."

"Well, we were glad that Monroe postponed a decision on the Georgia Treaty. Public opinion had some effect on that decision. I believe we can now go ahead with our plans for New Town, build an elegant capitol for the Nation."

"That's right in our own back yard."

"Yes, and I understand that Sam Worchester is coming to start a printing press there also."

"And I will write articles for him." Then she frowned. "But it's such a long time to wait."

Her father shook his turbaned head. "Tsika, you always want everything done in a hurry. These things take time."

"And," reminded Sean, "There's a new Dolan on the way."

"I know. I'm impatient for the baby to be born. And for Sam Worcester to come, for the press building to be built, because it all means that we can show the Georgians the progress the Cherokees are making."

"Come, our baby can't mean that much to Georgia, Tsika."

"You're exasperating at times, Sean. You know what I mean."

They said goodnight and Star called after them, "Remember what I told you to do, Tsika."

Sean waited until they'd closed the bedroom door, then he asked, "Pray what did your mother tell you to do?"

Tsika giggled. "You won't believe this. I'm to go to the Medicine Man."

"Because you're going to have a baby?"

"A papoose, remember, my mother clings to some of the old Cherokee customs. He would give me the inner bark of the wild cherry tree to relieve the pain of labor. Also brewed root of cinnamon speedwell and cones of the prickly pear tree. Then to make the fetus jump down at the proper time, he'd use ground spotted touch-me-not stems. You don't believe this, do you?"

"You're right. I don't believe it."

"I'm not through. To facilitate the actual birth, there's a herbal potion of slippery elm bark."

"It sounds to me as though the combination would make you so sick, you wouldn't care what happened." Then he noted her serious expression. *"You* don't believe this do you?"

"I believe that slippery elm might have some merit. Just saying the name suggests success," she grinned.

"Come on, you're so tired you're talking nonsense."

With a mischievous glint in her eyes, she added. "The

Medicine Man says I shouldn't wear a neckerchief or eat speckled trout, rabbit or squirrel. How does that sound?"

"Utterly ridiculous," he laughed, and he pulled the scarf from her neck. "But we can't take any chances, can we?"

"No, Eagle Dolan, we can't."

That spring Tsika wrote about the suggested plans for the new capitol of the Cherokee Nation.

"I'm too fat to do anything but wait, so I've written some of the things that John Ross wanted the world to know. Should I send it in to the *National Intelligencer* or to the Boston paper?"

"Doesn't matter as long as it gets there. Read it to me."

"Aware of the bribery by U.S. commissioners and Georgia officials in the past, the newly established Cherokee Legislative Council, decreed that:

1. The criminal codes be modified.

2. Silver and gold, copper and lead, found within the Cherokee boundary shall be the public property of the Cherokee Nation.

3. Surplus monies are to be loaned at six percent.

4. A new capitol is to be established, called New Echota, and located at the confluence of the Conasauga and the Coosawatti Rivers on the south side of the Conasauga River.

5. It was resolved to lay out 100 town lots, of one acre square on that river where the public square will embrace two acres of ground.

6. Main street will be 60 feet wide and other streets 50 feet wide.

7. Lots to be sold to the highest bidder and sales monies to be used to erect public buildings, i.e., council house, court buildings, print shop, tavern, stores, temporary shelter for visiting council members and permanent homes for the Reverend, Samuel Worcester, Elias Boudinot, and printer, John Wheeler."

"That's good, Tsika. And here we are, in on the ground floor. We'll help to make this a lovely town."

"It will be a period of renaissance for the Cherokees. Just

think, Sequoyah's syllabary will be in print for all the people to read, and I'll be writing for the paper."

"You're writing for a paper that isn't, and Worcester hasn't even come to town. You're accomplishing the impossible."

She laughed, "I know. Isn't it exciting?"

Sean again marveled at his good luck. He'd married a lovely winsome child, although she was capable of being maddeningly unpredictable. Everything in life was to be enjoyed and if of a serious nature, a cause to be pursued. She lived every day to the hilt and in her enthusiasm, drew everyone to her. Her pregnancy was just another interesting event to be savored, and entered into with verve. However, she had become a responsible woman in the past year and while still enthusiastic about everything, was a constant helpmate.

"Sean?"

He came to. "Oh, yes, exciting. Suppose we take a walk around the estate and give you your exercise for today."

"I'm afraid I can't. I've been having labor pains for the past thirty minutes."

"Oh my God!"

Melissa Dolan was born on May 15th, 1825, protesting with a lusty howl that the new world was not to her liking. Then she settled down to a quiet life, as quiet and peaceful as the Cherokee villages were at present. But Tsika took a long time to recover from the difficult birth. She wondered if she would be ready to take on her teaching responsibilities in the fall.

The Georgia officials hadn't harassed the Cherokees for some months and the year 1825-1826, when John Quincy Adams was elected president, was going smoothly. It was hoped that he'd be so involved with his new office that the peaceful atmosphere would continue.

Samuel Worcester arrived that fall and throughout the winter he worked on his translations. There was no sign of a printing press, and when asked when he would be able to get the presses, he said, "Soon."

The Council sent Boudinot East to raise funds for large presses with both English and Cherokee letters. Now that there were eighteen Missionary schools in the Nation and Sequoyah's syllabary was universally taught, it was necessary that the Cherokee people know what was going on in the world. Also he was to make a request for donations for a Cherokee National Academy.

During the winter months and spring of 1826, the buildings at New Echota were rising around the town square, and it was hoped that the first Legislative meeting would be held in the fall of that year in the new Council House.

Tsika started home on the final day of school in June, wondering whether she was wise to say she could raise a family and teach at the same time. She was almost due for another baby and felt daily fatigue. As she walked to her home, and passed the village square where the frenzied hammering and sawing went on, she marveled that so much had been accomplished. Yet it seemed that the Council House, the Court House, the homes and the stores had taken precedence over the print shop. It might not even be ready for business by fall.

"Oh, no!" Tsika said aloud. "It can't be. Not yet!" She bent over to recover from her first labor pain.

Hurrying as fast as she was able, she reached the end of the lane leading to the house, when she was gripped by such a severe stab of pain that she dropped to the ground.

She clenched her fists. "Oh, Dear Spirit, don't let me have my baby here!"

As she tried to rise, two large hands pulled her to her feet, then lifted her in strong arms and carried her up the path.

She struggled, "Put me down, I can walk, you—you—"

Ron Bullock laughed. "What? No thank you?" He set her on the top step, and loped off to the barns.

Of all people to find her like that. Damn him! "Oh—Manda! Help me!" Another pain and blackness.

The next thing Tsika knew, she heard a cry and someone said, "She's fortunate. This one came out like greased lightning."

She mumbled, "It was the slippery elm I took last night."

Sean's hearty laugh filled the room, then tenderly he took her in his arms. "My darling, Beth is a beautiful little Indian."

Star and Great Wolf visited the Dolan's home frequently, but this time, while their attention was mainly on their new granddaughter, Tsika's remarks drew Star to reprimand her as though she still lived with them at Springplace.

"Beth is a darling, Tsika. Now you'll have a full time job and you won't have time to teach."

Tsika nodded. "Since I'm doing so well this time, I can start immediately to write for the eastern papers. I'm anxious to begin. I wish the printing presses were set up."

"There will be plenty of time for that. Get your rest. Is this—this writing more important than your daughters?"

"No, Momma," she kissed the leathery cheek. "I just am not intent upon educating the children and teaching them how to combat the forces against them, and letting the easterners know how we have progressed that I feel there isn't time enough to do all I must do. I'll write to the eastern papers immediately."

"What's this about eastern papers?" Sean called as he came in slapping the dust from his heavy pants. "Been plowing," he explained. "It's high time people in the east realize what the Cherokees are accomplishing in their new capitol. When's dinner?"

Wolf looked up from his reading and smiled.

"All you men think of is food," Tsika scolded.

Sean winked at Wolf. "Oh, now I wouldn't say that, would you, Beth?" He reached into the crib and smoothed his little daughter's soft black hair.

After their dinner, the men went into the library for their brandy, Tsika and Star sipped their tea in the small parlor and Nilla took the babies up for their baths and night's sleep.

Star gazed at the satin drapes, the brocade chairs and the silver service, and said, "Such beauty, Tsika. Whoever thought."

"I know. I have to pinch myself sometimes. Our lives are so full and so happy. We have so much, I feel it can't last."

"It won't—" Star covered her mouth with her hand.

"What's wrong, Momma?"

Star bowed her head in her hands. "I—I shouldn't say."

"Yes, you should. What? Now speak up, please."

"The Cherokees have a saying. 'Enjoy today, smoke peace pipe today, tomorrow you wear war paint and die.' "

"You're making that up."

Star looked embarrassed. "Yes, but that's the way I feel. I try to hide my feelings, cover up what I know, but—"

"What do you know? There have been no recent harassments from Georgians, no ultimatums from the U.S. Government authorities. President Adams is concerned only with his people's rights and fairness to all. He has a keen interest in foreign trade, and since no one troubles the Cherokees, New Echota building progresses, and at Council meetings, plans were made to adopt a constitution. Much of it is written by John Ross and will be presented to the Council committee of the national Council in July."

"I know. Your father has told me. But this is something quite different. This is here," and she pressed her chest. "I—I feel—There's bad news already. Old Headchief Pathkiller has died and then four weeks later, Charles Hicks, Second Chief was killed. Tsika—I see your father being killed in the woods."

"Momma, now you're talking nonsense."

"No, Tsika. I have future sight, like my mother had. I never told anyone, for I fear it." Now Star was weeping. "Some terrible things I've seen have come true. It's a curse."

Tsika hugged her mother. "Don't worry Momma. Come, we'll tell Papa and then he can protect himself. I wish you'd told me about this foresight. I could have helped you through your worries. And about the chiefs, John Ross will make a fine Chief."

"That's not all."

"No, Momma come, no more tonight. Let's go into the library and tell Papa."

Although things were temporarily quiet in Cherokee country, Georgia Governor Forsyth and his staff were discussing the possibility that the Cherokees might demand citizenship on the chief's next trip to the capitol. It was moved they send a delegation at the same time to object to claims and to suggest removal.

On their exit from the meeting, Ron suggested a stop at a nearby saloon, and Cochee agreed.

Ron wasted no time. "I have a proposition to make to you."

"I only work for Johnson, McAllister and the Party."

"I know, so do I and what I'm asking you to do ties in with it, but I'm too damn close to this to do it myself. You've got to help me, and if it comes off all right, I'll give you another job later. I pay well. At the same time you'll be doing the Georgia officials a favor."

"So?"

"First off—kidnapping."

"Whoa there, I don't do nothin' to get me in law trouble."

"You already killed Chaim, so why you so squeamish? Wait 'til you hear my plans."

"Shoot!"

"All you have to do is take Melissa Dolan out a ways in the woods and leave her. If she dies, whose fault is that? The child just wandered off. She walks, she's over two. All done in the name of pushing the damned Cherokees to accept removal."

"When?"

"Watch the place. Get accustomed to when the nurse takes the kid out. You'll know when. Just watch for your chance."

Cochee nodded.

"Then when that dies down, get Wolf. As a chief he's so important we got to get him out of the way. And, of course we all take part in routing Ross from his fancy house, getting the treaty signed by the loyalists and harassing anyone who tries to get in the way."

"Yeah, I already heard that part."

"Finally, kill that damn boss of mine."

"No, by God, you do that! I'll not do all your dirty work."

On July 26, 1827, the Cherokee National Council adopted a Constitution that was modeled after the Constitution of the United States, with Executive, Legislative and Judicial branches. The people were proud of John Ross, the president of the National Council, who had written most of its contents.

There were six national festivals each year. The Cherokees, who clung to their customs, had just celebrated the Green Corn Festival, but this news was reason to extend the songs and dances to the rhythm of the flutes and drums for another few days.

At the Dolan's Riverview Acres, there was also cause for celebration. Daniel Gerald Dolan was born. Family and hired help waited anxiously for word of the birth. While Sean paced the floor and Wolf and Star amused the two little girls on the veranda, the mansion took on a grim, yet expectant atmosphere. When lusty cries burst forth, there was a loud cheer.

Wolf shouted, "The birth of a nation and the birth of a grandson all in one day—now nothing can quell our optimism."

Tsika's first words were, "See, Sean I had three children in three and one half years. Do I keep my jobs?"

He leaned over to kiss her. "Of course, my love. You've made me the happiest man in the world. Anything you say."

"Then I'll write about the new constitution immediately."

"Perhaps you'd better wait a day or two, and maybe—"

Tsika had fallen asleep.

Sean winked at the doctor and they left the room.

Smiling, Sean came downstairs and thanked the good wishers wondering what the Georgians would do when they heard about the Constitution.

After the excitement had subsided, he asked Wolf, "What do you think, are there bound to be repercussions? Violence?"

"The Georgia officials will go screaming to Washington. I believe we're in for trouble."

And within two days, The *Georgia Journal* was delivered at the Chief's doorsteps, where an article appeared in large print on the front page, stating that the Georgia officials would send a delegation to the Capitol to make further requests for removal.

John Ross announced they would also send a delegation, and when President Adams was prevailed upon to entertain both the Georgia and the Cherokee delegations, he accepted with some reluctance. His sympathies were with the Indians, but he felt duty bound to support the State of Georgia.

Again the Treaty of 1802 was brought up, again arguments were advanced that refuted its claims and again the issue of removal was a stalemate. In late August, both parties left Washington feeling disappointed no agreement had been reached.

By fall Worcester was printing a pamphlet in his home and asked Tsika to write an occasional article for publication. She went home the first day, with a smile on her face and enough enthusiasm to publish a paper all by herself.

"Sean," she greeted her husband, "in my article today I suggested our new government apply for citizenship. Then we could vote for Adams for president in November '28."

"You did what? Tsika, it's not up to you to suggest what the governing body of the Cherokee people should do."

"It's what we all want. Why not?"

Sean shrugged. "It's not the proper approach. Well, it's done. Wait for some response, from John—or—your father."

"Why can't John Ross do it?"

"The proper procedure, *if* the National Council accepts the idea, is to get someone like Senator Daniel Boone, who is sympathetic with the Indians to present a bill before

Congress."

"Could your father help us?"

"No, he wouldn't, not since I went against his wishes."

"Oh. I guess I was wrong to suggest it."

"The idea or a request to my father?"

"Both." Tsika felt deflated, but her good humor returned. "Won't that bit of news shake up Governor Forsyth of Georgia!"

Laughing, they ran up the stairs to see their children.

Worcester decided to shelve Tsika's article until Ross could be contacted and asked about its publication.

1828 - 1831

On February 21, 1828, the Cherokee Phoenix building, a one-story log structure, was opened for business. It had cases for the 85 characters of Cherokee type, a bank and stands that Worcester had purchased in Boston.

In the first issue, portions of the Cherokee Constitution were published. Not only this news but the fact that Cherokees were now so well educated that they could print a paper for their people to read was more than Governor Forsyth could stand. He immediately forwarded a copy to President Adams, demanding their removal.

In order to appease the Georgia officials, Colonel Hugh Montgomery arrived in Cherokee country two weeks later to urge a voluntary exodus to the land across the Mississippi River.

The Cherokee people turned a deaf ear to his eloquent speeches for they had more important things to think about. They were becoming concerned about the coming U.S. presidential election. If Jackson were elected, they had to be prepared, and what better way than to elect John Ross for their own president.

At Riverview Acres life moved along smoothly. Tsika was delighted to be doing what she'd always wanted to do. She felt a little guilty about leaving the children, but the newly hired nursemaid Ollie was excellent, and with Nilla and Manda nearby, nothing could go wrong.

As she walked to the Phoenix office, on that beautiful morning in mid-March, she felt uneasy. Something was wrong. But when she entered and saw John Wheeler with an ink spot on his nose, she forgot her qualms.

She giggled, "John, you should see your face. You surely have thrown yourself into the printing business."

He grinned and nodded, "Get busy, my girl. You have work to do. Worcester decided your last article was a little too sharp. He left you a note."

Tsika frowned, then became so immersed in her writing, she didn't realize it was lunch time. She stretched and decided to walk outside, and sit on a log to eat her sandwich. She glanced into the woods. It seemed as though eyes were watching her.

Leaving at four o'clock, she went to the back of the building, where a glass window blinked in the afternoon sun. Below it were the imprints of two booted feet. She followed the tracks into the woods. There was complete silence. Then she saw it for what it was: a limping track. Could it be Cochee? On a somber, thoughtful walk back to Riverview, she heard Quati's warning ringing in her ears. "Promise you'll be careful." Sean had said, "Don't tempt fate, my darling. There are people who would like to silence your people's claims to rightful ownership of the land and your writing sometimes—" Ah yes, she did have a way with words that incensed. She'd be extra careful.

When trouble struck, it was not where she had expected it: an attack on herself.

As she reached the lane, Ollie raced toward her, screaming, "Mam, Melissa, she go. Missy go. One minute she there. She gone. Come, come." Ollie pulled on Tsika's sleeve.

For a moment Tsika was in shock. Then she shouted, "Where was she last, girl? Speak up! Tell me, so I know where to look."

"Near the house, I—guess—"

"You guess," Tsika panted, running up the lane. "She loves to ride. We'll try the barns first."

Ollie lumbered after her wringing her hands.

"She no ride, Missus, she only two and a half."

"No, her daddy takes her on a horse with him, but she could be there. It's the first place she wants to go when you have her out. You take these stalls, I'll go on the other side."

"She cain't be, she just cain't be."

"Stop it, Ollie! Look and stop howling."

A cry came from behind the barns. Tsika raced around the haystacks and picked up the crying child.

"Oh my darling, are you hurt?" Her dress was blood-spattered.

Then she heard a groan. Benji, the young groom, lay a few feet away on the ground and blood covered the front of his shirt.

"Ollie, Ollie," Tsika screamed. "Get someone, hurry, Benji's dying. Oh, Dear God, let the boy live."

Where was everybody when she needed them? Thank Heaven, Missy was just frightened. What had happened? Who would be able to wound Benji and escape without being seen? She hugged the child closely until the crying ceased. Now, Tsika was frightened. Was someone trying to get to her through the child? Oh God, *no!*

When the boy was taken to the house, the doctor sent for and Sean had arrived, the situation looked somewhat better, but the cause for the act posed a question.

"I must talk to Benji, Doc. How soon?" Sean asked.

"Give him a little time, Sean. The boy has a nasty knife wound, but with rest, he'll be good as new."

Manda stood silently beside him holding his hand. When she moved he looked up at her and groaned.

"I'se all right, Mamma. He no see me. He try to take Missy, an' I push at him. He drop her an' come after me." Tears ran from the corners of his eyes. "I fight, I do. I hang on him. Then he hear a noise. He limp to his horse and go away."

"Was he a big man, Benji?" Sean asked.

"Yes, he big. He hear noise an—" his voice faded away.

"Enough, now the boy must rest, Sean."

Sean patted Benji on the shoulder. "You're a brave boy. He'll be rewarded for protecting our daughter, Manda."

"Thank you, Mr. Dolan, never mind, just so he get well."

Tsika added, "Take him into the den later, Manda. You can watch over him here better than in your cabin."

"Oh, thank you, Mam, but the dinner—it be burning."

"Don't worry, I'll get dinner tonight."

Still wringing her hands, Ollie touched Tsika's sleeve. "Mam, I do that. You been through plenty today."

That evening there was a knock on the door. Sam Worchester had heard about the attempted kidnapping and felt it his duty to warn Tsika.

After their greeting, he said, "I'll get right to the point of my visit, Tsika. I am sure this was in direct response to your last article about the tactics of the Georgia officials."

"Oh, I hope not, Sam." But hadn't she considered it?

"It might be wise if you would desist from any mention of the problems affecting the Cherokees for awhile. Hold all comments, at least until after the November presidential election."

"I'll agree if you'll allow me to urge people in the East to vote for Adams. I so want Jackson to be defeated."

Sam smiled. "I suppose there's no harm in that."

A week later Wolf stopped at the Dolans' to report the recent news from Washington.

"Adams is so busy concentrating on the upcoming election, he hasn't had any interest in checking Hugh Montgomery's progress. The man left for the Capital today. And I believe Adams was so impressed also by Henry Clay's, Daniel Boone's and Daniel Webster's articles in the papers that commended the Cherokees for their progress in education and government, that they caused him to forget us for awhile."

"That's all encouraging, but only if Adams is re-elected."

"Right," said Wolf. "If we could vote, he would be."

Sean smiled. "Perhaps." Then said, "Stay for dinner, Wolf. I have a question for you. He liked his father-in-law immensely and valued his opinions on cases that came up in the new court.

"I'm sorry, Sean. I must get back. I don't trust those Georgians for one minute since I lost my property in '24."

"I understand. We'll see you soon."

Since Chief Pathkiller and Second Chief Hicks had died, the people had become discouraged, even though John Ross had been selected as their head chief.

Tsika sat at her desk trying to write an optimistic article, when a message arrived from the U.S. Supreme Court stating:

> The Cherokee Nation is a distinct community occupying its own territory, in which the laws of Georgia have no force and which the citizens of Georgia have no right to enter except with express consent of the Cherokee. The Act of the State of Georgia is consequently null and void. The acts of Georgia are repugnant to the Constitution, laws and treaties of the United States.

Here was something positive. When Worcester read her article he shook his head. "The Georgia State officials have never observed the decisions of the U.S. Supreme Court before. Why should they now comply?"

"At least we can be optimistic that the people have elected John Ross to be their head chief," Tsika said stubbornly.

When Jackson won the presidential election two weeks later, the people received the information in stony silence.

However, Tsika felt optimistic and as she neared the house sounds of laughter came from within. Sean and the children were playing rough and tumble games. She smiled.

Arms outstretched, Melissa ran to her. "Mama, I'm going to have a horse for Christmas."

Tsika looked at Sean. "We'll have to talk about that."

After the Christmas wrappings had been cleared away and the children were happily playing with their new toys, Sean took Tsika in his arms.

"I have two surprises. First, come with me to the stables."

"A horse? Now Sean, you said we'd wait another year."

He grinned. "Perhaps. Bring all the children along. They must also see the surprise."

One stable stall held a sorrel with four white feet and a white mask. "For the lady of the house," Sean bowed.

"Oh, Sean, she's beautiful. I shall call her Shana."

Tsika stroked the soft nose and laid her head against the mare's neck. Before she had a chance to suggest a ride, Sean motioned to the next stall.

"And here's a Paint for Missy."

Squeals of delight out-shouted the protestations Tsika had to offer, and the rest of the day, with the exception of one large meal, was devoted to riding.

After supper Sean announced, "Now here is my other surprise. "We're going to Washington for a much needed vacation."

"Oh Sean, that sounds wonderful, but I have to—"

"Work at the *Phoenix?*"

"Yes, and I must help Juni get out of jail."

"I took care of that. Worcester says there's nothing of great importance at present, and Sam has Juni's case."

"I agree it would be nice for the children to see their grandparents, but it's such a long tedious trip for them."

"My parents are in New York for the holiday season and I wasn't planning on taking the children. This is to be a second honeymoon, my sweet."

Her eyes sparkled with excitement. "All right, we'll go, and perhaps I'll get to see the president."

"What makes you think President Adams would give us the time of day?"

"He might refuse to see the Cherokee, Tsika Wolf, but he would never refuse to see Mrs. Sean Dolan," she laughed. "And remember once you kept me from seeing a president. I was so in love I let you talk me out of it."

"Was?"

"Yes."

"And now?" He picked her up and placed her at the foot of the stairs. "Go pack up, princess! Washington, here we come."

"Oh Sean, I have to get supper. I let the help go this afternoon."

"Who will put the wild Indians to bed?"

"You will, my dear."

Sean laughed, "Did I ever say I ruled this household?"

By the next morning they were on the way to Atlanta where they would change stages for the long trip to Washington. There were already six people in the coach, three to a side, but the vehicle stopped for yet another passenger.

"Don't know where they'll put 'im," mumbled a rider.

"By Jove, it's Chuck." Sean greeted their friend. "Take my seat, I'll sit up beside the ribbon handler."

"No, I will," offered a well-dressed gentleman. "Your friend may sit here. I'll be dismounting soon."

Chuck said, "Thank you." The man bowed, then climbed up with the driver.

Chuck started the conversation as soon as he was seated. "I thought things were fairly quiet in Cherokee country, but Sam said something quite to the contrary today. I'm concerned."

"Oh, Sam. He's always pessimistic," Tsika sputtered.

The passengers either pretended disinterest or were feigning sleep, and Chuck became aware of it. He'd play out an act.

"Yes, perhaps there's nothing to be alarmed about. You're

looking lovely, Mrs. Dolan." He nodded slightly in the group's direction.

Sean took the cue. "We're off to Washington, for a small vacation. We figured the *Phoenix* and my Law office could manage for a few weeks."

When the coach reached Atlanta and the passengers had either left or gone to transfer to another, Chuck spoke freely. "Tsika once said she didn't trust Sam Kellog. She's right."

"You mean concerning Juni's case?"

"Yes. Originally when I told Sam I would testify on the man's behalf, he said there would be no trial."

"I know, Sam thought it would be better if he handled it his way." Sean acknowledged.

"I thought at first that was good, but now I wonder. It's purely a case of self-defense. God, poor Juni had only gone to the barn for his horse so he could get help to save his wife's life when Red attacked him. We would have done the same."

"Now Red's recuperating from a knife wound and Juni's in jail. And Sam's marking time? Is that your worry?"

"My main concern was that Sam said there'd be no use to have a trial, because even though the Indian might not be at fault, he'd not have a chance in a white man's court. He said it'll be on the books soon. What books? Georgia's?"

"Georgia doesn't even have a court."

"That remark indicated to me that Sam knows something of what the Georgians are going to do. It frightens me."

"Sam's a mixed-blood. He wouldn't go back on his own."

"I wouldn't be too sure. Last night I heard him talking to McAllister and Johnson. That's why I'm on my way to Augusta. Maybe a white can convince a white to do justice in this case."

"We'll go along with you. Maybe I can help."

"No, Sean. You work with Sam. It would be best if I'm alone and I have business to attend to about my delivering surplus produce from Cherokee farms to Augusta. It's a two-purpose trip.

"Tsika doesn't know of all my surprises, Chuck. We're going to see President Adams. I thought we'd better come to Washington before Jackson takes over in March."

"Oh, Sean," she breathed. "I'm overcome! Perhaps I'll be able to talk to him about out problems."

"It's a party, Tsika, a social evening. You're not to say anything about Cherokee business."

Chuck smiled. "I can imagine Tsika will do just as she wishes, Sean. You don't stand a chance. Now, goodbye, and have a safe trip and a fine time."

The couple waved from the Washington-bound stage.

They arrived at the White House at the appointed hour on December 31st, 1828, to see the New Year in with the elite of Washington society. Uniformed drivers maneuvered fashionable carriages drawn by sleek horses beneath the *porte-cochere*, to deliver bejeweled ladies and impeccably dressed gentlemen to the President's mansion.

Tsika decided she looked right in her empire-styled blue velvet gown, and Sean was handsome in his knee-pants and fancy long jacket. Jewels sparkled in the candlelight that glowed from crystal chandeliers and the sconces on the walls flickered beside pastel murals in the marble halls and in the pillared reception room.

As the Dolans waited in the receiving line to be greeted by John Quincy and Abigail Adams, Tsika felt all the butterflies she'd ever seen, flutter in her stomach. This was a lifetime experience. She must make Sean proud of her. He'd met and talked with Adams on numerous occasions, and looked very self-assured. She closed her eyes; she must remember every lovely moment. Then before she could gather her thoughts together, she was hurried past the couple, Sean had said his few words to the President and they were handed on to the next government official.

"Sean, I didn't even get to say, I'm pleased to meet you."

"True, my love. That's the way of Washington. Wait, then

hurry. It's different in the Army where it's hurry up and wait. Just listen carefully at dinner; you may hear something you can write about. But remember, don't talk business."

"Right. Listen, but don't talk."

However, when the Secretary of War and the President began to speak of Adams' plans for the next two months, Tsika could restrain herself no longer.

"If the government had been able to grant the Cherokees citizenship, Mr. President, you would have won your second term as President. Every Cherokee would have voted for you."

Conversation stopped; all eyes focused on Tsika. Sean was shocked.

He sputtered, "My apologies, Mr. President. At times my wife becomes too enthusiastic for her people's welfare."

The President responded with a wave of his hand. "It's quite usual for one to speak on behalf of one's people, and I commend you, Mrs. Dolan, but it would take the better part of two years to accomplish that purpose. First, a bill must be introduced to discontinue the annuities in order to release you from your dependent status, then a bill to grant citizenship, and passage of both must go through both houses you know."

Tsika nodded.

The conversation turned to other matters. She blinked back the tears, and Sean squeezed her hand beneath the damask cloth to assure her of his forgiveness and support.

On their way back to the hotel, she again urged Sean to ask his father to intercede for them."

"It takes too long. You heard the President. There's so much red tape."

"Still we must try it. Can you talk to your father's friend Senator Hyde? It's our only hope if we're to have any say about whether we stay in Georgia."

"All right, I'll see Senator Hyde. Now, forget everything except that you are in the capitol city and having the time of your life. It's our second honeymoon, Tsika, and you are my pretty bride of almost five years. Come, smile!"

"How can I ever resist you, Sean?" She laughed and her sparkling eyes told him all he wanted to know.

Sean could get no definite answer from Senator Hyde. Tsika was discouraged, but on their arrival in Cherokee country there was news that took their minds from a mere governmental request.

Jeremy jumped down from his high seat on the carriage shouting, "Massa Chuck, he no get home from Augusta."

"Oh Sean, we should have insisted on going with him."

"But he said not to. And he had business concerning his hauling customers. I thought we'd be interfering." Then he called, "Jeremy, go right over to Bronson's."

"Yass suh."

"Are the children all right, Jeremy?"

"They's right as rain."

"Is Ron back?" Sean asked.

Jeremy's white eyebrows drew together, and he shrugged, "He's back an' everythin's agoin' his way again."

Tsika turned her head and bit back a caustic comment. She'd say nothing about Ron unless he became too bold. Why didn't Sean see that no one liked the man?

They reached Bronson's, and when Tsika jumped down from the carriage, Sean said, "You go in, I must talk to your father."

She looked surprised. She wanted to go to her folks home also, but she nodded, "All right, Rena needs me. Maybe in a woman-to-woman talk I can find something out."

Samantha opened the door. The girl fell into her arms. "Oh Tsika," she cried. "It's so good of you to come. My father—"

"I know, dear, but we must have hope that he'll be back."

Sean lost no time. "Wolf, I find it hard to believe that Chuck would go to Augusta so suddenly without talking to one of us first. If it's on behalf of Juni, why did he wait three weeks to go? Why not when Juni was first accused and imprisoned?"

"He did talk to me, Sean, but I couldn't make out what it

was all about."

"He said he'd overheard a conversation between McAllister, Johnson and Sam that upset him."

"Yes, and he said something about their plans to talk to the treaty boys, and just as he came to warn me, Ulah and my two young ones came in. He told her he was going to aid Juni and left."

"Warn you about what?"

"I don't know, although there's plenty of people should be warned to be careful these days."

"I believe I'll go down to Augusta and see what I can find out about his disappearance. Do you know the names of his business contacts there?"

"Yes, one or two. He delivers our farm surplus there. Let's see, I wrote it down somewhere." He went to his desk. "Oh, damn, it must have been thrown out with the old papers."

"Never mind. I'll find out from Rena."

"She will know. Don't go alone and be careful."

"You know I will." His father-in-law patted his back and he left for Bronsons to question Rena and pick up Tsika.

Warning! The word haunted him. What had Tsika told him about a warning from her mother months ago? Something about being attacked and killed in a woods. Impossible! But was it?

But there was a plan that included two assassinations and an effort to convert enough of the Cherokees to the belief that the Treaty Party's pro-removal policy was right: Disunity was urged and disloyalty to Ross was necessary.

At a meeting in the rear room of the Moose Saloon in Augusta, an unholy group of five discussed possibilities of completing some necessary action to accomplish that plan. Big Red, Ron, Cochee, McAllister and Johnson thought there would be a great deal of money to be made from the land the Cherokees would leave, but it was wise to pretend they were functioning for the benefit of the Georgia officials.

"That guy Bronson's got to go," said Johnson. "He overheard our plans for Ross and Wolf and about the meeting at Red Clay."

"I don't believe he heard anything after we spoke of Wolf. I saw him leave shortly thereafter."

"But you don't know. He could have sneaked back in."

"Lemme take care of him." Red boasted, "I know how to shut up a snooper an' nobody'll ever find the body."

"What about Dolan?" asked Ron. "You said you saw him talking to Chuck."

"Yeah, but I was hidin' behind the shed, an' he didn't say nothin' except he'd talk to a lawyer about gettin' Juni out of the Lawrenceville Prison."

"When's the meeting at Red Clay?"

"Next week Wednesday."

"That'll be a shocker if Ridge comes through."

McAllister rubbed his hands together. "Then the Treaty Party can really move."

As Tsika left the house, the promised rain started to fall. She reached the end of the lane to meet Sean returning from Augusta. He jumped from the rented hack, tossed the driver a silver coin, and hopped into the carriage.

He kissed her, and immediately said, "No," anticipating her question about Chuck. "I found out nothing except that he saw his customers, planned to meet them for dinner that evening and never appeared. He'd made an appointment for the following day at ten to see his lawyer friend and didn't keep it. It's as though he's fallen off the face of the earth."

"What did you do?"

"Alerted the Chief of Police in Augusta. He said he'd put out a search and let us know if he found anything out."

"I guess that's all you could do."

"You know, I felt all the time I was there as if someone was watching me. It was eerie. I was kind of glad to get away."

"You'll want to tell my father. He'll be there today."

"I feel so sorry for Rena, not knowing where he is or—whether he's even alive."

"We'll stop at Rena's after the meeting, Sean."

They were detained by a driving rainstorm, and assumed they would be late. However, as they entered the enclosure, John Ross was rapping his gavel for silence. The respect and love for him was so apparent in people's attitude, log cabin and townspeople alike, that all conversation stopped at once.

Again Ross vowed the Cherokees could fight the forces that discouraged them by continuing to use the power of the press and the law to help them, and not resort to violence.

Major Ridge spoke also. His portly stature and strong voice commanded the people's attention by sheer force. His white hair, thick white beard and piercing brown eyes, added to his dignity. He said to use their reason; that perhaps it would be better for them to prepare what President Jackson had in store for them, to think of the possibility of leaving.

There was a collective murmur in the crowd of over one hundred people, then, "The Ridge," as he was frequently called, announced, "And now, my son John will address you."

John rose. "I've been to Washington and found that the President plans to align himself with the Georgia officials. My friends, John Walker and James Starr will attest to that."

There was a gasp from the floor, and silently the new chief, John Ross, the sub-chiefs and other council members filed out without speaking. This had become an intolerable situation.

It now seemed that the John Ridge faction, the Georgia Party and the Jackson Government were all against John Ross's Cherokees.

Throughout spring and summer of '29, harassment was resumed at an alarming rate. Agent Montgomery returned and hired pro-removal members to influence Cherokee chiefs, merchants, mill owners and farmers to join the pre-removal group. Three Western Cherokees (migrants of 1812) Head Chief Jolly and two associates came across the Mississippi

River to help recruit.

David Joshua, a mixed-blood, was cultivating in the fields one day when he was approached by two strangers.

One said, "It would be wise if you'd sign up to move."

"And if I don't?"

"You could have trouble."

"Well, I refuse."

"Your friend Wheaton signed yesterday."

"That's his business."

As soon as the two men left, Dave went to Weatherby's farm next door. "You know whether Wheaton has signed up to go West?" he asked.

"He'd never do that. I'd swear to it." Then he wasn't too sure. He scowled. "Anything can happen. We'll go ask him."

"Yes, I agree, anything can happen. Since Ross had to give up his farm, slaves, ferry service and post at Rossville and move to Head of Coosa—who are we to think we can't be affected?"

"But he didn't go West."

At Chuck Benson's a crowd had gathered. No one had as yet heard from Chuck. All thought the Georgians or the pro-removal were responsible for his disappearance.

Big Elk was shouting, "That proves it!"

One of the men Dave had seen on his property lay prone on the ground in front of the house, and Fox was coming out of the door with the other one, a gun at the culprit's back. He shoved the man against a tree, tied him securely, then faced the crowd.

"Do I hear volunteers to ride them out of our country?"

A cheer went up. The hills and valleys echoed with their voices. Donner offered, then questioned Fox about the details.

"He was holding a gun at Rena's head when I entered the house through the back door. She was seated at the kitchen table weeping, pen in hand, and he was shouting, 'Sign, damn you! Your husband ain't comin' back!' "

"I was fooled," a Cherokee, named Aaron, called to Fox.

"He said my brother had signed up to go, so I signed. My brother had no intention of going West. I aim to get even. I'll go with you." Several others volunteered.

"No violence, now," Fox said. "Just usher them out."

Five Cherokees left with their charges, and that night Donner's farm buildings were burned. His wife and children all perished in the fire.

The Cherokee's anger knew no bounds, and it was with great difficulty Ross was able to quell their lust for retaliation with a promise to hire William Wirt, constitutional lawyer, to take the case of Donner versus the State of Georgia.

The citizens temporarily shelved their frustrations and anger, and agreed to wait for results. They continued to farm, ignore the recruiters and refuse to sign anything.

After Tsika wrote about the meeting at Red Clay, she heard of the disturbance at Bronson's, and went to see Rena.

She told Sean, on her return, "It was so devastating for her, Sean, for now she believes what the recruiter said, that Chuck isn't coming back. That he's dead. You can't encourage her to believe otherwise when you yourself believe it's the case."

"So many things happen to the Cherokees, who want to stay, perhaps Ridge is right." He sighed. "Find peace in the West."

"Sean!" Tsika shouted. "You can't really believe that! I'll die before I'll leave."

"I guess not. Ross is still optimistic that you can overcome the adversity by using the law and the press, so I agree."

"That's better. Now, let's go to see Juni. It's a long trip. I'll tell Manda we won't be back until tomorrow."

Sean had finally managed to persuade the judge to place Juni on probation by asserting he was white and mistaken for the man who had attacked the horse thief.

He said, "I'll take full responsibility for him."

"It's beyond my understanding, how you did it."

"I can't understand it either Tsika; he just closed his eyes to the possibility that it could be any different when I showed him the papers."

"What papers?"

"I procured some citizenship papers for him. He's an Italian, called Gino Rossetti, taking on an Indian culture."

"Sean, that's dishonest."

"You wanted your brother out of jail, didn't you?"

Tsika giggled, "Sean, you're a good liar and I'm glad you fooled the judge, but don't you ever lie to me. You hear?"

After another visit to Rena's, Tsika and Sean returned to Riverview Acres to find visitors waiting for them. Jeremy opened the door, and Sean's father and mother greeted them. The children ran to them immediately to show the toys their grandparents had brought from Washington.

There were hearty hugs and some kisses, then a challenging evening ensued. Tsika tried hard to make the Dolans feel welcome and, although Sean was happy to see his parents, he was tense and apprehensive about this visit: the first since the stormy objection to his marriage and choice of future dwelling.

There was no need to worry, however, for the children had captured their grandparent's hearts.

Missy, now four, made a pretty picture, dressed in her favorite red dress and white pinafore. It brought pink to her cheeks and light to her blue eyes. When she curtsied, her raven-black hair flew forward.

Beth at three was equally friendly. Her blondness and sparkling black eyes resulted in a striking effect. Complete opposites in coloring, the girls complemented one another.

And Danny was a chubby little boy, who Lilla said looked just like Sean did when he was that age.

Anxiety and concern disappeared, and acceptance on both sides was assured. Instead of a few days visit as intended, the elder Dolans stayed almost two weeks.

Tsika entertained her neighbors, friends and relatives, and the Dolans left with a much different view of life in the Cherokee community than they had originally imagined.

Sean spoke of the coming worries concerning the removal policy and the harassment the people had endured.

"They now know President Jackson condones Georgia's acts of lawlessness."

Father Dolan said, "I'm determined to change the minds of those in Washington who deal with the Cherokee's problems."

"We hope to God you can."

But hope seemed to be on gossamer wings in 1829. News of President Jackson's first annual address to Congress in December in which he promised: "To initiate and propel through Congress in June, a bill to provide for removal of all Southeastern Indian tribes to lands west of the Mississippi River," even overshadowed the discovery of gold on Cherokee property.

On December 18th, eleven days later, Georgia's legislators were so inspired by Jackson's address they passed several laws for the Cherokees in their state. They were listed as follows:

1. Confiscation by Georgia of a large section of Cherokee land.

2. Nullification of Cherokee law within the prescribed area.

3. Prohibit further meetings of the Cherokee Legislative Council, and all other meetings within Georgia.

4. Arrest and imprisonment of any Cherokee who influences fellow tribesmen to reject immigration west.

5. Contracts between Cherokees and whites null and void unless witnessed by two whites.

6. Illegal for any Cherokee to testify against any white in Georgia Courts.

7. Forbidden to dig gold on their land.

These rules were posted in all the Cherokee villages and printed in both Cherokee and English.

On the evening they became public, Ross called a meeting at Head of Coosa, where the conversation centered on Jackson's demands.

He said, "We won't obey all of the rules: we'll still continue to have meetings, our government will still function at New Echota, and the miners will no doubt continue to mine gold. At whatever cost to our freedom, we will not resort to violence."

"That's mighty hard these days, John," Wolf remarked. After Donner's family were killed in their burning home, the cabin folk and farmers as well as the townspeople can't be held back for long. They're all enraged."

"The Intercourse Act gives us the right to chase intruders off our land, but I still believe it is in the best interest of the Cherokees if we refrain from violence."

Major Ridge took the floor. "John, you're too tolerant. There's trouble in the gold fields. The Georgia Militia has prodded the Indians out of the area with rifle butts and sword points. I aim to gather an army together, go down there and fight those forty thousand whites. That's Cherokee land. Elijah Hicks and your own nephew, Cooley, have an interest in those mines. John, what else do you need to convince you that something should be done?"

"It's only disrupting those in the Haweis area where farmers have left their plows to go to the gold fields, but I've seen no such foolishness here. Things will quiet down there of their own accord."

Ridge rose, stood his full height, which was imposing, and majestically strode out, boot heels clicking on the wooden floors.

John Ross continued with the meeting. "I think the main question here is how to fight the Georgia rules, and I believe the Council should appoint a delegation to go to Washington for that purpose. Also, with your approval, I would like to appoint William Wirt, constitutional lawyer from Philadelphia, to take our case to the U.S. Supreme Court."

That was agreed upon, four men were appointed to accompany John Ross to the Capitol, and the meeting was adjourned.

On the way out Sean caught up with Wolf. "Just breaking a few of those rules will keep the Georgians busy," he laughed.

"Indeed it will, and I believe in spite of what Ross says, he will oust intruders (per Intercourse Act) if the situation warrants, and he'll approve of fighting in the gold fields."

In Haweis, Aiku and Roper were among the Cherokees who went to the gold fields nearby. Their farms were productive, but they decided to try their luck. They fought the white miners for the right to work on their own soil until the Georgia Militia came in, arrested them and threw them into a filthy Georgia jail. U.S. troops arrived to quell the disturbance, but Governor Forsyth convinced the government it was Georgia's affair, and Major Ridge found himself and his Cherokees in the middle.

In August, Aiku and Roper were jailed, their homes were burned, and Tani and Alda and their children fled into the woods to survive. With others, they formed a small desperate group, whose members helped one another, and so, although some died, most survived.

As ill and weak from hunger and exposure as Tani became, she managed with Alda's good help to keep her children well. Alda's three boys chopped wood for their fires and snared small woods creatures for food. They dug roots and herbs.

"I think I'll never see a life of ease again, Alda," she finally admitted one night when the wolves howled and they had all climbed into the trees.

"We've managed for more than a month, Tani. We can hold out against all odds, just so we can get out of here before winter."

"It's lucky you had your gun and I managed to carry off some blankets." Tani's voice weakened.

By the time the men were out of jail, both women and two of the children were ill and undernourished. The wise move was to go back to Springplace where Ulah and Fox would care for them.

Jackson followed through with his promise. He introduced his Removal bill in early May, and it was passed through Congress by a small margin. Many Easterners and even Europeans expressed their horror in the press on the issue of removal. Public officials sought to defer the bill.

Jeremiah Evarts of the Foreign Missions in Boston, Editor of the *Christian Herald*, wrote a series of articles for the *National Intelligencer* under the pen name of William Penn, criticizing the general treatment of minorities. Senator Daniel Webster, Daniel Boone, Chancellor James Kent, Winthrop Sargent, William Wirt, and Representative Horace Everett, tried on May 19th on the floor of the House, to defeat the bill. All opposed Jackson's action.

However their efforts came to naught, for on May 23rd the bill was ratified and from then on, the Cherokees had not only the Georgians to fight, but the United States Government as well.

The members of the Cherokee Nation Council who had come home only six weeks earlier from Washington, now returned to plead their cause.

Jackson had completed treaties of removal with several of the Eastern tribes and requested members of the Cherokee National Council to meet him in Nashville to discuss terms of their Treaty Removal. They refused and at that point in time realized they not only needed William Wirt to defend them again but the firm of Underwood and Hill of Philadelphia also.

"What do you two lawyers think about that?" Tsika asked of Sean on the evening they heard the news.

"I hoped Wirt would be able to help, but as I talked with Sam, I realized the Cherokees have a flaw in their economy."

"What is that?"

They can't claim to be a sovereign nation while they accept an annuity of $78.00 each from the government. It is nationally not self-sustaining. We must do something to catch this oversight before the Georgia officials latch onto it or we won't have a chance at court."

"What did Sam say to that?"

"Sam immediately said he had an appointment he'd forgotten about. It was then I realized that what you thought about him was true. I should never have offered that bit of information. Now I am suspicious of him. I'm sure he went to report to the members of the Treaty Party."

"Is there really a Treaty Party, Sean?"

"Forming, yes. It's not official yet, but you know we've suspected John Ridge, Walker and Cooley of being pro-removal."

"Yes, and at the *Phoenix* office, I've even suspected Boudinot. He has refused to send to the Eastern papers some of the information I have been writing. What can we do?"

"Except for offering to go to Washington again, there's nothing we can do."

"It doesn't seem to do much good, Sean. Since Jackson is President, we're at a standstill. Some Eastern tribes are even leaving for the West, signing separate treaties."

In July, in spite of Georgia's rules, a meeting was held at New Echota to hear a report from John Ross on William Wirt's success concerning their case and of retaining the law firm of Underwood and Harris.

The trial would not come up until December. Other items were discussed, among them the news that the Indian tribes in the East, the Seminoles, Choctaws, Chickasaws and the Creeks, had all considered moving. One group would leave on September 27. By the first of the year, Ross reported at council meeting that Wirt cited as an example the case of Tassell in the Supreme Court on December 12, 1830. It concerned a writ of error and the Georgia courts had ignored the Supreme Court's decision, and executed the man.

Governor Lumpkin of Georgia, who was enraged at the Supreme Court for dictating to Georgia, wrote to the President on January 3, 1831, and Wirt, anticipating such a move, had another Cherokee case ready. He stated that the Cherokee Nation was a sovereign nation and therefore the State of Georgia had no cause to infringe upon her rights. The counter-argument stated, "There cannot be a nation within a nation." And Wirt lost the case.

It fell upon Ross to advise his people of yet another failure to be released from Georgia's constant harassment.

At the *Phoenix* the news was reported with fury and resentment, but Wirt had been dedicated in trying to help them, so Tsika toned down the first article she'd written. Boudinot was setting type and Wheeler was busy inking the press when Isaac Proctor, the blacksmith and Daniel Butrick burst through the door bearing an edition of the *Georgia Journal*.

"Look at this," shouted Butrick. "This article circled in red ink says it will be a penal offense for a white missionary to remain in Cherokee country after March 1st."

"Why so excited?" Boudinot asked. "They're just using scare tactics. Jackson made many rules to be implemented by spring, but much can happen by then to discourage that."

"Well, we're not waiting," said Proctor. "We're leaving for Tennessee."

"Isaac, they won't do anything about it until March. I'm staying here, come Georgia Militia or U.S. Troops." He laughed. "Let them fight over who's going to take me first."

"It's not a joking matter, Elias," Butrick accused. "You know Jackson has a mean disposition. He hates Indians and he's fighting tooth and nail to oust us."

"I know. We scribble away and they shove it down our throats."

"I wouldn't say that," Tsika interrupted. "I'd say we have done a lot of good, made some headway in the East, changed opinions. Davy Crockett of Tennessee, Horace Everett, member of the House from Vermont, Senator Daniel Webster, and Joe Everts, all are on our side to help revoke the removal bill."

"You're right, Tsika. We mustn't give up. Ross is determined to win. He even says there will someday be a State of Cherokee."

"Do you believe that?" Her eyes widened.

"No," said Boudinot. "But I try to be optimistic."

"So do I," said Worcester, on entering the office. "But to be safe, I decided to write to the Missionary Board in Boston and ask for advice."

"The year of '31 started out on the wrong foot," mumbled Boudinot. "I'm going home and wrestle with my sons."

When Tsika arrived home from the *Phoenix* that day, the nation's problems seemed dwarfed by her own.

Mellissa met her at the door. "I told Beth she was too young to go riding alone, Momma, but she said I couldn't boss her."

Sean had the account books spread out before him in the study. Tsika shouted, "You were supposed to watch Bethy, Sean, since Manda and Nilla are off today. Where did she go?"

"She's around somewhere."

"No, she's not. Missy says she's gone riding."

"She was here ten minutes ago." He looked at the clock. "Oh my God, it's five o'clock!"

"I'll ride out to look for her. Coming?"

"Be right with you." He began to pick up his papers. It was maddening. He was so slow.

"I'm going." She rushed like a demon to the stable, then into the woods at the far end of the property. *Kidnapped*, kept hammering on her brain. It couldn't be an attempt. Not again! Oh, God no, Bethy!

Where would she go? Which direction? Calm down now, look for tracks.

Sean pounded after her. "Go east, I'll go west and Jake'll go south."

There were several horseshoe tracks, then she saw small ones that led away from the others. Beth's pony? She followed it, then it disappeared into nothing. She dismounted, calling "Bethy, Bethy, answer me. Please!"

Ahead was a small canyon. With fear, yet with confidence,

she approached its rim. For a moment, she had her mother's ability to foresee the future. Beth would be here.

"Oh, God! There she is!" Tsika cried, sliding to the bottom unaware of brambles and jagged rocks, spraining her ankle and cutting her head. "Speak to me, Bethy. Oh, my darling!"

Tsika cradled the unconscious child in her arms, rocking her to and fro, then felt of her pulse. "Becky!" she screamed. "Oh someone help. She isn't breathing. Sean, where are you? Oh Dear Cherokee Spirit, don't let her die."

Tears rolled down her cheeks. Be calm. Do something. She tried to lift the child. "Oh, Becky come back!" She sat holding her daughter, for how long, she didn't know, but darkness had settled in the canyon. She shivered.

A voice came from far away. "Tsika, Tsika, where are you?"

"Here," she answered, but no sound emerged. Lanterns swung on top of the rim. She tried again to answer, but only a moan escaped her lips.

However, it was enough to direct the searchers.

"Tsika!" Sean's descending boots scattered pebbles. "We've searched—Where are you?" The lantern light from above was so dim he had to feel for her. "You've found her. Thank God!"

She could only nod as she handed the child to him. Jake got a foothold on the cliff and took her from Sean. Her pony lay on its side with a broken leg.

"I'm sorry, Bethy. I must put him out of his misery," he called, as the shot rang out.

Then Sean helped Tsika to the top of the cliff. "She's—she's—dead, Sean. Bethy's dead," Tsika sobbed.

"No. She's out to be sure, but she's breathing. She'll be all right. You just thought the worst thing possible had happened when you found her."

Tsika continued to shake her head. "No, Sean. We've lost her. See, she's limp. Just like her rag dolly."

There was a certain amount of comfort in the doctor's report that Beth would recover in time from the concussion and broken back. But time did not seem to help much. She came out of her coma, but her legs were paralyzed. Tsika was inconsolable.

"Mrs. Dolan will be able to help Beth better than any of you, given time," predicted Dr. Bevans, from Nashville.

That too was debatable, for Tsika remained static. After three weeks, she still sat gazing into space, saying almost nothing.

Sean was becoming hopelessly mired in impatience and frustration. He snapped at the children and at the help.

It was not until Star and Wolf came to stay with them for a time that Tsika responded to anything positive. Sean sighed with relief and gratitude.

Her mother said, "Come, Tsika, you can't help Beth this way, and Missy and Danny don't understand why you won't talk."

She just shook her head.

"Do you want to lose your husband?"

She snapped, "Of course not. What do you mean?"

Wolf interrupted, "I'd leave Star in a minute if she didn't talk to me," and he winked at his wife. "Where's your spirit?"

"Beth will always be a crippled child. It isn't right. She was such a happy little girl, so sunny and active," she sobbed.

"Beth will be strong if you are strong. I know you're sad, but life is not over yet for either of you."

She hugged her father, "I know, Papa, I'll try."

"That's good. Now with that in mind, I'll be on my way."

For the moment, for Wolf, National matters took precedence over anything else. Fox and Big Elk were waiting for him in the Dolan library discussing the missionaries problems with Sean.

When he entered the room, Fox was saying, "Georgia's rules have so frightened some of the missionaries, they're leaving."

"They're cowards," Big Elk asserted.

Wolf joined in the conversation. "I'll judge them when we hear what they have to say for themselves."

"Maybe William Wirt can do something for us in Washington."

"I'm still hopeful," said Fox. "The wheels of justice work slowly, so I expect we won't hear the results until summer."

"We'll be on our way, Sean." Wolf patted his son-in-law on the shoulder. "I think Tsika will be all right now. Her mother and I gave her a little jolt."

"Oh? I hope it works. What—"

"Never ask," Wolf smiled.

By the end of April, Tsika was herself again, and Sean's joy knew no bounds. As he left the law office for the last time, he pondered on what it was Wolf had said to her. Well he might never know, but whatever it was, it was good.

"I'm home," he called at noon.

"So early, Sean? Did you take the day off to make love?"

"Of course, princess." He kissed her. "I'm through at the law office as of now."

"You've finally left Sam. I must say I expected it. Did he suspect why or did you tell him outright?"

"I told him. Some sharp words flew about. I accused him, he denied ever being in sympathy with the Treaty Party and, calling it by name assured me our suspicions were right. He stormed out, I cleaned out my desk—and here I am: farmer Dolan again."

"Good. Now you can get rid of that arrogant manager."

"Not just yet. Why are you so against him, Tsika? He takes a lot of the work from my shoulders."

She shrugged and hesitated. Should she tell him? "I—I just don't like him. He makes me feel uncomfortable."

"That's hardly a reason to fire a man who's been a good manager, Tsika. He also gleans some news for you at times.

He's the one who told me about the missionaries."

"What's that?"

"I thought you'd be interested. The white missionaries were required to take an oath of allegiance to the State of Georgia or be imprisoned for a four year term."

"So Georgia's earlier bluff didn't work. Now they're serious. That's the thanks the missionaries get for educating our children and aiding the Cherokee farmers. Can we help them?"

"I doubt it, but perhaps we can do something when we go to Washington in June."

Both Tsika and Boudinot wrote scathing articles concerning the plight of the missionaries, and in May, Boudinot was approached by the Georgia Guard for writing liberal articles and warned to desist or he would be jailed.

Before Sean left for Washington he had taken on many of the responsibilities that had before fallen to Ron. When they rode on the farm together, Ron decided now was the time to act.

Newly released from his law duties, Sean reveled in the beauty of his land. He stood at the top of the rise behind the mansion and admired his ripening fields, the glistening river with the mountains rising in the background, and breathed his thanks.

It was truly a lovely land, this Cherokee land where the Tennessee *(Long Man),* supplied its many tributaries with clear water for the farms. No wonder Georgia wanted its western section for settlers and resented the Cherokee ownership. Well, get on with your farming, sir, he chided himself.

He called ahead to Ron, "I enjoy being a farmer again."

"I thought you *were* a farmer."

"I was dormant for awhile. I'm glad to be back."

"Does that mean I'm out of a job?"

"Of course not. I'll occasionally have law cases of my own."

"I'm relieved. I thought you might be taking my place."

"No. You're a good manager." Maybe he should not be so

fast with the "No." Tsika had often disagreed with him about
Ron. Ah, well. "What do you think about the recent ruling by
the Georgians?"

"Which ruling is that?" Ron smiled.

"That the missionaries leave or be imprisoned if they don't
swear allegiance to Georgia."

Ron shrugged, "Probably more bluff."

"I don't think so. They've done everything from burning
cabins to stealing livestock and murdering Cherokees."

"We—" *Oh God, he'd almost made a break.* "We don't
want to be pessimistic, do we?"

"Guess not. Well let's get on with our tour. Tell me how
much fencing you need for the far pasture."

He smiled to himself. What a chance for that accident!

At that moment Jake rode out from behind the barns.
"May I ride with you, sir? I have a question to ask about the
cotton."

"Sure, come along, Jake. What's on your mind?"

Damn, breathed Ron. A good opportunity missed and all
because of Jake's whim. How long would he have to wait?

Business attended to, Sean announced, "I'll be going to
Washington in a couple of weeks, Ron. Keep things hum-
ming."

"That I will, sir." And how he would! Tsika would be here.

But Tsika left Riverview Acres when Sean went to Washington. He rode with her and the children as far as the Stage Station, where he would wait with Ross, Wolf, Lowrey and Ridge
for the coach going east.

He kissed her goodbye, then advised, "Be careful, love.
There are spies about, even in Springplace."

"Don't worry. I'm indestructible."

Here the children waved goodbye and they went on in the
old wagon. The wheelchair rested in the rear with bricks for
blocks and Missy held the arms so Beth would feel secure.
Danny rode on the high seat in front with Tsika.

On previous visits, Tsika's mother and grandmother planned activities for the children, but this time it would be different. They would play indoors with Beth, but they weren't disappointed. Great Grandmother Niahmi searched in her old trunk for dress patches for making doll clothes. On some days Star took Missy to shop at Big Elks or to the Ridge emporium and young Danny was just a happy little boy delighted to have all the attention given him. Bedtime stories consisted of tales of brave Cherokee warriors or of Niamhi's childhood experiences in a woodland village in North Carolina.

The weeks Sean was gone passed quickly. Tsika worked in the rich red earth, gardening as she did as a child. She even felt like a carefree child again, turning back the pages of time and reverting to Indian customs. She wondered about the doeskin dress she'd made for her wedding. She was moved to look at it, to see if it was as she remembered it.

In the storage place above the lean-to was the box of old relics of the Cherokee past. She looked through the mementoes: The leather strip of deer's teeth, the tomahawks, the dress. She held it up, admiring her workmanship. It was still beautiful. She tried it on and was surprised it fit. In the recesses of the box were the beaded moccasins and headband, and the leggings. She put them on.

As she handled them, they called her to the woodland. It would be so nice to ride through the fields again on Paint, and feel the wind in her face. That was when Aiku first called her his woodland princess. It wouldn't hurt to go out for a short time. The family members were all occupied with various pursuits.

She left the house through the back door, went to the barn and mounted Greta's pony. She wouldn't go to the same hillock where she and Aiku had met so many times, but she'd ride—ride recklessly and enjoy every moment.

She galloped through the flowering fields and into the wooded hills. Coming to a clearing she looked ahead to the river. Across the river, trees bearing the light green leaves of summer stood out against the darker green of the pine forest, and with the grandeur of mountains in the background, the old feeling of being in tune with nature returned to her. Earthly problems ceased to exist.

Tsika tethered her horse and walked to the bank of the river, to linger where the gentle rush of water over the rocks could lull one to sleep. She moved to a soft grassy area and sat cross-legged watching waterfowl dip and churn for their noon meal in a quiet pool formed by a circle of rocks at one side. A mallard's iridescent feathers glistened in the sunlight.

"Where are your friends, little duck?" she said aloud.

A voice answered, "Here, my woodland princess."

She was dreaming. It was the lull of the rushing water. She turned her head to look directly into Aiku's gentle brown eyes: eyes that were full of love. The nostalgia? "Is it really you? I—I thought you were downstate mining."

"You are a beautiful vision, Tsika."

Uttering apologies, she started to rise. "I—I just couldn't resist living in the Cherokee past for a moment."

"Don't go, Tsika." He pulled her down beside him and took her hand in the same manner of so many years ago. "I was mining. I was looking for a nugget to bring you like the one you lost in the fire."

"You remembered that?"

"Just now, I remembered it," he laughed. It would be wise to talk of impersonal things.

"You can't imagine what that southeast corner of Georgia was like. By January '31, four thousand rough whites had arrived with kegs of whiskey, pick axes and shovels, food and tents, and from nearby Haweis, Dr. Butler's Missionary headquarters, Cherokee farmers dropped their plows and rushed to the gold fields. Roper and I were among them."

"Sean said that in the first nine months from October when gold was first found, $230,000 was received in Augusta, but it didn't go into the Cherokee treasury, did it? It's all personal gain for the whites, John Ross's nephew, Cooley, and Elizur

Hicks have an interest in the mine. Did you find much gold?"

"Enough to rebuild our burned homes. After the crowd assembled, and fighting broke out, the Georgia Militia came in to oust the Cherokees. On our march to jail, the Federal troops met them and made the guards release us. Then the Indian Agents warned the whites off the land, arrested some of them and took their firearms. We cheered, but later 100 Georgia Guard came back, demolished the equipment, and arrested us."

"Where were you? In Lawrenceville?"

"Yes, but we were finally freed. Did you know Ridge came down with an army of Cherokees to help us fight the battle?"

"I heard about that. Ross wanted no violence, but closed his eyes when Ridge asserted the Intercourse Act allowed action. I believe everyone thought it was a good idea. Did you fight with Ridge?"

"Sure, and he helped us. How's your family, Tsika?"

Tears came to her eyes as she told him about Beth. "I am devastated, Aiku. My beautiful little girl will never walk again."

He ached to take her into his arms to comfort her. He interlaced his fingers with hers. Just the touching might show her how much he still cared for her.

Suddenly she was in his arms and he was kissing her.

"Oh, no—Aiku no. Forgive me. I—I must go."

As he released her he heard his name called.

"Here," he answered in a voice hoarse with emotion.

Al Wheaton appeared at the edge of the woods. "Come quickly, your father asked me to get you. He's gone to find Chamberlain. Samuel Worcester and Elizur Butler have been taken prisoner by the Georgia Guard."

Aiku nodded, jumped on his horse and followed Al Wheaton into the woods.

Tsika stood. She was shaking. What ever had possessed her? What must Al Wheaton think of her? Married and found in another man's arms. She loved Sean with all her heart. How could she allow herself to be carried away by nostalgia—and

Aiku? Did she still care for him? He hadn't said a word about Tani.

No. Forget it. It never happened. Go back home. Fast!

As she rode through the fields, she saw a rider at the edge of the woods. Who was it? Where had he been? Had he seen her?

When Tsika hurried into the house, Danny was not up from his nap, Grandma Niamhi was reading a story to Beth and Missy and Star were still in town with Micha and Greta. She breathed a sigh of relief. Apparently no one had missed her. She hurried to the bedroom to change into her ruffled skirt and blouse and return the doeskin outfit to its box.

Shortly Star came up the path laughing and singing, as light-hearted as a child, with the three children in tow. They joyfully displayed their purchases and she recounted the information she'd received concerning the missionaries.

"I know you're disappointed not to stay longer with Grandma and Grandpa and Niahmi, but I must get back to report the news to the *Phoenix*. Get ready children."

"Can't we stay here while you're gone?" Missy complained.

Star agreed it would be sensible instead of hurrying Beth away. "You can come back tomorrow."

"If you think it's all right." She kissed them goodbye and was gone within ten minutes.

As soon as she opened the door she was greeted by the typesetter, Wheeler. "A messenger just left. He told us Isaac Proctor was picked up by the Georgia Guard at Carmel Mission headquarters and they're marching toward the *Phoenix.*"

"Carmel Mission is forty miles away. It will take them awhile to get here," said Worcester. "Don't be concerned. I'll go with them peacefully. You'll have no trouble."

CHAPTER

V

1831 - 1832

The soldiers, who arrested Isaac Proctor from his blacksmith shop at Carmel Mission on July 7, 1831, had other ideas, promoted by second-term Governor Gilmore of Georgia.

One of the twelve armed Georgia Guards made a comment to his nearest comrade, "I thought we were supposed to arrest the white missionaries who wouldn't sign the oath of allegiance. Why a blacksmith?"

"It's all right; the missionary from here was arrested last week with ten merchants from all over Cherokee country."

"So what now?"

"We go to New Echota, about forty miles from here."

"I won't touch that missionary school. You know who's there? Sophia Sawyer and she's a stiff eastern—"

"You afraid of a woman?"

"You're damned right I am. I had a run-in with her, when I was sent to reprimand and warn her she'd be fined from $1,000 to $5,000 for having two wooly-heads in her classroom."

"She said, 'What does that have to do with me? This is Cherokee land, not Georgia land. The negroes have a right to be educated too,' and she ousted me. Nobody can get along with her. She was sent from Brainard, to Haweis, to New

Echota."

"All right, I'll take her on. You get Worcester and Wheeler at the *Phoenix* and Butler too, if he's there."

"What about the Indian woman?"

"Gilmore said Ron asked to take care of her," he smirked.

Within three hours, half the guard stormed into the *Phoenix* building. Worcester was at his desk; Wheeler was packing some typesetting equipment, and Tsika stood beside him assisting him.

A soldier pulled Wheeler roughly from his work and handcuffed him. Another shoved the letters from the workbench.

"Get Worcester, you damn fool. We came for people, not equipment."

Worcester was helping Tsika get out of the rear window when he was yanked away. He protested he was coming with them of his own accord, but he had to let Tsika go with a thud.

She gasped as she fell to the ground. There were two guards waiting for her, but oddly enough, they helped her up and advised her to go home.

She ran for her horse, galloped around to the front of the building in time to see Worcester and Wheeler being tied by their necks with ropes to a horse's bridle. She jumped down and over the din of loud curses and neighing horses, shouted, "Stop that!"

"Shut up, lady, or you'll go too." His rifle butt pushed into her side.

Butler rushed from the building, calling, "Let the man go. He must see his new-born daughter before he leaves."

"You want to take his place, maybe? Move! Get in line!" Surprisingly, the sergeant said, "We'll stop at his home on the way back from High Tower, where we pick up Thompson."

It sounded generous and kind, but at the same time a soldier was knotting the rope. How ever could they stand it to be pulled all the way to Lawrenceville headquarters like this?

They moved off. Butler, however, was allowed to ride his horse. Tsika waited until the sad procession left before she started for Springplace.

She wished she could go back inside and print the day's happenings, but her better judgment told her to get out of the area fast. What about the Mission School? Would anyone dare to bother Sophia? Then she smiled. If so, Sophia would probably send them off in a hurry.

When Sean returned from Washington in August and heard the news, he said, "I wish they could have fought off the guards."

"Sean, you know better than that. How, with ten armed soldiers coming at them, could they possibly have done anything?"

"I know. Perhaps I can help them. A white lawyer going to defend white missionaries could have some weight."

"Wouldn't you have to wait for their trial in September?"

"Yes, but I'll go over now and at least talk to them."

After they returned to Riverview, they both settled into their usual routine: Sean was busy with the farm work and tried a case now and then and Tsika was at the *Phoenix* every day.

In late August Georgia Guards came to arrest Boudinot for his libelous articles, threatened him with whippings and marched him to prison. And just as suddenly, Worcester and Thompson were released.

Worcester said, "We weren't treated badly. In fact the civil authorities sympathized with us. They said it was a matter of 'Jurisdiction rather than Opposition,' because Thompson and I were Federal Agents (postal masters) in our districts therefore not subject to Georgia rule and we could leave."

But their freedom was short-lived. When Sean returned, he reported, "Gilmore has fixed that." Two days later, he relieved them of their postal duties. "Also, Tsika, here's a message for you: Boudinot has appointed Stand Watie, his brother-in-law, to take his place at the *Phoenix.*"

Again, the guards came back, arrested Worcester and this

time there was no sympathy. Chains instead of ropes were used and the only time any compassion was shown was when Samuel Worcester became ill; then he was allowed, for short periods of time, to ride in a wagon.

Elijah Hicks was appointed to help at the *Phoenix*, so for a time Tsika's load was lessened, but the news continued to pour in. Isaac Proctor became ill and was released, had to walk the ninety miles home. The jailors were unpredictable. Some prisoners were given blankets, but had to sleep on the cold dirt floor. They were to stay there until the hearings in Lawrenceville. On September 16th, John Ross, Wolf, Fox, Tsika, Sean, and several lesser chiefs attended the trial of Worcester and ten others. Those who agreed to take the pledge of allegiance to Georgia were released, but Worcester and Butler refused, so were sentenced to four years in Midgeville prison.

William Wirt had been hired to take their cases, but was ill, and when Sean offered to replace him, was refused on the grounds that, knowing the defense, he would not be impartial. A local Lawrenceville attorney was called in, so of course the verdict was guilty. Sean had not even been able to get their sentence reduced.

For some unknown reason, on that day Boudinot was released and two weeks later, by October 1st, he was sent to the east again to lecture for Cherokee funds.

The month of October in all its beauty couldn't help to raise the spirits of the Cherokees whose beloved missionaries were imprisoned. Tsika went to interview Ann Butler and Amy Worcester about their husbands, but they knew little. No one was allowed visitation at the prison. However Samuel had written.

Amy handed her a letter. "I am learning carpentry, mending shoes and, along with my continuing work of translating the Bible, am doing well. I even like the peace and quiet."

"It sounds as though they aren't treating him too badly."

"No, but he misses his family and his school."

"I know. And it's hard for you, Amy. I'll come in to help you whenever I can."

"That would be nice of you, Tsika." She smiled, "I had news of what some of your kind people are doing. A group of the older students have labored over writing him a letter in English. It took five of them a whole day to accomplish the feat and I could picture them with furrowed brows and firm lips in concentration.

After talking to Ann Butler, she returned to the *Phoenix* to write up her article. Stand Watie stood over her. It was usual, but unnerving.

"I heartily approve, Tsika," he complimented. "That's the kind of article you're good at. Keep up the good work."

She resented his patronizing attitude, and was upset that he frowned on some of her articles about the suspected treaty group. In fact he had deleted some of her remarks. She had never called suspected men by name, but she had left little doubt as to their true identity.

He was surely of the pro-removal group himself, but she never accused him or objected when he edited out some of her news. However she told Sean of her suspicions.

"I've added Stand Watie to my list of suspects, Sean: Ron, Sam Kellog, John Ridge, Cooley and now my boss. It seems as though the list grows too fast. It makes me feel uneasy."

"Maybe you see trouble where it doesn't really exist, my love."

"You men! You don't have women's intuition, or foresight."

"Thank God for that! We can see things as they really are."

"Sometimes, I wish I was like that."

"Like a man, Tsika? Heaven forbid!"

She laughed. "No, that would be worse than foresight, wouldn't it?"

"Yes, I wouldn't be doing this." He kissed her soundly.

But the uneasy feeling persisted for several weeks as more Cherokees seemed to doubt whether Ross was right, thinking it would be better for all concerned if they would travel West.

With a heavy heart, Tsika walked from the *Phoenix* building in a light November snow. It was unusual in this area where the winters were mild. Children were delighted to see a little snow. When she arrived home, Melissa and two of the Boudinot children were coasting down the hill behind the house. She joined them in an effort to feel a bit of light-heartedness.

At eleven o'clock that evening as she and Sean retired, a loud knock on the door summoned him. A sleepy Jeremy said, "Mr. Fox downstairs, askin' is you up."

They donned their robes and hurried to the lower hall. Fox was apologetic. "I must ask you to come with me, Sean. We have some trouble in Springplace."

Questions by them both brought forth no information. Fox just stood shaking his head and urging Sean to hurry. Finally to avoid further queries he said, "I'll wait outside," and left.

Tsika followed Sean upstairs as he went to dress. As he pulled on his shirt and pants, she continued to wonder aloud what it could be that would call him out so late at night.

"I knew it. There's trouble. I felt it all along. I'm worried. Hurry back, Sean." She kissed him.

"Be home in three hours."

"More like four," she groaned. "I'm going with you."

"No! Goodbye," and he rushed down the stairs.

"It's not fair, Sean," she shouted after him. "I'm going to follow you," and she started to dress. Then a wave of nausea washed over her and she thought of her mother's words: Your father, I see him being attacked—"Oh, God, *no!*" she screamed aloud. Then clapped her hand over her mouth. With almost too much calm, she went to the kitchen and made coffee. She was still there when Sean returned four hours later.

On his way back he couldn't decide how to tell her what had happened. He repeated phrases over and over in his mind. None of them would ease the pain. He was surprised to find her in the kitchen.

"You waited up for me, Tsika?"

"Yes, I couldn't sleep."

"It's—it's about your father, Tsika. I'm—"

"I know. Indians know when death stalks. I felt it, but I somehow couldn't relate it to me."

She was far too calm and tearless. Sean hugged her. "Oh, my dear, I am so grieved for you, I know—" then raised his hand in a helpless gesture as she pulled away.

"I will seek revenge. Tell me how it happened. As my mother prophesied three years ago?"

"Tsika you can't be thinking of revenge."

"I will do what I have to do. Now, tell me exactly what happened, then we will tell Manda to care for the children and we'll leave for Springplace."

Sean resigned himself to her request, took a cup of coffee and sat at the table. It was difficult to have to repeat what Fox had told him.

Fox had explained immediately, "I just couldn't tell Tsika what had happened to her father. Either he tried to take the bullet for Ross, or one was also meant for him, or perhaps the three roughnecks were just robbers bent on stealing, and he was shot by accident. We don't know," came out in a rush.

"Slower Fox. Tell me exactly how it happened."

Sean reported to Tsika, "John Ross, Wolf, Andrew Ross, two sub-chiefs and Fox were riding single file along a wooded path, on the way home from a meeting concerning the missionaries. The only stop had been at Ridge's Store. They were enjoying the crisp evening, singing and talking. The moon was shining through the trees lighting the way and suddenly three men pointing guns at them jumped out of the woods and blocked their way. The horses reared and Wolf and Morgan Owi dropped to the ground returning shots as they fell. One of the robbers was killed. The other two fled. Ross said he knew one, he wouldn't press charges. It was robbery and not of a political nature."

"I don't see why he said that. He's not sure," Tsika objected.

"Apparently he doesn't want to stir up any more trouble."

"Well I do. I shall dig until I find the cause."

One arm about her, they rode to Springplace and for thirty miles only the sound of horse's hoofs on the wooded path and the hooting of owls broke the silence.

When Sean wakened in the Wolf home the next morning, Tsika was gone, not only from their bed, but from the house.

"Oh my God, no!" he moaned. "Revenge!"

He opened the back door. Star was feeding the chickens. He rushed out, shouting, "Where's Tsika? Where did she go?"

"I haven't seen her this morning, Sean," she answered so calmly he realized she was in shock over her husband's death.

"Ron was here, asking for you, but now he's gone."

"Plantation business can wait. Tsika can't." He took off without the white man's saddle.

Even in her grief, Star had to smile at that. Something must truly be bothering him. Then she realized he wanted to find Tsika. Where could she be, Star wondered listlessly.

Sean rushed to Coosa to find out the exact spot where the attack had occurred. He was sure that's where Tsika would be. Ross explained directions carefully and Sean hurried away.

Ron smiled as he left the Wolf's farm for the wooded section north of Springplace. Ross had escaped the bullet meant for him, but the shot hadn't been wasted. Cochee had bagged one valuable enemy. Almost caught waiting to follow Tsika, Ron complimented himself for telling Star a believable story.

Ohahaty cussed at Cochee for missing his mark. "The Georgia bosses won't be happy you missed. Go back an' tell 'em! Butch 'n me'll go get Harris later tonight." Cochee galloped away.

"Come on, Butch, we gotta go get him afore the police do. The place'll be crawlin' with 'em by noon."

"I need more sleep."

"The hell you do. Come on." He yanked at his partner.

They rode in silence to the area. Between the trees they saw a figure scuffing the leaves in the path.

"Sh!"

"My God, it's a girl!" Butch whispered. "What'll we do?"

"Take her, that's what. Hey, it's Wolf's daughter."

"Me first. I'm creepin' up on 'er."

Tsika was so concentrated in her quest for clues of Cochee she failed to use her Indian-born gift of caution. By the time she was aware of someone near her, it was too late. Powerful arms caught her in a vise and she was thrown to the ground. Before she could utter a sound, her skirts were pulled up.

Muscle and cunning were needed and at the moment she felt bereft of both. She bit, scratched and clawed at her attacker and then heard a cackling laugh come from behind her head. Another one! Oh, my God, help me!

As the bearded face and ill-smelling breath sought her lips and hands pawed, she struggled to free herself. And what for? To be raped by another man? In one last effort, she brought up her knee with all the force she could muster and he rolled off as suddenly as he had pinned her down. Then she was struck on the side of the head.

In the foggy distance, a voice came through, "Get the hell out of here, you filthy swine! Go back to Cochee and Walker."

That voice. It was Ron. *He* was her savior.

"Oh, Ron," she said fuzzily. "Thank you, thank you."

"Take your dead partner and get out, fast, or I'll have your damn hide."

Then he turned to help Tsika up. "You're quite welcome, my lady," he bowed. "Now what's a nice girl like you doing out in the woods all alone?"

"Tracking. I had to find out who killed my father. I guess he found me first. I thought it was Cochee, but—" Then she realized that what she'd heard in her daze proved Ron was in with Cochee— "You're one of them. I knew it!"

Roughly he pulled her to him. She looked so appealing in

her anger and state of disarray, he blurted, "Guess I'll take you for myself. You seem to prefer kissing men in the woods."

She pounded him on the chest, and brought her knee up. He dodged, backed up and said, "Whoa, no force my little demon. I don't need force with you. You'll come to me, when I'm ready."

"Never, you beast! Why would I?"

"Because, I saw you and Aiku out by the river that day in July. You wouldn't want me to tell your husband about that, now would you?"

So, Ron was the man on horseback. She might have known.

The sneering, gloating, satisfied expression on his face made her want to slap him, but she was at his mercy at the moment.

To think he'd misinterpreted her innocent act made her feel nauseous, but she pretended acquiescence.

"Let's go back, Ron. I am so grief-stricken now. You can't expect to take advantage of my misdeeds, can you? I will see you later at Riverview and I do want to thank you for saving me from those men."

He smiled knowingly and boosted her up on her horse. She waved to him and he galloped away. Sean came into view as she rounded the first bend on the wooded path.

"Thank God, I've found you, Tsika. What were you thinking of to—" he exploded, then stopped short when he saw her torn dress.

She answered her husband with black eyes blazing. "I came to avenge my father's death."

Her hair hung in two braids over erect shoulders. She carried a rifle.

Sean could only stare at her. "Have you forgotten you are the wife of an Irish planter?"

"Forgive me! I thought I was the daughter of Chief Wolf." Her chin firm, her head held high, she was the picture of an Indian princess.

Then emotion choked her. "I—I. Oh Sean, I'm glad you're here." She leaned toward him.

He pulled her from her horse and seated her before him, and hugging her, rocked her to and fro. He smoothed her hair. "There, there, tell me what happened, my love."

"Hold me tight." Then she laughed nervously. "You must have been in a hurry, Sean. You never rode without a saddle before."

"I was. I rode down to ask Ross how to get here. That's why I was so late."

"You were right, Sean. I shouldn't have come. It was so horrible. I'll never come back here," she sobbed. "Take me home."

While Ross grieved for Wolf's family and his own loss of a loyal chief, he pressed no charges. He said one of his men shot the robber who'd shot Wolf. The attack was simply an attempted robbery, and not one of a political nature.

When Tsika went to the *Phoenix* several days later, she told Boudinot, "My father was killed and I am not supposed to ask why or by whom?"

"Harris and Ohahaty are known horse thieves; no one seems to be able to tie them in with Georgia officials."

"Cochee was that third man. I'm going to press charges."

"No one will listen to you, Tsika. No Indian has rights in court. You know the Georgia rules."

Tears came to her eyes. "I know, but I saw Cochee's limping footprints. I have proof he was there."

"The only thing you can do is write an article intimating that the Georgia officials had something to do with it. You can't actually blame them for the attack and killing."

She shook her head in frustration. She wrote, but with lack of purpose, tore up the paper and threw it away. However, before she left the office that day, her spirits rose when Wheeler told her that Ron had left for Augusta.

Silently, she thanked the Great Spirit for this fortunate respite, although she knew he would be back sometime to claim—what she would never do—she had to *tell* Sean about meeting Aiku. She should have told him a long time ago. Ron must have gone to see Cochee, or be busy with some Georgia business. Maybe if she could prove his involvement with them, she could keep him from coming back. Get Sam to slip.

"Sean, I have an idea. I know you don't want to remain at odds with Sam even though you've had difficulties. Suppose we have them over for dinner some night."

"That's fine with me. We have always enjoyed a social evening with the Kellogs."

Sam Kellog agreed and the date was set. Tsika invited her mother, grandmother and the children. Kellog's two girls, ten and twelve, loved to play with the Dolan and Wolf children.

At dinner the conversation centered around both men's cases, market prices and farm produce.

"Concerning the farm," Sean said, "Jake has been doing well since Ron left."

Tsika interrupted. "Yes, but I wonder how you'll have enough hours on Monday to try cases, leave orders for Jake, finish the work for Ross and prepare for the Washington visit."

"You plan to go with the delegation, Sean?" Sam asked.

"Yes, we leave on Tuesday."

"What do the Cherokees expect to accomplish this time?"

"We're concerned about the missionaries' imprisonment."

"I'm not against you, you know, but from what I've been able to gather, it won't do you much good."

Tsika snapped at that opening. "Who informs you of these things, Sam?"

Sam smiled, "Well now, if I told you Ron—" There was absolute silence for a moment. Sam shifted in his chair. "—Ron's been a good manager."

Star interrupted. "Let's go into the living room for coffee Tsika, and let the men discuss their problems."

Tsika was furious with her mother. Just when Sam had made a slip, which she could pursue, and say "Ron what?" Star had spoiled it, but one didn't take issue with a mother even in one's own home.

She called Nilla to serve coffee and the ladies left the table. Tsika managed to carry on an intelligent conversation and be polite, but she seethed within. Then the children rushed in to join them and all serious conversation was abandoned.

She complained to Sean later, "That remark was left hanging in mid-air like one of Sophia's dangling participles. Sean, I'm furious. Why didn't you pursue it?"

"Why, Tsika? You accomplished your purpose. I saw through Sam's poor effort to catch himself by pretending interest in Ron's job here. And what about Renee's hurry to get the family home because Sam had a long trip to Augusta tomorrow to meet with Ron and Colonel Bishop?"

"Then you're convinced about Ron, and that he and Sam are thick as thieves. But who's Bishop?"

"Only the head of the Georgia Militia and Gilmore's right hand man. Does that impress you?"

"Oh, heavens yes, it ties them both in nicely to the pro-removal group. What will Ross do about it when you tell him?"

"Nothing for the time being. These meetings in Washington take months, and if there's no further harassment, we wait."

"I hope this will be your last trip. The children don't know they have a father."

Sean shook his head. "You're the one who urged me to go to help Wirt organize for the missionaries' trial. Remember?"

She smiled, "Did I say that? I take it back. We miss you so."

"This time I won't stay the full three months. I'll be back by the end of February."

"I suppose I must bear with that. Come, I'll help you pack." She gave him a meaningful glance and pulled him upstairs.

The concerns of the Cherokee Nation fell at the doorstep of the *Phoenix,* and since Wheeler, Worcester and Boudinot were all away, Tsika was not only writing and proof-reading, she was also aiding Hicks and Stand Watie in type-setting.

From December into the first two months of 1832, the pace heightened in spite of having no harassments to report.

There was news about the missionaries' upcoming trial, marketing, trading, building and a letter had arrived from Boudinot expressing relief at the present unity of Cherokee governing leaders.

February 22, 1832 was a holiday for the school children, so Tsika took her three to Amy Worcester's Mission for a visit and some first-hand news about Samuel Worcester.

Amy threw her arms around Tsika. "I'm so happy to see you, dear. I just received a letter from Samuel."

"What does he say about his treatment in prison?"

"He's well, but feels sad because they allow no devotions. However, my most distressing news comes from a man named Reese. I heard him speak yesterday, and he urged the people to go West. He said my husband thought it was best for them to go now. I don't believe Samuel said that. He would never go back on his word to the Cherokees, Tsika."

"I know. The man is just saying that to sway the people."

"But the people who have been trying so hard to get him out of prison will believe it." Tears glistened in her eyes.

"Have you asked Butrick to help get him released?"

"John Ross asked him and he refused, saying a man of religion shouldn't be embroiled in politics."

"As soon as Sean returns we'll go over and talk to Sam."

"Will they let you in?"

"A white lawyer? Yes, I'm sure Sean can get to see him. Now let's take the children for a hike. I'll get Beth into her traveling chair. See, Jake put small pony cart wheels on our armed kitchen chair and it works beautifully. Get your brood together, Amy."

"No Mamma, I can do it." Beth pushed Tsika away, and

reached for the seat of the chair and bracing her feet, slowly swung her body up.

Tsika watched, shaking her head in amazement. Missy, Danny and the Worcester girls clapped. Tsika's tears flowed as she hugged the child to her and smoothed the blond curls.

"Oh Bethy, this is wonderful. How? When did you learn?"

"We've been showing Beth how to do it, Nilla and me," Missy explained. "We wanted to surprise you."

"My dears, I can't believe this. How could you be doing this miracle under my very nose? For how long?"

"Long time, Mamma. Now, when Papa brings us his surprise package from Washington, we have a surprise for him."

"Indeed you do, my dears. We've worked on those little legs for so long with no results. But there *are* results! Oh, children, I'm so happy! We'll keep trying to walk, Bethy."

"You forget we're taking a walk now, Mamma?"

"No, let's go, a-singing, 'Great Spirit, we thank Thee,' for we are so humbly grateful." The wheel cart rumbled along the walk, to the rhythm of the time-worn song.

1832 - 1835

Before the spring meeting in March, the delegation members returned home with the cheerful message that the U.S. Supreme Court, in the person of Chief Justice Marshall, declared, "Georgia's rule be null and void: the Georgians have no right to enter Cherokees land without the consent of the Cherokees."

The *Phoenix* published the news in Cherokee, and the people were overjoyed that they could read it in their own tongue.

But Sean wasn't optimistic. When he returned home, he said, "When did Georgia ever abide by any laws except her own."

Before John Ross left the capital, that fact was proven. It was reported President Jackson said, "John Marshall has rendered his decision: now let him enforce it."

In April, 626 Cherokee immigrants left for the West because they were frightened by Jackson's rules.

In Washington, in late May, Jackson's Secretary of War, John Eaton, spoke of removal to the Cherokee delegation members, who had not yet left the capital: John Ross, William Coodey, John Ridge and James Martin. James Starr and John

Walker, two men who were very interested in the success of the treaty for removal, had engaged him to speak at the meeting. All except Ross were impressed.

Up to this time all the Cherokee resistance to removal had been fought by legal procedure, newspaper articles and trips to Washington by delegations such as these. Would they eventually need force to meet force?

In May Boudinot resigned from the *Phoenix* and when Ross returned from the capitol in June, a worried and concerned man, he advised the people to fast and pray. They gladly complied.

At the July 23, 1832 council meeting at Red Clay in Tennessee, U.S. Commissioner Elisha Chester insisted Cherokee removal would save the Nation suffering.

Major Ridge, who had groomed his son John for just such an occasion watched with pride as the young man rose to address the members, but felt shock as did others at John's first words.

He welcomed the members, then stated, "Some of you won't like what I'm going to say. Afterwards you may take the floor to debate or comment. Removal is imminent. Your rights will not be reinstated. Georgia's rules will be enforced. The Government, in the person of President Andrew Jackson, has declared that Cherokees would do well to observe those rules and sign the Removal Treaty. You should know the truth. John Ross has led you to believe you have a chance, but it would be wise if you move now before a forced removal is instigated."

Ross jumped to his feet, his five-foot-eight looking tall and formidable. His blue eyes flashed fury. He scowled with indignation. "It takes two sides to ratify a treaty and neither Georgia nor President Jackson can force us to sign."

Then he turned to Elias Boudinot and said, "Mr. Boudinot, I'd advise you not to report any of this discussion in the *Phoenix* for fear it will provoke trouble, even violence."

"You are suppressing free speech, Ross," Boudinot

shouted, "to forbid any information that comes out of this meeting. What is the *Phoenix* for but to publish information, to publish the truth, and yes, even to publish Cherokee rights?" Then he added, "You've brought up an issue for the Supreme Court to decide."

Chief Hicks took the floor. "What about an instance, when a decision is made by that U.S. Court and Georgia officials ignore it, like the Tassel case, when the man was hanged after the Supreme Court said to try him, and the President doesn't defend the decision? Seems as if that's where we are."

"We're getting off the track, Hicks," said John. "The *Phoenix* should advise the American people of the Cherokee grievances, so they can be solved by discussions in Washington."

"John, I'd like to speak," said his nephew, Coodey, looking as self-satisfied as the proverbial cat. "Your situation is hopeless. You really have only three avenues open to you and your people. One, fight and be annihilated, two, submit to oppression and suffer death, or three, remove to the West voluntarily."

Boudinot said, "I see hope in the third avenue only."

Ross snapped, "I believe in your integrity, Elias, but your judgment is poor. I blame you for giving comfort to the enemy: those in favor of removal."

"My intentions are misunderstood, and I hereby resign from the National Council." He strode from the room.

"Meeting adjourned." The chairman pounded the gavel.

Many left murmuring their discontent: some remained, adding their names to the list of removal advocates. Starr and Walker headed the list, followed by John Ridge, Andrew Ross, William Coodey, William Hicks and William Rogers.

The meeting had ended in bitterness and disunity. It would split the Cherokee leaders into two factions: The Ridge Party or the Treaty Party and the John Ross Party. Life-long friends, Major Ridge and John Ross, had come to a bitter parting.

Sadly, John admitted to his loyal supporters, "The Major

has not yet signed his name, and he looks innocent, but I fear
he will go the way of the son. I intend to hold a meeting on
October 8, at Coosa where the whole Cherokee Nation will be
represented. We must strive for UNITY if we are to survive."

The man who had written most of the tribe's constitution,
been head-chief and had served the Cherokee Nation as
President of the National Committee for more than a decade,
was devoted to them and was beloved by hill Cherokees, farmers, townspeople and merchants. They would turn out in full
force.

A caravan of visitors arrived at the head of the Coosa.
Carts and drays loaded with pots and pans, children and animals set up camp on the Ross grounds. Blankets were draped
over the surrounding fences. Cooking fires burned and the
odor of roasting meat permeated the air. The atmosphere was
festive in spite of a drizzle of rain that started to fall.

Some wore complete Indian regalia, others part Indian
garb and part white's clothing. The leaders and the sub-chiefs
wore turbans, but otherwise, they and their wives were dressed
as for any white social affairs. Everything was normal for a
gathering of all the people until the meeting started, and an
uninvited stranger appeared. It was John Lowrey, a representative of the Federal Government. His visit was unannounced
and the Cherokees observed him with some concern.

The Council stated its business, then Lowrey addressed the
people. John Ridge translated to them the message that was
sent through this man from the Secretary of War: "To conform
with the Removal Bill, Cherokee land will be surveyed and dis-
tributed to Georgia citizens by lottery. It will include the gold
mines." He droned on for fifteen minutes, and ended his
speech with, "And what will become of you?"

Major Ridge introduced a resolution to send a delegation
to Washington during the winter of 1832-1833 to discuss
Treaty Removal with Jackson. Ross advised they wait until after the coming presidential election in 1832 between Henry
Clay and President Jackson. The people left hurriedly as

though to escape more controversy. Discouraged, they packed their belongings and trudged home.

The meeting had ended in a stalemate. Later, Ross realized that to wait for Henry Clay to become President was wishful thinking, so he accepted the suggestion that they go once again to Washington. To tackle the issue now would be better.

"This is the beginning of the end," Tsika said to Sean, as they returned to their home in the pouring rain. "It's as depressing as the weather."

"Many in the government are on our side. I still believe that men like Davy Crockett and Daniel Webster can aid us."

"What about Major Ridge? Do you think John has influenced him to join the Treaty Party?"

"I'm afraid so. Also Boudinot and Worcester."

"Worcester! When we talked to him in prison, I thought he'd never forsake the Cherokees."

"He's being released because he signed the oath. He said perhaps he's been wrong and it might be in the best interests of the Cherokees if they would go West peacefully."

"So many are going over to the Pro-removal side, it's hard to know who is still loyal to Ross, and Eastern tribes are leaving for the West. This month three have accepted treaties."

"Three quarters of the population still choose to remain on Cherokee soil. That's a good thing to remember when you get discouraged."

"Up until now, John Ridge, Elias Boudinot, Stand Watie and Andrew Ross have been within Constitutional law, but since they've tried and failed, I'm afraid they'll resort to force."

"Perhaps." Sean's mind was wandering. Now his eyes took on a pleased expression. "Look, here come our little Indians. Tsika, this calls for a picnic."

Missy and Danny were running down the lane, pushing Beth's chair ahead of them. Sean called "Whoa," stopped the team and, picking up each one, pretended to toss them into the rear of the carriage, then gently set them down. Squealing and laughing they tumbled about until they heard they would be going on a picnic, then started planning what they'd take.

But nature protested: the wind began to blow, rain pelted them as they emerged from the carriage, and a bedraggled family group entered the house.

"Postponed until further notice," Sean addressed the children. "I hope you're not too disappointed."

"Missy is," said Beth, "but I don't care. I don't have much fun at picnics anyway."

"Spoil-sport," called Danny.

"Enough, Daniel. Beth can't run and play like you and Missy. That's enough reason why she doesn't like picnics."

"No, that's not the reason, Papa. I just don't like the bugs."

Her remark brought laughter. She'd diverted the immediate concern about her incapacity. With perception beyond her years she realized that to pretend her crippled legs didn't matter was important to the family. For the first time Tsika saw her daughter in a new light. Beth had come just so far, but had made up her mind to adjust. Love, humor and caring made for a good family relationship. Silently she prayed, "Great Spirit, let us all live to enjoy it."

The next day dawned clear and fresh, a right day for a picnic. "Manda has everything ready for the day's outing, girls. Get things together. Papa has gone to the barn with Danny for the horse and cart."

The sun was trying to poke through the mist that hung over the valley and the hills beyond were a hazy blue-green. The wagon was loaded with children, baskets, blankets and two dogs, Dodge, the shepherd and the sheep dog, Wooly. It was an excited, noisy group. They bumped over the country roads singing, "Oh, Susanna," and banging the sides of the wagon.

At the end of a busy day, Sean and Tsika were packing the wagon for the trip home.

"Get Bethy's chair, Sean, and carry her over here, please."

Missy squealed, "Come, Momma, Papa, see Bethy."

Beth was standing beside a tree, unsteadily reaching one foot forward as she hung onto the small trunk with both hands.

It brought them both hurrying to her. The child was shaking her blond curls. "Don't help. See, I can do it."

They stood back allowing her to show them how she went from one tree to the next, and holding back tears of gratitude, joined Melissa and Daniel in clapping for her success.

Beth's face was wreathed in smiles and as they placed her in the wagon, she said, "Papa always thought I could do it."

Her father's girl, thought Tsika. Just as she had been determined to please her father, so had Beth been anxious to please Sean since her toddling days. It was so right and good.

Beth's exercise had tired her and almost as soon as she was placed on the pad in the wagon she fell asleep. The other two, worn out from the days play, drifted into dreamland, tousled heads on the wooly dog.

"This has been a wonderful day, Sean. One we'll always remember."

Sean placed his arm around Tsika's slim waist; his other hand turned her face to his for a kiss, and a slice of new moon smiled through the clouds.

"Sean, we'll go off the road," she mumbled.

"Domino knows the way home, my sweet. Don't deny me the feeling of a newly married man. We don't seem to find time for this lately."

"I'll quit my job like you did."

"The trouble is, I accepted another one."

"You're not going back with Sam!"

"No, Ross had to make a few changes when he was elected and gave me his old job, handling the finances for the Cherokees."

"I'm proud of you Eagle," she smiled. "Now you're a true Cherokee."

He laughed. "Micha's old name for me. I haven't thought of it for a long time. I'll see if I can measure up to the courage it represents."

On their return, Jake helped them from the wagon. "Mr. Dolan, there's been men here all day marking trees. They said

Georgia officials sent 550 of them to Cherokee country to survey the land. They left a paper—"

"So soon?" Tsika said. "We knew it was coming, but—"

"I'll check on it, Jake." He kissed Tsika and the children, saying, "I won't be long," and ran to the barn for his horse.

"Go with him, Jake."

Sean was still gone long after Tsika had tucked the children in bed. She parted the living room curtains and looked out across the side yard to the barns where a lighted lantern flickered in Jake's tack house. Two shadowy figures running toward the house alerted her to trouble. Where was Sean? Pounding fists brought her hurriedly to the door.

Benji and another groom stood there; frightened faces staring at her.

"Benji, what is it? Speak up!"

Finally he squeaked, "Master, he hurt *ba-ad*. Come! I think Jake hurt too."

Tsika raced after them, her wrap forgotten in her haste. She was led down the lane to the field adjacent to their property. Sean lay unconscious in the weeds. Jake was moaning, his foot bent at a grotesque angle beneath him.

"Oh my God Jake, what happened?"

"Sean and I followed them. They turned mean—"

Benji said, "We didn't think we should carry him. Sammy's gone for the doctor."

Tsika ripped open Sean's shirt, the stab wound was just below the left arm. "Oh dear God, no! Sean can you hear me? You'll be all right; the doctor is coming." She pulled off her petticoat, rolled it up and placed it under his head.

Jake was struggling to rise; he was speaking through swollen lips, "Missus, we went over to Boudinot's where they said they were going to stay and Sean said, when Elias and Harriet saw what kind of men were supposed to stay with them, he threw them out."

"So the men were fighting mad when you found them."

"One pulled a knife on Sean, before we even had a chance

to talk to them."

Tsika became furious with Jake. "And where were you while this was happening?"

He pointed to his mouth. "Mam, I was fighting the other two."

"Forgive me, Jake. I'm upset. Oh thank God, here comes Dr. Ainslee."

He staunched the blood flow, cauterized and bandaged Sean's wound and sent Benji after the cart and blankets.

"It's the lottery, Tsika," Ainslee explained. "It's a way of harassing us. They hope we'll get weary of all this and leave."

Tsika shook her head. "I know, but when it comes this close to home, and you know they mean everything they say, we will really resist. Once Sean said, 'If the Cherokees are willing to die fighting for their country, so am I.' Sean is one of us, Doctor. I can't bear it if he doesn't recover."

She wiped her tears on her sleeve. "My apologies. I'm no stoic Indian when it comes to my husband."

"I understand." He placed his arm around her. "Sean will be as right as rain when he regains his strength from blood loss."

When had she heard that expression from a doctor before?

However, this time the doctor's prediction was true. Sean felt stronger every day and by the time the delegates were ready to go to Washington on December 3rd, was able to go with them.

On the 16th, Melissa bounded in from school with a frown and a complaint. "Miss Sophia makes us work too hard. She's an old—old—"

That's enough, Missy," Tsika reprimanded. "That's a disrespectful way to speak of your teacher."

"Well," her daughter pouted, "she said I should learn to behave like you did in school."

"And how did you misbehave?"

Her hand flew to cover her mouth and she shook her head.

Tsika took her by the shoulders. "Look me in the eyes, Missy, and tell me exactly what you did."

Those blue eyes so like Sean's always melted her heart, and she couldn't bear to punish her daughter, but she had to know.

"I went into town. I—I wanted to see the burned black-smith shop."

"You left school?"

"It was just during recess time. Oh, Momma don't be cross with me. I just wanted to give you news to write about like Papa does—and he wasn't here." The blue eyes filled with tears.

She hugged her daughter. "I understand, but Missy, that was wrong—and it was dangerous."

"That's what Miss Sophia said."

"There are some people in New Echota who could harm you. You must stay away from town. Promise?"

Missy nodded. "But, Miss Sophia will punish me."

"I'll talk to her. Now up to bed, my darling."

Tsika didn't have long to wait. There was a knock at the door. Miss Sophia Sawyer had come to Riverview Acres.

"Hello, Sophia. Melissa told me. We've settled the problem. It won't happen again."

"I came, not to talk about your daughter, but about you."

"About me? Why, Sophia?"

"Ron Bullock is in town. He's one of the men running the lottery in New Echota with a man named Reese. I don't like to think of you're being here without Sean after what you told me about him."

"Thank you, dear. I'll take them to Springplace to visit my mother until Sean returns. We plan to spend Christmas with my family there anyway; we'll just go a little early."

"Good. I'll give you the children's lessons for the week." Her angular features softened when she spoke of the little ones she taught. They loved her as did the Cherokee parents, but it seemed impossible for her to get along with the mission-aries.

She suddenly brought her handkerchief to her eyes. "Tsika, I'm asked to leave at the end of the term."

"Surely not. What will you do?"

She was a stormy, opinionated woman with a difficult disposition that caused a shift when she'd been at odds with Worcester and was sent from Springplace to Haweis and thence to New Echota.

She smiled through her tears. "Worcester says I express myself 'out of season and out of reason.' "

"Where will you go? Surely not back East."

"No, I will go to the Ridges to teach their children. I have been welcome there ever since I came from New Hampshire. I feel at home at Running Waters. The Major is a good friend."

"Who asked you to leave New Echota?"

"Barker, a Georgia councilman fell heir to my Missionary building by way of the lottery."

"Lawyer Dolan will come to your aid, Sophia."

"It wouldn't help me and would only cause them to hate him. There's no dealing fairly with the Georgia officials. I'll be happy at the Ridges."

"Don't let him convert you. You know John Ridge is a member of the so-called Treaty Party. He's influencing his father."

"I'll watch out, my dear. Now you pack up the children and leave in the morning. You must be careful, Tsika. We cannot trust anyone these days."

"I know. I met Katherine on the street yesterday. She advised me to send Missy to the Ladies' Seminary in North Carolina in January."

"Do that, Tsika, by all means. She'll be safe there."

Just as Tsika and Nilla had finished packing the luggage for the trip to Springplace, there was a knock at the door.

"Who could that be, Nilla? It's almost ten o'clock."

"Jeremy's calling, Mam. He say it's Ron Bullock."

"Tell him I've retired."

In a moment Nilla rushed upstairs. "Mam, he pushed right

in. He say you'd see him."

Tsika's lips pressed together. "I'll go down, but stay nearby. I don't trust that man."

"Oh, yes Mam. And Jeremy be there too. We be in the kitchen."

Tsika's knees were shaking when she came down the stairs.

"Aren't you going to invite me to be seated?"

"No. I'm going to ask you to leave."

"I came to collect."

Act ignorant. "Collect what?"

"A little promise made in the woods one day as a favor for keeping my mouth shut."

Bluff. "You think I meant that? I said it just to get away. Surely you don't think I've neglected to tell Sean about my harmless meeting with Aiku."

"I don't believe for one moment you've told him about that. He stepped forward to clasp her in his arms. "Come on, be nice."

She stepped back. "Don't you touch me. I'll scream, and the entire house staff will be in here."

He bowed, then went to the door. He turned to look at her, green eyes blazing. "I'll be back."

Tsika was weak with fear and disgust. She'd make sure she'd not be alone. It would be wise to take Nilla along tomorrow.

She looked out of the bedroom window at the trees swaying in the breeze against a full moon. It was beautiful, but no, she'd not open the window this night.

It was a long time before she fell asleep. Around midnight Beth screamed. Another nightmare about falling over the cliff. She went to comfort the child. Then Danny cried with an earache. She called Nilla and together they quieted him with drops of oil and heated pads laid against his head. He finally drifted off to sleep. Would they get to Springplace tomorrow?

With all the activity, she forgot about Ron, and when she went to bed this time, she slipped into a deep slumber.

Ron slammed into the saloon where he was to meet Cochee, pushed up to the bar and said, "A bottle of that rot-gut stuff you sell here."

"You look like the devil's got you by the tail. Too bad you didn't get what you wanted," Cochee grinned. "You go about things the wrong way to."

Ron glared at him. "Mind your own damned business."

"It's my business too. You're supposed to get the boss first, like Johnson told ya. Then you kin go get her."

"Shut your big mouth, Cochee."

"No cause to go off the deep end. Red hair sure means temper. Here, have another drink. Improves the disposition."

Tsika wakened to a scratching sound. She thought it must be the cat and sleepily rolled over.

Suddenly she felt a presence in the room. She turned to see the shadowy figure of a man in the moonlight at the window. Oh, my God, a thief. She held her breath. If she remained silent, perhaps he'd take what he wanted and leave.

Then he slurred, "You won't get away from me this time."

"Oh, no, Ron!" She screamed. But who would hear her? The servants quarters were on the other side of the house.

He reeked with alcohol. A pillow muffled her screams. She bit and clawed and kicked to no avail. When she managed to turn her head and gasp for air, she screamed again and took a sharp blow to the face. She tasted blood, and another punch reduced her to unconsciousness.

At the first sound of pounding feet, Ron climbed out of the window onto the balcony. He fell from the trellis to the ground. Damn! He was clumsy from the liquor. He limped away.

Frantic voices came through the mist to her consciousness.

"Oh, Mam, is you all right?"

"Did I waken the children?" came out in a mumble.

"No, the child's is asleep," Nilla assured her.

"How did you know?" Oh dear, was she going to faint again?

"Benji was comin' home late an' thought he heard a scream, then shrugged, an' said, it's imagination, or perhaps a wild cat. He thought he better check the chickens an' the horses an' on the other side the house, he heard it again an' knew where it came from. It took him awhile to rouse us."

"You came. That's all that matters."

"Now have a nice warm bath, Mam. You'se not going to travel today."

"Oh yes I am, Manda. Nilla is going with me to Springplace. You'll protect me, won't you, dear."

The child's nurse looked surprised, but nodded, "Yessum."

"Greetings," Tsika shouted, as the three children burst into the Wolf house.

"Grandma, we've come to stay with you for a long time and for Christmas," Missy shouted.

"Good." Star hugged them all. "We will go to Reverend Clauder's service on Christmas Eve." She turned to Tsika. "He was assigned to the Springplace Mission by the board to take the place of Brother Gottlieb and is Dean of all the Moravian Missions. He's so pleased to be here because of the lovely Herb Garden. Everyone is so very fond of him and he has a nice family."

"My he's made a great impression on you."

"When is Sean coming home?"

"Not in time for Christmas, but soon. I hope this is the last time. The children and I miss him so much."

"Tsika, something's wrong. What is it? I can tell, you are not your exuberant self."

"Nothing that you're good food and company won't fix, Momma."

Reverend H. J. Clauder was in his study preparing his Christmas Eve service when there was a knock on his door.

Several men stood on the threshold. Ah, visitors! He would follow his custom of inviting them in for food and lodging and inquire about their businesses.

Before he had a chance to speak, one of the men said, "I represent the owner of this property, who drew it in the lottery. He will move in tomorrow, but you are permitted to stay in part of it for $150 a year."

Shocked, Clauder was speechless. Another man said, "In the future you will pay your rent to me."

The missionary angrily slammed the door shut, bolted it and returned to the study to write to the Board of Missionaries in Boston for help.

Clauder did manage to give his Christmas Eve service.

"I can't understand it, Tsika. The Reverend's address is so halting, and he acts as if someone's looking over his shoulder."

"People are buzzing. I don't know why, but I'll find out."

After the service, Tsika left her family to speak to White Fox. "Do you know what this confusion is all about?"

"Yes, the Reverend's property was up for lottery drawing and now belongs to Colonel Bishop of the Georgia Militia. He plans to make that his headquarters."

Tsika felt actual physical pain. "It isn't right." She wiped her eyes.

"It means the U.S. authorities condone Georgia's acts."

On Christmas morning, Colonel Bishop pulled up to the doorway of the missionary in a carriage followed by a wagon-load of furniture. His driver knocked on the door but there was no answer. The door was bolted and the Colonel was forced to sleep outside in his carriage. Reverend Clauder took satisfaction in the fact that he was not going to give in easily.

However, the next day, when he heard the lock being forced open, he knew sheer panic. This time there were eighteen soldiers of the Georgia Militia, who tramped through the mission and the house, and moved the family possessions to a back room.

"What will happen to us?" Mrs. Clauder wailed. "We can't

live this way. We're used to—"

"Hush, Myrtle," Clauder cut her off. "I'll talk to Star. The Wolfs are kind people and I think will allow us to stay with them until we find another place. Best we go over and talk to them immediately. Get the children dressed."

Star and the family opened their arms to the Clauders, and offered food and shelter for as long as they needed to stay.

But this was a matter to be solved as quickly as possible, so the Reverend went to see Big Elk, who would advise him.

They seated themselves in the back room of the newly built Post.

"Have a mug of my home-made corn whiskey, Reverend."

"That's just the kind of fortification I need, my friend."

They discussed the deplorable situation in which Clauder found himself and his family, the lottery and how settlers in covered wagons were moving into the area and taking over the property.

Big Elk leaned back in his chair, his pipe dropping ashes on his waistcoat. "The only good thing to say about them is that they're not pony thieves or miners, but something has to be done about it."

"I heard the citizens have formed a group to fight it."

"Since the blacksmith shop was burned, we have plenty who want to get even. When John Ross gets back he'll calm them down.

"At the moment, I feel as though I'd like to start a group myself to fight this invasion."

The front door banged and there was a scuffling of boots.

"Ross says a treaty must be agreed upon by two sides to make it lawful." Boudinot's high-pitched voice carried into the back room.

"He says, but we can get around that. Just get a few men to sign in Washington and round up a few Cherokees and you've got it made," said John Ridge. Then he shouted, "Who's mindin' the store?"

Big Elk nodded to Clauder and strode to the front of the Post. "Hello," he boomed. "What can I do for you gentlemen?"

Mr. Boudinot placed an order for the mission. Ridge took some parched corn and jerky.

"Taking a trip, Mr. Ridge?"

"Just going by coach to Washington."

Elk knew the Ridge family could afford to go in style, so who was this dried meat for? Someone who didn't want to show his face in the Post. Cochee? Ron Bullock?

"Have a good trip. Thank you, gentlemen. Mr. Boudinot, your order will be delivered to the Mission."

Elk had a bitter taste in his mouth when he bid them goodbye.

He returned to Clauder, "What do you make of that?"

"Sounds as if there's someone who wants to stay out of sight. And I don't like the idea of signing a treaty by those who have no right to do so."

"I aim to ask Ross about that as soon as he comes back."

A light snow had begun to fall as Tsika, Sean and the children prepared to leave for Riverview Acres. By the time they had reached the Vann's home they were in a white world of swirling feathers.

"It's so beautiful, I even like the cold weather a little bit, Sean. However, not to walk in. Look ahead. There is Mr. Vann and his daughter, and someone's unloading furniture. Oh no! They're dispossessed. The lottery again."

They stopped, asked him and Clara to climb into the carriage. The new owners had not even allowed them to take a horse from the barn.

"Martins was taken last night," Vann said. "The lovely home of marble mantles, Persian rugs and famous paintings is taken over by those damned ruffians."

"Where are the other members of your family?" asked Tsika.

"They're with my mother in Atlanta, thank God."

"You'll come home with us and I'll take you over to Atlanta in the morning," Sean offered.

The snow was clinging to trees and shrubs creating a veritable fairyland, but the beauty of it escaped them now. A frightening thought took its place. It could happen to them.

In Augusta, Governor Lumpkin called a meeting of his officials to hear a report by members of the harassment group headed by Cochee.

Limping and with a deep scratch on his face, Ron Bullock wondered if his information would be valuable enough to compensate for the derision he'd get from the members. He and Cochee arrived late.

Lumpkin was speaking. "My policies concerning the Cherokees are identical with the former governor's. Lottery drawing is in progress and we'll hear a report from our representatives."

After the report, Ron said, "John Ridge and Walker are doing a fine job of recruiting new members to the Treaty Party and will leave for Washington shortly with a delegation to sign."

"Good," said Johnson. "It doesn't matter if we have to falsify signatures or even bribe a few important people, like John Ross. We'll run them out of Georgia somehow."

Tsika wrote scathing articles in the *Phoenix* concerning the lottery tragedy. One stated: "Lottery numbers aren't even needed for some of the smaller properties. Settlers have come into the area in their covered wagons, chased the owners out at gunpoint and appropriated their buildings and lands. In other instances, where some farmers were fond of liquor, they were approached in the grog shops and, while under its influence, urged to sign their property away."

She was ready to take it to Wheeler for type-setting, but he was coming to her desk. Hesitantly he handed her a paper that had been brought to him by a messenger only moments before.

"I hate to be the one to do this to you, Tsika. It's—it's about your brother."

"Juni! Oh, no! He couldn't! John, tell me it's not true!"

"I'm afraid it is, Tsika. Unah, his wife found him in the barn—a—he'd hung himself."

Tsika was too stunned to cry. She pressed John for details. "Why? When?"

"They say he'd been drinking, and was despondent because he'd signed away his farm."

"Oh, God. No! Not one of those I just wrote about."

To herself she mumbled, "What will Unah and the children do? I must go to them."

Tsika was gone in a second. John added a paragraph to her article and doggedly went about the duty of publishing the unpleasant news. One more victim of Cherokee oppression.

When John Ross received the report concerning the proremoval group that planned to descend upon Washington, he quickly returned. He planned to refute their claims to sign any treaty and also to object to the lottery.

There had been some doubt whether William Hicks had turned against the Ross Cherokees, but in February, word came that no one was to claim his property by lottery and that was proof positive that he was with the Treaty Party one hundred percent. Also properties of John Ridge and Elias Boudinot were safe.

When Ross returned in April to Coosa, he brought Butler and Worcester with him. The two missionaries found things much different in Cherokee country than when they'd left. Grog shops were set up along the highway, next to the stores and Cherokee businesses. Drunkenness was seen everywhere.

"Demoralizing. That's what it is," said Worcester. There is nowhere to go when there's a take-over of the large properties and the missionaries by Georgia militia except leave the land."

"I'd debate that, Sam," Ross said as he bid goodbye to the missionary at his doorstep in New Echota. "You let them talk you into that in order to be freed."

"A messenger came to Ross as he left Worcester's New Echota mission. "Mr. President, your—your house has been taken."

"Speed up driver!" John shouted, standing in the cab as if it would accelerate the horse.

He pulled up to see Tsika and Sean at the side door.

"We just heard, John. We've come to see how Quati is getting along," Sean greeted him.

"Thank you, friends. *I* just heard." He pushed past the nursemaid who'd opened the door. "Mena, where is she?"

"She sick, Mastah. I don' know what to do. The childs is all upset."

"We'll be glad to help if we can, Mena," said Tsika. "Perhaps we could take the children over to our house? Or we'll leave until John needs us. We don't want to interfere."

"I don' know." the girl stood by wringing her hands.

They left, vowing to do something soon. The livestock, fields, orchards and buildings were appropriated and some of the barns were being torn down to make room for—what?

"That's criminal, Tsika. What will he do?"

Ross's first concern was Quati. It had been a shock to her when she was so ill with fever she could hardly stand, to be roughly herded with her children into a small back room. He cared for her day and night until she was able to travel.

Two weeks later they moved across the Tennessee River with several other dispossessed landowners. He was discouraged, but now more than ever he was determined to get the Georgians out of Cherokee land.

"He did have one bit of good news to report when he spoke at the council meeting," Sean told Tsika at dinner that night. "Elbert Hemming of the Department of Indian Affairs has promised to help keep the lottery intruders out of the Cherokee Nation, even saying that he would send the U.S. Military to accomplish the purpose."

Tsika smiled at that. "Do you really think that will ever come to pass, Sean?"

"We can hope, but it goes on. Worcester and Butler have been home for only a few weeks and their missionaries at New Echota and Haweis have been taken."

"And," Tsika added, "Chief Lowrey's property is gone. He joined Ross across the river in Tennessee. At the *Phoenix* offices today, Wheeler said news came in that Reese has returned to recruit for pro-removal possibilities. He and Chief Jolly from the Western Cherokee lands are to be joined by McAllister, James Starr and John Walker. Isn't that a lovely combination? All bad news."

Recruiting went on all spring and summer without any remarkable results. The Cherokees went about their everyday duties, and except for the few who preferred to spend their time in the grog shops, the people were loyal to John Ross.

Even Katherine Brown was apprehensive. One day when she chanced to meet Tsika on the street, she said, "Since the blacksmith shop was burned, I have been frightened to come to town."

Tsika answered sharply, "And for good reason. Your friends, the Ridges are going pro-removal. You should fear them."

"You can't mean that, Tsika."

"Partially. They could influence you to agree with them."

"Oh, I didn't realize. I've been teaching in the missionary school down in the southern part of the country for so long, I've quite lost touch."

"Have you had no recruiters there? No trouble?"

"No, only a few settlers have moved in and taken property, but it was worthless land."

"Be careful, Katherine. Things are changing. When Samuel Worcester came back from prison, he was amazed at how much the Cherokees had changed. From a quiet, industrious, progressive people, many have become quarrelsome, drunken and violent. He said it grieved him and he could see why

Boudinot urged him to tell the people to move. Under Georgia rule there would be certain deterioration and death."

"Do you believe that?"

"No, but many are being convinced. My husband and I are fighting along with Ross to save the people and their land."

"I'll do my bit in spite of my friend's beliefs."

"I know you will. Good luck."

News of the next delegation, sent by Council in January '34, came to the desk at the *Phoenix* for publication. Jackson had made an offer of $2,500,000 for the remaining Cherokee lands. Ross refused, saying, "The gold mines are worth more than that."

Then an offer of $3,000,000 was made, with assurance of protection in the West if the Cherokees moved voluntarily and he responded, "How can you guarantee protection in the West when you can't protect us from Georgia?"

Big Elk had reported to John Ross the plan he'd heard revealed: one instigated by John Walker to sign a treaty for removal by representatives who were unauthorized to do so.

John decided to ask Major Ridge about the plan. It was more or less a conciliatory move to patch up past differences, but it only assured him that Ridge thought it would be in the best interests of the Cherokees to move. The man sincerely believed it was best. Nothing could be done to change his mind. John left his old friend with the sad realization their ways had parted. There was now a Ridge Party and a Ross Party. There was no meeting ground. He pulled his coat collar up around his ears.

The weather was bitter cold. The Cherokees called it a Lapland Winter. Some of the people hovered miserably in their cabins. Some, encouraged to drink too much, were dispossessed by crafty recruiters who urged them to sign their farms away; some were told their relatives had signed which influenced them to sign and others were driven from their homes, by sheer force. They were convinced they should go West.

Crude shelters had been erected near Hiwassee to house them while they awaited transportation.

Many were ill from exposure before they started, and rations of food were either sparse or not nourishing.

News of all this led the people to believe what had long been suspected, that there was a Treaty Party, composed of Cherokee leaders who had gone pre-removal and had no feelings of responsibility for the people.

When John Ross visited them in the inadequate dwellings, he felt heartsick, promised them aid and vowed he'd see that they were housed in better facilities.

Throughout the spring and summer, after the emigrants left by way of the Tennessee River on barges, news of their welfare came trickling in. Before they reached the Mississippi one barge had capsized, throwing all the passengers into the water. Sixty seven were saved, but their possessions were lost. Their leader Harris attempted to herd them into a camp to await the next boat, but a number escaped into the surrounding woods to either return or hide out indefinitely. The *Phoenix* published their fate.

Letters finally arrived saying, "Don't leave. There is nothing but grief, sickness and death from exposure, and poor food. We became snagged on a sand bar in the Arkansas River and had to climb out, carry our bundles, wade to the banks and walk to our destination. Some of us stole wagons or horses and got here. Others died of exposure and poor food or from cholera. It's been a nightmare. Of the 475 who started from Hiwassee, 50 died, and most are ill. Along the way some scattered into the woods where the living would be difficult, but free. And half of the people died on arrival. Don't leave!"

The article ended with Harris's words, "The first emigration was a fiasco."

On November 24, 1834, at a meeting held at John Ridge's home, Running Waters, the Treaty Party was officially organized and by the end of the month they were again on their way to Washington to push treaty terms. This time, however,

John Walker wasn't with them. He'd been found dead in his home from a bullet wound in the chest.

On hearing this, Sean immediately went to see Big Elk. The big man's report might have caused this.

"It was murder, wasn't it, Elk?"

Elk was reluctant to look directly into Sean's penetrating gaze. Finally he said, "Perhaps. Walker's name came up whenever Ross talked of Unity. He introduced *disunity*, and was in on that attack when Wolf was killed."

"Are you sure about that, Elk?"

Elk looked sheepish. "No, but he's been a main recruiter. Lots of people wanted him out of the way."

"I'm not blaming anyone. I just thought I'd come down and offer my legal services should they be needed."

There was a murmur as the eight men who were meeting in Elk's back room started to comment.

"So, a meeting!" Sean raised his eyebrows. He glanced into the smoke-filled back room and said, "Just a word of warning. I could have been the law on an investigating spree, or someone from the opposing faction. Probably the less said about this the better, even among yourselves."

"There's righteous indignation over the treatment we've received, Sean," Fox explained. "Something had to be done about it. It's like saying, 'let that be a lesson to you.' "

"Ross won't condone that, you know. Well, for what it's worth, I've said it. Good day, gentlemen."

There was a desultory investigation in the town that produced no results, and soon Ross was notified from Washington that he and his council would be held totally responsible for murders of Treaty members that were committed by his people.

Ross read the note carefully. That surely tied the Jackson machine to the Georgia officials and the Treaty members. There were, however, so many of his people involved in this, it would hardly be worth the Government authorities' time to investigate it thoroughly—and they knew it.

He tore up the note and called a meeting of Council to discuss a matter of more importance: his desire to explain in detail the exact terms of a treaty so his people wouldn't make the mistake of signing anything that would put them in jeopardy.

"The Removal bill calls for a treaty to be ratified by the majority of each nation involved," he stated. "Remember that if you're ever approached. It is vastly important."

Before the meeting was adjourned, Ross was directed to go again to Washington to forestall any action by the Georgia officials and the Treaty Party, to deal with the people directly; to crush any procedure to gain signatures for the Removal Treaty. He agreed.

The meeting in the capital this time dealt with price.

The Treaty Party had unlawfully put Cherokee lands up for sale and the Ross Party had no choice but to block the sale by objecting to the price. Jackson offered $3,000,000 for Cherokee lands, and when that met with refusal, offered $4,000,000. Ross was tired of the constant government official's acceptance that money would make any difference in his stand, and decided to wake them up.

"We demand payment of $20,000,000 and a promise no more sales will be negotiated."

For a moment there was shocked silence, then, of course the suggestion was refused by Jackson. Again the Cherokee question hung in mid-air.

Sean returned in good humor, telling Tsika about the trick Ross played on Jackson.

"Wouldn't he have been one surprised leader if his offer'd been accepted. That was a dangerous thing to do. I thought Ross had better sense."

"It might be that he really meant it. Even Ross is sick at heart over the things that have affected his people."

"I can't believe he meant it."

Danny burst into the room. "Papa's here, Papa's here!" he shouted with glee.

Sean tossed him in the air as Missy came running and Beth pushed her chair before her.

"Good Beth, you're doing well. Now the chair is a crutch. I'll have Jeremy carve you a good one."

He ruffled Missy's black hair, which she immediately smoothed. He laughed. "A young lady all of a sudden."

"You're here so seldom, Sean, that's why you noticed."

The children were unaware of Tsika's sarcasm, and soon bounced back to their own pursuits.

She persisted. "Sean, you're away so much I'm amazed they know you."

"Now, now, it's not that bad. You know it takes more than two months to make the trip and to accomplish our business there."

"More than two months?"

"Come, sweet, what's come over you?" He hugged her.

She pulled away and he laughed. "When I'm home, you're not."

"Oh, Sean!"

"It's true. You spread yourself too thin. You're either at the *Phoenix* or helping Amy Worcester or Ann Butler."

Tsika sniffed, "I—I know. We're like leaves blowing off a tree. We greet one another briefly and float away. You go hither and I go yon." For a strong person, she sounded weak.

"Come, dry your tears. It's time we do something about this. I didn't realize."

"No, you surely didn't."

"Sit here on my lap. Now what shall we do. Take a vacation?"

"No. Just stay home once in a while." She hugged him.

"All right, I'm home. I'll be here until Tuesday. Let's make the most of it."

"Oh, good! All of three days. I dance for joy."

"I'm going down to Atlanta to try a case."

"You still don't understand, do you Sean? You go on with your work and I'm supposed to quit mine?"

A scream from the nursery brought them to their feet.

"Mamma, Bethy fell. She's hurt. She's crying," Missy called.

"Damn!" said Sean. "I've got to get something made for her support other than that clumsy chair."

"Are you all right, Bethy?" Tsika picked her up, hugged her and smoothed back the blond curls.

"I was just frightened," she sniffed.

Missy laughed. "Yes, it was like falling down a cliff."

Tsika frowned, ready to reprimand Missy for the reminder, but Bethy was laughing with her sister.

Tsika smiled. Those two understood one another better than she understood either of them. And a frightening thought occurred to her. She was away from them far too much. Sean was right. She was spreading herself too thin: missionary help, and newspaper, especially since Boudinot and Stand Watie had left. She'd been on occasional forays into the surrounding farmlands and woods to check on reports of harassments by spies. Did she want to miss the joys of seeing her children grow up?"

Missy was saying, "You don't have to Papa. Micha is making Bethy one."

"Oh?"

"Yes. He's been here almost every day, working in the shop."

"Well, this I have to see. Did you know about this, Tsika?"

She admitted, "No, I didn't. My brother is as secretive as I am out-going."

Sean shook his head. On their property, in their own shop —her own brother? And she didn't know.

"That's what I mean, Tsika. You're really not home very often either."

She nodded, but was not quite ready to verbally admit her failure, or, as the Missionaries said, her sins of omission. She promised herself she would do better in the future.

Her good intentions failed to materialize when she thought

of the Treaty member's attempt to sell Cherokee land. She was drawn to the *Phoenix* to write a criticism of policy that allowed such a move to take place. Where was the Blood Law?

No one paid much attention to it except the Ross Party members. The Cherokee villages were caught in the vise of the coldest winter the old ones could remember. The cabin Indians and farmers couldn't plant their second crop that year and worried about their future. They had no concern about national affairs, and the townspeople weathered through the winter of 1834-35 with fewer sales, but acceptance as long as they were allowed to function without interruption from the Georgians. There was one advantage in the bitter weather; it was too cold for harassment.

At Big Elk's one evening, however, the Ross Party was geared for action if the plan met with unanimous approval.

White Fox addressed the group. "This will take careful planning and when we ask for volunteers, names will be written on a paper and drawn from a hat. It's best if we don't even know who's chosen for the eventual act and remember what Sean said, don't even talk about it among ourselves."

The meeting progressed and a date was set for the action.

In March, when the Treaty Party returned to Cherokee country from Washington, the members were accompanied by Reverend J. Schermerhorn, a U.S. Commissioner, appointed by President Jackson. He was instructed to get the Ridge Party's treaty ratified by the Cherokee people before the Presidential election in the coming November.

News of the Treaty Party members' determination to push the Removal Treaty through prompted Ross's Cherokee members to issue warnings to John Ridge Jr., Major Ridge, Elias Boudinot and Stand Watie: "Sign, and you face what happened to Walker."

John Ross heard of their intentions and approached his followers. "I have said no violence and hope that order will be observed. You are reminded that our own courts could convict you and, if they don't, the Georgia courts will. You have no proof until the document is actually signed."

John had a hard time convincing his supporters, but they finally agreed to temporarily postpone the murders.

John felt despair. It was then that he determined on March 22, 1835, to write a letter to Mr. de Costello y Lanzo, *chargé d'affaires* of Mexico. He wrote, "My people would, at once, move out of the limits of the U.S., provided they could effect an arrangement with your government so as to secure them lands sufficient for their accommodations—and also the enjoyments of equal rights and privileges of citizenship."

He requested the reply be sent to his brother Lewis Ross, near Calhoun, Tennessee, but nothing further was ever heard of the request. Either Lanzo refused to answer or it had been intercepted and never reached Mexico.

There was reason to suspect that mail going in and out of Cherokee country was subject to postal spies on either side.

By candlelight on the evening of March 29, 1835, at Elias Boudinot's home, the treaty for removal was secretly signed by the Treaty Party leaders and now, the Ridge group hoped they could convince the Cherokee people to sign.

In May, Tsika resigned from the *Phoenix*, and just in time for shortly thereafter, Colonel Bishop raided the *Phoenix* building, destroying some of the equipment. It sent Hicks and Wheeler running for their lives. Hicks managed to return and save some of the type and presses, and continued for a time to publish the paper in his home, but soon it and all its contents were appropriated by the Georgians. He and other Ross party members, Elijah Hicks, Walter Adair, Thomas Taylor, old chief Whitepath, James Trott and John Martin were arrested. Ross found it very difficult to free them for his lawyer William Underwood and Judge Hooper had been bribed by the Ridge party members.

Another fortunate reason for Tsika's retirement was the joy of spending this summer with the children: the free-roaming, riding, romping time, while they were still young enough to make the most of every moment. Tsika realized what she had missed. The affairs of the Cherokee Nation still occupied her mind, but except for the wishes to thwart the Georgians and the U.S. Government edicts, she was concentrating on her family.

Missy galloped ahead to meet Sean when they reached the end of the trail. He handed her the mail and she galloped back.

"Papa said read this." Her black hair fell forward as she leaned to reach her mother's hand, and her azure eyes sparkled. "It's from Grandma Dolan. They're coming to visit. Isn't that the best news of the month?"

At ten, Missy's enthusiasm knew no bounds. She raced her horse to the barns, then danced her way to the house.

Tsika's thoughts were churning. She must get new curtains for the guest room, have the rugs beaten and do a thorough job of spring cleaning. Since Manda had been ill, there had been a lull in the weekly duties. She'd help.

Activity began at once. After Jeremy and Benji had hauled rugs into the yard, and the wooden beaters had punished the rugs enough, Tsika stood back and nodded her approval.

Hands on hips, her skirts tied up with a cord around her waist, she looked like an Indian maid. She felt she was back on the farm doing some of the chores she'd learned from Star.

She had scrubbed and polished and moved furniture and now, after overseeing the carpets, picked up the brooms and beaters. She straightened her headband and untied her skirt.

She saw Sean and Micha leaving the farm shop. "Come Micha," she called to her brother. "Help Benji carry the rugs. They're too heavy for Jeremy."

"She's sure turning the house upside-down, Eagle."

"It doesn't pay to get in her way, Micha. She's putting us all to work."

"Looks like I'm already caught," he signed good-naturedly, and lifted one end of the huge rug as Benji lifted the other.

"Where to Madam?"

"In through the side door, please, then to the living room."

"Doesn't everything look beautiful, Sean?" she asked her husband. "Come 'round to the front. I had Jake paint the porch."

"You'd think we were preparing for an annual ball."

She grinned. "Let's have one while your parents are here."

"Slow down. You take my breath away. Like you did when we first met. Is it because of that get-up or your enthusiasm?"

"Both!" Her black eyes sparkled and she whirled around.

"Come, let's see the front." He took her by the hand.

The mansion was washed by pinkish rays of the setting sun. The pillars stood tall and proud as did their owners. Tsika was moved by the effect it had on her.

"Sean, it's almost frightening, it's so beautiful. What does the future hold for us? Are we going to be able to keep it?"

"I don't believe they'll bother us, because I'm white."

The children waited on the front porch while Sean went to the stage depot in Springplace to pick up his mother and father.

"When will they come, Mamma? I'm tired of waiting," Danny complained, bouncing up and down on a wicker bench.

"Danny sit still. You're making my new dress get wrinkled."

"She's too fussy, Mamma."

"No complaints from you, Beth?" Tsika asked.

"No, I'm thinking how Grandpa and Grandma will see how well I can walk."

Tears came to Tsika's eyes. How the child could have so much cheerfulness and patience was a miracle. And perhaps that's why the miracle had happened: that, and exercise and prayers.

"But Papa left hours ago," Missy insisted.

"Perhaps the stage was late."

Missy sighed. "It takes forever."

Suddenly Danny shouted, "Here they come!" And all squealed.

The carriage soon approached the port cochere, and
Melissa and Danny ran to meet it. Beth and Tsika went slowly
down the steps and around to the side of the house.

Hugs and kisses were accompanied by exclamations about
their growth and Beth's ability to walk. They went into the entrance hall and immediately Lotta Dolan remarked about the
beauty of the mansion.

"Children, your home looks even larger and more lovely
then I remembered it. Everything sparkles."

Sean couldn't resist. "Tsika's been polishing ever since she
heard you were coming. Brow-beating us all into helping."

Danny giggled, "And she even beat the *rugs.*"

If Tsika were embarrassed it disappeared with that remark.
They all laughed. Jeremy took their luggage upstairs and Tsika
suggested a rest before dinner.

"I will, my dear. It's a long weary trip, this stage ride. Accommodations are not the best along the way. However our
stop at Lewis Ross's estate in Tennessee was delightful. He's a
charming man."

"He is the only brother who has rallied at John's side during this whole confrontation with the Georgians. But no more
of that now. We'll have dinner at eight. Do you have everything you need?"

"Everything, and that lovely canopied bed looks delicious.
Please tell Gerald to waken me in time to dress for dinner,
dear."

Tsika looked around the room and was satisfied that it was
just right for her mother-in-law's taste.

Gerald Dolan preferred to visit with his son, while Tsika
attended to the children and checked the table for last minute
details. The crystal sparkled, the silver and linen napkins were
placed just so and a large floral arrangement with three-tiered
silver candelabra on either side, graced the center of the table
set for seven. Tonight, even at this late hour, the children were
to join the adults.

At the table Sean continued the ribbing. "Things were out

of control here. I holed up in my farm office at the rear of the house. I couldn't stand the confusion in the study."

"Poor man," said Tsika. "We feel sorry for him, don't we children."

They were used to this banter, and laughed, then proceeded to monopolize the conversation with their individual accounts of accomplishments: Danny's newly acquired ability to trap, Beth's claim to be able to read faster than Missy and Melissa's riding and dancing, each vying for Grandma's and Grandpa's approval.

By the time the meal of roast venison, sweet potatoes, greens, wild berries and cakes was over, there were tired adults as well as very tired children, and the evening hours after Nilla took the children to bed were short by mutual consent.

The days passed by pleasantly. Sean took his father to see some of the headmen of the tribe, but when Cherokee problems were discussed they came away frustrated and with a feeling of sadness. Gerald felt helpless for the first time in his life.

He knew his money could do nothing to aid his son and family—unless—"Sean, come home with us. Things look very dark for Tsika's people and surely you want your family to be safe."

Sean nodded, "I know. I have told her no one would disturb us because I'm white, but—I don't really believe that. I'll speak to her about it."

Tsika and Lotta went into town, but shops had little to display after the exceptionally cold winter when Cherokees came to the stores, took what they needed and couldn't pay for want of their late annuity.

"We could go to Atlanta, but Sean heard that some of the stages on that run have been robbed. He wouldn't allow it."

"I'm perfectly contented to stay here, Tsika, and don't forget you have a party coming up tomorrow night."

The Treaty Party members who had been guests the last time Dolan's visited were conspicuous by their absence, but with all of Ross's supporters, family and friends there remained a number large enough to fill the mansion with gaiety. It would be remembered as the last large party anyone enjoyed in Cherokee country. Ever!

On the last evening of their visit, Lotta remarked, "I miss the drums of the native dances, Tsika. Are the people so converted to American customs that they don't have their tribal celebrations any more?"

"No, but they're held up in the hills now. In town, the Dances have been interrupted by Georgian violence so often, the people are afraid to hold any kind of a celebration within its borders. The large stockade fence surrounding the town has long since been removed, but sometimes I wonder if it was wise. Were it still there, we could hide behind it and wage war on the enemy."

"Things are pretty bad now?"

"They are indeed. We act lighthearted, but carry a constant pain here." She pressed her chest. "We've tried peaceful means to keep our land: hired William Wirt, constitutional lawyer, written articles for the Eastern papers, found many people on our side, but when the delegations arrive in Washington they have been disappointed. President Jackson seems to be able to block our every move. It's still *Removal* as far as he's concerned."

Sean, Gerald and the children came into the room bubbling over with enthusiasm about their ride into the hills to check on Danny's traps.

"Grandpa said he'd like to set traps for some of those men in Washington who are against us," Danny shouted.

"I wish it were that easy. Come, say your good nights.," Tsika ordered, "then off to bed you go. We must get up early to take Grandpa and Grandma to the station."

"Grandma says I can come to visit them sometime." Missy's blue eyes sparkled. "Can I Mamma?"

"Perhaps."

"Why not now, Tsika?" Gerald suggested.

"You can't go, Melissa," Beth interrupted. "How could I ever get along without you?"

"I'll take her place, Bethy," Danny offered. "I'll go pack right now."

Tsika laughed. "This is getting out of hand."

"Not so," said Sean. "It's not a bad idea. In fact it's not a bad idea if we all go East before we're forced to move."

"Sean, you don't mean that." She called, "Nilla, we're ready for you to put the children to bed."

Sean went on as though there had been no interruption. "To protect my family, Tsika. That's what I want to do."

"But you said—you didn't think—It's not imminent, the actual removal. The bill hasn't been ratified by the people. Am I supposed to turn my back on my people?"

"My dear, no. But *we're* your people also," said Gerald, "and I believe it would be wise for you to consider a move to the East."

"We will, Father. Tsika, surely you can see the move would be reasonable," Sean urged.

"No, I don't. I vowed to protect the Cherokees at all costs."

"We'll think about it and talk again in the morning." He nodded a good night to his parents.

"I'll feel about it in the morning exactly as I do tonight," she snapped. Infuriated she turned on her heels and preceded them all up the stairs.

In their bedroom, Tsika charged into Sean's arguments. "You can't mean you actually want us to desert. I thought you considered my people your people."

"I do, but common sense tells me that you can't hold out much longer. You don't want to be here when things fall apart."

"I wonder if you know how I really feel."

"What about the safety of the children?"

"It seems you just want to make things difficult."

"They're difficult already, and not of my making."

"Maybe not, but you're as bad as the turncoats."

"I think we should all go back with them for the summer."

"Then take the children and go! I'm staying here."

"Maybe I will."

"Oh, Sean, I didn't mean that. What will we do?" She rushed into his outstretched arms.

"Go, while we still have a choice. Before we're forcibly sent West. Wouldn't you rather live in the East?"

"Maybe we could send the children with your parents for the rest of the summer? And see what the end of August brings?"

"That's better than nothing."

She couldn't sleep. The Dolans would have to postpone their departure for a couple of days so packing could be done. Two days' reprieve. What could she do to change Sean's mind.?

She overslept. When she looked out of her bedroom window in the morning, she saw Sean riding toward the woods with Danny on the saddle in front of him and Missy riding her pony beside him. It was a picture she loved and couldn't bear to think of any time when it wouldn't be exactly so. How could they ever live throughout the summer without their lively brood. Hurriedly, she bathed and dressed. She must get them packed up. Tears welled up back of her eyes. She hoped she'd not disgrace herself. Where was her stoicism now?

How could she bear to send them away? She'd so miss Danny's teasing and laughter and Missy's concern for her, but for Beth it was wise. There were good doctors to help her in the East.

At the breakfast table, she announced, "If it's still all right with your Grandparents, you may all go along for the rest of the summer."

Danny beamed, "Oh, good. Will I have my pony along?"

"No, I'm afraid not Danny," laughed Gerald. "He wouldn't fit in the stage."

"And I won't be able to play with my friend, Jackie."

"Not in Raleigh."

"Will I have to go to school, Grandma?"

Lilla smiled. "No, remember it's summertime."

"All right, then I'll go."

"Beth, I'll pack your things," said Melissa, and skipped from the room.

"That was sudden," Sean commented.

"I believe she's a bit emotional now about leaving."

"It will pass." Sean, lighthearted as usual cancelled it from his mind.

The evening before their final departure, Tsika went in to tuck the children in bed. Missy was crying.

"What's the trouble, Missy?"

"I—I—guess I don't want to go after all."

"You don't have to, dear."

"But what will Bethy do without me?" she sniffed.

"Ask her. She'll tell you the truth. Bethy is always honest and straightforward."

"And what would you do without me? I don't know what to do."

"All our lives we have to make decisions, Missy. There's a right one for you." She kissed the child. "It's a sign you're growing up when you begin to weigh possibilities pro and con."

"I—I don't want to grow up. I don't like what Papa says will happen to us."

Who could tell what went on in their little heads?

"There are many people who think we should move away, but I think we will have a long time to weigh that decision. Now, don't worry about those things, dear. Go to sleep and pleasant dreams. You'll know when the sun comes up what you want to do."

Tsika thought, she so wanted to say, stay. It was going to be so hard to be without them all. But there came a time when one had to let the fledglings fly from the nest, perhaps this would be a trial run.

The following morning, Sean called, "Everybody ready?"

Everybody was, and they were on their way.

As Tsika waved goodbye to them, crowded in the stage coach, she wished with all her heart she'd said, "Positively no."

They returned to an empty house: no noise, no laughter, no quarreling. How could she ever stand it? Not even the *Phoenix* or housework to do, but she was determined not to complain to Sean. He kissed her goodbye, saying nothing about the children's departure and she was left alone. She fought back bitter tears, went upstairs and tackled the attic storage area like a windstorm, until she came upon a baby crib. Then tears flowed, all those unshed tears: for Wolf, Juni, Beth and her people.

At noon, Sean came home, took her in his arms and kissed her. He said, "I'm sad too, my love. We'll give it a week, then go East to visit them."

"Oh, thank you, Sean. I'd like that."

"But first we'll go to John's meeting."

John Ross had urged his people, 2,000 strong, to attend the council meeting at Running Waters in July in order to vote no to the proposed annuity. If accepted, it would mean that they were accepting removal. Of course, it was voted down. Aiku and Roper attended. It was the first time Tsika had seen him in five years. He smiled tentatively and nodded. She felt a flutter. Why? Because she remembered their hug and kiss? Ridiculous!

Belatedly, Ron heard of Gerald Dolan's visit to Riverview and damned himself for not being able to bag two birds at once, but Johnson had kept him busy in the southern part of the state.

He'd been almost killed by an immigrant who'd survived the first migration and went for him with a pick axe. He'd suffered a deep leg wound when he attempted to take the Missionary at Creek Path from Katherine Brown. He, Red and Cochee had gone in confidently, expecting no trouble and found she was prepared.

Four boys hidden in a back room immediately set upon them. It was a fiasco. Ron suffered a shot in the leg, Cochee was knifed on the arm and Red was killed.

Katherine fled to New Echota. She arrived at Tsika's sobbing. "I can't go back and I won't go to my brother's."

Tsika hugged the frightened girl. "Of course not, but now you're going to stay here."

"You were right, Tsika. Oppression came to my mission, and it was frightening. If some of my boys hadn't come to warn me that they'd seen Ron Bullock in town, I'd be dead."

Tsika gasped, "Oh, no, Ron's back again?"

"Oh, that's right, I forgot. He used to be your farm manager. Well, he can't walk now. Billy shot him in the leg."

Tsika nodded. "That's good."

"They are just big Indian school boys, but they surely protected their teacher when she needed it most. Tsika, what can I do for Marcus; the one who killed Red?"

"Oh, my God, I don't know. Self defense, maybe. I'll ask Sean to defend him. And you said something about Cochee."

"Yes, he was the third man; he was knifed in the arm."

"Good. They all had their just desserts. Now come, have some tea. "I'm a bit lonesome these days. Our children are in the East with Sean's parents for the summer."

"I wondered why it was so quiet. I'll go to visit Ulah and Roper in a couple of days. I don't want to wear out my welcome." As Tsika poured the tea and Nilla served Manda's crunchy cakes, Katherine asked, "Have you seen the Chaims or Aiku and Tani lately?"

No. They seem to by-pass us. Roper and Aiku are busy with their hauling business, so they're out of town frequently."

Now a wistful look had replaced the frightened expression on her pale face. "When you were going to marry Aiku, I was in love with Roper, and he never knew I existed. Even back in the Brainard days, I thought I was going to marry him, but he couldn't see anyone but Alda. I've never loved anyone else."

"But you married."

She nodded, "Yes, then left him after a year and took back my maiden name."

"The boys at the nearby college thought you attractive."

Katherine shrugged, "I guess I wasn't interested."

"If you are still in love with Roper, is it wise to go to stay with them?" Tsika frowned. "Guess I shouldn't ask that."

"You can ask, and I do. I suppose it's not a good idea." Abruptly she said, "Are you still in love with Aiku, Tsika?"

Tsika was shocked. No one had ever asked her that question before. "Of course not. I'm in love with Sean, Kate. He's a wonderful husband and we have always felt love for one another."

Katherine looked embarrassed. "I'm sorry, Tsika. I shouldn't have asked. It's just that, I—I can't seem to get over my love for Roper."

"It's been twelve years since those days, Katherine. I believe you should try. Meet some nice man and forget the past."

Katherine shrugged, "I suppose so."

"You won't forget him living under the same roof."

Sean stormed in, shouting, "Anything left for lunch?" Then he saw Katherine. "I'm very sorry, Katherine, to hear of your horrible experience. I'll help any way I can."

"Perhaps you could defend Marcus. You see, he killed Red."

"I'll be glad to. Now, let's have lunch."

Tsika grinned. "Men and their appetites."

After Katherine retired for a nap, Sean said, "By the time Katherine leaves, it will be too late to go for a visit."

"We'll go anyway, and bring them home."

"Oh, I thought they were coming home by themselves."

"Sean, you can't mean it! That's a gruelling trip. They're only ten, nine and seven. I don't believe for one moment your mother would permit them to come home on their own."

"Then let her bring them."

"You're so anxious to protect your children, you want to send them to live in the East, but you're willing to let them make that trip—Oh! I give up! We're going after them."

Sean smiled. "Of course, we're going for them."

"Sean you're impossible! You were teasing me all the time." She went for him with the hairbrush, and they tussled.

After the children's bubbling accounts of the summer, life settled down to comfortably moderate confusion again. School started and the missionaries that had been taken over were functioning in the homes. By permission from the board and the owners, Butler maintained the New Echota Missionary School at Riverview. Eleven children were present, including the Dolans.

The October meeting was held in the open-sided council house at Red Clay. The brilliant scarlet Sumac and red-yellow foliage rivaled the colorful turbans, sashes and tunics worn by the people. After second-chief, Lowrey and the sub-chiefs had each led their group to a spot of advantage, they were seated on a platform next to Chief Ross. Also seated on the platform was a guest. Howard Payne, historian and author of "Home, Sweet Home." He had come to visit the chief for information about the Cherokees and their customs and was invited to attend.

Both Ross and Ridge Cherokees attended, and Commissioner Schermerhorn was appointed by President Jackson to present the terms of the Removal Treaty to be approved and signed.

He read: "The most important provision gives the Cherokees $3,500,000 for their eastern lands; $150,000 for depreditive claims (including Creek War losses of 1814); restated a guarantee for 13,000,000 acres of western territory, granted in 1828 and 1833 to previously emigrated Cherokees, and gives an additional 800,000 acres in that same region to those leaving voluntarily now."

It was rejected by both parties. Then Schermerhorn offered $5,000,000 which also was rejected by both and meeting adjourned.

"Something strange is going on," Fox said to Elk. "I thought this was just what the Ridge faction was striving for."

"Perhaps they thought that if they signed openly there'd be a few assassinations." Big Elk smiled. "And I believe there would have been, Jake."

Sean's present manager nodded in agreement. "We'll wait to see what happens before the December meeting."

Aiku and Roper sat with Fox, Big Elk and Jake and commented from time to time. Since their move back to Springplace from Dohlonega, they became interested in Cherokee National affairs and had attended several of the meetings.

Today, Aiku was thinking more about Tsika than what had been said from the platform. When he didn't see her, there was no problem; Tani and the children were his life. But something alerted him about the way she had responded to his gesture of greeting in July. She's actually blushed. Was she still thinking of him once in a while? He tried to cast the thought from his mind. They were both married. Tani was ill much of the time, but that was no reason to think about Tsika. He pushed back the lock of hair that persisted in dropping from his headband.

Again Tsika felt moved when she saw that endearing gesture. What was the matter with her? Was she thinking how she used to smooth those wisps from his forehead?

Abruptly she turned to Sean. "Shall we go now?"

"I want to talk to Fox before we leave. Come, you usually like to find out what the others are thinking after a meeting."

She shrugged. "You go over to them. I'll go speak to Katherine; I haven't seen her lately."

Was this peculiar feeling connected with Aiku or with the fact that she had sadly separated herself from her tribal customs; the songs, dances and rituals when she married Sean: that the customs and Aiku were just bound together in some way. That must be the answer, for she loved Sean.

The five members of the Ross Party, who had been expected to sign the treaty papers, reasoned that Schermerhorn would write out another treaty, and present it at the December meeting.

Fox said, "That would give us more time."

"Yes, the procedure sometimes takes months, years," Lowrey answered. "If you remember, the removal bill was first introduced by Jackson in early May, 1830, pushed through Congress and ratified by the Senate on May 23. Then the terms were set up and the treaty had to be signed by both parties: the Cherokees and representatives of the Federal Government.

"And since the terms weren't agreeable to us, we caused postponement. That's good. And we'll be prepared for them in the same way at the meeting on December 23rd."

By December 5, 1835, Howard Payne was making good progress with the material Ross had given him: the important Cherokee papers were spread out before him on a table. He was in deep concentration when he was startled by a loud crash at the cabin door which brought Ross running. The minute it was opened, soldiers rushed into the room.

"What's the meaning of this intrusion?" Ross demanded.

And his answer was a rough push from the cabin. "Mount your horses. You and your friend Payne are under arrest."

They complained, but complied. It would be sheer folly to resist so many guns.

The valuable papers were scooped up, and in a blinding rainstorm, they were led to Fort Benton by twenty-five Georgia Guard and thrown into a dark dismal cabin that was used as a prison. Except for weak candlelight they were met with almost total darkness and a fetid overpowering odor.

"Get Dolan," Ross shouted. "I want a lawyer."

As the door clanged shut, he muttered, "This injustice overwhelms me, Howard. Forgive us."

"It's not your fault, John. Oh, my God, look! Eyes became accustomed to the dim light revealing a corpse hanging from the rafters, decomposing, odoriferous, and gruesome. Payne was sick.

The son of Crawling Snake, chained nearby, awakened. "Welcome to the hell hole, Ross; I been here for months."

"I've been trying to get you out, since your father told me about your unjust sentence. Have heart. We'll manage it soon."

Finally, after thirteen days of making much disturbance, asking for Sean or Colonel Bishop and suffering cold and bad food, Ross was released. In four more days, Payne was freed.

At his first opportunity Ross went to see Colonel Bishop and demanded, "What were the charges, Colonel?"

"There were none and arrest across the state line is unlawful," he shrugged. "I blame just a few ruffians in the militia for the mistake."

"A mistake of thirteen days? And no one is to be punished?"

John Ross left immediately for Washington to complain about Georgia's Militia, and so incensed was Howard Payne that he wrote scathing articles about their treatment for the Knoxville *Register*, the Georgia *Constitutional*, and all the Eastern papers, blaming the Georgia Guard.

This publicity raised criticism of an administration that would allow such injustice, but as in the past, press and the law had little effect on officials in Washington. Jackson, the Georgia machine and now the Treaty Party members were in full control and aligned against the Ross Cherokees.

On December 28, 1835, White Fox, Sean Dolan, Al Wheaton, and Joseph Vann gathered at Big Elk's Post. Discussion was concerning the meeting proposed by the Ridge Party for the next day at New Echota.

"They're taking advantage of Ross's absence," White Fox remarked. "Hadn't we better go down, see what's going on?"

"Few will go," said Elk. "All Cherokees'll stay huddled in their cabins in this icy weather, with the wind blowing a gale and branches blowing off trees. Besides, they're hungry and weak since Jackson cut off annuities for refusal to leave."

"In spite of that," said Sean, "I'm going."

By dawn on the 29th, the wind had slackened, but it was sleeting and the paths were icy. The horses were sure-footed, but the men arrived at New Echota too late for the meeting.

Elk admitted, "I'm amazed at the hundreds of people who are waiting in this drizzle for voting results."

Sean looked inside. "I don't believe Schermerhorn has a chance of passing his new treaty. It's not a large crowd."

Fox shrugged, "Look, Ridge is shaking hands with Boudinot."

Elk edged inside the door. "I'm going to find out what the voting results were."

Immediately John Ridge came up to him. "You're not welcome here now. The voting's over."

"Not that mine would have made any difference. I see you're congratulating one another. Apparently you came to a decision. Surely all the votes cannot be counted yet."

Ridge turned his back to Elk and walked to Schermerhorn. They conferred. Suddenly, two Georgia Guards, who stood near the door, strode toward Elk, grabbed his arms and marched him outside. A full fledged fight ensued, Elk took a savage blow to the head by a guard's gun, and as he fell to the ground, a dozen men rushed at the guards. Shots were fired. Some of the hundreds of people waiting outside fled; some came to the rescue of Ross's loyal followers, and amidst shouts, cries and pounding feet, there was the sound of horse's hooves. The rest of the Georgia Guard had arrived. Soldiers flailed their bayonets at fleeing people, then galloped off and all was quiet.

Fox and Sean helped Elk to his feet and led him to his horse. They left hurriedly by way of the woods to go to Riverview for bandages and sustenance.

1835 - 1837

The Ross Party members awaited their leader's return with keen anticipation, hoping to hear good news, but as of that date, President Jackson's ultimatum was discouraging.

When Ross came home in February, he spoke bitterly about the New Echota Treaty. "Unlawfully, John Ridge, Major Ridge, Elias Boudinot, Stand Watie, other members of the Treaty Party and 100 disloyal Cherokees have signed what is called the New Echota Treaty. It was taken to Washington, presented to President Jackson and he termed it a valid treaty for removal. It comes up before the Senate for approval on May 23, 1836."

Loud objections could be heard from all sides. "It can't be valid. The men who signed had no right."

Ross read, "It states, 'That the Cherokee Nation ceded, relinquished, and conveyed to the United States, all the lands owned, claimed or possessed, by the Nation east of the Mississippi River, for $5,000,000, to be expended, paid and invested in a manner stipulated and agreed upon. Those lands given them, are never to be annexed by another state or territory without the Cherokee Nation's consent.' We'll fight it."

White Fox asked, "Just how do we plan to fight it?"

Ross's blue eyes flashed. "There's one hopeful note. Senators Bell, Calhoun, Clay, Webster and White have assured me that the Removal Treaty will never pass the Senate, and I propose to take a delegation back to Washington with me to help influence the Senators who disagree with them."

Delegates, Situwakee, Whitepath, and Elijah Hicks returned to Washington with John Ross on March 1, 1836. These faithful Cherokees, who had accompanied him many times before, had their arguments well prepared for the grueling days ahead. To prove that the document was not valid they stated:

1. Schermerhorn had no authority to sign the treaty.

2. The Cherokee people had never made such a treaty.

3. John Ridge, Elias Boudinot, Major Ridge and Stand Watie were not members of the Cherokee National Council, therefore they had no right to sign. We have proof of that.

Up until May 22, 1836, the day before the treaty went to the Senate for ratification, Ross was assured of negative votes by Senators Bell, Clay, Webster, Calhoun, White and many more.

But on May 23, 1836, the Cherokee's doom was sealed by one man's change of heart. The results were in favor of removal by *one* vote. Senator White had switched his allegiance at the last moment, and the deadline set for removal was May 23, 1838, allowing them two years to get their emigration in order.

The Secretary of War notified John Ross that, "The President had ceased to recognize any existing government among the eastern Cherokees, and any further effort by him (Ross) to prevent the consummation of the treaty would be suppressed."

When the news became public, there was a storm of protest by citizens and government authorities as well.

John Q. Adams, House member from Massachusetts called

it "Infamous—it brings with it eternal disgrace upon the country."

Major W. M. Davis, appraiser of Cherokee improvements, told the Secretary of War, "The Treaty of Echota is no treaty at all. It was made without sanction or assent of the great body of Cherokees. The delegation taken to Washington by Schermerhorn had no more authority to make a treaty than any other dozen Cherokees picked up for the purpose."

General John Ellis Wool, commander of federal troops was sent to Cherokee country to disarm the people and enforce the fraudulent treaty. By September, after a summer of close contact with the people, he was disturbed by what the country was doing to the educated and wealthy landowners as well as to the poor. He asked to be relieved of his post as soon as possible. He and his men had no enthusiasm for punishment and for building pens for the retainment of Cherokees awaiting removal.

Although the storm signals had long been in evidence, the people were stunned at the news of the removal treaty.

Some thought Tsika expressed it best when she said, "We can carry on as normally as possible, ignore the impositions placed upon us and keep faith with John Ross that we will be able to stay in our beloved land. Perhaps we can even help by making the soldiers feel welcome by inviting them to our homes."

"Optimism is fine, Tsika, but I believe Ross sometimes chooses to hide his head. We've got to be realistic. Prepare to leave, if we have to, or possibly before."

She scowled. "No, Ross says when Henry Clay is elected in November he will help to get the ratification nullified."

"All right, *you* hope, I'll get my affairs in order."

"Sean, sometimes you're exasperating. Once, you said you'd even fight for us, remember?"

Sean smiled. "So I did, but now I am aiding you in this entertaining process. Come, you must get ready for your third gala event.

"Oh, you!" He could always change her anger to amusement with just one remark. She hurried to the kitchen to confer with Manda on the trays for the evening's refreshments.

As dusk fell on Riverview Acres, lighted lanterns danced in a mild breeze that carried with it the seductive fragrance of gardenias, whose bushes lined the walks.

The festive look gave early arrivals a lilt to their approaching steps and anticipation of a pleasant evening ahead.

Star, Rena Bronson, Katherine Brown and Ulah Chaim entered the kitchen to help Nilla and a new maid serve.

"Everything looks lovely, as usual, Tsika," Rena greeted her hostess.

"Thank you," Tsika grinned. "Entertainment is paying off. You know I believe John Ridge is getting uneasy, because there has been a noticeable difference in the attitude of the soldiers. They're dragging their feet about the building."

A wooden platform had been erected for musicians and dancing. Already there were soldiers in their dress uniforms draped along its edges, chatting and drinking the liquor Jeremy served. Missy was entranced. It was the first time she had been allowed to stay up for one of the parties. She went outside to observe the soldiers.

"Papa," she called to Sean. "They aren't too old for me. See that one is about the same age as my friend, Little Owl. You can fall in love at any age."

"Missy, you're only eleven. All are too old for you at the present time. Even Little Owl."

"Mamma was friends with Aiku when she was my age and her Papa didn't object. Grandma Star said so."

Sean sighed. How did Tsika handle things like this? "Friends yes—but." Oh, hell! He called, "Tsika, come here!"

The mansion upstairs and down looked out from its windows with beckoning light and warmth. All the friends and relatives began to pour in, were greeted, and as soon as the soldiers came in, were introduced.

"I get to stay up late tonight, Grandma," Missy edged up to

Star, who carried a tray of sandwiches to the long table.

"And that's good, little one?"

"I'm almost twelve, Grandma, and I have a friend, Owl."

"And?"

How much could she tell this Grandma? She shrugged, "Oh, he kisses me." She waited for the reaction.

"So?" Star was shocked, but thought it best to toss off the confidence and tell Tsika to watch her little daughter.

Katherine came in on the last of the conversation. "Watch out for those handsome soldiers, Missy. Some are only seventeen."

Melissa grinned. *There* was someone who thought of her as a grown-up.

"Now Kate, she's only eleven," Star frowned.

"But she looks fifteen. Some Indian girls marry at twelve."

Tsika joined them, laughed at the remark and playfully ruffled her daughter's shining black hair. "Careful or it's to bed with you. I'll not have you flirting with my soldiers."

The newly arrived soldiers from Tennessee were entranced with the lovely well-educated Indian girls, and it was not long before they had coupled off and were dancing on the platform on what was a glorious moonlight night.

Missy was ecstatic when one soldier asked her to dance, even though it was General Dunlap, who was as old as her father. And she was glad she'd been taught to dance like the girls who went to eastern colleges. She smiled broadly as they waltzed by her parents.

"Guess she's safe enough with Dunlap," laughed Sean.

At their departure, the Cherokee guests complimented them and said the soldiers seemed like nice young men. They were surely right in entertaining them.

She answered them all. "Yes, I believe they're changing their opinion of us. It may help."

The soldiers remarked, "It is so nice to eat home-cooked food," or "Thank you for your kind hospitality," and Dunlap shook their hands with his firm grasp, shouting, "It was so good of you folks to invite us, when we're sent here to send you off."

Missy's flushed cheeks and dancing eyes told the story of her first evening party.

"Now the guests have all gone, I suppose you're willing to go to bed?" her mother laughed.

"Yes, yes, and thank you. It was ever so much fun. Maybe I'll go East to school someday if the boys are that mannerly."

Sean winked at Tsika. "So be it. Now off with you."

Tsika sighed. "She's growing up too fast, Sean."

"They have a way of doing that. To go back to the party. I heard today that our entertaining the U.S. soldiers has John Ridge worried."

"I know. It's good they're not the Georgia Militia or we wouldn't have a chance no matter what we did."

"I also heard that Ron Bullock almost died of an infection in the leg that was wounded at Katherine's missionary."

"Too bad he didn't."

"Them's unkind words, Tsika. However, he didn't. He's enlisted in the Georgia Guard."

"Oh no! It can mean nothing but grief for us if he's ordered to come here. Oh, I hope not, Sean."

"We have to know these things and be prepared, like sending the children to my parents."

"Let's not start that again. Come we must get to bed before we argue about it."

"Beat you upstairs." Sean dashed up two steps at a time. Tsika followed. Who could stay angry with him for long?

Plans were made for 600 Treaty Party members to leave voluntarily for Western Cherokee land in early January, 1837. Elk informed Sean and Tsika of the time of departure.

"They've stocked up on supplies. It will be an exodus of style and plenty," Elk assured them. "You'd better come down and see how the elite manage to travel in comfort."

Tsika said, "I feel self-conscious about going, Elk, and I hate to give them the satisfaction that I'm interested."

"Well come along anyway. It should be a good show."

Sean said, "Perhaps the leaders think they'd better go before they're assassinated."

"Could well be," Elk nodded.

Sean turned to Tsika, "I'm glad they're leaving. I feel like celebrating. Let's take the children and go."

On the appointed morning, crowds of Ross Cherokees lined the street to watch the Treaty families assemble for their trek.

While negro slaves loaded provisions, children cried, sad about leaving their little friends, women were busy tucking in this and fussing with that, in order to hide their true feelings and the men struggled to calm their horses who danced with impatience to be under way.

The clatter of hoofs, the shouts and murmurs of voices and the bellowing of cattle and oxen shook the earth like some monster's steps. Soon the cold morning mist would be warmed by the sun and dissolve and Major Ridge would lead them on their way.

Remaining were about 15,000 emigrants who refused to go voluntarily. When Van Buren won the presidential election in November, 1836, his policies followed Jackson's as closely as the man's shadow, and there was no hope of nullification of the New Echota Treaty. By the time of his inauguration in March, the removal was in full swing. He lost no time in forcing the Cherokees to leave.

On the morning of March 3, 1837, a party of 465 persons left by way of a flatboat from Ross's landing.

"We don't want to go," said the spokesman, Howard Nelson, "but we were threatened with death if we hesitated another day."

"Howard, they can't drive a white man from his land," Elk assured his neighbor.

"But they are because my wife is Cherokee. We heard Ridge's party arrived safely, so we're trying to be optimistic."

Sadly Elk waved them off, wondering how well they would

fare on that water route via the Tennessee, Ohio, Mississippi and Arkansas rivers, particularly the Arkansas with its shallows and sandbars.

Sean went to see General Dunlap to inquire when the next emigration would take place, and to observe the structures being built for those Cherokees awaiting transportation.

The answer from the general proved Tsika's theory that the soldiers were half-hearted about the removal tactics.

"We're purposefully slow, Mr. Dolan. We feel guilty to be following President Van Buren's orders to oppress a people so decent and progressive."

"How will you go about it?"

"We're supposed to disarm and threaten, and if that doesn't work, bodily force the people into the shelters. I'm not proud of this and hope to be relieved of my duties soon."

"I know, you're under orders. I understand."

Dunbar sighed. "I am actually glad some of the Cherokees have escaped into the hills, yet wonder how they will live."

Sean nodded. "They'll survive. The Cherokees are survivors and you can be sure of it."

"I surely hope so. The Georgia Militia will be here soon."

They shook hands. Dunbar's grasp was firm and meaningful.

Sean returned to Riverview, determined to convince Tsika the children should be sent to his parents.

"Hey, I'm home."

"Oh, Sean, I wondered where you'd gone. The children want to go on an early spring picnic."

"It's early all right. There's still frost on the ground in the mornings, but since we won't be able to do it much longer, we'll go."

"And just what do you mean by that remark?"

"The Georgia Militia is due to come in a week and the removal will be stepped up. I'm going to send the children to my parent's home."

"*You're* going to send them, Sean? I thought we made decisions together."

"Usually we do, but this time I think you're hiding your head under a bushel basket."

"I don't believe it's necessary, Sean."

"It *is*, my darling. I can see both sides of the question and, while I'm proud of you for feeling committed to your people, our main concern should be the safety of the children."

"All right, take them and go, but wait a few weeks, Sean."

"Until April. I'll write my father to come for them. I'll not leave you, my girl."

She produced a weak smile. "Thank you. That gives us a little more time. You are sensible, Sean. I love you for it, but sometimes it exasperates me no end."

The ride along the trails to their favorite mountain picnic area was more lovely than ever this morning. The fields abloom with spring beauties, bluettes and wild daisies along with the unwanted jimson weed and its thistle companions, led to the forest trail. Here were violets, sweet gum trees and budded sweet shrub. Fragrant wild honeysuckle climbed the tree trunks at the edge of the path. Tsika breathed in the faintly perfumed air. The greening woods, clean and fresh, promised lovely summer.

Song birds greeted them at every turn with lilting melodies or with a scolding that meant they were too close to nests. There were no thoughts now of removal or soldiers. There could never be another way of life.

But there could be. She shook off the forbidding thoughts that there could be suffering and possibly death.

"Look ahead Mamma," Bethy called to her. "See the dogwood."

The hill was covered with the pink and white blossoms of the lovely spring bush. Mountain laurel should be blooming soon and the magnolias and azaleas. It was a good world to live in, this Cherokee country.

Bethy now could ride horseback and was as untiring as any

of the others. Yes, it had been wise to send her to visit her grandparents that summer. Perhaps it would be good for the children to go to Raleigh again—for awhile.

Soon, they all stood on the pinnacle exclaiming as always about the way the mist would soon leave the valley and reveal their peaceful looking toy town. Surrounding it were the blooming fruit trees and the red earth ready for plowing.

The children started their usual chatter with games, and their laughter echoed off the high cliffs.

Tsika spread the bright blanket on the ground and placed the picnic hamper on it. Tears smarted behind her eyelids. She couldn't force the depressing thought away that this would be the last time for a picnic for a long time. "The last time, the last time," kept drumming in her mind like a tom tom.

Sean and the children seemed not to worry about anything today. She'd join them.

They climbed down beside the waterfall to the small lake. They swam, then climbed back up for a meal of cold fried chicken, potato salad, corn bread, salad greens and cake Manda had packed. Sean announced it was time to play the game of "See what I found."

"Off with you all now. See what you can bring back."

Ten minutes later all had congregated. Tsika started the game. "Beth what are you chewing?"

"I found some gum oozing out of the sweet gum tree. It's good. What did you find Danny?"

He approached with a huge bouquet of leaves. "I brought a bouquet for Mamma."

"Thank you, dear. Oh my God, help us. It's poison oak. He'll be covered. Throw it away—immediately!"

Danny cried, but Missy laughed. "Don't worry. I rubbed him with that oil plant before he picked it. He won't break out. Grandma says it's what you used when you were little. And if he does break out, here's spider bean leaves for rash."

Tsika sighed. "I hope you're right."

Danny muffled his sobs. "What—what did you get, Papa?"

"What I needed most for my work shop. Resin. Now, Tsika, what can we expect, something exotic?"

She laughed. "Of course. I looked for mint for stomach cramps, for iris roots for earaches and—"

Oh, Mamma," Missy fumed. "Tell us what you *found*, don't mention those ugly things."

"Here is what I found. Buds from the sweet shrub. You put it in a dresser drawer and the scent is delightful."

Missy was laughing. "I have something besides cures for Danny's poison oak. It jumps."

Beth giggled. "I know, but I won't tell."

"Out with it Missy."

She reached in her bulging pocket. "Look, a baby rabbit. Can I keep it, Mamma? I saved it from certain death. Wooly had it in his teeth."

Tsika looked at Sean. "Another rescued animal? Missy, I believe you're going to be an animal doctor."

"I'd like that. Can I keep him?"

"Of course," Tsika laughed. "Just don't let the dogs know you've shifted your affections."

Before they realized, it was five o'clock and time to return home. They gathered the picnic things together and for a long moment Tsika gazed at the scene below her. She shivered. There was a feeling she would never see it again.

Gerald Dolan arrived, stayed for two days, then the day of departure came too soon. Sadness prevailed as tears were shed and admonitions were given.

"I'm so sorry, Tsika, you and Sean must be parted from the children. I wish you would change your mind and all come home with me."

He was kind; they were all upset; Tsika just nodded her head. She couldn't speak. She had wanted this moment never to come, yet wanted it over with. Oh Damn! Damn the Georgians! She grabbed her cape, flung it over her shoulders and angrily wiped the tears from her eyes.

Sean helped Jeremy load the luggage. Tsika kissed each child.

"I know you'll be just fine with your grandpa and grandma, and that will make us both happy."

"Then why you cry, Mamma?" Danny asked, his blue eyes wearing an appealing expression so like Sean's.

She laughed. "The showers are over, Danny. Now we'll have sunshine. Smile everyone. You're going on an exciting trip."

As they went out of the door, Missy hung behind. "I—I can't—can't go, Papa," and she burst into tears. "I've got to stay here." Frantically she clung to her mother.

"You must, Missy. Please don't make it so hard. You must go to be safe."

"But you two won't be safe. I'm grown up now, Mamma. I'm twelve years old. I must decide these things for myself."

"Well, ride along anyway, Missy. Maybe you'll change your mind when we arrive at the station."

Once there, she pulled away when Sean tried to help her into the stage.

"Papa, don't! I won't go." she screamed. Then she ran to Tsika and frantically clutched her mother around the waist.

"Calm down, dear. We're not forcing you to go. Now wave goodbye to your grandpa and Beth and Danny."

The sobs and the hiccups stopped and the tears subsided to quick sighs.

Two sad little faces peered from the stage window until Sean handed them each a package. "For you to open on the way," he said, as he jumped down and waved them off.

Tsika wrapped her arms around Missy on the ride back to Riverview Acres, smoothing the shining black hair and murmuring a few assurances she didn't feel.

"We'll go to visit your Grandma Star and Greta soon."

The child nodded. "I'd like that. Greta is such fun, and at home I have my animals."

"And us," Sean chimed in.

Missy laughed. She never held a grudge. Forgiven already, her father always brought humor to any desperate situation.

"Of course, Papa. I love you more than my animals."

In late April another party of emigrants was scheduled to leave under government supervision. Some of their friends were leaving so Tsika and Sean decided to wish them "God Speed."

"We'll take you up to Grandma's today, Missy. Drop you off after we've said goodbye to the Hicks and the Andersons."

"Good. I'll get packed. Can I take my rabbit?"

Tsika sighed. "I don't believe so. Grandma has enough cats and dogs and chickens. I think you'd better leave Mo at home."

"This contingent is going by way of Calhoun Agency, Tsika. We'll drive there first before we go to Springplace."

"It's such a beautiful day. Perhaps we can walk the last mile. Let Jeremy take the carriage to my mother's and wait for us there."

"Fine. A walk will give us our daily exercise."

"Can we go the back route where we went last summer?" Missy asked. She loved to hike through the hills and vales like Tsika and never missed a chance to ride or walk the woodland trails. "Maybe I'll find another rabbit."

"Heaven forbid," laughed Sean. "That would surely cause our menagerie to increase in very short order."

Today, as on the picnic, Tsika seemed to be more aware of all the sights, sounds and smells of the surrounding countryside.

The hillsides were covered with pink and white dogwood, and magnolias that lined the path turned their delicate petals to a cloudless blue sky to face the sun. Tsika breathed deeply of the spring air, and felt the breeze was wafting the wild honeysuckle's fragrance just for her. Azaleas were budded, and would soon burst forth in all their colorful glory, transforming the hillsides from pink and white to all shades of pink, apricot, lavender, yellow and red.

"Hear the birds, Sean. They're particularly happy today."

"They are indeed. Look, Missy. A bird's nest. A thrush just flew out, scolding us away." He parted the branches of a low spruce to reveal two speckled brown eggs.

"Don't disturb it, Papa, or the mother bird won't come back and hatch them." Then she skipped ahead of them.

Tsika stopped to pick a leaf from a low growing plant, rubbed it between her fingers and sniffed its aromatic fragrance. "Umm, smell this, Sean. It's some kind of mint. Nice?"

Sean took her hand. "Yes, nice. I like your long way home." He bent his head down to kiss her.

"Mmm, that's nice too," she grinned. "It gives me the same feeling as the walk through the woods today. Utter bliss."

Missy rushed back to them. "Will the soldiers make us leave like those emigrants, pushing them around?"

Sean spoke first. "No, don't worry about that, Missy. When we have to leave it will be with preparation and dignity."

"I see, but Mamma and Grandma *do* have to worry, because they're full-blood Cherokees."

"I see Jeremy up ahead. We're almost at Grandma's," Tsika noted, glad to change the subject. Missy's words and worries bespoke her own. What was going to happen to them?

"Sean, Missy is growing up; she even has grown-up worries. I feel such deep sadness for her. She should be looking forward to a lovely life of romance, and perhaps a life's work and what she has are worries."

Sean shrugged. "She wouldn't go along with the others."

They hailed Jeremy.

"Wait a few more minutes," Sean called. "We'll be ready to go home as soon as we leave Missy and say a short hello and goodbye to Tsika's mother and sister."

"Umph. Oh, Master Dolan, I didn't hear you a comin'."

Sean chuckled. "No wondering about time there. He napped."

The apprehensive mood remained and as they rode back

to Riverview, Tsika held Sean's hand as though she needed assurance. "Jeremy's whistling that mournful Negro spiritual
doesn't help, does it?" she said. "I wish we'd stayed at
Mamma's awhile to visit with my ever-cheerful little sister.
Missy's right, Greta's fun."

Sean rallied to her thought. "We'll go back and tell Jeremy
to bed down in the tack shop with Enos."

She laughed, "Oh, Sean, you really would do that?"

"Sure. On the other hand, I'd rather have you all to myself
tonight. This is a rare opportunity, my girl. And just think, I'm
all yours. Aren't you the lucky one?"

Her mood lightened, as always, when Sean assured her of
his love for her. She raised her head for his kisses.

On the tree-lined road into New Echota they passed a
troop of the Georgia Guard.

"They're always in evidence," she moaned.

"Yes, all the more since the Federal troops came in. They
stand around like vultures, sometimes not even waiting for the
emigrants to leave before they snatch the property for settlers.
Forget them for the time being, my sweet. We have much
more interesting things to think of. When I get you home—"

"Look ahead," shouted, Jeremy. "Up the lane, Masta
Dolan, we got trouble."

Twelve mounts of the Georgia National Guard were tethered to the porch railings at Riverview.

In a small voice, Tsika moaned, "No, no, it can't be true."

"Damn," Sean exploded. "I didn't think they'd bother a
white. Act calm, my darling. We'll brave it through."

With a perception born of anxiety, Sean took the situation
in at a glance: some of the soldiers guarded Jake and the help
at the barn and negro cabin area east of the mansion; one
stood guard at the front door; the others were inside.

"Stay here," he told Tsika. "I'll go see what's up."

"No, Sean—"

Rushing past the guard, Benji rushed out. "Don't come in.
They's pushed by me. I couldn't—couldn't—"

The guard stopped him with one sweep of his gun butt. The boy dropped to the porch, bleeding from a head wound.

Sean jumped over him and rushed inside, shouting. "What in hell's going on in here?"

Tsika and Jeremy hurried to the porch to Benji, and suddenly the guard pulled her up and pushed her into the hall. There was a shot and Jeremy dropped beside Benji's inert form.

"You beast!" She clawed and bit and kicked but he pulled her hands behind her back and held her firmly.

"Keep your hands off my wife and get the hell out of here!"

Two soldiers grabbed Sean and while he struggled to free himself, a familiar voice came from the area of the dining room.

"You don't have much to say about this house, Dolan. I drew it in the lottery. I finally got you where I want you." The man stepped forward pointing a gun at Sean.

Tsika's screams pierced the rooms. "Ron, you can't!"

Ron's green eyes blazed with fury and madness. "I can and I will. He killed my family and I'll get even." He cocked the gun.

Sean was puzzled and angered beyond reason. He jerked loose from the guard's hold and rushed at Ron, yelling, "I killed no one, you fool!"

Before Sean had gone two steps, Ron pulled the trigger. Tsika screamed; Sean's hand flew to his chest as he fell to the floor.

The shocked soldiers released their hold on Tsika and she ran to her husband, falling on her knees beside him.

"Sean, talk to me, *Sean!*" she sobbed. Then she shook him. "Please talk to me. Sean—" she whimpered. "Oh, my dear, what has he done to us?"

Blood covered the front of his new blue shirt. His birthday present. Such inconsequential thoughts when he lay dying. "Oh, my God! No! *No!* It can't be!"

She shrieked, "You killed my husband," and, all in one movement, rose and lunged at Ron.

He laughed and grabbed her wrists. "Now you'll do as I say." Then he shoved her toward the guards. "Lock her up."

Kicking and screaming they bore her out to the horses, her feet barely touching the steps. In a final brave struggle, she yanked herself away for a moment, only to receive a blow that brought unconsciousness. She was thrown over a horse's back, the three guards mounted, and they rode away.

The three soldiers, who were left in the living room with their sergeant, still felt shock at Ron's actions.

"Take these bodies out and tell the niggers to bury them."

They hesitated after he'd barked out his orders.

"Don't look so surprised. You joined the Guards to promote change around here, didn't you?" Suddenly saneness returned and he felt he had to explain. "And I had a personal vendetta going. His father killed my family, so I had to pay him back. She aimed at me and shot her husband. That's your story or you'll end up like him. Got it? Now move! Oh, and send Jake up here."

They saluted their sergeant and, with the bodies slung over their saddles, they departed to join the six guards at the barns.

One soldier turned to the other two, "Tough bugger, eh? *I'm* not talkin', that's for sure."

The others nodded, only too anxious to agree.

When they rode up to the barn area, the blacks gasped when they saw Sean and Jeremy and cringed in terror for fear of what might happen to them.

"Sergeant's orders are as follows," said the soldier who seemed to be in charge. "You there," and he pointed to Jake. "Get spades so the niggers can bury these dead, then you're to go up to see Ron."

The bodies were laid on the ground. The women wept silently and the men swallowed hard, lowering their heads in prayer and quiet acceptance.

Someone had to know about this. Jake had to get away.

The soldiers who had been guarding at the barns and cabins left the burying duties to the three and rode off.

Jake appealed to the remaining guards, "Let me take the boy to my cabin. You'll be well rewarded."

"How can we trust you?" asked the tall one in charge.

"One of you come with me."

"All this to save a worthless nigger?"

"Let him go," said one of the others. See what he's got he's so anxious to part with."

"All right, go with him. If there's any funny business, call. Or better yet, shoot."

Jake carried Benji to the cabin. The guard, gun aimed at Jake's back, followed him closely.

Once inside he reached under the pillow of his bunk for a sack and surreptitiously lifted his gun as well. He might need that to get away.

"Here's my life's savings if you'll let us leave."

The soldier shrugged, looked at the gold and marched out.

Jake picked up the spades. The guard showed the money to the others; they talked, and as the digging began, Jake started to go back to his cabin. Two of the guards took chase and Jake was suddenly halted, not by them, but by an oncoming horseman. The soldiers stopped. He looked up. It was Cochee.

He dismounted, shouting, "The boss says the niggers are his property now. And you," he pointed to Jake, "go up an' see Ron!"

"I have something of more important to do at the moment."

Roughly he grabbed Jake's arm. "Nothin's as important as what Ron wants. I said come!" He gave Jake a clout on the head. A full head shorter than Jake the blow landed on the ear.

Jake whipped the small gun from his vest and assuming a brave stance ordered, "Stand back, all of you. I'm not going to see Ron. I have more important things to do around here."

Backing up, gun raised, he started again for his cabin. He planned to go out the back way, through the woods and down the far side of the lane to town.

Cochee pulled his gun from its holster and at the same moment both men pressed the triggers. Cochee's shot went wild as Jake dodged and Jake's bullet found its mark in Cochee's shooting arm.

The man dropped his gun, held onto his arm and yelled, "Get that damned bastard!"

As the soldiers ran for Jake, the blacks attacked Cochee and no one knew who dealt the final blow. By the time the soldiers had returned without Jake, the limp body of Cochee lay on the ground and not a negro was in sight.

The guard, who arrived first, felt for a pulse, raised a limp arm and let it fall. "What do we do? Tell the sergeant?"

"I guess we have to report it or bury the body and go after the murderers, but three against all those angry niggers: Not me!"

By the time Ron heard of the murder, the field negroes and even Benji and the women had gone from the farm.

That night he reported to headquarters at Colonel Bishop's at Fort Benton, the old Springplace Mission building.

Searchers were sent out immediately, but the negroes had nature's protection at night, and by morning, there was no trace of them. It was as though they'd been swallowed up by the earth.

Churning up red dust, Jake galloped into Aiku's drive, dismounted, rushed to the front door, and pounded on it.

It was answered almost immediately. "Well, greetings, my friend. What—something's wrong."

"Aiku, I must go to see Star," he panted. "You must get your father."

"Take it easy, man. What is it?"

"They came home to find Ron there. He'd taken over the property—lottery drawing. He killed Sean and Tsika's blamed.

She's been taken to jail. The negroes are to be slaves again."
Jake bowed his head in his hands. "Help them to get away."

"Tsika, in jail? My God, we've got to get her out."

Tani came into the room. "I overheard, Aiku. We must try
to free her. I'll go with you." She turned aside, coughing.

Jake looked at the young girl, old before her time due to
the lung disease, contracted from exposure in the woods down
in gold country, and shook his head. How strange that a girl,
whom Aiku and Roper found living on roots and berries in the
woods for years had succumbed to that horrible coughing
sickness.

"You must be careful of your health, Tani. Aiku and I will
go to the prison after I talk to Star."

"The best thing you can do now is to get Jake something to
eat and I'll pour him some of our corn whiskey."

The boys rushed in. "What's wrong, Papa?"

"There's been an accident. Melissa will be getting some
bad news. You two go over to Wolf's and visit with her a bit
after Jake leaves. You might help her bear it."

Aiku hurried out.

Accustomed to obedience without question, Little Owl and
Jumping Rabbit sat beside Jake while he ate the corn bread
and gnawed the chicken legs, asking for no explanation.

"Give me about fifteen minutes, then come over," he advised.

They nodded.

Aiku determined he had to talk to his father or Arapho.
Would Tsika's brother be able to help through his father-in-
law, McAllister? That he doubted. First he'd go to Big Elk's
where they were holding their meeting tonight. Several heads
could think better than one confused one—his. What could
anyone do? No Indian was allowed his day in court, particularly in Georgia Courts.

In the midst of a serious discussion concerning the grog
shops, the frequency of drunkenness and violence in the
towns, and how to stop it, and the fees to be paid them for

their transportation to the West, the door burst open.

Aiku shouted, "Sean's been killed, Tsika is arrested, but Ron did it."

For a moment there was shocked silence, then all the men were talking at once.

"Sean killed. Oh, my God!"

"Ron? What was he doing there?"

"Tsika jailed?"

"Unbelievable. Why only last night—"

"Please listen to me. I need advice. We must get Tsika out of jail. How can we do it?"

Fox came to his son. "Aiku, just tell us slowly what happened. How did you hear this? Are you sure it's true?"

"Jake came to my house, breathless and almost in a faint. He'd gotten away from the soldiers after shooting Cochee."

"This gets more complicated the more we hear," said Arapho.

"Give him a chance to continue, Raph," Elk scowled.

"Sean and Jeremy were killed when they got home. Jake said it was horrible. The guards from the house brought their bodies out to the barns and told him to get spades so the 'niggers' could bury them."

"Ron was in the house?" asked Micha.

"Ron had drawn Sean's house in the lottery and he made the soldiers hold Tsika and Sean while he taunted them. He heard Tsika scream while the rest of the soldiers were guarding the house servants and the field hands." Words tumbled out fast now.

"Cochee came to tell Jake that Ron wanted him up at the house. There was some trouble over that because Jake wanted to come to tell us, and that's how Cochee got shot in the arm. Now who's going to help me get Tsika out of jail?"

Fox used the reasonable approach. "We must first go through lawful channels, Aiku."

"What good would that do? The Indian's never allowed a fair court trial. Look at Tassel's death."

"Perhaps Sam Kellog could help," Elijah Hicks suggested.

"No, he's a member of the Treaty Party now."

"What about the soldiers who were in the house when Sean was killed?" asked Micha.

"Jake said after one guard told the soldiers at the barn, one of the guards shot him."

"His own soldier?"

"Yes, they'll stop at nothing. They'll never rat on Ron, for if they did, *they'd* get shot."

"Well, son, for the present, go over to the prison and ask the jailer to allow you to visit Tsika. At least that will give her some comfort."

"We'll go with you," Micha and Arapho offered.

Aiku nodded, appreciating her brother's offer, then said, "It would be better if I went alone. Even one Indian requesting a visit might cause trouble."

"Perhaps you're right, but wait until morning. It's late," advised his father.

He knew his father was right, but he'd try to see her tonight. He galloped to the temporary Springplace prison. He hoped they hadn't taken her to Lawrenceville. If she couldn't be lawfully freed, then he'd just have to do it some other way.

VIII

1837 - 1838

A thousand bees were buzzing. Tsika moved her head to get away from them. She was back on the farm, helping her father capture the sweet honey for the breakfast table. But her head ached. She heard the rushing stream beside the cabin. It was misty; she couldn't see it, but she knew it was there. She squinted her eyes to view the cabin and the sparkling water, but she saw a low ceiling, dark walls and a barred window outlined in the moonlight.

She was lying down. She felt panic as she reached for something—anything to grasp, and touched a dirt floor. She tried to rise and felt pain in her ribs and head. Her arms and wrists hurt. Then she remembered.

"Lock her up." He's dead! Oh, God, Sean's been killed. What will become of us? Tears flowed onto the dirt floor, and she made no effort to stop them. Tears of regret that she hadn't done as Sean had wished, tears for her children, and tears for her people. What was to become of all of them?

Slowly she rose moving each limb cautiously to determine how badly she was hurt, then took stock of her desperate situation. Always impulsive, it was hard not to demand action, but she had no choice: this she had to think about.

She still felt confused about what had happened, but she would try to be optimistic. When the authorities found out what had occurred at Riverview, they would accuse Ron of murder and she would be freed. But losing Sean was something she would never get over and tears came again. She was cold, hungry and she began to wonder whether anyone knew she was here besides Ron and the Georgia guards. She heard the distant clang of a metal door. Perhaps she would be released. It was all a mistake.

Footsteps approached her door. A scraping noise sent a plate sliding beneath the barred door.

"Wait, let me out," she called.

"What's out? You'se in here to stay," a gravelly voice responded. A loud cackle gradually receded.

She pounded on the door and screamed, "You've got to get me some help. Get someone in here from town."

Raucous laughter and hoot calls from other cell occupants told her that approach was hopeless.

"Oh, Sean," she moaned. "What can I do?" Even if she could get out, life would never be the same without him, her very being, her soul. "I can't live without you."

But she had to for the children's sake. Thank God, Danny and Beth were with their grandparents and Missy was with Star. Dear Danny, the small image of his handsome blue-eyed father, whose hearty joyful laugh was stilled forever. It would never again echo through the halls of the mansion he'd so proudly built. He would never come in after his day's work and toss the children into the air.

Sobbing, she covered her face with her hands. She couldn't think of this thing that was so devastating, so overpowering and so utterly hopeless.

"No, I won't believe it. Sean's coming for me," she moaned.

"Shut up over there!" came a gruff demand.

Frowning, she nodded, then decided she'd be strong and think someone would come to release her soon.

Meanwhile, she'd think of the green woods and the cool rushing stream beside the cabin her mother and father built after their move from Hiwassee, and draw strength from those memories. She'd ride Poncho through the meadows, black hair flying from beneath a beaded headband, learning to shoot an arrow and a gun, straight as her brothers, helping her father, Great Wolf, with the horses, and Niamhi, her father's mother, and her mother Star with the planting of vegetables, corn, cotton and flax. The sun was warm on their backs and a cool breeze wafted from the nearby mountain tops.

Tsika fell into a fitful sleep on the lumpy cot, dreaming of soldiers, Ron, judges and lawyers to be feared. Not only made uncomfortable by aching bones and the laceration on her head, her troubled mind conjured up nightmarish qualities of torture and death. Several times during the night she startled herself by crying out. Would this night never end?

There was no way to tell until the first fingers of dawn crept in at the high, barred window. There was stiffness in every joint as she moved to the small bowl of rank water left for washing and to the slop jar in the corner.

A scraping sound sent a plate of grayish gruel sliding beneath the cell door. She tasted it, gagged, and pushed it aside.

At mid-morning, she heard a grumble of voices in the corridor. Were they coming to let her out? In spite of the dire thoughts of the night before she was optimistic.

There was a rattle at her door, and a command, "Get over here!" It was a relief from doing nothing. A huge red-bearded white man fumbled with the lock. "Jack, you lazy nigger, come here!"

In one motion, she was pulled off her feet and dragged between them along the dark hall. "Hurry, damn you. The judge won't wait forever."

Good, she thought. She would appear before the judge and get out. She was pushed into a room that faced the east. Sun attempted to shine through a dirty window, and seated in front of it was a heavy-jowled man who looked like a Buddha.

When her eyes adjusted to the light, she saw a scowl on his face as he ruffled through the many papers on his desk.

Then he mumbled, "Your gun was found beside the body of Mr. Sean Dolan. There are several witnesses who observed the shooting." He never once looked up from his papers. "Guilty of murder." With a wave of dismissal, he rose from his chair and walked to the door.

"You can't do this. I didn't shoot my husband," she cried after him. "Who said I shot him?"

She was pulled back to her cell screaming, "I could never do such a thing. I want to see a lawyer."

"Get along, Indian bitch. Think you'll get a lawyer?" the jailer laughed. "You'll rot in jail 'afore that day comes."

Again locked in her cell, she wondered how long it would be before someone could help her. Was she to be just another forgotten case like those unfortunate Indians, who had been picked up for minor misdemeanors and never heard from again? It was a frightening thought.

The noon meal, gluey-looking gravy over stringy meat, looked no more appetizing than the others, but she was so hungry she forced it down, only to lose it five minutes later. She lay on her cot feeling utterly wretched with stomach discomfort. Was she coming down with an illness? She wished she had some of Niamhi's herb for pain.

She called, "Guard, could I have some medicine?"

There was no response to her several calls. Maybe if she'd just lie down on the cot the pain would go away.

She wondered what had happened to Benji. Poor Manda. How horrible for her to learn of Jeremy's death. And what did Ron expect of Jake? She shook her head to clear the thought that she was blamed for Sean's death. Ron had shouted, "You killed my father!" What did he mean? In Ireland? How could he? Sean was here. "There's something about Sean you wouldn't want to know." Was that what he'd meant? Surely it wasn't Sean's fault.

Late in the afternoon, the sound of boots clacked on the

corridor floor. They approached her cell. Then that voice!

"Well, look what we have here," Ron's leer greeted her.

"Get out! I never want to lay eyes on you." She shuddered.

"I'll get you out, Tsika."

"No," she gasped, then snapped. "You killed my husband, blamed me and now expect me to let you rescue me? There are no words in my vocabulary to describe you, you vile— beast!"

He laughed, but his eyes, as hard as mossy river-stones, bore into her. "You'll sing a different tune when you've been in here for a few months."

Tears stung her eyelids. "Get me a lawyer!"

"When hell freezes over! You never learn, do you? Still ordering people about. Someday maybe I'll help you out of here, if you agree to a few rules I'll insist on, and no bossing."

"Never! Get out of here!" She retreated to a corner on the side of the jail cell door where he couldn't see her and covered her face. Tears flowed. She'd never depend on him for anything, no matter how miserable she was.

Refused by the sleepy jailer when he requested visitation, Aiku was debating whether to knock the man out and find her cell or bide his time when another guard joined them.

"What's the damned red doing here?"

"Just someone wants to see the Indian woman. I said, no."

"Get out of here, scum, 'less you want a cell too."

Aiku left in haste. He crept around the building trying to locate Tsika's cell. He called once, then heard the guard's footsteps on the gravel path behind him. He disappeared into the woods, jumped on his horse and rode away. He'd be back.

The next morning Aiku went to see Sam Kellog. When he knocked on the office door, a familiar voice called, "Come in."

"Mr. Kellog, could I speak with you for a moment?"

"Oh, hello, Aiku. Of course. Sit down."

Aiku's only contact with Sam was as his errand boy years ago, so his nervousness and Sam's membership in the Treaty party made for a self-conscious rush of requests.

"Tsika Dolan is in jail, you know, for murdering Sean. She didn't do it; do you think you could defend her and could you get me in to see her?"

Sam scratched his beard. "Well, I might, but I'd have to know more about what the circumstances were and who made the charge. We were friends. I'd like to help her if I can."

"Some of the Georgia guard saw Ron shoot Sean."

"My hands are tied. I can tell the judge we must have a fair trial, but you know no Indian's testimony is allowed against a white in Georgia courts. I have applied several times to the War Department and to the President to right that injustice (we want the same rights for all races) but we hear it is 'Not a matter of rights but a matter of remedy': the remedy of removal to western lands. There you will have lands where you'll have that right, and I quote, 'It will endure as long as grass grows and water runs'."

"I know many have accepted that provisional treaty and left, but—" Aiku insisted, "*we* will stay."

Sam sighed, "I doubt that you are wise."

"What of our immediate problem. Are you saying you can't take the case?"

"No, but I'm not a criminal lawyer, Aiku. I can but give it a try. I'll try to see Judge Hooper today and also ask that you be allowed to visit Tsika. That's the best I can do."

"Then her case may never come up for trial," he mumbled.

"That's a definite possibility."

"All right. I hope they let me in today. I'll tell her you'll try."

When Aiku left, Sam shook his head. Why were the Cherokees so stubborn? He disliked being so evasive. She wouldn't even have a hearing. He knew Judge Hooper had accepted bribes to detain the Cherokee headmen who were arrested in September '36.

That afternoon when Aiku told the same jailer his lawyer said he could come to see Mrs. Dolan, the small man blew a

whistle. Two strong guards appeared and he was bodily taken
from the entrance room, thrown to the ground, kicked in the
ribs, spat at and warned.

He was no match for them together, but should he ever get
a chance at each one—well! Think of how you can get to see
her.

That night he waited in the woods behind the prison until
about midnight. The air was cool, the moon was high overhead, and he crept stealthily from window to window calling
her name.

Just as he had finally given up hope, she answered, "Aiku,
is that you?"

"Oh, Tsika, I'm glad I found you. They wouldn't let me in.
I'm so sorry for everything."

"You don't believe them, do you?"

"Of course I don't. I've talked to Sam. He's going to talk to
the judge."

"That man! He's heartless. He'll never listen to anyone."

"What are you doing to remain calm and hopeful?"

"I think of my childhood on the Hiwassee River. It helps
for awhile, Aiku, but I've got to get out of here."

She stood on her cot on tip toe and reached up to touch
his hand. It wasn't right. He was a married man, but she
needed the physical assurance that he was really there.

His heart ached for her. "Somehow the truth will come
out. Think of the pleasant times we had on picnics on the river.
I must go. I hear someone coming."

And the shadow at the barred window was gone. She was
alone again, in her dark cubicle with her cot, and slop bucket.

She started to weep for those days and for all the happy
days since then, until—No! Don't think of it! Think of the
pleasant times.

She still stood on the cot and breathed in the cool April
air. Only the croaking of frogs and the occasional hoot of an
owl broke the silence of the night, promising spring. What
promise did it hold for her? Out there was the change that

comes in spring when there's the pungent odor of leafy mold and the delicate fragrance of blooming shrubs and trees. She inhaled deeply trying to transport herself to the banks of the river. She welcomed the spring, but couldn't see it and it was the seeing that gladdened the heart.

Think of the past: as winter faded and the miracle of rebirth occurred in nature; when rushing water cascaded over mossy stones; air smelled fresh and there was a misty green on budding trees; and when, one day she'd been walking through the woods and heard a cry. That day when Aiku saved Micha from drowning, and he'd laughed, "Imagine a sixteen-year-old Cherokee boy crying. But I am so grateful I came along when I did and—" dripping wet, the three, hugging one another, he added, "Tsika, I also have discovered I'm in love with you."

"You can't be! My mother says I am still a boyish child of fourteen with no ladylike qualities because I like to climb trees and shoot arrows."

Then he smiled and kissed her cheek. "Then I love a girl who can climb trees and shoot. You have much time to learn woman's work while I farm my father's land or learn a white man's trade."

She had blushed under her dusky tan.

"The awareness of my intentions becomes you. Tsika, you are beautiful."

She was pleased. Her future with Aiku would be perfect. She had loved him ever since she was eight and he'd taken her hand to lead her over rocks and out of ruts on the road from Hiwassee to Springplace. Perhaps it had been for only a short time, for usually the children and women rode in wagons, but she could still feel the firm clasp of his hand.

Then there was the day on the trek when he took her to his father's cart while Star delivered Micha.

She dreamed that she would marry Aiku when she became seventeen. It was the right age for Cherokees to wed, but she was sent away to school and a blue-eyed knight in shining armor came into her life. He bore an aura of romance, because in her English class at Brainard, Miss Sophia Sawyer presented the students with "The Knights of King Arthur's Round Table." Sean Dolan was Sir Lancelot and she was his Lady Elaine. She'd die for him. But—ultimately he died for her, didn't he.

She fell asleep dreaming of their whirlwind courtship, Aiku's sadness and her parents' delight over her good fortune. Mixed marriages were acceptable, for they made the Cherokees feel they were being wholly absorbed into the white world they wished to emulate. It gave them a sense of security.

She awakened at dawn to the honking of wild geese announcing their glorious freedom in flight. She turned on the hard cot, straining to see the gracefully flowing triangle. They were beyond the small square of dim light of the barred window.

Oh, to see them feeding in the ponds, white chin-straps on the long black necks stretched out from the soft grey bodies! And when they took off on the wing again, some feathers floated down onto the water's surface for the boys' arrow shafts.

She looked around the dark cell. This was the place where Ross and Payne were imprisoned and saw a Cherokee's body hanging from the rafters. She shivered. There was no dead body, but a musty foul odor hung on the heavy air; the floor was damp; the walls were encrusted with mold and cobwebs hung from the rafters. She shook her head in disgust at the lumpy cot and the thin soiled blanket. How could she, who had such a beautiful clean home, exist in this filth? She closed her eyes.

The small slot in the door slid open and a guard threw her a prison shift. "Put this on and shove your clothes through here," a gravelly voice commanded.

"I'll tend to her, Matt," a woman yelled at him.

The door banged open and before Tsika had a chance to obey, a burly woman burst in, ripped off the ruffled skirt, and reached for Tsika's necklace.

"No!" Tsika clutched it.

"Yes, my fine lady," she sneered, "and I ain't sayin' please." She pulled hard on the chain of the diamond necklace; it broke in her firm grasp and then the woman reached for Tsika's rings.

Tsika was shocked, then anger surmounted the surprise and she lashed out in fury. "You greedy witch, stop it! I'll give them to you if you'll act human. Stop trying to humiliate me!"

In turn she suffered a smart slap to the mouth. "Shut up, slut!" The rings were ripped off her fingers and the woman stormed out.

Overcome with emotion, Tsika wept.

She told herself, the prison attendants were supposed to humble and break the spirit of their charges. She sniffed, well, they wouldn't break hers. She was a Cherokee and Cherokees were brave. Didn't Aiku say he'd talked to Sam Kellog? After all Sam was half-Cherokee and even though he'd signed with the Treaty party, he'd not let her down. She drifted back into her shell of reveries.

She'd live those carefree years of youth again: the years when there was no fear of whites, when the affluent Cherokees were building fine homes, marrying whites, raising mixed-blood children and formulating a court system and government modeled after United States institutions.

How lovely it was to help build their new cabin on the 100 acre plot at Springplace. Although only eight, she dug the clay and handed her father tools, while her brothers, Arapho and Juni, chopped trees and flattened the ends to fit one another. The red clay, spread between the logs, sealed the cold out in winter and the heat out in summer.

But winter wasn't too severe. Fall's hazy, smoky time drifted into a few days of frost, then suddenly buds were on the trees and it was spring again.

Star and Niamhi, her father's mother, built the stone fireplace, then planted corn, flax, cotton and vegetables. The boys brought wood to the cabin for the cooking fire. A heavy iron pot hung on a crane containing redolent rabbit stew or wild fowl and, when Great Wolf shot a deer in the woods surrounding the village, the little cabin was steeped in the delicious aroma of steaming venison.

Tsika's responsibility was the care of her small brother, Micha, while her mother and grandmother planted, wove cotton, spun flax strands or preserved foods.

This noon was the same as many others. The fragrant stew bubbled in the iron pot above the wood ashes, when her grandmother called to her, "Come, Tsika, put the boy on his bear skin rug for a nap. You're old enough to help me with the dyeing."

How she had longed for the time when she could take the yards of material her mother and grandmother had woven on their loom during the winter months, and help to transform them into a beautiful rainbow of colors.

She hurried to obey. "Will I have a red dress to wear to the Mission School in the fall, Grandmother?"

"Aye. Bring me the dye in the clay bowls on the top shelf while I prepare the indigo for the boys' shirts."

Tsika reached for the bowls of walnut, maple and hickory bark mixtures and carefully set them on the table. Thoughtfully she regarded them. Which one could she claim for her very own? Maybe the one containing red sumac berries.

The hickory would produce a lovely green for Grandmother's dress, and since the mission-lady-teacher Sophia said the women must be more modest and wear full ankle-length skirts instead of short buckskin tunics, the maple would dye her mother a purple skirt, then mixing the maple and the hickory would make a color like the cabbage butterfly, a lovely yellow for a sash for her father. Walnut and indigo would blend for dark pants and jackets for the boys. They must have clothes like the whites if they were also to attend the school.

Then her eyes lighted when she saw the last bowl on the shelf; the one that contained the precious red: the red made of crushed sumac berries.

"And this is for my new dress, Grandmother," she called, pulling the earthen vessel to the edge of the high shelf.

It tipped, the lid fell off, and, in the next moment, Tsika was covered with red dye.

She screamed. She wasn't hurt, but startled and worried, for she expected her grandmother to scold her and that ultimately her mother would use the switch.

But Naimhi laughed. "Tsika, you should see yourself— you're truly a Red Indian now."

Hesitantly the child smiled. Grandma Niamhi could even joke about the white man's name for the Cherokee.

"But I won't have a red dress for school," she wailed.

"What is that you wear, already dyed?"

Tears still flowed, "But it's not a new dress and it's only red in front."

"Turn around. I'll splash the rest on your back."

Tsika frowned, then she saw a twinkle in Niamhi's eyes. "You're teasing me again. But what will Mamma say?"

"Don't worry. I'll take care of your mamma. Take the dress off, go wash yourself and in two minutes we'll have a pink dress and a pink rug. I'll get a pail of hot water."

"Oh, thank you, thank you, Grandmother."

Niamhi hugged her granddaughter. "When your mamma returns from Benton's, where she cares for the new baby, she'll never know what happened."

There was a feeling of closeness Tsika would hold dear whenever she thought of Niamhi. She loved her mother and father and, yes, even her brothers sometimes, but for Niamhi and Aiku there was a special fun-loving love.

Aiku? Yes, for only a short time ago, when her brothers were teaching her how to shoot, Aiku had cemented their already close bond of friendship and made her love him for his courage in standing up to them.

Her first attempts at marksmanship were so successful that Juni taunted her. "Just luck. She can't do it again."

Arapho said, "Hit the leaf hanging down on that oak."

Her arrow pierced the leaf. "Good," Aiku shouted.

"You guided her hand," Juni accused.

"I wasn't near her hand."

"You were too. You helped her. You're a cheater!"

"Nobody calls me a cheater." Aiku strode toward Juni, fists clenched and a scowl on his face.

Aiku gave Juni one punch and Arapho jumped into the fight knocking them all to the ground where they rolled and punched and Aiku's bloody nose announced a serious intent.

Tsika thought she had always loved her brothers, but now that Aiku was unfairly being beaten, she joined in the fray, pounding and pinching. More bloody noses and swelling eyes resulted.

She smiled. It was a good fight. But enough of that. It was well to dream, but she had to think of another way to make the time go faster: mark the days, clean the cell, anything.

She looked around the cell again and called, "Guard, could I have some soap and water and a rag?"

He opened the door and a hard shove pushed a pale slight girl into the cell. She fell to the floor, and ragged blankets followed her. The girl looked up wearing the expression of a wooden doll.

"Here's a bad 'un wants to meet cha and here's her bed."

The cot was shoved in barely missing the girl. She hitched herself into a corner like a frightened mouse.

As soon as the prison guard left, the girl smiled wanly and extended a bony hand. "I'm Blossom, a Pawnee. It pays to act dumb in here." She showed angry red welts on her back.

"Oh, my dear, why did they do this to you?"

"I was beaten for not telling where my husband was after we were taken from Haweis Mission. He escaped the soldiers en route to the prison. I—I never knew what happened to him. I've never heard from him. Dr. Butler thinks he's been killed."

"Dr. Butler will do his best to find him."

"I know. He's a good man. He comes to the prison about

every three months to dispense medicines for dysentery and rash. He's overdue: it's April isn't it?"

"Yes. My friend has given me some paper and a pencil. I keep track, keep it hidden beneath my straw mattress."

"They allow someone to visit you?"

"No." Tsika smiled. "He comes to the window at night."

"Oh, my God, if he ever gets caught—"

"He's very careful. It's Aiku Fox, a friend from childhood. I didn't introduce myself. I'm Tsika Dolan."

"I know. I saw you once when you visited Dr. Butler at the missionary. Your husband was trying a case in Haweis."

"You were the teacher there?"

She nodded.

"You've been here for over a year. How can you stand it?"

"One does what one must do to exist, even eat the mealy bugs." Sadly she shook her head. "If we live long enough, we'll get out."

Tsika grimaced. "Maybe we should do something to try to forget what might be in store for us—like clean up this filthy cell. I'll ask again for cleaning supplies."

"You're right. We should, but there's not a chance."

"My grandmother says, if you're oppressed, take positive action, attack and your courage will return."

Blossom nodded. "I surely need more courage."

"Here comes the guard bringing our mealy bugs."

Tsika asked him, "Please, sir, will you bring us some soap and water and rags. We want to clean up this—place."

"No need. You're trash. You should feel right at home in trash."

"You're trash!" spat Blossom.

"Sh." Tsika placed her hand over Blossom's mouth. "Honey is known to get better results than vinegar, Blossom."

Tsika turned to the guard. "Please, will you help us just a little. We'd be so grateful."

"What right you got askin' fer anythin'?" He shuffled away.

Two days later he left a pail of water, a cup of gel (soap)

and a rag.

"Oh Tsika, thanks to you we'll live in a clean room." And immediately Blossom set to scrubbing the metal cots.

Aiku came to their barred window two nights a week, bringing family news, herbs for the rash, and bits of food. A letter from Beth made her sad, but again she felt thankful the two younger children were in the East with their grandparents. Missy and Star sent small notes regularly.

Notes, pad, sometimes even left over food was hidden under the straw mattress, and at times it bulged, but they thought the buxom matron knew the mattress was bumpy and would suspect nothing. As days dragged into weeks and weeks wore into months, the girls became careless.

One morning in August, Matron Buxom came in as Tsika was writing on her pad. An attempt to hide it was noted and quickly the woman yanked the mattress off. Letters, last night's chicken bones and a spool of thread fell to the floor.

"So! *You* have some questions to answer. Come here!"

Tsika suffered a sharp slap on her face. "Where did you get these things?"

She shook her head.

She was grabbed by the arms, marched to the warden's office and pushed in front of his desk. "This one needs the persuader."

Aiku would be arrested, or worse, if she spoke his name.

She remained grimly silent throughout the arm-twisting and the threats of branding. Finally the warden said, "Take her out for twenty lashes. I'll gladly see to it myself."

Flinching, but never once crying out, she bit her lips until they bled. *Crack! Crack!* She'd die before she'd tell them Aiku's name. At the fifteenth lash, she fainted.

"Take her back to her cell. I'll finish her up later. Make no mistake, we'll get the name out of her."

Blossom tended the welts with the last bit of ointment Dr. Butler had left in March. It soothed Tsika's wounds and after two days and a night of agony she was able to rise from her cot.

The next night they heard Aiku at the window. She warned him to stay away and asked him to tell Dr. Butler to come.

It was time for his prison visit, but the doctor didn't appear until late September, and by that time they badly needed medication for diarrhea, fever and rash.

Along with the medicines, he brought news. As soon as the guard had left, he leaned close to them and whispered, "It's rumored you will be transferred to Midville prison in the middle of October. Plans are made to take you from the prison wagon. Hold them up. You must be in the last one."

The girls could hardly contain their excitement.

Tsika held her hands to her mouth to keep from shouting for joy. "What can we do to hold them up? Who planned this?"

"Sh. Here comes the guard. I must go along now. Take the Blazing Star for the dysentery."

He patted their shoulders. "Be brave, girls. Have hope," and departed.

By the end of September, the plans were almost complete. Aiku, Micha and Roper had enlisted the help of Fox and Big Elk.

The two older men met in the grog shop that was located at the former site of Springplace Mission where Jake had recently been hired to tend bar.

"I've heard there is less brawling here and who, except for a couple of old codgers like we, would go into the dark on such a sunny warm September day. We'll be alone."

"The boys will be along later to finish making plans."

"Do you think it's wise, Elk?"

"Yes, it's as good an opportunity as we can expect. While the prisoners are in transit and there's much attention given by the residents of Springplace to the next groups of emigrants due to go West. Who's going to notice our activities?"

"All right. We'll go along with the boys, do our part and hope they'll be able to get the girls out of the prison wagons and up to Ross Landing in time for the Reese-Starr journey."

"Once in Tennessee the State of Georgia can't stop their escape."

The young men came in. After a whispered conversation and final plans were made for October 15th, they discussed other things of import for an orderly exodus in May.

"I've hidden some money in a clay vessel in the first row of my corn field, Aiku. Should I not be able to get to it, you must take it with you."

"Pa, you're just being pessimistic. We'll be allowed our carts, horses, and money."

"I wouldn't be too sure."

"You're place is out far enough that you haven't been harassed as we have been," said Roper. "Part of your Pa's property has been taken, my ma's, and some of the Wolf lands. I'll leave my carts and horses at Aiku's."

Big Elk laughed. "You'd think we were going tomorrow."

Fox mumbled, "I still have worries about the escape plans."

Aiku placed his arm around his father's shoulder. "We'll be successful. You'll get along well and be off into the woods before the Georgia prison guards know what hit them."

All shook hands. Aiku said, "Dr. Butler alerted the girls. I'll drop a note in their cell the night before so they'll be ready. Until October 15th, goodbye and good luck."

"Will Aiku ever come back?" Tsika worried aloud. "Perhaps he's been caught and jailed for coming here."

"You told him not to come, remember, Tsika?"

"But it's been two weeks."

Finally on the night before the prisoners were to be moved to Midville prison, there was a tap on the window bars. Aiku whispered, "Be ready tomorrow. Act sick enough to cause your wagon to be last."

And he disappeared as Tsika called, "We don't have to

act."

The girls couldn't sleep for excitement. It was early morning before they dozed, and then in almost minutes they were roused. Even the rain couldn't dampen their spirits.

"Git ready. We're goin' on a little trip," called the red-bearded guard. "Yer bound fer Midville. That'll hold ya."

They were handcuffed and led by twos to the carts. Tsika dropped to the ground pulling Blossom after her.

"The sun hurts my eyes. Oh, my head!" she groaned.

"Git up, bitch!" She was whipped to join the others, but by the time they were in line, their purpose had been accomplished. They were pushed into the last wagon.

On each side within the wagons were wooden seats. Metal rings above were used to chain the handcuffs securely, but because the wagons were so crowded the guards couldn't attach the girl's handcuffs. They hurriedly slammed the rear door.

"Happenstance?" asked Blossom.

"God's wish," Tsika answered.

Two mounted guards led the procession and two brought up the rear.

In a downpour, weeping women and children lined the streets. Few of the townspeople of Springplace had gone to see the emigrants off at Ross's Landing. Led by Reese and Starr, it was the second voluntary group to leave Cherokee country for Western lands under government supervision. On this rainy October morning there were approximately 365 people ready to travel the overland route.

Worriedly, White Fox and Big Elk checked the crowd for spies, who might follow them, but it was to their advantage that so many people had remained on the square. They were unobserved as they left for the rendezvous with Aiku, Roper and Micha. Each took a different path to meet at the designated bend in the valley road with the others who had started in the misty dawn.

The three young men had tethered their horses in the woods near Cross Creek bend and progressed the rest of the way on foot. The wind had dispersed the rain clouds and sun shown through the trees along the dappled path. Aiku felt a full measure of confidence in their plan. Just so Tsika had been able to stall the loading of prisoners long enough so they would be last in line. He hoped he'd have a chance at the red-bearded guard who had kicked him in the ribs.

White Fox and Big Elk arrived at the appointed spot. Ahead was a valley where daisies nodded their heads in the sunshine. From their high position, Cross Creek sparkled on one side of the gravel road and a pine woods offered good protection on the other. Around the next bend was where the action would occur. The quiet was incongruous with the planned violent acts about to take place.

After a fifteen minute wait, Roper, Aiku and Micha arrived and within a half hour, the slow-moving caravan rounded the bend.

"Now," called Aiku, and Fox and Elk charged forward.

There was a scuffling sound at the rear of the procession, but no cries. One mounted guard fell from his horse, uttering only a low moan as Fox's knife wounded him and their horses collided. The other guard turned and pulled out his gun as Elk struck the man in the thigh. The soldier's horse reared and came down on his rider. The two Cherokees dashed up the slope and into the woods.

On signal, Aiku jumped into the rear wagon. The driver turned, reached for his gun and before he'd drawn it from the holster, Aiku slashed his shoulder.

Micha and Roper pulled the weakened girls from the wagon and dragged them to the horses. Chained together, they were boosted onto the same mount. The boys jumped on their horses and all charged into the woods.

The procession stopped. The other drivers jumped out and trained their guns on the rest of the prisoners. While guns blazed, the two lead-guards took chase. Shots echoed against the hills, and wounded horses screamed out in agony as they and their riders were thrown to the ground.

Roper escaped. Wounded, Micha was picked up along with the prisoners and Aiku and taken to the wagons. The girls were roughly shoved into their places. The wounded driver was taken to the nearly empty front wagon along with Micha, the dead soldier, and the wounded rear guard. Aiku, a rope tied around his neck, was made to walk and pulled along beside a mount.

For their part in the attempted escape, the girls, already weak and ill, received fifteen lashes. Their incapacities were ignored for the day, then some healing ointment was dispensed.

Tsika and Blossom lay prone on their cots until late the second day. Perhaps then, even the jailers were alarmed, for a doctor was called. They were tended in the prison infirmary until they were improved, then taken back to their cell.

They heard through the prison grapevine that Aiku and Micha were on the chain gang. Tsika wept for her would-be rescuers. Everything that happened to the Cherokees these days brought on more grief. Now nothing could give them hope for freedom.

Even after the care in the prison hospital, they were still weak and ill. Tsika wavered between hopes that she'd die and the return of the old Cherokee spirit of never giving up.

She said, "Blossom, this is a better prison. We'll do kitchen duty, have an exercise time and be able to eat in the hall with the others. There's the bell for lunch. Come, Blossom, we must try to go."

"No, you go. Bring me some bread."

"So, she's able to eat," rasped the woman guard. "Kitchen duty for you."

As Tsika washed dishes, she looked from the window at the end of the room. There were Aiku and Micha leaving the compound under guard and chained to one another. They were on their way to do road work. Tears came to her eyes as she watched.

"Back to work, slut!" came a command.

The buxom white woman gave her a shove.

Go on the offensive. Defiantly Tsika said, "I want some rags and soap and water to clean our cell."

"Now, she orders!" Boxom gave Tsika a slap on the face. In her weakened condition, she fell to the floor breaking a wrist.

Conditions worsened. Utterly dejected, both girls became lethargic, hollow-eyed from lack of sleep and during the cold days of winter, developed chills and fever. Driven to work in the kitchens, fainting at times, contributed to colds and flu. They tried guessing games, learning one another's language and marking the days, anything for survival, anything to get through the days.

One day in January Tsika returned to their cell, exclaiming, "It's rumored Ross has asked for the release of all Cherokees in Georgia prisons by May, 1838, so they can go West with their families."

"If we last that long, Tsika. I don't care anymore."

"I know." Tsika held her head in her hands and laughed hollowly. "Sometimes I think I'm losing my mind."

Boots scuffled along the hall. The scraping sounds approached their cell, and a reedy voice called, "You ready to go home with me?"

Tsika jerked to attention. "Ron! Never! I'll die first."

"You just might, unless you come now."

"Go away!"

Blossom whispered. "Go with him, Tsika. We can't last much longer."

Tsika cried, "I can't—can't. He's a beast. And I won't go without you. Hear that, killer?" she screamed loudly.

But he had left.

Blossom said, "Tsika you've got to go if he comes back. Don't worry about me. I'll get along. I'll live. I'm strong."

Tsika's tears fell. It was so easy to cry these days. Where was her spunk? Gone with her physical strength? She denied it had gone with her hope of escape.

Maybe if Ron came back she'd go. Anything to get out of here. No! She couldn't do that. She wasn't even thinking straight lately. Maybe it was the fever, but she felt cold. She needed to rest. She fell on the cot. She'd have to go to keep her sanity, but she couldn't—couldn't do what he wanted.

Those were her last conscious thoughts. When she came to, she was lying in her own bed, looking out of her own ruffle-curtained windows. Outside, trees swayed in the winter wind. How? It couldn't be. She was dreaming.

Tsika pinched her arm. It hurt. It *was* real. She looked around the familiar room. She really was home. Oh, Dear God!

She raised her head to call out, then fell back when sharp pains seared through her head. Then Ron's piercing green eyes skittered across her sphere of vision. Had she submitted to—

"No! No! No!" she screamed.

The door opened. A small black woman tip-toed toward her bed, and a faint voice said, "You come back to us, lady."

"Um," Tsika moaned.

"Lie still. You need care. I put salve on your back. Now you have some good soup. You get well."

"Blossom?" she whispered.

"No blossom in February, dear. The trees is cold outside."

"There's no one with me? I came here alone? When?"

"No. You be alone. The boss he say, 'Take good care, Dora,' so I takes care. It be three weeks. You rest now."

After her ministrations, the dark woman drew the shades and left.

Now she knew. She'd really been ill, and Ron had brought her here, expecting her to thank him. She had to get away before he locked doors and put bars on the windows. First, she had to be able to get up and walk. Again she tried to rise and fell back.

As the days went by, she gained strength and asked Dora many questions. The woman answered them in an evasive manner that told Tsika nothing. Dora seemed bent on telling her own story, that she had been picked up on the street, homeless until Ron found her starving and brought her here. "As long as I not talk about him, I keep my job, so you see?"

It was maddening. The day finally came when Tsika felt strength in her legs, and with Dora's help could walk around the room. She'd wait her chance. In another week or so, she'd try for an escape.

One morning as she was having her breakfast, she heard a key turn in the lock and Ron swaggered in. "So, you're feeling better."

Glumly, she nodded.

"Soon, you'll be able to stroll the grounds with me."

"I didn't come here of my own free will."

"You begged me to take you out of jail, my sweet."

"I was delirious," she snapped.

"I snatched you from certain death. You should be a little grateful." He stooped and placed a kiss on her cheek.

Scowling, she pulled away.

Ron left chuckling, "You'll come around, before too long."

He was dressed in tight beige pants, a brown velvet waistcoat and there were ruffles at his neck and wrist. He was stylish, she'd give him that, but he was still his same arrogant ugly self. She groaned. She had to get out of here.

But it was such luxury to bathe in scented water, sleep between clean sheets on a soft bed and eat good nourishing food again. She sighed with almost a kitten's contented purr.

Here she was back in her own Riverview, but not her own. Sometimes she could nearly shut her mind to what was expected of her. She was obligated to Ron, that was true. But, Oh God, not that way. The truth was she had sold herself to have this comfort, if not consciously, subconsciously . . . to a most despicable man. Oh *no!* Somehow she had to escape at night. This very night!

She tested the bedroom door. It was locked. She went to the dressing room. This door to the hall could be pried open if she could find a sharp instrument. She searched in the drawers of the highboy, long since emptied, then in her bedroom dresser and night stand. Her sewing cabinet? For a scissors? Frantically she pulled the things out. Beneath a petticoat to be mended, there it was, just as she had left it so long ago. Thank God! After opening the door, she slipped the scissors in her pocket.

Soundlessly, she crept down the dark hall, weak, but knowing every step of the way; down the servant's stairway to the kitchen and out through the back door. She ran to the first stable, where a lantern dimly glowed. A groom lay asleep on the hay in a corner. As she patted the horse, to assure him, he whinnied and the boy shouted.

She mounted the horse: and suddenly powerful hands pulled her from the horse's back and dragged her to the house kicking and screaming. Ron appeared at the head of the stairs. He said nothing, but the green eyes blazed with fury and one glimpse of his smirking mouth told her she would now never avoid rape or worse.

He took her by the arm and led her to the bedroom, calling, "Thank you Bruno for catching my prize."

Again, she thought of Niamhi. "Sugar will take you farther than vinegar." But could she grit her teeth and bear it? Then get away while he slept? Surely Bruno had to sleep sometime too. He'd not expect her to try to escape again so soon.

The thought of Ron taking her was repulsive. She couldn't do it! She had to do it! She'd never feel clean again. Never! Oh God, let this be over in a hurry! Then she thought of the scissors and hid it beneath her pillow. Just a small stab might cause him to release her so she could run from the house. She dressed in her warmest nightgown with ruffles up to the neck and long sleeves, and waited.

The key turned the lock and Ron said, "So you're finally going to pay me back for rescuing you."

"I didn't say so." She rose to face him.

"You were willing in the Georgia prison to promise anything to get out."

"I said I didn't know what I was saying. I was delirious."

He pushed her down on the bed. "Enough talking. If you won't cooperate with me, I'll have to do a little persuading."

Before she could move, he was on top of her, ripping her gown, pinning her arms down. His weight was a factor she'd not taken into consideration. How could she ever get at the scissors? She struggled twisting her head back and forth to avoid his kisses, and somehow managed to bring her knee up for a weak blow to his groin.

"You she-devil!"

It was enough to cause him to relax his hold on her arms. Though his weight impeded her movement she quickly reached for the scissors and brought her arm down onto Ron's neck. Blood spurted from the jugular vein onto her face and gown.

Ron groaned, "Bitch!" and went limp.

Tsika, shaking and horrified at what she'd done, pulled out from under his dead weight, ran through the dark halls, and out of the house through the back way again to the woods behind the barns.

The same startled groom saw her. At the sight of her bloodied gown and her disarray, his mouth gaped, and his eyes rolled, showing luminous white against the black skin. Then he shouted, "Bruno, get her!"

Between them, she was dragged, again struggling and scratching to the house. "What you do? Why you bloody?"

She remembered a blow to the head and the next time she opened her eyes she was back in the Georgia prison.

Had she killed Ron? What would they do to her now? Hang her like they did Tassel? Would she ever see her children again? She was stiff and sore all over her body, but her next conscious thought was of Blossom. She asked the woman warden about her former cell mate.

"Nobody by that name here."

"But she was here two months ago. Was she freed?"

"I doubt it. Not many get out of here."

"Could you find out for me?"

"I can try."

"Oh thank you. You see we grew to be good friends while—"

The woman had gone.

Tsika's life here was much the same as it had been before except that now she was alone.

When asked for an explanation, she was told, "Killers gets special treatment. Solitary and bread and water."

"Oh, dear Heaven, then Ron had died."

Again days became weeks and weeks became months. She grew weaker and this time there was no Blossom for company and no visits from Aiku. Time extended into merely vague stretches of misery. Thin and always cold and hungry, she was now burdened with a new hopelessness when she learned that Reverend Butler was forbidden to come to the prison.

He had always offered a prayer for them. Perhaps it would help if she tried the Christian prayers along with the prayers she had said as a child. The missionaries said they should keep their religious customs, but also learn the Christian ways. She bowed her head and said the Twenty-third Psalm, and as she prayed a calmness came over her and knew she would survive.

On March 14, 1838, President Van Buren had sent General Winfield Scott with 7,000 federal and Georgia state troops to round up all Cherokees from towns, villages and woodlands. He was to bring them before the removal date of May 23rd, to the temporary shelters built near Calhoun Agency or Ross Landing, to await transportation to the West. He urged the Cherokees to leave of their own volition on the next government supervised trip, due to depart shortly.

While in Washington, John Ross had met this six foot four, dignified commander and while they had vastly different views on removal, they were on good terms with one another. When Scott left, Ross stayed on, to present to President Van Buren a list of 15,665 signatures, and an appeal to have the Treaty annulled or to at least postpone departure.

The President was polite and was on the verge of allowing a postponement when Gilmore in his third term as Governor of Georgia refused any negotiations and insisted on the set date for removal, so Ross stated his other reasons for coming:

1. To collect back annuities.

2. To arrange for some 200 old and infirm Cherokees to remain in their respective communities and be allowed to become American citizens.

3. To release Cherokee prisoners in Georgia jails so they can migrate with their families.

From the time of General Scott's arrival in March, there were problems. To round up 15,000 willing Cherokees, and maintain living quarters, would be difficult, but a forced exit impossible without violence.

A report came to the Nation that Congressman Dolan was initiating an investigation into the death of his son and Charles Benton, whites murdered in Georgia. Georgia officials sought to keep the facts hidden, and had Red murdered. It was ironic that the very cause he worked for caused his death.

When word came that the prisoners were to be freed on May 22, 1838, the night before the first enforced migration, Fox approached Elk and Okemas with plans for a rescue operation.

"We'll be prepared to take Aiku, Micha and Tsika from the prison wagons the moment they arrive."

"Good, there'll be a crowd of people and much confusion. While the prison guards try to get them transferred to the carts for the trip to Ross's Landing, we'll kidnap them," Elk agreed.

"Whoever happens to be nearest them, give a signal and we'll each do what we can to divert the guards."

Then the prison door was opened and the emaciated inmates poured out, they wandered in confusion until guards corralled them into the waiting wagons.

One guard cackled, "Ha, even the jail don't want Injuns."

At first, her mind felt so numbed, Tsika didn't know what

was happening. Her eyes hurt in the sun's glare. The morning air was chilly in spite of the sun and she shivered in her thin shift. She hesitated at the doorway.

"Go on, scum, git in the wagon!" A guard pushed her ahead into another prisoner.

The elderly woman peered at Tsika from glazed blue eyes, grasped her wrist with a claw-like hand. "What'r we s'posed to do, girl? I see butterflies out there."

The woman was a demented scarecrow, yet there was some comfort in the touch of her hand. Tsika responded, "I—I guess we're free to leave."

Some staggered away as fast as their weakened legs would carry them. Others, dazed by their sudden freedom, stood staring at the wagons.

Suddenly Tsika did see butterflies out there. They had beautiful blue-green gossamer wings. She grasped the woman's other hand and led her in the steps of a Cherokee Indian dance of gratitude. Ross had managed to have them released.

Silently, they rode in the swaying wagons, each with their own worry of what would happen to them next. The elderly woman began to cry and Tsika patted the matted grey hair, soothing her like a small child.

"Sh, we'll be there soon. What's your name?"

"Bertie. I—I started West with a wagon—got captured by Indians—family all killed." She continued to sob.

Tsika blanched, and felt shame for her race. Yet, there were some good and some bad in every race. She found herself saying, "I'll take care of you. Don't worry."

"There they are," Fox shouted, as the ragged passengers began to descend from the prison wagons.

Hearts sank as the freed prisoners lurched forward into the waiting arms of friends and relatives only to be pushed toward the waiting military conveyances ready to deliver them to Ross's Landing.

Due to the huge crowd, soldiers had difficulty in rounding

them all up and amidst the confusion, Star and Greta managed to get Tsika and the woman she insisted on bringing to Big Elk's covered wagon. And soon Micha and Aiku were spirited away by Fox to Aiku's home on the outer fringes of Spring-place.

The 800 had been rounded up from Creek Path, the gold district in south-eastern Georgia, Haweis and Echota for the first forced emigration. There had been little resistance among the townspeople, for their guns had been taken, but some of the cabin Indians had escaped into the surrounding forested hills.

Because of illness in the temporary prisons and the search that went on, the trip was postponed.

After additional supplies arrived, the first trip was sched-uled for June 6th.

At that time General Winfield Scott made a speech to his 7,000 troops concerning the treatment of the emigrants.

John Reese and William Starr, who were chosen to lead this first group of 800 to Ross Landing, stood on either side of General Scott.

Scott spoke of the Cherokee's advanced progress in farm-ing education and citizenship, and issued the following warn-ing:

"The American public sympathizes with the Cherokees and because of this and their progress, every possible kindness must be shown by the troops, and if in the ranks, any despica-ble individual should be found capable of inflicting a wanton injury or insult on any Cherokee man, woman or child, it is hereby made the special duty of the nearest good officer or man, instantly to interpose and seize and consign the guilty wretch to the severest penalty of the law."

He also remarked there must be extra concern for the ill, infirm infants and women in a "helpless condition."

The people listened dully to the speech, wondering whether the soldiers would obey. So far, prodded by bayonets, the guards had routed them from their homes, and pushed them into the improvised shelters, allowing them only the clothes they wore.

Although a few had been rescued from the group, and taken into hiding, the rest of the poorly clad, unhappy families were herded forward to board the steamboat or one of the several two-decker flatboats that awaited them at Ross's Landing, where Superintendent General Nathaniel Smith was in charge of removal.

The next group was to leave on June 16th, and during the previous week, Ulah and her small son and daughter were taken from the Wolf barn while Greta, Missy and Star were out.

At first, Tsika had been determined to survive for her children, but the gradual suffering and numbness from misery and hopelessness took over and a death-wish pushed itself into her mind. Now suddenly, with this new found freedom and returning health, she felt like shouting, I live! I live!

She would see Missy, Greta and all her friends again. She'd send for Danny and Beth soon. Just to see them, hear their dear voices. That's what she'd struggled for for so long, before the profound disparagement had overcome her.

Would they be different? Would they recognize her, so pale and drawn? She felt of the sagging flesh on her bony frame. Large bones and tall frames showed loss of weight so definitely.

After Micha and Aiku and Tsika had been hidden at Tani's and Aiku's for several days, the good care and good food began to bring them all back to a resemblance of their former selves, and Roper brought Star, Greta and Missy to see them.

Laughter and tears mingled with kisses and shouts of joy as she hugged them to her. "Missy you look like a young lady. Your grandma is taking good care of you."

"Yes, Mama, but was it awful?" she cried.

"Yes, but now we'll not talk about it. We will only think about how we will keep our family together and make that trip."

While Micha was in prison, Star and Greta had been harassed by settlers, and although they had managed to keep two horses, a wagon and a few pieces of furniture, they had been moved out of their house to the barn by a Georgian family.

Star couldn't withhold the sad news of Ulah's capture from Tsika.

"We don't know what to do for her and the children and last night Rena Chaim, her daughter Kim and the baby were taken away."

"Maybe Roper can figure how to help them. We'll ask him."

The Fox property had also been taken over bit by bit until only the sparsely furnished house was left.

Elks, Chaims, Wheatons and Rena Benton and many others had suffered losses, but Aiku's and Roper's properties had been missed, probably because they were located north of Springplace and hidden by the hills.

Here also were two children, Grey Bird and Elna, whose parents had died of exposure in one of the prison camps.

Little Owl and Hopping Rabbit, Aiku's and Tani's sons, helped Atta and Fox on the farm while Aiku was in prison, but by now Aiku was able to work for short periods of time.

The fever many had suffered during the spring months had returned to plague those in the damp stockades. Ulah and the children, Rena and her daughter and the baby were the first to sicken. There was a center at one of the missionaries for the ill, and they were taken there to recuperate.

"Now is our chance to get them out," Roper told Okema.

That night, when they visited Ulah and Rena, one caused a bit of confusion by calling "Fire," while the other whisked the families from the church and took them to Roper's home.

"We'd better move the rest to Aiku's."

When John Ross returned in July, he visited the prison camps and found that something had to be done about the way his people were being treated. At camp Herzel they were herded together like cattle in foul pens, ill and undernourished from poor food.

He went to General Scott. "Sir, I demand that living conditions be improved for the prisoners, medications sent to them
immediately, the date set for removal be extended to October
because of the extreme drought and that the Cherokees be
allowed to manage their own emigrations."

Scott granted his requests, so John Ross said, "We would
also like more coffee, sugar and soap for the people and sixteen cents per person per day for food."

Scott's response was, "I'll try." Also he told Ross, "I'll rec-
ommend you to take over General Nathaniel Smith's removal
duties."

Smith wrote to Andrew Jackson, now retired and living at
the Hermitage, and, furious, Jackson sent a written order:
"Get Smith back and arrest Ross."

Neither Scott nor Ross, however, were disturbed by Jackson's written order. After all, he was President no longer, and
Ross, reacting in his typically optimistic manner, made claims
for restitution for stolen livestock, property, firearms, books,
planted fields, race horses, slaves and expensive items such as
paintings and silver, and asked for remunerations for homes
that were burned or taken over by the militia.

All of the requests weren't granted, but Ross received approval for dividing the remaining 13,000 evacuees into groups
of 1,000 each, secured a postponement for departure and
managed to contract for more food, supplies, wagon masters
and physicians for each group.

It reportedly cost the Bank of the United States and the
office of Indian Affairs between $500,000 and $650,000, after
the June, July and early September trips.

On August 1st, Ross met with his council members, who
were at Aquohee prison camp, on the subject of taking the
Cherokee Nation's government papers, on Cherokees removal
and what would be needed for comfortable travel.

He held one last council meeting at Rattlesnake Springs,
where it was unanimously decided to retain the Cherokee Na-

tion's constitution and laws in the West.

The first detachment of those 13,000 numbered 1,103 and was scheduled to leave on October 1, 1838, under two civilian leaders picked by Ross, George Lowrey and John Benge. A company of Scott's troops would accompany them. The government furnished 645 wagons, but many of the Cherokee elected to walk or ride horseback.

From October to December, the groups would be leaving Cherokee land, either by water, up the Tennessee River to the Ohio to the Mississippi and eventually up the Arkansas, or by land, following the rivers at times, but traveling north then west and south.

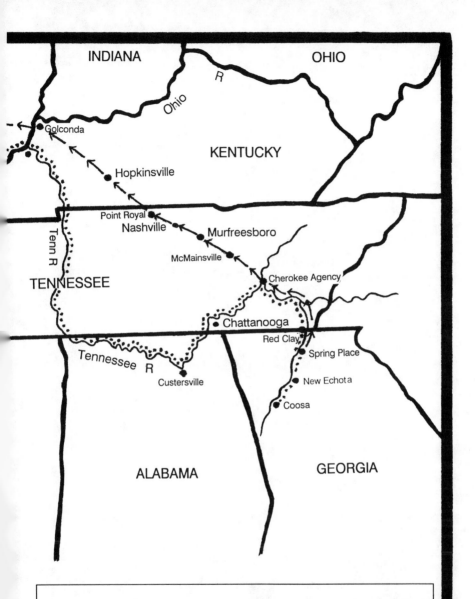

The Cherokees traveled from Coosa, New Echota, Springplace, Red Clay, and the surrounding farms in Georgia to the Cherokee Agency in Tennessee.

From Cherokee Agency, they went by land → → → → or by water • • • • • • to lands west of the Mississippi River.

M. KLEIN • 1992

1838 - 1839

The summer and fall months had given the prisoners from Georgia ample time to regain their health. Tsika, Aiku and Micha were packed to leave.

Fox, Elk, Okema, Roper, Micha and Aiku stretched canvas over strong metal frames. The covering would protect them from rain and cold and keep their belongings dry. Within, wooden bunks were built on one side; a wooden bench on the other side for storing blankets and clothing; a cabinet at the front end for cooking utensils and food, and at the rear, two steps were attached where the canvas flap opened.

Tsika watched as the passengers sorted themselves out for the covered wagons. Mounted riders were Micha, Fox and Elk. Each led his own wagon: Attu followed his father whose wagon took Ulah and her two children Robin and Jeff; Rena, very pregnant Samantha, Kim and her baby entered Elk's and Okema's wagon. The two men, the bachelor and the widower, had pooled their resources and they would spell one another driving and riding. Tsika smiled; they were both interested in Rena.

The next in line was Aiku's and Tani's wagon with little Owl and Hopping Rabbit and two orphaned children, Grey

Bird and Elno. Roper drove his wagon for Alda and their
three children and now Micha got in line to lead the Wolf
wagon and Tsika climbed up to the driver's seat.

"I was going to drive, Tsika," said Greta.

"It's been so long, Greta, let me. I feel strong now and you
can spell me."

"All right. Missy, climb up beside your mother and let me
know the minute she tires."

Finally all was in readiness on this rainy chill October 1,
1838. The first 1,103 of the remaining 13,000 were in their
places. John Ross offered a prayer, the army bugle blew and
amidst the bellowing and neighing animals, crying children,
shouting soldiers and wagoners swearing at their teams, whips
cracked, wagons creaked and the cavalcade was on its way.
Mounted soldiers led, followed by Benge and Lowrey and the
motley collection of emigrants: some carried all their worldly
possessions in bundles over their shoulders, some walked beside a loaded mule, others rode in open wagons or in covered
wagons.

The faces of the travelers told of sadness and suffering,
their mood, a reflection of the weather. Hopefully the wind
would soon push the storm clouds away.

Niamhi, Star and Greta settled themselves as comfortably
as possible in the wagon. Bertie was riding with Rena in
Okema's wagon, helping to care for Jo-Jo, Okema and Rena's
grandchild.

Tsika looked at the familiar green hills. Rounded with age
they seemed to beckon beneath the rainy mist.

She sighed, "Missy, they remind me of the first trek that
took us from our home in the Great Smoky Mountains years
ago."

"Look forward," Niamhi called from within the canvas
covered wagon,

Tsika smiled, "Leave it to Grandmother to give us the right
outlook. Yes, we must look forward, no matter what comes."

She followed Okema's wagon and about half-way to Ross's

Landing, when they slowed their progress, a child ran back to them, calling, "Can I ride with you? I'm Jo-Jo Okema."

She smiled. The direct approach like Sean. She liked that. The Shawnee man Okema had joined the wagons at the last moment, and it was well, for otherwise there would have been no one to drive Elk's wagon. Until now, she hadn't met him or his son.

"I'm Tsika Dolan, and I'm anxious to get to the Tennessee River, but I'll slow down," she smiled. "Jump on the hub. Missy will pull you up."

He squeezed between Missy and Tsika. "How do all these people get across?"

"On ferry boats and barges."

He sighed and looked ahead and behind them. "It will take a long time."

"You're right. We may not all get across today. There are 645 wagons and our five covered ones and some are walking."

"And dogs. Who owns that nice black one?" He pointed ahead.

"That belongs to Aiku Fox. His name is Chien, the French word for dog."

His eyes grew large. "You know French!" Then without a pause said, "While they take people across we can have picnics, and maybe get to sleep by the river."

Rain continued to fall and the skies were still dark. It had grown cooler.

"I wish this rain would stop," groaned Missy. "It makes me feel sad. Where can you picnic when it's raining, Jo-Jo?"

"In the wagon, Missy. I can make a picnic anywhere. You just have to sing and laugh a lot."

"That's good advice any time, Jo-Jo." Tsika smiled. "I guess we'll have to make do with the weather."

It was well the children regarded this trip as an adventure and had no worries about the future: the wearisome possibilities of food shortage, broken wheels, illness and even death. She touched the paraflech of dried corn and jerky tied to her waist and felt somewhat secure.

"Now go back to your wagon, Jo-Jo. Your papa will wonder where you are."

"He doesn't care like my mama did."

"Oh I'm sure he does. He just has other duties now."

"My mama died, you know."

"Yes, I'm very sorry."

"My Auntie Blossom died too"

"Blossom?"

"Yes, in prison." He brushed his hands over his eyes. "I—I loved her. She taught me in the Cross Path school."

Tsika held her breath. Oh, God, no! "She was your aunt? I knew her, Jo-Jo. I was in prison with her."

She hugged the little boy. "I loved her too."

"Can I stay with you and Missy?"

"Of course, for awhile. Go ask your father."

When he left, tears rolled down Tsika's cheeks.

"Mama, it's terrible she died, but please don't cry."

"I can be brave about some things, Missy, but the way she had to die—alone—horrible. It was my fault."

"It can't be, Mama. You weren't even there when she died."

"I know. I'm sorry I lost control like that. I'm not being a true Indian to show my emotions."

Melissa patted her mother's arm. "You're caring."

Oh, why couldn't she have stayed conscious long enough to insist that Ron take Blossom too? But Niamhi would say, "What will be, will be, and, Trust the Great Spirit," so she must make the best of it and help Jo-Jo as much as possible.

She wiped her eyes. "There, Missy, I'm better."

The procession finally reached Ross's Landing, and the soldiers lined up prepared to direct the crossing of the Tennessee. Ferry boats tooted, horses pawed the earth anxious about climbing up the ramps, and the general excitement lasted the rest of the day and far into the night.

From the other side they would progress north for a time

through the Cumberland Mountains. While it would be difficult, and longer than the water route, it would not be as dangerous. Reports from the earlier migrations told of capsized
boats, snags and sand bars in the river that impeded their
progress and of illness and death.

By the second day the rain had stopped, the skies were a
clear blue and the sun shone brightly. The travelers climbed
hills, descended into valleys and the drivers manipulated their
teams around S curves over rough, rutted roads. Those riding
in the wagons suffered motion sickness and bruises from the
rocking and jolting, while the emigrants who walked were
buoyant, and thrived on the fresh air and exercise. Thus they
arrived at McMinnville.

After six days, however, the trend was reversed, and at
evening camp there were footsore patients lined up at the doctor's tent. The twisting, climbing road toward Murfreesboro
took its toll. As they climbed even higher the temperature
dropped. Some who had no warm clothing were helped by the
ones who did, but there were too many in need. The emigrants
in the covered wagons were better equipped to endure the
cold weather and had now become used to the swaying
bumping travel.

Dark clouds scudded over the sun at noon and skies
turned murky grey as the cavalcade reached the summit of a
hill overlooking Murfreesboro. One more steep incline, then
down into town.

White Fox, as usual, led their wagon on horseback, and
called back to Aiku, "Look ahead, we may be in for snow."

"Freezing weather may halt the sickness. That's good."

"Here comes Elk. What ho?" The big man rode up beside
them.

"A wagon just went over the side of the cliff back about a
half-mile. The whole train must stop while it's pulled up."

After a half-hour's wait, the wagons started up again,
creaking as the oxen and horses struggled to climb one more
hill, then they must brake for the descent.

Aiku was followed by Okema, then by Tsika and Roper. They slowly started the down-grade trip. Okema's wagon responded to his pull on the horses reins, then suddenly the wagon bumped into the rear of his horses and they reared. It gained speed with each bump and finally, to avoid crashing into Aiku, he ran into the cliff on the right side of the road.

Tsika screamed when he crashed, but unable to stop, she continued to descend, the momentum carrying her down the steep slope. The rest of the procession continued to by-pass the accident on the narrow winding road.

Fox and Big Elk galloped back to assist Okema, who jumped off unharmed. The three men pulled Rena and the two boys from the tipped wagon, then reached in for Bertie, Kim and the baby Marci. All were frightened, dazed and bruised, but the only casualty was Jo-Jo, who had a broken arm.

Then six men with the aid of the oxen, that were sorely gashed by the jagged rocks, managed to pull the wagon upright and back on the road. One side was splintered, the canvas was torn and an axle and a wheel were broken.

The spare wheel from below the wagon was in good shape.

One soldier, feeling particularly generous, said, "Have the blacksmith bend the metal bar from the supply wagon for the axle. Our supplies are so low, we don't need it now."

So the job was done, and now they brought up the rear with thirteen soldiers.

Tsika took Jo-Jo into her wagon again, and at the foot of the hill, camp was set up. The doctor erected his tent and began to treat the foot-weary sufferers. When she took the boy in Okema went along.

After the wrist was set, he gave Okema some white powder, saying, "This will help."

"I recognize it, doctor," Okema said. "It's called Kinnikin-nik. I'm Shawnee."

"Yes, I use it on occasion. I was given it by a doctor, who lived for a time with the Shawnee tribe."

"There are so many going to the doctor, he will never get to look in on the children," Tsika told Rena.

"We can try. I'll stand in line and ask him if he will come over when he gets through here."

Tsika limped as she left the rear steps.

"Are you all right?"

Tsika laughed, "Yes, just weary bones from rough roads, Rena, but I'm grateful every day for this kind of soreness instead of the kind I felt in prison."

"How's Niamhi doing?"

"Not well, but she never complains. I get provoked at my mother's and Greta's groaning about trivial discomforts at times and snap at them, thinking of Tani and little Robin."

"I know. I wish we could help them."

"Surely the doctor will come by tonight."

"You're caring for them, also Jeff and Hopping Rabbit?"

"No, now only Tani during the day, and Micha drives our wagon. Oh! Look, here comes the doctor."

"And what might be amiss among the elite?" he asked.

Tsika resented his snide reference to their covered wagons and snapped, "The same troubles that come to the others."

He looked directly at her from tired eyes. "No offense meant. Guess I'm worn out."

Tsika shrugged. "So are we all, weary of the whole trip." Then she checked her anger. "I know you can't help our situation or our weariness, but we've been waiting so long for your visit."

He poked and tapped, looked in ears, noses and throats and said, "Looks like measles."

"The children are worse. We've tried willow bark for fever and wintergreen for stomach cramps, and when our remedies produced no results, I began to worry about cholera."

"It's true we have some cholera. The people who were penned up in filth for so long came down with it. Just you be careful not to eat the same food or drink the same water or milk."

"How can we do that if it's all dispensed by the government and comes to us by the same supply wagon?"

He shrugged and threw his hands up, "Just be careful. The children will no doubt have a rash in a day or two."

"Then I'll know what to do. Comfrey tea helps."

At that moment Tani had a coughing spell.

"I'll see that little lady as long as I'm here."

"No need, Doctor," Tani gasped. "I'm all right."

"I'll take a look at you anyway." He took a packet from his case. "Give her one of these powders every two hours and have her rest as much as possible." He smiled. "It's a mixture of mullein, sage and lobelia. Steep it. You see I've learned to respect Indian remedies."

The doctor motioned Tsika to step outside the canvas wagon. "The young lady is desperately ill with tuberculosis, the lung disease that kills."

"I suspected it," said Tsika. "What else can we do?"

"She needs rest. Can you take the children to your wagon?"

"Of course."

She took Owl and Hopping Rabbit to the Wolf wagon. Although Star and Niamhi weren't able, Greta would care for them.

It was ironic to be caring for Aiku's wife, but to Tsika's surprise she was doing it out of sympathy for the girl, and not to repay for the days in hiding in Aiku's home. And she had become very fond of Tani.

After she took Tani a meal of stringy meat stew and some corn bread, she sat around the camp fire with the other women discussing their progress.

"It's maddeningly slow," said Rena. "We'll all be ill before we can even get to Nashville to get more supplies."

"Maybe there's something to be had at Murfreesboro."

"It's too small, Tsika. It's only a crossroads."

"Why do you suppose we've run out of food so soon?"

"Someone probably didn't know how to plan for so many people, and—"

Suddenly, there was a scream and a shout, and they heard Elk call, "We're coming."

Then there were pounding hoof beats and sounds of sobbing.

As Tsika jumped up ready to find out what was happening, Roper road by shouting, "A damned soldier raped a negro girl up there," and pointed to a stand of fir trees ahead.

"I'm going over there." Tsika started to run.

She met Aiku carrying the girl to his wagon. "She's calmed down now," he said.

"Oh, my God, it's my Nilla. Where was she riding?"

"Not riding. She's a slave. She was walking."

"Oh, I'm glad you're taking care of her. What can I do?"

"Go back to your wagon!" An expression of fury darted from his black eyes. Then in a kinder voice, he added, "She'll be all right. She can help you with Tani and the children later."

"Yes." For a moment, their eyes locked in an expression of mutual desire. Then thoughtfully, she went back to her wagon.

In the morning frost was in the air and a light snow was falling. What would the next few days bring? More food, more supplies or just more snow?

Bundled in wool coats and snug caps, Tsika and Missy climbed onto the driver's seat. "Put the blanket around you, Missy." Then she called to her passengers, "Is everyone set inside? They're ready to go."

"Mama, when will we get to the Ohio River?"

"Who can tell, Missy? Fox thought we'd reach Nashville tomorrow and it's many miles to the north from there. It depends upon how well the wagons do and what repairs are needed."

Each man, woman and child had his assigned place and the procession started. Toward evening two days later, Aiku's wagon lost a wheel and the horses slid to a struggling stop on the icy road. In succession several others then skidded into a ditch and one in the rear fell off into a deep ravine. Rescue operations began, but they were held up for a day making repairs.

When the doctor made his rounds again he said, "It was one of the two cholera wagons that crashed to the bottom of the ravine and all except one of the six passengers were killed."

He sounded sympathetic, but those who heard him felt he was relieved for them and himself, for he could do nothing for them in their extreme suffering.

Along with the dysentery and rashes that plagued everyone, the constant complaint to the doctor was of stomach pains.

"Relieved of their guns, the men have gone into the woods with their bows and arrows to hunt for deer," Tsika told him.

"We'll wish them luck. I hope the supply will be plentiful enough to feed many."

Roasted on a spit over the fire the tantalizing odor brought a crowd of emigrants to the few cooking fires that were blazing. The women cooked roots and herbs for a stew to stretch the meat and feed as many as possible.

There were five deer for so many. Tsika couldn't wait to taste the lovely food, but at the same time shed tears for the many who still had to do without. Each small family group tried to supplement the inadequate government supplies, so some managed to survive the hunger pangs.

At her first opportunity, Tsika went to Aiku's wagon to check on Tani and talk to Nilla.

"I'm so sorry, Nilla." She hugged the girl. "I didn't know you were on this trip or I'd have had you join us."

"Oh, Miz Dolan, now I know what you went through at the big house. It was horrible." Then she smiled, "But now I help Tani."

"That's good, and in turn you're helping me. Tell me about Manda and Benji."

Her white teeth shone in the black face and her eyes

sparkled. "We outsmarted them Georgians, we did. We hid in the woods 'til they left, an' then went to Tennessee."

"But you're here."

"Yassum. I'se here. I tried to get to your mother's an' they put me in the stockade."

"Well, I'm surely glad you found us, though it was not the easy way."

"With all those 1,000 people, it was hard and when I finally saw where you was, that's when—the soldier—"

"We'll be thankful. Now I'll visit with Tani for a few minutes then I must get back to the children."

That evening as wind clouds collected, the skies scowled with a promise of snow. Fox turned up his coat collar and hurried to the Captain's tent to voice the people's complaint.

"Captain, many of these people can't go any farther without adequate food, warm clothing and rest. Could several of your men go ahead to Nashville with the supply wagon and bring supplies back here to them?"

"No, we have to keep moving, Fox. Look at that sky. It means snow, and while we're still in the mountains it could mean trouble."

"I know, but—"

"Get back to your wagon. You're protected. What are you worrying about?"

"The others—"

The captain turned away, lit a lantern, proceeded to take a paper from his packet and handed it to Fox. "See this! Orders to be in Ft. Girard to cross the ol' Miss by November 1st. We'll never make it if we don't move. We should be doing 20 miles a day and we're way behind schedule. Wagon breakdowns, illness, funerals."

Fox shrugged. Was there no compassion in the man? He felt compelled to remark, "There'll be more funerals if they can't have something to eat and wear soon."

At dawn as usual came the galloping trooper with orders to "Move on."

Tears froze on Tsika's face as a cold wind whipped snow at
the travelers. Even in the covered wagons there was illness and
suffering. How could those in the open wagons and on foot
bear it? She shivered. There were bloody footprints in the
snow.

She worried about Niamhi's weakened condition and Star's
heart and she worried about Little Grey Bird and Elno. They
were so ill. Perhaps at Nashville, when supplies were purchased, things would be better. *I must be optimistic, like Missy.*

She was told the soldiers had forgotten Scott's orders to
treat the emigrants kindly. At times the whips were not only
used on the horses and oxen. Tears again. *Oh, it was all so
hopeless.*

Micha rode up beside the wagon. "Let me spell you for
awhile, Tsika."

Gratefully, she climbed down as he tied his mount to the
rear of the wagon. It would be good to get inside and relieve
Greta and Missy of their nursing duties.

"How are the little ones, Greta?"

"Quiet, which is more alarming than crying and coughing."

"In Nashville the doctor will get more medicine."

"I hope it's in time. Grey Bird's cough is so harsh."

"He's got the croup, Tsika," claimed Star. "Just give him
some of that wintergreen or comfrey. That should help."

"Mama, that was gone some time ago." She glanced at
Greta and whispered, "Forgetful?"

"Then try Niamhi's steeped mullein, sage and lobelia."

"Niamhi's is all gone too, Mama."

Finally the long line of sad, emaciated emigrants reached
the edge of Nashville and set up camp. Even in a protected
spot at the foot of a hill, in the lee of the wind, the wind
swirled snow into the wagons.

There was dire need for food, warm clothing, boots, shoes
and woolen hats, mittens, socks and blankets, so four of the
soldiers accompanied the mounted leaders into Nashville for
supplies. The rest of the militia were to remain in camp, but as

soon as their superiors had left, they too left for town.

The people built fires to keep warm and heat the sparse bits of food left. Carefully they apportioned most to the children, then went back to their wagons.

After Star and Niamhi had been settled for the night, Tsika asked Greta, "Where has your spark of humor and your light-heartedness disappeared to, little sister?"

"Mama," said Missy, "how dare you be so personal?"

"Greta doesn't mind. We've always been frank and honest with one another, but, granted, we're not dignified Indians."

"Everyone can't have your optimism, Tsika," Greta snapped.

"It's not just optimism you've been lacking. You look the other way whenever Okema comes in. Are you in love with him?"

"You think you're perceptive? I care nothing for a man who prefers a woman almost twice his age."

"Rena?"

"Who else? Both Okema and Elk are making fools of themselves, vying for her attention." Tears came to her eyes.

"Why, Greta, you surprise me. You used to fight for what you wanted. Do you want him?"

She sniffed, "It's such a crazy time for this. Everyone is suffering from lack of food; there's illness and death, and here I am falling in love."

Tsika placed her arm around her sister. "It's not a bad time to fall in love, Greta. At a time like this, a person's true nature comes forth. You know what stuff they're made of."

She thought of Aiku's expression when he ordered her back to the wagon.

Greta wiped her tears and smiled, "You know, I believe she loves neither the bachelor nor the widower. She loves Fox, but with Samantha's death in childbirth and Bits to care for—"

"That would surely be a repeat. Poor Elk. He was so in love with Laura when Fox married her. Now he loves Rena and she loves Fox. It's a strange world. I believe I'll go over and talk to Rena. She might say something about Okema. Do you mind?"

"Of course not. Just don't say anything about my feelings."

"I won't, dear."

"Rena, would you like a visitor?" she called at the canvas flap. "It's Tsika."

"Come in. I was just getting the children settled for bed."

"I'll help. Maybe our stop here will give us a chance to catch up on some much needed rest. Where's Okema?"

"Helping the blacksmith shoe a horse. You want him to help you with something?"

"No, I just wondered. He's usually here."

"Well, the wagon belongs to him and Elk, so they're free to come and go. I do the cooking and care for the children. They tend to the repairs, drive and such. You know that. What is it Tsika? Something's on your mind besides rest for the weary."

Tsika looked embarrassed. "I don't do very well hiding the purpose of my visit, do I?"

Rena laughed. "No, and I believe I know what you're thinking. I thought when Charles died, I'd never in my life care for another man. But—well, you guessed it. I'm in love."

Suddenly horses whinnied, there were shouts and a sound of galloping hooves. Men at the camp were alerted, as were Rena and Tsika. They looked outside and saw lighted torches blazing and men riding, rounding up their horses, then the young Cherokees followed the thieves. She knew nothing more about Okema.

Shots heard in the distance were of deep concern, until the men returned with twelve of the fifteen stolen horses.

"What about the horse thieves?" Fox called to them.

"They got what they deserved," Aiku answered. "One was hung."

Fox turned to his friend. "Elk, that seems a bit severe."

"They got carried away. That's what happens when people take the law into their own hands."

"I'll bet we haven't heard the last of this."

"Maybe not, Fox, but we can't be blamed in a situation like this. A horse is mighty important to any of us."

"Agreed. It could be a factor in whether we live or die."

"Right. If we get short of food, we can eat 'em."

"Elk, you wouldn't. Not your favorite, Roger."

"Oh yes I would, and from what I've heard from up front, if we can't get a good supply at Nashville—"

"We'll get enough."

"I'm not so sure. How much food will it take to feed almost 1,000 people in the next sixty days? Remember our jerky and corn is all gone. We're staring hunger in the face."

"We'll be able to reach Galconda and find more there."

"You're more optimistic than I. Somehow I think I'd like to be one of those twelve men who escaped into the woods. At least they'll have clean water and uncontaminated food."

"They won't catch cholera there, but wintertime is a bad time to be hunting food in the wilds."

Tsika's frantic call for help interrupted their immediate speculations.

"Micha, go for the doctor. Little Bird is choking."

"On my way," he shouted, and he hurried off.

"It's a matter of constant vigil for the women. When one cries, the rest awaken and cry either from hunger or illness."

Tsika was thinking the same thing. When Star and Niamhi became worse, it became more difficult to attend to the children. Tomorrow she must take them back to Rena or Tani and let Bertie or Nilla care for them.

She rocked Grey Bird in her arms. Why must the children and the elderly be the first to suffer? Suffer because the whites wanted to settle in Georgia and Tennessee. She felt an ache around her heart that wouldn't go away. Suddenly the child gasped and was silent.

The missionary was offering prayers for five others who had died, so Fox offered to say a few words at the gravesite. The sad message was short. "Great Spirit of our ancestors, take this small soul to join his parents and be blessed by thee."

He expressed the feelings of the group.

Police rode in from Nashville to question about the hanging of the horse thief. There were some tense moments, until the captain convinced them no one would confess, and all of the emigrants couldn't be arrested.

After the burials in shallow graves at the foot of a hill, they moved to their wagons.

The soldiers took half an hour to distribute the food and clothing, then it was "Move on" again.

"Missy is the only cheerful one in our group of wagons. How she remains so optimistic when she feels as weak and miserable as the rest of us is a miracle," said Tsika entering the wagon with Greta.

"Maybe it's love."

"At almost thirteen? I doubt it."

"You were in love with Aiku at that age."

Tsika smiled. "I suppose it's not to be ignored."

She felt uncomfortable talking about Aiku, even to Greta. Or was she afraid to express aloud what was edging into her consciousness; that she was thinking of him more and more.

She quickly changed the subject. "Hopkinsville is next, then hopefully across the Ohio River and safely on our way to Jonesboro, Illinois."

"Yes Tsika, travel is safer to discuss than our personal feelings," Greta smiled. "And I'll be glad when we reach Springfield, Missouri, and will start in a southern direction."

"You guessed."

"I know you pretty well, big sister."

They hugged. "We'll make it through and make new lives for ourselves. I know it."

Greta nodded. "We'll have to face another day of sleet and cold. Climb up."

Fox stopped in that evening to visit the women and Micha. He reported, "There are five more deaths from cholera, two from gangrene and a woman and three children were killed when their wagon lost a wheel and turned over on them."

"It never ends."

After he left, Star said, "Does he always have to tell us the bad news?" She started to cough. *"Will* it never end?"

Gaunt and weak, Niamhi, who was seated on a box across from Star, and had been quiet during the conversation, now offered her sage advice. "Probably not, but we can pretend we're in the West already and sing. Come Star, sing along with me."

Grey braids swinging beneath her head band, she began to hum a melody known only to her.

"Grandma, sing the Cherokee song your parents taught you."

"The one when things looked hopeless?"

"Yes, that's the one."

In her weak cracked voice, Niamhi started to croon.

> *"We're but sun or wind or rain,*
> *Fleeting, gone as we in pain,*
> *Sent to nourish our good earth,*
> *To bring about a good rebirth.*
> *But enjoy today, my child,*
> *It beckons you to fields and wilds.*
> *Nature's bounties yours to hold,*
> *And love will all of you enfold."*

Tsika had to turn her head to hide her tears.

"Come on, sing, Greta, Mama," Missy urged. "Grandma needs you."

The child could see what adults shut out, the encouragement that comes from group participation—in everything— even in a sad little song of long ago. It would help them to survive. During the night, Niamhi quietly slipped away. In the morning when Tsika made her rounds to check on each family member, the little grandmother was cold. Tsika kneeled to pray.

Star seemed to know. She awakened immediately saying, "She's gone." She was dry-eyed.

Tsika nodded.

Then tears came and Tsika rocked Star to and fro in her arms. She looked so pale, Tsika shed tears not only for Niamhi, but for her mother. She knew Star couldn't live much longer.

Star sobbed, "And we sang her song as we parted."

"Yes, Mama, I believe we made her leaving us a little easier for her. She's at rest."

"What's wrong, Tsika?" Greta asked, wakened by the sounds of their conversation.

"Niamhi's gone. She slept away peacefully." Tsika wiped her eyes.

"I can't grieve," said Greta. "She suffered so and was so patient through it all."

"I know, she was a strong lady," Tsika smiled. "She told me her warrior husband would strike his chest and say, strong squaw here, and have many papooses here, and rub his stomach."

"Yes," added Star. "Niamhi and he had Great Wolf, then he went off to war and was killed." She grimaced and grew paler. "Oh! Oh!" She clasped her chest.

"Lie back, Mama. I'll get your medicine."

Tsika felt inside the deerskin medicine pouch and frowned. Only one pill left. She gave it with water to her mother.

Greta nodded, "I know. What do we do when they're gone?"

"Wait for supplies to come and hope the doctor can get something to help her."

"Maybe we could find some herb that would help until the doctor can get something. Oh, dear, Niamhi'd know what to do."

"I'll try to find some foxglove. Steeped, the leaves exude digitalis. But here? In the winter under the snow?"

"I'll go with you, but I don't even know how it looks."

"I do. It has fuzz on the underside of the leaf. It would be all dried up now. I guess it's hopeless."

"Oh Tsika, if it were only any other season but winter, we could search the woods and fields for greens, buds, flowers, all edible: new green leaves of dandelions, pig weed, nettles, wild lettuce, berries, nuts and even the sweet sap from the inner cambium bark of the pine and birch trees."

"Stop it, Greta! We can't, so forget it!" Then her face brightened. "If the soldiers would give us enough time perhaps we could dig deep enough to find dried roots to grind for flour instead of using the weevil-infested cornmeal."

"I'd settle for frozen roots or bulbs today."

"Grandmother used peppery tiger lily bulbs, licorice root, wild onion, garlic, salty colt's foot and lemony sorrel, all good for flavoring the stringy beef we get for rations. I'll start looking for some of those. I used to help her find them."

"Or we could use them to add to the wild game or fowl the boys may bring from their forest search."

"They keep trying and we should too, though there's never enough to go around."

"Look, I found some wild sweet potato roots. Look beside the marshy area. Maybe you can find some lily bulbs."

Returning to camp somewhat encouraged, they prepared to grind the roots.

Missy greeted them. "Ah, a good dinner tonight."

"Dare you be funny at a time like this?"

"Yes. Mama, you're too pessimistic lately."

Tsika smiled. "Perhaps it's because I'm hungry."

"Owl and I will go to the stream and catch you some fish. That should help." She grinned, kissed her mother, and ran to the Fox wagon.

Ears flopping, Aiku's big black dog bounced up to her. "Come on Chien. Let's get Owl and go fishing."

He followed her into the wagon. She asked Bunny, "Where's Owl?"

"Gone to help Okema fix a wheel."

"Oh, then I'll just take his fishing rod and you tell him I'm down by the stream."

She turned to the dog. "Come on Chien."

But Chien had other plans. He looked at her with sad eyes and headed in the opposite direction. Missy started for the woods.

At the camp outside Hopkinsville, camp fires were lit for warmth and in the hope that the men would bring some wild life from their hunt to cook with the roots. Tsika was stirring a pot of rabbit and some unknown creature Okema said was good for the blood. They all questioned it but anything was better than the last government meat.

They heard a scream and Tsika, immediately aware of Missy's promise, shouted, "It's Missy, at the stream."

Owl ran from the Fox wagon, and by the time Tsika had reached them, she saw Aiku pull a soldier up from Missy, who was lying on the ground. Aiku stabbed him, then ran into the woods.

Tsika ran to her hysterical daughter and hugged her. "Missy, are you—did he—?"

"I'm all right, Mama," she hiccuped. "Just scared. What if Aiku hadn't come. Oh, Mama, he—"

People collected, soldiers surrounded them.

A sergeant bellowed, "What in hell's going on here?"

"He—he—" Tsika pointed to the dead soldier, "attacked my daughter."

The sergeant pulled Tsika to her feet. "You're under arrest for killing a guard."

"Owl pushed through the crowd shouting, "I killed him."

"Ha!"

"No," Missy shouted. "I did it."

"I laugh even louder. Where'd the woman hide the knife?"

The captain approached them. "I'll take over here."

The sergeant shrugged, then saluted.

"Break it up! I warned you young bucks to leave the Indians alone." Then he turned toward the women. "And you, get back in your wagons and stay there. What can you expect when you run around half-naked?"

Tsika ached to snap at him, "What other clothes did you provide?" but held her tongue. So much worse could have happened if the captain hadn't come.

The captain said, "The search is on. I know who killed him. I'll get the damned Red."

Several soldiers searched through the night, and by dawn, marched in with Aiku, a rope tied around his neck.

He was tied to a tree. Crack! Crack! The sound of twenty lashes descending on Aiku's back cut through the frosty air. Some watched in horrible fascination; others covered their ears; still others cried.

Tsika wept as the leather whip came down again and again. She prayed, "Stop, stop. He can't stand that."

He didn't cry out, but fainted before the last lash.

He sagged on his ropes, and they left him, saying, "You'll get over it, and when you come to, we'll shoot you."

Fox and Atta lowered him to the ground, cut the ropes and carried him to the wagon. There they bathed his lacerated back, bound his wounds and spirited him away.

When the soldiers returned, they searched the two wagons, and when this was to no avail, one bellowed, "We'll find him, he can't get far in this weather. We can trace him in the snow."

Half the soldiers dispersed into the woods. The other half moved the caravan forward to the Ohio River and Golconda.

On the second day the searchers caught up with the train and reported no sign of Aiku. On the road some of the people dully followed as usual, bleeding feet and stomach cramps slowing them. In their emaciated condition, they cared not whether they reached the river.

When word reached them that they would receive food and clothing, sheer will propelled them forward, to fall exhausted into a snowy field across from the river town.

By dawn the following morning, the horses and oxen were hitched to their wagons and ready to cross the ice-covered Ohio River. In some spots where the water was turbulent, a thin sheet of ice said, "Beware," and the wagoners searched for a safe place to cross, but narrow bridges accommodated some of the small conveyances and pedestrians.

Some of the more courageous or foolish tested their manual dexterity by hopping across ice floes near the rapids. To the young boys this was a sporting challenge. Bunny joined the venturesome and fell, hitting his leg on a sharp floe, and slipped into the freezing water.

At his scream and the shouts of the other boys, Atta jumped in to rescue him, calling, "Hang on." Good God, he muttered to himself. Let nothing happen to that boy!

Since Aiku was gone and Tani was ill, responsibility for their children lay heavily on his shoulders. Clothing freezing on their bodies, he carried Bunny to the wagon. A painful, swollen knee told him the boy's injury was serious.

Tsika called, "Bring him to our wagon, Atta," and ran for the doctor. "He's in terrible pain."

Later Nilla could care for him, but now she and Atta would have to take Aiku's and Tani's places. She pulled the wet clothes off and covered him with a blanket. He was made as comfortable as possible. It was Star she was worried about.

Her mother was rapidly losing strength. A chill shook the frail body and she wrapped Star in another blanket. Now there were no tears. They were spent four days ago at the time of Niamhi's death, when she knew Star couldn't live much longer.

Some of the wagons were moved to the far bank. The doctor's visit was delayed, for he had saved a three-year-old girl when a wagon went through the ice and her parents were drowned.

On arrival, he immediately said, "It's not serious; the knee is dislocated. I'll give him a dose of laudanum, and when it takes effect I'll need your help." Still the same gruff man.

The boy was crying. "What should I do for Bunny?"

"Bunny, that's a nice name, young man. You're going to be brave for me, aren't you? You'll be walking again in no time."

The boy nodded slowly. The drug was taking effect.

"Now," said the doctor, "hold his arms down. I'll pull."

It took one jerk; there was a dull thud, and quickly, he wrapped a tight bandage around the knee.

"Now," he said. "I'll take a look at your mother, then I must get into town to pick up some medical supplies. The soldiers have gone to replenish the food and clothing. The women will be starting their cooking fires."

He bent over Star and pronounced her better. Both he and Tsika knew her condition was one which couldn't get better, only worse, and it was a kind way of addressing the patient.

A look of deep understanding darted between them.

He looked into her dark eyes. "I admire your stamina and courage, young lady." He smiled, showing even white teeth.

His candor surprised her and his smile, even more so. He looked younger without the strained frown. He was a nice looking, tall man, who reminded her a little of Sean. Funny, she hadn't noticed before. He was about forty and prematurely grey.

"I hope the young man, Aiku, gets along well in the wilderness. He looked capable."

The man was very perceptive. How did he know she was so concerned about Aiku?

He seemed to read her mind. "I saw you praying at the time of his punishment."

"Oh, yes," she admitted, dreamily. "I'm worried about him."

Suddenly he asked, "How's his wife doing?"

That brought her back to reality. "She's holding her own." Did he think she forgot Aiku was married?

"Now, I'll check your mother," he said abruptly.

He was caring, but disconcerting. Was he interested in her? What was his purpose in asking about Aiku?

On leaving, he took both her hands in his and pressed them. "Your mother is very ill, my dear. I hope you will hang onto that courage. It will be best for her, you know. And as for Bunny, he'll be hopping around in a few days."

Yes, he was caring, but hard to understand. He didn't go to other wagons. The people had to come to him no matter how sick. She reached in her pocket for a gold coin.

He shook his head. "No, my dear. You'll need that when we get to the West. By the way, my name is Elias Swan."

Tsika thought, "My dear!" It's as though he thinks I'm a child. I'm almost his age. But she thanked him.

He had a strange effect on her. He made her feel calm—calmer than anytime since Aiku had left; optimistic that he'd live—that they'd survive. Suddenly a weight seemed to be lifted from her shoulders. Elias Swan. Even his name sounded peaceful, and she hadn't even bothered to call him by name.

Anyway she had no time for worry or wonder. There was noise and confusion. Elno was crying, Greta was tired, Missy brought the tiny three year old, Leah, to their wagon. Surviving the icy bath in the Ohio River, she was now happily chewing on the last piece of jerky. Thankfully, Bunny still slept and Tsika went to sit beside her mother.

That night Star's breathing became labored; even digitalis didn't help and, true to Dr. Swan's prediction, she weakened rapidly. She had succumbed to the rigors of the trip; the cold, dampness, confusion and constant jolting; all adding to the burden of an already damaged heart.

Tsika held her closely, gently rocking her to and fro. "You'll feel better in the morning, Mama," she soothed.

"No, my daughter," Star was alert. "One by one we older ones go to make room for the younger ones. God grant they survive.

"That's like you, thinking of others, but you're not old."

"No, just tired—so tired." Her voice drifted to a whisper. "So—so—" It was like a dry leaf floating to the brown earth.

"I have the children quieted," Missy whispered. "Now let me sit with Grandma."

"I—I can't leave her, Missy. Thank you—"

"Then I'll sit with both of you. I can't leave you alone at such a sad time. I'll be quiet so the others can sleep."

Tsika nodded. "You're such a comfort, Missy. I couldn't have made this trip without you."

Missy sniffed. "I miss Bethy and Danny, but I'm glad they're not here and I am."

"Yes, so am I."

"Owl and I will take care of you, when we marry, Mama."

"Oh Missy, you—"

Star stirred, gasped once for breath, then her frail body jerked in a final death-spasm and she was gone.

Tsika leaned her head against her mother's dark braids. "She's at peace now."

"She suffered for so long. I think it was something besides her heart, Mama. It's best, you know."

"Yes, I know. It's just that I feel a part of my life has been cut away. Except for Arapho, I'm the oldest one in the family now."

"I wonder if they made it safely to the West on that river route," Missy mused.

Already they were thinking of the living. That was good.

Seven had died during the night and early morning hours, so, as the first rays of sun streaked the eastern skies, the emigrants buried their loved ones. The last rites performed, family and friends bid farewell to Star in cold southern Illinois, so far from their hilly woodland home.

"Move," came the starting call, and again the cavalcade was on its way, but this time it was through swamp lands on narrow roads and across streams over rickety bridges. It was surprising they bore the weight of the large covered wagons.

The Elk-Okema wagon stopped in the middle of the first bridge. The Wolf wagon followed it, waited for it to continue, and when there was no movement, Tsika jumped down, and went around it. There, on the narrow road, Greta and Okema stood in close embrace, Okema placing a firm kiss on Greta's willing lips.

A grin on his moon-shaped face, Jo-Jo held tightly to the reins and shouted, "Whoa, whoa."

Tsika laughed. "You two love-birds, get off the bridge before it collapses."

Their faces were wreathed in smiles. "Jo-Jo approves and Okema will shoot a buffalo to prove his love for me."

You two! You're in a dream world. Ride with him all the way to Ft. Gibson if you want, but move now."

She returned to their wagon, shaking her head. "You won't believe this, Missy."

"Oh yes, I will, Mama. I told Greta she could capture her Shawnee if she told him about Wolf's buffalo hunt; that she knew all about scraping skins and because of that would make a good squaw," Missy giggled. "He finally got the message. Of course, he loves her for other reasons. He just hadn't realized it; she had to show him the way."

"Missy, you're wise beyond your years. Did you use the same method on Owl?"

"I didn't have to. He said he's known he would marry me ever since he came over to Grandma's to see us when—when Papa was shot and—and you were taken to prison."

Tsika nodded. "That was a bad time. Worse, far worse than this, Missy. Here, at least, we have fresh air."

"And now that we'll be on the prairie soon, we'll have game to eat. We'll get along better."

"Yes. Game, good roads, Ft. Girard, but first we must get to Springfield, Missouri and replenish our supplies."

"Owl says that will take at least a week."

Tsika smiled. "Then it must be so." Ah, the confidence and love of youth! "When will the wedding take place?"

"What wedding?" Then Missy laughed. "Oh, not for a long time. Next year maybe."

"What about school?"

"We won't need school. I'm going to help Owl start his own business. Building. There'll be lots in the West. Look at all the people who'll need houses." She spread her arms wide to encompass the traveling emigrants.

"That's an excellent idea, but where will he get the money

for building supplies?"

"His father has some and John Ross will loan him some."

"He has it all figured out, doesn't he."

"Yes, we've planned this for a long time. I'll be the secretary and treasurer."

"Then, by all means, you'll have to go to school to learn accounting. And then, with all your knowledge, courage and optimism, anything is possible."

"Oh, Mama, you make it sound so hard."

"No, only sensible."

When they reached the eastern banks of the Mississippi, it was still bitter cold. There was a long way to go and they were weak, but a new strength of purpose flowed through their veins. Also the scene of activity at the docks inspired motivation.

Steamboats whistled, tug boats honked and keelboats tooted their horns. There was even a steam engine that pulled cars loaded with freight for the boats. Many had never seen such a frightening, puffing monster before and stood well clear of its belching smoke and immense wheels. Others were curious and, after they cut logs for anchors to use under wagons, were anxious to go aboard.

The crossing began. When the Fox wagon was hauled onto the barge, Fox pushed a log against the wheels to keep them from rolling. The barge lurched, one wheel slipped off the edge, the horses reared and Fox was pinned beneath the wagon. Finally the frightened horses were quieted, and after a heroic effort by his horrified friends, the wagon was lifted and Fox was carefully taken to the river bank where Dr. Swan advised how to bear him to the small dispensary. White Fox had fainted from the excruciating pain of a crushed and broken leg.

Rena immediately ran to them. "I'll help you, Doctor." Always calm and efficient, she took his acceptance of her offer for granted and followed him into the tent.

"Yes, sterilize these instruments and get out antiseptic bandages and laudanum," he ordered, gladly accepting her offer.

"May I aid, also?" Tsika asked, coming into the tent.

"Yes, I'll need a man in here as well. Get Micha. He's young and strong. I may have to amputate."

Tsika hurried and almost bumped into Atta and Micha on their way in. "Quick he wants you, Micha."

Swan looked up. "Send Atta out of here. Sons don't help much at a time like this."

"Look, I've got a right—"

"You heard me. Get Okema. If I need another man, I'll want him."

"Will you need the cauterizing iron?" asked Rena.

"Yes, if I amputate, and to cut away some of the flesh or he'll infect."

She worked quickly and efficiently.

To the anxious group waiting outside, the cries from the patient were more than some could bear. Women wept openly and the men bowed their heads. Strong whiskey was all that could be given for pain during any operation. After what seemed an interminably long span of agonizing screams, there was silence.

Finally, Dr. Swan came out wiping his brow, waved his arm in helpless resignation. "I've done what had to be done. Now it's up to Mother Nature, Fox and God to do the rest."

Prayerfully the group dispersed.

"I'm afraid it will be a long time before White Fox is able to get about again, my helpers," he told them. "And then only with the aid of a wooden leg," Swan sighed. "Now he will sleep for a time, then, when we move on and he's transferred to his cot in the wagon, he will be in much pain. Laudanum may help a bit." He gave Rena a supply. "Use it as little as possible."

"Thank you. I'll care for him. Bernie will look after Samantha's baby, watch over Jo-Jo, Kim and Marci."

The pain and discomfort lessened a little each day as the

jolting wagons threaded their way through the towns of Jonesboro, Illinois, then Jackson, Farmington, Potosi, and Rolla, Missouri en route to Springfield.

Here, as well as at other designated stops along the way, leaders, John Benji and George Lowrey, reported their progress to John Ross's detachment wherever it might be on the road.

Many of the people gathered around the post office. John said, "I've sent a report and received one from Ross from Paducah, Kentucky. Quati is ill and they have been advised to go the rest of the way on the rivers. From then on it would be impossible to know where they'd be at any certain time, therefore to cease all communication."

After the period of rest, a supply of food and an issue of clothing, the vast prairie lands of the west beckoned them. The nights were cold, the days cool and the emigrants believed they'd seen the last of snow. Climate these days was of minor concern. Finding game now was of major importance for survival. The last thought was of an attacking Indian tribe.

On the second morning out from Springfield, word came from John Benji, who scouted a half-mile ahead, that he saw a line of Indian braves on a rise on the far horizon. There was immediate action to form a circle, hopefully to frighten the band off and make the Indians think there were many men with guns and ammunition.

Shielding his eyes against the rays of the rising sun, Seeing Far, an Osage chief, saw a large company of Cherokees and decided to lead his braves in an attack against the life-long enemies. Ever since Cherokees had come to Arkansas Territory and taken over Osage hunting grounds, there had been trouble.

He raised his right arm, for a charge, and the small band thundered downhill and onto the plain. Dust rose around them, whirling in such thick clouds, it was hard to tell how many were in the attacking party. War paint streaked their faces, and amidst the war whoops, the thudding hoof-beats and the frightened screaming of the emigrants, it was impossible to hear the captain's orders.

There were gun shots, and the Indians came closer. Still shouting, the captain courageously rode toward them waving a white flag.

The women and children were scurrying for safety beneath and between the wagons. The men were running for their arrows and the soldiers for their guns. Rena, Greta and Tsika watched.

"My God," said Rena, "I thought we'd come to the end of all the trouble, and now this!"

"Maybe if we're taken prisoner, we'll have a good meal before we're killed. Should I wave my shift at them?" Greta's thin once beautiful full face stretched into a grin.

"Greta, how can you joke at a time like this?"

"Why not? We can't help by worrying."

"Oh, look the white flag. Do you suppose they'll observe it?" Tsika asked.

"I don't know. They're Osage. They hate the Cherokees."

"They look surprised. I can't believe what I see. The chief has halted his warriors."

Okema rode over to them. "All's clear. You can come out now. The chief spoke fairly good English. He said to the captain he saw suffering on our faces. He said the Osage warriors would not attack, for there was nothing to take from a tribe so destitute."

Greta grinned. "They're afraid of our great numbers."

"More like afraid of our sickness."

"No Indian is afraid no matter what his tribe, but I think they were sensible."

Tsika grinned. "Then it's the first time."

Everyone young and old fell into a jovial mood after the Osage left. They decided to camp early and Lowrey led some of the soldiers into the hilly section to the east to hunt.

Okema went on, "Ladies, that was an unprecedented act

on the part of a Native American. Never have I heard of any Indian, bent on attack, leaving before he did some damage. It was a peaceful gesture considering the fact that the Osage have resented any Indians settling west of the Mississippi."

"No wonder they came charging down upon us," said Tsika. "They probably thought we were going to take over some of their land. We're going too far west to bother them. Anyway now we prefer farming to the hunting-waring life."

"We still hunt," Okema insisted.

"But we extend a hand in friendship to many," said Tsika. "Didn't we welcome you into our family, Okema?"

"Tsika!" Greta shouted. "He hasn't—"

"Don't worry, dear," said Tsika, purposely misunderstanding her admonition. "We welcomed Okema by taking Jo-Jo under our wings. Now will you watch the children, Greta. I'm leaving to go hunting."

"No you aren't, Tsika," Micha said. "I'll do the hunting for this family."

"All right, hurry, we need venison for our fires."

Greta said, "I'm going over to see Fox and Rena. Coming, Tsika?"

"I'll be along later. I have something to do first."

As soon as they left the wagon, Tsika collected her bow and quiver of arrows, crept to a low hillock behind the wagon, and ran to the stand of willows beside the stream. Then she went through the woods to a small canyon about a mile distant.

Arapho, Juni and Aiku had taught her well. "Tread silently, get downwind, be patient, then get your sight and be quick and accurate."

She saw grouse, pheasant and quail, as she hid in the thicket, but she awaited game. She looked at the sun. It set early in the winter and it was well into the mid-afternoon. She'd wait another two hours, then shoot a fowl if nothing else.

A turkey cock strutted out on a rocky ledge. She lifted the

bow and fitted the arrow against the string. There was a swoosh below to her left, and out of the wooded area of hickory and ash a doe poked her velvety nose. Tsika aimed, then hesitated, for following the doe was a tawny, little spotted fawn. She lowered her bow. She couldn't shoot the beautiful animal and leave the fawn to die.

Just as she laid down her bow, a buck charged out into the open. The doe and fawn fled, she reached for the bow and aimed, but the arrow zinged into a nearby tree. *Damn!* To miss a chance like that, and it was an eight-prong stag.

Philosophically she mused, "Be aware, be watchful." She was not. All right I'll give it one more hour. I'll not go home empty-handed.

She changed her position, wandering farther down into the canyon. Beyond there was a pool where several small animals were apparently alert to something in the water. Also, there was a doe and no fawn this time. This time she aimed carefully and zing, the arrow struck the doe in the jugular.

Never once had she thought how she would get her quarry back to camp. Calling in this wilderness would produce no needed hands. However she called, "Help!" several times, and her voice echoed against the canyon walls.

Dusk came suddenly, and there was nothing to do but dress the animal, hang it on a tree so the night scavengers wouldn't get it, and climb the tree herself to protect it. Her family would worry about her, but that would not be of much concern.

How to protect it, she wondered, as she gutted the animal, washed it out and dragged it to a nearby tree. Many times, she had helped her father prepare a deer or an elk for food and its hide, so she worked almost automatically. Getting it hoisted was another matter. She took the rope from her waist, tied it around the animal's front legs, cut it, then tied the rest to the two back legs and decided a piece of tree branch would make a lever. That wouldn't do. She needed four hands. The only thing she could do, if she was to take her prize home, was to build a fire, sit beside the creature all night and throw stones or oranges at the wolves or coyotes. These predators were stealthy, savage and greedy, but were cowards, and not as vicious as the gray timber wolf. And who was to say one of those couldn't be in the area, or even a pack of them.

At that moment, she heard a wolf howl in the distance. She shivered. Maybe instead of sitting by a fire all night, she'd climb a tree and throw stones from there if one found the meat.

First she went to the top of the cliff to dig up some sweet potato roots she'd found earlier, when she'd awaited her game, then picked some hard Osage oranges to throw at the predators.

It was the longest night she'd spent since her first night in the prison, and just about as uncomfortable, but here she had fresh air and—yes—company. Wolves. There were two. One came first to check out the meat, then called the other. She bounced rocks off their bodies until they retreated. When one sneaked back in the early morning hours, she used the oranges.

Finally at dawn, she heard a call, "Hello, Tsika! Hello, Tsika!" It echoed against the canyon walls. "Hello Tsika!"

"I'm here, here," she scrambled up to the top.

"Dammit girl," said Micha. "You had us all worried sick. We've hunted for you all night. Wolves howled and coyotes barked and a bear growled at us this morning. There are caves in these hills where bears live. We had no idea where you were. I thought you joked about going hunting."

"I'm glad you found me. I'm sorry I worried you all."

He frowned. "You ought to be spanked, even at thirty-two."

"I'm properly chastised. Now let's get along with the butchering. I know a lot of hungry people who will be glad to see this animal. By the way, what did you bag yesterday?"

"I didn't think you'd ever ask. Elk bagged an elk, I got two bucks and Okema shot four turkeys and a wapiti. It has an exceptionally soft skin for the new baby's cradleboard. All in all fifty-two wild animals were shot and some of the men are still out. We'll be ready for a real feast."

"I'm glad you waited for me," she laughed.

"We waited for you to roast them," Attu smiled.

On Tsika's arrival at the camp, Greta tearfully greeted her with open arms. "Oh, Tsika we were so worried about—"

Missy interrupted, "I knew you'd be all right, Mama. You are always able to take care of yourself."

"There were moments when I wondered; when two wolves came to my kill and I was seated up in a tree tossing stones and Osage oranges at them.

"Oh, you didn't!" she giggled. "I wish I'd been there to see that."

"I'm very glad you weren't. Then *I'd* have been worried."

Even Dr. Swan, ever attentive to his patients had left them long enough to welcome Tsika back. There was a hoarseness in his deep voice when he took her hand in his. "I thought you were more sensible than to go off alone, but, since you did, I knew you'd bravely face any danger."

After the compliments were over and Greta's tears were wiped away she laughed, "Okema will want to marry you, Tsika. I can only scrape the hide of a deer. You can shoot one."

"I'll settle for the scraping, Greta," Okema remarked tenderly taking her in his arms. Still a little self-conscious about their new relationship, he blushed as he looked over her shoulder at the group. Then suddenly he shouted, "Look at the clouds of dust. Those are buffalo out there. Let's go after them."

"Okema, work-worn horses and work-weary men could never ride down a herd of buffalo," said Elk, "unless—"

"Unless what?"

"We could ride them over a cliff the way the Sioux do, and it feeds the whole camp for a winter."

"Only trouble there are no cliffs near here."

"Oh, yes there are. I scouted the area over yonder where the buffalo are headed."

"Then let's try our weary horses, or—better yet, borrow the militia's. We'd need their permission anyway."

"They wouldn't trust us with their mounts."

"They would if we let them come along."

"Let them. They wouldn't let us out of their sight."

"Let's ask the captain anyway."

Immediately Captain Benjamin bellowed, "You're out of your minds, men. I'd never subject my men or my horses to such a foolish venture. You have to know how to use a rope and divert the leader from the herd to divide them. You're not Plains Indians. I absolutely refuse your request."

So the herd of buffalo passed by and the Cherokee's mouths watered at the thought of all that good meat traveling north.

"It's just as well," said Fox, when Elk told him of their disappointment. He smiled feebly. "There are even accidents when experienced hunters go after buffalo. As the captain says, we aren't Plains Indians."

"Buffalo stew would taste mighty good," admitted Attu, "but I'll settle for Elk's elk."

Fox rallied. "Get the pot on, son. I'm ready for venison."

There had been time for the children to play games while the men were hunting, but now everyone in camp concentrated on the cooking. The pungent odors of herbs and roasting meat permeated the whole area. It was time to revel in their good fortune and dance to thank the Great Spirit. There were only two tom-toms in the whole camp, but the emigrants made enough noise with the rattles and improvised horns to make up for their lack.

Lafayetteville was the next stop. Then they turned southwest on the final road to their destination, Ft. Gibson and the Three Rivers area: the lush green river valley of the Arkansas, the Verdigris and the Neosho or the Grande Rivers.

Finally the crooked line of willows ahead designated the

winding banks of the Grande River. Waving prairie grasses and cool breezes beckoned them to hurry. The soil looked fertile. Maybe this Western land would not be so bad after all. It was just getting there that was so difficult especially for the ill.

"This is the place where Sequoyah came in 1828 and again with the Treaty Party in March 1837. Remember, he told us how every green thing seemed to grow twice its normal size?" Tsika asked Missy. "I'm going to *make* myself like it. How about you?"

"I'll like it wherever Owl is," she smiled.

How simple youth makes forced decisions sound, Tsika thought. Perhaps I'll be able to do the same, if only we knew where Aiku was. Fox and Dr. Elias Swan said he would survive and I guess I think so too. At least this is better than the drive-on, drive-on existence of the past three months. She smiled, "Yes, Missy, I'll like it too. It will be delightful to lie down under a thatched roof instead of under a moving canvas top of a wagon."

"I heard that," said Greta. "Whose thatched roof? Who'll take bedraggled emigrants in?"

"You're pessimistic, Greta. We'll find a few friends here and just maybe the Western Cherokees will welcome us."

"Don't you believe it. They'll resent us."

"Where's your good sense of humor, Greta? You can't change my optimism. Missy converted me. We'll make ourselves indispensable. We'll build a house and become good citizens of the West. You'll plant and weave and make pottery just like you used to do for Mama, only now you'll get married and keep house for Okema."

"I like that part of your optimism," she smiled.

1839

On entering Fort Gibson there were more Cherokees walking than riding, for so many wagons had met with accidents or had fallen by the wayside in disrepair. Any wagon owners who still had a working vehicle were crowded and uncomfortable because they were sharing with those who needed food and clothing. All were discouraged and the rain that greeted them matched their mood. The travelers found few Western Cherokees to meet them. One fourth of the emigrants in John Benge's and George Lowrey's group had died en route. The travelers disembarked.

"Oh, Tsika," a familiar voice called out, and Sophia Sawyer rushed to embrace her. "It's so good to see you, my dear."

"We look a bit weary I fear, but Sophia, we made it!"

"*Why* did John Ross leave in the fall of the year?"

"There was nothing to do about that," said Greta. "It was a forced migration, you know."

"Yes, and I told you—"

"Now, Sophia," Katherine Brown came over to them. She hugged Tsika. "They must not look back, only forward now."

"Is there a hospital here?" Greta interrupted. "Okema is terribly ill."

"There's a dispensary at Honey Creek, operated by a Dr. Elliot," Sophia said, "or there's an Army doctor here at the fort and a small military hospital, but I don't believe—"

"I'll take him there."

Sophia frowned, then snapped, "Do what you want, but you'll probably regret it."

Tsika smiled. The same Sophia; she didn't like to be twice interrupted.

"Sophia, you haven't changed a bit."

Sophia's blue eyes flashed. "I believe I have mellowed. You know age does that to us."

"Age will never affect you, my dear, and I have a project that will interest you and Katherine."

"How do you propose to propose projects when you don't even have a place to rest your weary heads?"

"Temporarily, we have our wagon?"

"Temporarily, you have my home, Tsika," said Katherine. "I insist you stay with me. Let me pay you back in part for allowing me to live at Riverview when I was sent in tears and fright from New Echota."

"We do thank you Kate, and will do all we can to help."

"Of course, Missy, Greta and your—"

"Both Mama and Grandmother have succumbed to the rigors of the trip. Missy says it is best for them, but I miss them so."

"It must have been terrible for you all. Oh, here comes Missy—with a child?"

Tsika laughed. "Not Missy's. Hardly. Little Leah is three years old. Her parents met with an accident on the trip."

"Hello, Missy. You're a grown lady."

"Yes, Katherine, I grew up on that journey," she said seriously, then grinned. "How do you like my little blond baby?"

Not hearing Tsika's explanation, Sophia gasped, "God *no!*"

Everyone laughed. It was good to be among these friends once more and share in their happiness.

Sophia smiled. "Now I realize the impossibility of Missy's

having this child. And speaking of children, Rena and her family are staying with me for awhile. Also Jo-Jo, if he wishes."

Knowing that Sophia had come to the West at John Ridge's bidding, Tsika couldn't resist asking, "What will John Ridge say to that, Sophia?"

"He built me a school, he gave me a house and furnished it, but he doesn't tell me what I may or may not do. I pay for all his kindnesses by teaching his children and helping Sally. Also the Major and Sarah." Again the blue eyes flashed.

"Don't take offense, dear. I just thought—"

"Well, there is still a great division here, but I don't take part in political doings. I'm my own woman. I took your advice when I went to live at the Ridge home so long ago. I'll never understand John Ross: how he could let you come out here in the winter? But I can't understand John Ridge's Treaty Party either. They're both too stubborn for their own good."

"No political opinions, Sophia?" Tsika laughed.

"Oh, it's good to argue with you again, my girl. You're one of the few people who can challenge me."

"Just where are you living, Sophia?"

"At Honey Creek. You will come to visit me. Katherine is near me between the village of Honey Creek and Park Hill, where some of the Cherokees who came earlier have built houses."

Ever thoughtful of others, Missy asked, "Where will all the other people live before they have their own houses?"

"At the fort, or in other's homes or barns. The soldiers at the fort have orders from the government to feed and clothe them until they can provide for themselves."

"But think of all the others to come. We were the first of the Ross group of 13,000."

"I know," Katherine said. "Believe me, we've given that lots of thought and have planned ahead. In fact some homes have already been started, but of course people have to pay for them. Were many of you allowed to bring any money along?"

"Some of us managed to hide some sewn in our clothes; others were pulled away from their homes and thrown into holding pens before they could rescue anything."

"It will be hard on them unless they can find work to do in the area. Come get into your wagon. We must get you settled in my house, then we'll talk at great length. We have so much to catch up on."

Tsika sighed. Ah, the first good bath in months, and at Katherine's table, the first good cooked-in-a-kitchen meal. She would have to eat sparingly for awhile, for her stomach wouldn't take the good food in quantities.

As soon as the meal of lamb stew and dumplings was done, Katherine asked, "Did Roper come with your party?"

Tsika looked at her friend in alarm. "You're not still in love with him, Kate!"

"Well no, not exactly. A good solid citizen of the Western Cherokee community wants to marry me, but—if Roper's not—"

"He is, Kate. Get married to your Western Cherokee." Then Tsika laughed, "I'm not here an hour and already I'm advising you."

"That's all right. I needed someone to give me a push. He's really a good chief. You'll like him."

"The question is, do you like him as well as love him?"

She nodded, then changed the subject. "What do you think of John's giving Sophia a school and a house?"

"I think he's bribing her with the house, but the school is a fine idea."

"Oh, Mama," complained Missy, "you're always praising schools. Do I have to go, Katherine?"

"Indeed," Tsika asserted. "If you and Owl plan a business."

"They're going to get married?"

"Kate, they're only thirteen. And Missy, it's Miss Brown."

"Yes, Miss Brown, Owl is planning to be a builder and wants to start now. He wants me to help him."

"I'm surprised. Where's Aiku? His father should help him."

"Where is Aiku? That's what we're all asking," said Tsika. "Is he out in the woods somewhere in Kentucky? Has he been captured by some Indian tribe or picked up by the militia? Is he on a river boat? Is he dead or alive? He escaped the soldiers. They caught him and he suffered twenty lashes. They tied him to a tree and told us they'd come back and shoot him when he came to."

Missy interrupted. "He saved me. A soldier tried to rape me."

"Oh Missy dear, and Tsika, what a terrible experience."

"We hope Aiku has managed to survive," Tsika continued. "The weather was so bitter cold, but Fox and Atta say he's immune to hardship. He's a survivor."

"My aunt can take Tani and the boys in," Kate offered.

"Tani is very ill and must go to a hospital, but have her take the boys. Fox has serious trouble with his leg; it hasn't healed since he had an amputation when his wagon slipped off the barge as we loaded to go across the Mississippi. Greta says Okema is terribly ill—they must go to the hospital too."

"Even though he says no, Fox must be worrying about Aiku."

"You're right, but he has faith."

After Aiku escaped the soldiers, who were sent to bring him in the second time, he crawled into the hollow of a tree trunk. Chien guarded him and he slept for fourteen hours. From the exertion of pulling himself from his hiding place, the wounds on his back again began to bleed. He looked for sassafras to clean the wounds to no avail, then settled for moss to stop the flow of blood. Chien caught a rabbit and they ate it raw.

He started to run in a northerly direction as easily and steadily as only a Native American is trained to do. He ran through the forested hills of Tennessee and southern Kentucky with only short stops to snare small game and to eat or rest.

Until the wind whipped the snow against the higher hills,

he had found a sleep-place on the pine strewn forest floor or in the crotch of a tree. Now the freezing nights demanded a search for a more sheltered area.

He saw an old cabin half-hidden in the undergrowth several hundred yards ahead, watched for an hour and when there was no action, he decided it might be abandoned, and he could use it for a short rest.

The faithful dog stood close to him. He rubbed the soft ears. "We're a good pair, aren't we, Chien. First, we catch ourselves something to eat, then rest a bit. All right? Now, we wait in the brush on the hillside."

He moved forward and up-grade for about one-fourth mile, dragging a branch to cover his tracks in the snow. They climbed into a cave-like hollow overlooking an open space where a stream laden with ice flowed sluggishly over the stones. "Now, quiet, we're downwind of any game that comes to drink."

Within the next hour came a doe and a fawn; then in moments there was a crackling of brush, and a strong buck appeared. Aiku crept forward silently, and was almost close enough to strike, when a shot rang out. He heard a yelp. The doe and fawn loped away and the buck charged into the woods and disappeared. Aiku pivoted in time to see Chien drop to the ground, and a few feet away, lowering his gun, was a bearded white man.

Aiku took the situation in at a glance. Chien had come out to warn him. He positioned himself to throw the knife at the man. He had to move quickly before the white man could reload.

The man held up his hand. "Halt, mein fren'. I only came to hunt, not to kill a dog. He got in the way."

He was evidently taken by surprise by Aiku's haunted, wild appearance, and quickly added, "Come to my cabin! Get warm, get some food in your belly." He pantomimed by pretending to place a blanket around his shoulders and patting his large stomach.

Aiku thought, he's frightened. He'll treat the savage kindly, then go for help. But no, the man could have shot him.

Aiku nodded. He couldn't speak, not because he feared the man, but because he felt so devastated about Chien. He followed the burly be-whiskered man to the cabin in the woods.

When he was satisfied the man was alone and sincere in his offer, he warmed up. He looked around the sparsely furnished one-room dwelling and asked, "You live here alone?"

The man registered shock. "Ya, you speak good. What tribe speaks so good English?"

"I am Cherokee. We believe in good education."

Quickly he responded, "From the wagon train, ya?"

"No, I left home when the Cherokees were forced to move. I heard we were to be sent west and I wanted to go north."

"Then you need something warm and boots for the feet," and he handed Aiku a blanket, a pair of cord pants and high boots.

Judging from the expression in his blue eyes and the tightness of his lips Aiku didn't believe him, and the next remark was a message. "Be on your way."

"I have to go by the village for supplies. I be back soon. The hassenpfeffer's in the pot. Eat and rest yourself."

Perhaps the big German was just being kind, but would he go to the police across the river to Galconda? Had the soldiers posted a bounty for runaways from the forced removal groups?

He would not wait to find out. He ate some stew, put on the pants and boots, then picked up the blanket, some bread from the box on the table and left for Cairo. It was definitely not north. He'd get a job on a riverboat going down the Mississippi River to the Arkansas and up to Fort Gibson.

He could cover many miles before the German could get a search party going north. He solemnly thanked the white man for a full stomach, the boots, the warm pants and the blanket, then left with a heavy heart as he thought of Chien.

In the rough river town of Cairo it was difficult to find a job. No one wanted to hire a "Lazy Injun," even though he could speak good English.

Each evening when he passed the saloons on the waterfront, somebody usually came crashing through the swinging half-door to land in the street, definitely not of his own volition. One night he followed a riverboat captain into a saloon and stood nearby as though he was protecting the man. He had but a few minutes to wait for a brawl to erupt.

This time when trouble started there was a voluntary bouncer, who caught the captain's eye. Aiku was small, but had enough strength to throw a larger man, and the captain was impressed. Captain Starr led him from the saloon directly to his steamboat, *River Queen*, and put him to work as a stoker.

"Me man got drunk, got stabbed an' the knifer pushed 'im overboard on the last trip. He's so damn mean, he'll give the fish a bellyache. So yer on. At go, ye stoke; at stop, ye go ashore and cut down trees fer our steam 'n maybe shoot a deer or two. Got to have meat fer the table, y'know. Maybe even shoot a rattlesnake, a real treat."

"I'm not a seaman, sir. I'm a land man."

"So ye'll be larnin'."

He learned to stand up against the roughest, toughest men on the river, and the trip down the Mississippi proved to be a matter of survival. Fights and knifings were daily fare.

When the *River Queen* docked in Memphis and began to unload cargo, a huge box slipped into the water. The two negro slaves responsible were whipped as their owner, a balding, screaming merchant stood by directing the procedure.

A little farther downriver, a pregnant girl who'd followed a dapper gambler to the boat, jumped overboard when rejected.

Otherwise the trip was uneventful, until the boat came to within a mile of the confluence of the Mississippi and the Arkansas Rivers. A severe storm lashed at the *River Queen* and no matter how hard the helmsman tried to keep it on even keel, or how fast the stokers worked, the boat floundered. It was swept quickly and violently amidst thunderous applause from above into a floating log and onto a sandbar by the waves. It shuddered, gave one sudden lurch and, as lightening slashed through the darkened skies and passengers panicked, the boat listed, then began to take on water. They were near enough to the shore to swim.

There were only two lifeboats and when Captain Starr ordered, "Man the lifeboats," twenty-two passengers rushed to fill them.

The women, children and three men were rowed to shore and the rest jumped into the water or waited for another boat to come along and rescue them before they sank.

Suddenly those on shore found they were not alone. War cries and pounding hooves announced a party of Sioux warriors bent on capture.

Aiku had stoked to the last moment, then jumped overboard and swam to shore where he felt the hoof beats on the ground long before the others knew what was happening. He jumped back into the water and allowed himself to drift downstream a ways then, hoping to avoid capture, ran like he had never run. Those who had clamored for seats in the lifeboats now wished they'd remained on the listing vessel. Aiku felt he should go back to aid them, but how could he be assured he would not be in the same danger? He fled into the surrounding woods going west to eventually reach the Arkansas river. It was live off the land again, but he felt trouble and he moved cautiously. Some of the Sioux had spotted him, and lost no time in searching for him.

If only it was dark! Aiku dove into a rocky crevice just wide enough for his slim body, and it was protected by weeds. He stuffed his red blanket beneath him.

One rider jumped his horse across the small depression and as the weeds moved from the motion, he saw a tip of red. The brave jumped down from his horse, and before Aiku could scramble out and use his knife, the Sioux was able to lift him out by his scalp-piece, and shouted, *"Takpe!"*

Aiku knew a few Siouan words and that shout of
"Revenge!" meant death. How he wished he'd shaved his head
like the rest of the boatmen or worn a turban like his brothers.
Damn the red blanket!

Although a captive without a chance to fight, he tried to
strike the brave only to end up with a blow to the head with
the side of a tomahawk. The Sioux could have shot him right
there for *takpe*, but chose to kick him, throw the limp form
over a horse's back and ride away.

Aiku awakened beside a stream with an aching head, bruised
ribs and a bloody face.

He was thrown from the horse. "Wash," a brave ordered in
English, then they spoke in Siouan. He understood part of the
chatter. "No kill. Take to Chief. He loco."

Aiku saw the boat captives at a distance at times, when the
Indians stopped to rest in shifts or roast game they shot. They
looked ragged and forlorn, but most of them were making the
best of a bad situation. The little children and the women cried
at times. Captain Starr and most of the men were brave. Evidently the captives were kept separated from one another
most of the time, probably so they couldn't plan escape. It was
a long tiresome trip to the Dakota Territory.

When the odor of roasting game became too tantalizing to
bear, and Aiku begged for food, he was given a bone to gnaw
on. He presumed the others were given just enough to keep
them alive. But for what? To be tortured for the chief's pleasure? Often he heard a shot. Was it for game or for one of the
party?

The braves rode, laughed, ate and slept. The captives were
hungry, cold and frightened. It seemed impossible that the
prairie grasses could still be green, that the streams could still
flow serenely in the sunshine and the stars and the moon light
the night sky when there were people who were suffering.

The brave's arrival with their white prisoners caused noise
and confusion at the camp, then agonizing days dragged by

while the Sioux squaws danced around their white captives and one by one were tortured to death.

Cherokees were once warlike too, but never had Aiku heard of scenes like this. He was sickened and vowed to do something about it. Up to this point he had acted the imbecile for he'd heard the Sioux either were frightened of them or revered them, and if the former, might turn him out. But no. Maybe magic would work. He asked to see the chief.

He bowed low. "Good Chief, I am a witch doctor of the Cherokee tribe," he said in his best Siouan language. I have magic at my finger tips. May I show you?"

"No, I have Wapia, a sacred healer."

"I can make tall ears appear where there is none and let tied Sioux Dog free."

"Show me! Knot tie Sioux Dog tight."

"I must have my red blanket."

Chief Kettle clapped his hands together. "Bright Sun, bring red blanket!"

Aiku wafted the blanket in front of the dog, saying, "Stay!" while he untied the cord. Aiku hoped his training had resulted in obedience. Then he said, "I must get my knife," and left the chief's tepee.

A boy captive, Rollo, had caught two rabbits barehanded, which had impressed the chief. He said, "He good boy, no weapon," so Rollo was allowed to keep the animals.

Now with his excuse to get his knife, Aiku passed the rabbit hutch, picked up a rabbit, hid it under his tunic and hurried back to the chief's tepee. As he produced the rabbit, he called to the dog, "Come, Sioux Dog." And Sioux Dog came.

On the day Captain Starr was to be brought to the whipping post, Aiku was determined to save him. He had collected a flat piece of dry wood and a sage brush stick for the twirler to start his fire. He had stolen gun powder from the chief's pouch and had sprinkled it from one end of the staked area to the other. Now at daybreak he was ready.

The Indians were gathered in a circle around the stake.

Captain Starr was tied securely. The chanting began and when the braves prepared to torture the man with lighted torches, Aiku stepped forward and held up his hand. The seer Wapia rose, but Chief Kettle motioned him to be seated.

Aiku announced, "If I can produce the magic fire that will travel from one end of the compound to the other, will you allow this man and the others to go free?"

The chief shouted, *"No!"*

Although the Sioux people didn't understand the words, they saw their chief's signal and also shouted, "No! No!"

"Chief Kettle, I will stay and cure your bone illness."

The chief reconsidered and answered, "You have my promise."

Aiku twirled the sage stick on the flat wood, fire flared and he threw it to the ground. The powder caught immediately and the fire traveled at an alarming rate. People scurried out of its way, and soon it arrived at the far end of the area.

They admired the feat, but were fearful. The seer bowed to him and left the scene, relinquishing his position. Chief Kettle clapped his hands in delight; then those remaining at a distance followed his example.

Aiku bowed. The captives surrounded him and wept with gratitude. He untied the captain.

Captain Starr clapped Aiku on the shoulder, saying, "It's a saviour you are. I'll ride ye anytime on me new boat for free."

The captives were supplied with a gun, two horses and some food and told to go on their way. It would be a hard trip, but one that meant freedom. There was mourning for those who had died, but, they had to live for their children and tomorrow.

Aiku went to the fields and woods to collect herbs for the chief's aching bones and swollen joints. Kettle had kept his promise, so even though Aiku was anxious to get away, he should honor Kettle's words. He would remain awhile and hopefully cure the chief's rheumatism.

Tsika said Niamhi used a poultice of comfrey and winter-

green. It was the first day of May. Would the herbs be leafed
out this far to the north? Or would they grow here at all? He
recalled comfrey was a knee-high plant growing pointed leaves
that seemed to grow together and were fuzzy underneath. It
had dark berries and if the plant wasn't grown, the roots would
do just as well. Wintergreen was low and grew everywhere,
with small spear-like leaves and small red spots inside.

Even horseradish root steeped and drunk with apple juice
was warming and helped sore joints. Also along the river, he
cut some willow bark and found jimson weed for fever.

Within two weeks time, Chief Kettle pronounced himself
cured and grateful, but sad because he'd lost his Wapia, his
first healer, sacred man and seer. "You no see what comes,"
he complained to Aiku.

He suggested, "Now you go. Take magic and goddamn
dog. Sioux Dog my dog no more. He follow you like shadow
since you come."

Aiku smiled. He believed Chief Kettle knew he was a fake
magician and wanted him to leave. The chief really was a soft-
hearted fellow but wouldn't want anyone to think so. It would
make him seem weak. No doubt he was cruel in his youth, but
had mellowed with age. Aiku noticed he wasn't present when
the braves tortured their captives.

They grasped one another's arms in farewell and Aiku said,
"Some day I will come back to visit you."

"Better you not come. Young braves not like. Goodbye my
friend."

When he reached the tepee to collect his red blanket and
his few possessions, a young horseholder handed him Dakota's
lead. "I go too," said Istahota, Little Grey Eyes, "I run side."

"Thank you Istahota, but I prefer to ride alone. You thank
the chief for my horse and go back to your parents. Some time,
when you're old enough, you go with me, aye?"

He patted the five-year-old boy on his slim shoulders,
mounted Kettle's parting gift, and trotted to the southeast to
the Missouri River. Sioux Dog happily jogged behind Dakota.

Sioux Dog wasn't like Chien. His hair bristled and his eyes were green, one a bit white, so it gave him a rakish look. He could never take Chien's place, but he was company and he tried to please. He raced ahead when Aiku took him hunting, frightening any wildlife in his path. He needed a little training in that department. It would come later.

Aiku traveled along the Missouri River for several days, forded the Osage River, then headed for the banks of the Arkansas that lie a few miles to the south.

The waving prairie grasses had beckoned him to this spot, a wooded area of low hills leading to the river's bank.

There was nothing to impede his progress thus far, so possibly he became lax about watching for signs.

Ah, here was a good sleep-place. He decided on a rocky cave-like area in the woods. A good place, for it was late May and the former inhabitants were through hibernating. He tethered Dakota to a tree, took his gun from the saddle strap and called, "Come Sioux Dog, we hunt."

Aiku was ready to begin the training, but Sioux Dog didn't charge ahead as usual. He lagged behind at quite some distance.

"Don't you want to go, old boy?"

Then the dog wagged his tail and loped up beside him.

"We're two of a kind. My hair is as bristly as yours and I look a bit like you in the jowls too. Kind of lean and hungry."

Then he started training in earnest. And soon he spotted a deer. The dog behaved well for a beginner, and, after shooting his quarry, Aiku quickly constructed a travois for hauling the deer back to his temporary camp. Sioux Dog loped along very pleased with himself, until they reached to within a few paces of the woods. Then he whined and his ragged ears shot up.

"What is it boy? Stay." Instead of reloading his gun he pulled out his knife and rushed toward the spot where he'd tethered Dakota. Suddenly, he heard the screech of a wild cat, and then a final high whinny and a death scream from Dakota told him what he'd suspected.

He was too late for Dakota, but he threw his knife in an arc at the cat's neck. It made its mark and the bleeding cat turned to attack him. He jumped to the side and the cat fell. He could use its pelt, get a couple others and trade them for a ride up the Arkansas on a flatboat to Fort Smith or Fort Gibson.

Now to collect Sioux Dog and the deer, dress both wild animals and hang them on a tree beside the cave. He and Sioux Dog would guard them well tonight sleeping at the entrance.

He investigated within. The air was fetid. Aiku hurried out into the fresh air, Sioux Dog's bristly hair stood up high on his back and neck and he growled. That should have told him to beware, but, as before he ignored the warning.

He completed his task. After he and Sioux Dog had their good meal of venison, they slept the deep slumber of the weary.

Suddenly the dog growled, rousing him and before he could defend himself a huge claw ripped the back of his tunic from top to hip, batting him out of the sleep hollow.

A quick rolling movement sent him far enough to unsheath his knife and stab at whatever part of the animal's anatomy he could reach without being crushed. He finally gouged a large slit in the bear's neck. The man and the grizzly fought viciously for five minutes. Aiku received a slash from the great claw down the side of his hip through the tough hide pants.

Just as he thought his life was over, Sioux Dog's dust-colored body hurled itself at the beast's foreleg, and with a howl, a swipe from the bear's claw sent him flying through the air. For a fraction of a second the bear seemed to be off-guard and Aiku yelled, "Mahtoh, go away!"

The Sioux name made him hesitate again, and with mouth open, tongue lolling in agony from the wounds, his eyes held an almost human baffled expression as though begging for mercy. Then the bloodied old fellow fell to the earth with a thud.

As Aiku fell also, he thought, So, I die here? Fighting a sick old bear? So far from my destination, yet so close. Did I come all this way only to suffer through the prison and the Sioux camp—to—

Two soldiers from Fort Smith on the Arkansas were hunting on a strip of forest between Osage and Cherokee lands, when they heard war whoops and galloping horses first form one side of them, then from the other. In an open area, beyond the woods to the north, the two tribes met. Shouts, screams, and the whinnies of horses, told the soldiers of the habit of battling, that had gone on since the Cherokees had come across the Mississippi River onto Osage hunting lands.

The clamor finally receded and the silence was as sudden and tomblike as the earlier surprising, wild attack was explosive.

"You think it's safe for us to come out of hiding, Jake? It sounded so close, I hated to think we might be captured by Indians."

"Don't apologize. I was the first to dive into the brush. I wanted to keep my hair too," Jake laughed.

"We'll wait a little longer, then take our quarry to the river and paddle downstream. The Indians won't be moving south."

Private Al Bowen and Sergeant Jake Shean puffed as they pulled the buck along by its antlers.

"We can't move it far this way," said Jake. "You go back to the fort and get help. I'll stay here with Mr. Venison."

"Aye Aye, Sergeant sir."

Al had been gone only moments when he returned. "I heard a whine and look at this." He was carrying a limp, tan wolf-like dog. Half-covered by bloody matted fur on one hind leg was a foot-long gash.

Sioux Dog still whined.

"Put him down. He can wait with me. Go on to the fort."

Jake took out his emergency kit and immediately began to cut the bloody hair away.

He soothed the dog. "There, there, pup. This will hurt a bit." Then he cleansed the wound with alcohol. "When you feel better you'll lick it to heal it."

Sioux Dog struggled to stand up. Still whining, he hopped a short distance on his three good feet, then whined and looked back at Jake, hopped a little further and repeated the performance.

"I'll be damned! You want me to follow you? So be it, but not too far away from my buck, laddie."

Not far from where the soldiers had hidden was the cave, and here lay a huge grizzly bear and a man. The dog nuzzled the man and whined.

"Oh my God! Your master sure took a beating." He immediately stooped to take Aiku's pulse. The dog panted; he looked for all the world as if he smiled.

The man was still alive, but the pulse was weak. On a tree nearby hung two carcasses, a deer and a cat. His buck-rescuing party would have a surprise load.

He smiled to himself. "An Indian, you'd know it. No white man could hold off a grizzly that size. He didn't like Indians much, but he had to give this one credit for doing a good job. But the soldiers better get here soon or this poor, ragged red would be no more. He started to cut down some saplings.

He heard a distant shouting and breathed, "Thank God."

"What a picture you make, Sarge," one of the men remarked.

"No funny stuff, Bill. Get busy, make a travois to carry this poor guy. Gotta hurry."

"You must grant, it's a scene out of a picture book, Jack," said Al. "The two animals hanging on a tree, the man and the giant bear, a dead horse, blood all over."

The Indian wore a head band. There was a scalp lock; both sides of his head that had been shaved had bristly stubbles of hair growing now. His doeskin tunic was torn and blood-stained, the heavy cord pants were ripped and the raw thigh showed through with caked blood on the wound. At least he wasn't bleeding to death. How to carry him all that distance without having the wound open up again would be a problem. Jake bound the thigh.

Then he saw Aiku's travois. "Look here. Put him on this one he used for his deer. While the rest of you stay here and work on a travois for the animals, Al and I'll get him to the fort soon as we can. Bill, you come with us and bring the dog."

Aiku's fever raged for several days, then just as the infection was under control, he developed pneumonia. He was a fighter even in his unconscious state, and while he tossed he mumbled about surviving in a Georgia prison and from a Sioux capture. He called upon Wah-to-ton to cure him and cursed Mahto.

"I wish he could be conscious long enough to tell me what Indians use for pneumonia," Doctor Blair said. "They have some pretty good remedies."

"I'll sit with him all night, and if he wakens, I'll call you," Al volunteered.

"Good. Now I'll get some much needed rest."

On the day Aiku became conscious for the first time, and looked from eyes that were no longer clouded or glazed, he found himself surrounded by soldiers, and wondered if he had another obstacle to surmount. Soldiers meant trouble in Georgia and on the trek West. What did these know of the migrations?

"Hey he's awake," said one soldier. "Get the doc."

"Well," the military doctor declared, "you made me out a liar, young fellow. I said you'd never make it."

Aiku grinned feebly. "I guess I'm tough."

"Where were you going when they picked you up?"

"Up the Arkansas to Fort Gibson to be with my people— the Cherokees, who were sent from Georgia."

"Oh, that! Infamous! Everyone I ever talked to about that was horrified. For Jackson to introduce the removal bill was bad enough, but for the Congress to vote it through was inexcusable. Then get Georgia's support besides!"

"Yes, we suffered at the hands of the Georgia militia."

"Why did you say Mahto, go away, in your delirium?"

"That's the Sioux name for bear, and I was a captive in their camp for several months. I learned many of their words."

He mumbled, "I thought Mahto would be long gone from his hibernation cave in May, but he must have been ill. When he smelled the deer cooking, he came out. Hungry, of course." Aiku shook his head. "I should have been cautious and investigated its depths. If only I had heeded my dog's warnings when he growled. Sioux Dog—where is he?"

"I'm extremely sorry. Your dog is gone. He developed an infection in that gash in his leg. You can feel very lucky he saved your life. He alerted the soldiers to your plight. Sergeant Jake Bowden and Private Al Spears brought you to the fort. Here they are. They're anxious to talk to you."

He shook hands white man style and said the correct words, "Pleased to meet you. I'm Aiku Fox."

"You speak beautiful English, Aiku."

"Thank you. The Cherokees believe in good education."

How good it was to go to the Cherokee Mission schools long ago. In his waking moments and during dreams, the scenes of school came back to him time after time. How Tsika looked, and how—ah yes, how they loved one another at one time. Tsika. How did she get along on the trip? How were Tani and the boys?

Now he wondered, when could he leave to go back to them?

"Doctor, how soon will I be able to travel?"

"I'll let you know. Rest now. You've talked quite enough for the first time."

Tsika and Sophia frequently visited Fox and Rena. Since the couple had married, they had moved from the temporary dwelling in town to a farm between Park Hill and Honey Creek. On the land the government provided, Atta, Micha, Jake and Okema had built a two-story home and Atta had planted a large vegetable garden and a sizable orchard.

As the two women neared the Fox home, late one morning in middle of June, they marveled at how much the emigrants had done in six short months.

"It seems we're all just about settled and except for the few who sit in their doorways and mope, we are developing into a good productive community."

"When I see all the lovely buildings and the planting, I think of your home in Springplace."

"We've come a long way since then," she laughed. "I often think of our beginnings; how we had hand-woven hemp rugs on the cabin's dirt floor in Hiwassee; a two-story house in Springplace, with all of my mother's Atlanta-purchased furniture and, then of course of Riverview in New Echota, where I wore satins and laces and we'd throw back the oriental rugs for dancing parties, while servants went about with tiny sandwiches and drinks."

"Emulating the whites."

"Exactly. It all seems so far away now, like another world."

"And we are back to stage two except for the Worcesters, the Boudinots and the Ridges, who have large farms and homes here. The Major takes great pride in his orchard and garden, particularly in his apiary. He vows he'll have enough honey to supply all of Honey Hill and Park Creek."

"According to Elias Boudinot, the bottom lands are fertile. We should be able to have good crops." Then she changed the subject. "Sophia, what about Katherine and her Western Cherokee? Do you think it is a marriage of convenience since Roper is still married?"

With raised eyebrows, Sophia asked, "Didn't you know?"

"Know what?"

"Jake is over at Katherine's a lot lately."

"That's interesting. Big Elk told me *he* was courting her."

"And I see Micha and Atta are vying for Kim's attention."

"Sophia, you are a gossip, a matchmaker and a meddlesome so and so, but I love you." She hugged her former teacher.

Sophia smiled and in a voice that purred like a comfortable kitten, she said, "I have one more match to make."

"Who?"

"I can keep some secrets to myself, my dear."

The ladies turned into the path that led to Fox's home.

They're coming, dear," Rena called to Fox. "Now remember, don't say anything about Aiku."

"I'll let you do the talking. Take Sophia to the kitchen for coffee or something and tell her in no uncertain terms that she's not to say a word about him to Tsika."

"Don't worry, dear. I can handle Sophia. I'll do my part. I just hope you can lie."

The door knocker sounded and Rena hurried to let them in. She greeted them with her usual enthusiasm. "We're delighted to see you both. Fox has been anxiously awaiting your visit."

After the initial light chatter, Rena said, "Sophia, keep me company in the kitchen while I fix some sandwiches for lunch. We'll leave Tsika to visit with Fox."

They entered the cheery kitchen and Rena poured coffee.

"Sophia, do you think Atta is in some kind of trouble? He's been going out and coming in at such odd hours."

"No, I haven't heard anything about him, but there is a group of Ross party men who are being maligned by General Abernathy at the fort. The Ridges and Elias Boudinot have told him and the Indian agent William Armstrong that most of those who came in after February are drunkards, murderers and arsonists. I think Atta's been trying to quell such rumors."

"I worry about him. He's such an upright person and so sympathetic. I think he can't bear to have anyone unfairly treated."

"Then you don't need to worry about him. He can cope."

"All right, I won't. Oh, here are Kim and the children. Say hello to Miss Sawyer, Marci."

There was no response, and Kim explained, "She's shy. Wait until you have her in school. There'll be no holding her down."

"Heaven forbid, Kim. I hope I'll be retired by then."

Rena laughed. "Sophia, you've been saying that for years."

She nodded, "Yes, I know. It's hard to admit I should quit."

Kim and the children departed. Now Marci shouted, "Bye, bye."

Rena laughed. "Now she'll talk. That's typical."

After they left, Rena remarked, "Sophia, you have so much interest in town affairs, time won't hang heavy on your hands."

"You mean I don't mind my own business. I don't. For instance, I see something in this room that would give away a secret you're all trying to hide. What's Aiku's tunic doing on that chair in the corner? Better hide it."

"Oh merciful heavens! I told Fox—" she hurried to put the tunic in the closet. "I—"

"Don't worry. I've been with Tsika all morning. I can keep some information to myself."

"Thank you, Sophia. You're a dear. Now, let's join them."

They entered the living room with coffee and corn cakes.

"How nice," said Tsika. "Just like Mama used to make. I so miss both Niamhi and Star, and will always miss them, but I have decided not to miss my children any more." She grinned, "I've asked Dolans to bring Beth and Danny here in July. They're going to New York from Washington to take the Tuscarawas, Coulter, Decatur railroad to Wheeling, then the rest of the way by boat."

"Tsika, that's wonderful," Rena exclaimed, "but—"

"Will they like it? I don't know, but I said only for the two months, July and August. When they're here they can decide."

"After all that glamour of Eastern society in Washington with a grandfather who's a Congressman, and the schools in North Carolina? I wonder," said Rena.

"Now Rena, don't be so pessimistic," Fox scolded.

"I'm just telling her to look at the possibilities so she won't count too much on their staying. Look at the bad side first, then when things turn out for the best, you're happy."

"Don't worry, Rena. She's tough," said Sophia.

"One is, except where one's children are concerned."

"I'm prepared, Rena."

"Now Tsika," asked Fox, "what did you say about trouble with the old Treaty Party members?"

"Just that I heard through Kate there are still many who resent the way we were herded together and sent here, that the Treaty members sided in with Georgia and the Jackson removal policy."

"Is Ross upset?"

"I don't believe so. He grieves for Quati. While I believe he'll remarry someday, he now seems to be just concentrating on getting the children settled, the house furnished and the planting done. He's morose and pensive, not angry or vengeful. I believe he ultimately wants to get the Western Cherokees and the Ridge group to agree with him that there should be one chief and one government for all the people."

"In fact," said Sophia, "the Western chiefs have called a council meeting at Park Hill for June 18th and invited Ross to attend."

"Not the Ridges, Boudinot or Stand Watie?"

"Not that I know of."

"You can bet they'll turn up anyway."

"Come Tsika, we must leave to meet Katherine and go to our meeting for the "Move Forward" group. We're trying to get some of the cabin Cherokees to plant," she explained. "They've been given seeds, young trees, cows, chickens, a plow and horse and sit in their doorways in the sun. We're putting a fire under them."

"Go about your good deeds, ladies. What you're doing is admirable."

"Thank you, and since we're throwing bouquets at one another, I'm pleased you look better today."

"That's because my older son's com—" He stopped just in time and raised his hand to his mouth. Fortunately Tsika didn't see the gesture.

"Good," she said. "Keep that optimistic attitude."

Sophia immediately covered the slip, saying, "Aiku will come, because he has your courage."

"I know he'll survive in the wilderness. He can charm the birds out of the trees and the wild animals from their dens."

Outside Tsika said, "I hope he's right. He seems to be just waiting for Aiku to come. He's getting so weak. What if Aiku doesn't make it?"

"I thought you were optimistic, Tsika."

"I am. I'm just thinking of Fox. It's been seven months since Aiku left us in Kentucky."

"You were saying something about the former Treaty Party members to Fox as I came into the room."

"Just mentioning that the people are still resentful over the forced move. It wasn't right and I am bitter about it."

Sophia sighed. "You don't give up easily, do you, Tsika?"

"No, not when it killed Mama and Niamhi and so many others. Can you believe it, Sophia? Four thousand out of 18,000 people died from illness, starvation or exposure."

"Are you a sympathizer of the Revenge Group?"

"Is there such a group?"

"Yes, and I've had suspicions about some people for a long time."

"But not me. Is my brother Micha involved?"

"I'm certain he's not with the group, but he's been trying to stop the violence that's bound to erupt at the meetings."

"That's a relief. He's been acting so strangely of late."

"Come, Tsika, we must hurry to our meeting or the ladies will leave."

"Katherine will hold them down until we arrive."

Shortly after Tsika returned to her house and began to prepare dinner, there was a knock at the door.

She called to Missy, "Get the door, dear. I'm feeding Leah."

"Oh Mama, come quickly. Look who's here."

Carrying Leah on an apron-covered hip, she looked the picture of domesticity, one he'd dreamed of for months.

And all he could say was, "Hello, Tsika."

The shock of seeing Aiku paralyzed her. She was so overwhelmed, tears stung her eyes. She shook her head. "Is it really you, Aiku? You're *alive.* You're really here?"

"I wants my dinner," Leah shouted. And they all laughed, relieving the tension and bringing them down to earth. She wanted to dance and sing, thank the Great Spirit and hug him all at once, but sedately she asked, "Where have you been?"

"Feed your little charge, Tsika. We'll have plenty of time to talk later. I plan to be here for awhile."

"I'll take care of her, Mama. You go ahead and get dinner."

"Sure, I'll stay." Aiku grinned, "Even if I'm uninvited."

Tsika laughed at the old familiar remark. Aiku looked so at ease and happy. His dark eyes sparkled with humor and tender with love for her.

Tsika thought, he looks as handsome in his white man's suit as an eastern business man, but he doesn't have to emulate Sean to appeal to me. He smiled and the lock of hair that always persisted in dropping down on his forehead still looked to her as endearing as ever.

She said, "You must stay for dinner, Aiku, but you didn't have to dress up for me."

"It was for myself. I had been in Indian rags for so long I was beginning to feel like a renegade Indian," he laughed.

By the time he'd heard about his father's marriage to Rena, Tani's death and his boys' progress, Greta's and Okema's whirlwind romance and wedding, the interesting news about Big Elk, Jake and Katherine and the rivalry for Kim's hand in marriage by Micha and Atta, it was well after nine o'clock.

Then he was ready to tell of his wilderness trip, his time in the Sioux camp and the soldiers at Fort Smith.

At ten o'clock, Micha came in. "You didn't meet Atta to go to the meeting, Aiku."

"I was having a more pleasant time here."

"Micha, you knew he was here and didn't tell me?"

"It was to be a surprise."

"That's an understatement, if I ever heard one. I was overwhelmed."

Tsika decided it was good they'd had their conversation, before Micha got home, for he immediately demanded Aiku's total attention with news of the Western Cherokees, the former Treaty Party and John Ross's proposals.

"Some of the Ross followers act demented. They're determined to seek revenge for the suffering and death of their family members on the trek west and they resent the former Treaty members' efforts to govern them here. Atta and I have been trying to calm them down, but they want action."

"What kind of action?" Now Tsika was interested.

"Nothing specific yet, just talk of getting even. They're talking of waiting until after Ross's meeting at Park Hill with the Western Cherokee chiefs."

"Who's the leader?" asked Aiku. "Could it be Ross?"

"No, if he knew about it he'd quell such talk."

"Maybe that's all it is, just talk, letting off steam like the new railroad. I saw one once; it makes an awful fuss."

"No, Aiku. That threatening talk was serious. They mean business. We have our work cut out for us. Tomorrow morning Atta, you and I will go to each man and preach peace."

"Of course, I'm with you. Have most of the people done well or are all discontented?"

Tsika answered, "Most of them are trying; some are waiting for handouts from the government. Sophia, Katherine and I have been urging the cabin Indians, who sit at their doorways and nap, to get out and plant vegetables. I believe we've made some headway. The government gave them the land and some livestock."

"The ladies are doing a fine job," complimented Micha.

"How did the Western Cherokees accept a deluge of thousands of people last winter?"

"Philosophically," she said. "They're an easy-going lot, content if they plant enough for their family's food and have shelter. They figure why want more. They're not interested in education except for learning the Sequoyah Syllabary. He takes time off for a week or so from his saltworks to teach them, some send their children for a couple of months to the school John Ridge built for Sophia."

"There's a mill for grinding their grain," Micha added, "a blacksmith shop, a post and a little building company."

"That they need. Can you get building supplies there?"

"Some, or order them from the government, which travel slower than a river boat. Ever since John Ross arrived in late February, building had gone ahead fast. Orchards and vegetables have been planted and we think we look very prosperous. John Ross's home and gardens at Park Hill are very beautiful."

"Tell me more about this Western Cherokee council meeting."

"The three western chiefs, John Brown, John Rogers and John Looney have invited Chiefs Ross, John Lowrey and Ed Gunther to submit his resolutions for a governing body to include both the recent arrivals and the residents."

"That sounds like great progress."

"It does. Now we just have to await the outcome and hope the rioters won't spoil it."

"Amen, I must leave for my new home," Aiku yawned.

"Bernie and Nilla have been working on it, Aiku, but it's not quite livable yet," Tsika admitted.

"Then I'll be denied that pleasure and go back to my father's and sleep on the kitchen cot as I did last night."

Tsika gasped, "You were there this noon when Sophia and I visited? That was cruel."

"Perhaps, I decided I'd rather come to see you after a hair

cut and a good long bath."

She laughed good naturedly. "Everyone knew you were in town except me."

"I guess so." His brown eyes twinkled in spite of his professed drowsiness. He reached over and took her hand. "I'll be back tomorrow."

It was almost dawn before he fell asleep. He'd felt dubious about the way she'd react, even outfitted in Atta's good suit, but she was the same girl. Her luminous dark eyes that filled his vision showed her feelings so openly. There was a shy blush when he took her hands. Yes, he still had a chance. He felt a remote sadness for Tani, but for a long time he'd felt deeply for Tsika. She was all warmth, desire and his lost love.

As Tsika braided her long black hair, she thought, I do love him still. Or is it again? Time is a strange thing. Nothing except the rocks and hills and rivers and sky and earth last forever. When she looked at Missy it seemed as though the lovely years between 1824 and 1838 were a pleasant dream; those before, but memories and the ones since Sean was killed, a nightmare. She'd wavered between the nightmares and the reality of the present these days. Niamhi'd said, "The past you cannot change, so forget it, the present you live to the best of your ability and the future will take care of itself." So she would glory in Aiku's attention. She saw love in his eyes.

There was a tap on her door. Missy tiptoed in. "Mama, you look positively luminous. You're in love."

"Go on with you. You're only fourteen, and judging me?"

"You look the way I feel when I think of Owl. That's how I know, and I think it's very wonderful. I approve. You've been so serious lately. I think Papa would approve also when he looks down at us. Also don't feel guilty about Ron. Nilla told me."

Tsika's eyes filled with tears. "You're a very perceptive young lady." She gave Missy a big hug, then looked into her daughter's blue eyes. "Thank you, dear. Now, off to bed."

She'd felt sad and dubious about how Missy would feel if—

she decided to marry Aiku. Now, she knew all was well. A weight was lifted from her shoulders. She whispered, "Sean, I loved you with all my heart, but there comes a time when I must live for the future. Suddenly I feel released to love again."

On June 18th, the meetings at Takattokah began. Aiku and Micha represented the Ross sympathizers. Members of the Treaty Party were present. No one was forbidden to enter, but Micha thought it best if only a few of the Ross people were there, to allow the chiefs to do the negotiating without too much interference.

They reported the events of each day to Fox, Big Elk and Atta. At the end of the fifth day, the men met at the Fox home and Aiku told them of the activity. Aiku said, "The first three days went well. The two groups acted like brothers, seated on the same blankets, before the same campfires. Today, Ross was asked to submit his resolutions. They were as follows:

> *Whereas* the people of the Cherokee Nation East, having been captured and ejected from the land of their fathers by the strong arm of the military power of the United States Government and forced to remove to the west of the river Mississippi, and
>
> *Whereas* previous to the commencement of the emigration, measures were adapted in general council of the whole nation, and on July 31 and August 1, 1838, wherein the sentiments, rights and interests of the Cherokee people were fully expressed and asserted, and
>
> *Whereas* under those proceedings the removal took place and the late emigrants arrived in the country and settled among those of their brethren (who had presently emigrated) and,
>
> *Whereas* the reunion of the people and the adoption of a code of law are essential to the peace of the whole nation; therefore be it
>
> *Resolved* by the committee and the council of the Eastern and the Western Cherokees, each to wit: John Ross, George Lowrey and Edward Gunther on the part of the Eastern Cherokees, and John Brown, John Looney and John Rogers, on the part of the Western Cherokees, are hereby authorized and required to associate with themselves and three other persons to be selected by them from the respected council or committee, and who shall form a select joint committee for the purpose of revising and drafting a code of laws for

the government of the Cherokee Nation, and they be and are hereby required to lay before the general council of the Nation to be held at Takattakah on the *21st* day of *June* 1839, and which, when approved will be immediately submitted to the people for their acceptance.

Be it further *Resolved* that the respective laws and authorities of Eastern and Western Cherokees shall be continued to be exercised and enforced among themselves until repealed and the new government, which may be adopted, shall be organized and take effect.

"That's quite an order," said Fox. "Do you think they'll accept it?"

"We'll know tomorrow. We're doubtful because the Western chiefs were joined by some of the old Treaty Party, who probably were trying to influence them against it."

Fox smiled. "This is aside from the subject, but John must be a popular name among the Western Cherokees."

"Or it may be that anyone named John can be elected chief," Atta remarked.

Fox laughed. "What about our own chief John Ross?"

"We were educated by the missionaries who taught us about John in the Bible. Whites use the name, John, often."

A knock on the door announced an arrival. Roper burst into the room, shouting, "I found out what the western chiefs decided."

"Where *were* you? I didn't think any other Ross supporters were supposed to be there," Aiku accused.

"Hiding behind the chiefs blanket," he laughed. "Don't be so important, Aiku. Don't you want to hear my news?"

"Of course, Rope, shoot."

"The chiefs acted huffy, so I went to the end of the council hall with them and really did hide behind the chief's blanket. There was one fastened to the wall near them. They were so busy arguing after everyone had left, they didn't notice me."

"Go on," said Aiku.

"The Treaty Party members who were there, uninvited, advised Rogers, Brown and Looney to reject Ross's resolutions and wait. Looney and Rogers seemed to go along with Ross, but Brown refused."

"So they weren't to be submitted to the people?"

"No, and since the head chief John Brown, declared that the Eastern Cherokees had come to the West and were welcomed by the Western Cherokees they should accept the western government."

"Then we wait for tomorrow morning," said Aiku.

"Well, I'll be off," said Roper.

Rena came into the room with a tray. "Stay and have some coffee and cakes, Roper."

"Thanks, I know what I'm missing, but I must leave. I told Jack Donner I'd stop to tell him what happened at the meeting."

"He's a very unhappy man," said Micha.

"And for good reason. He's in ill health, lost his wife and children when the Georgians torched his home and arrived here without a cent. He came on the same trip as Arapho, Wheatons, Weatherbys, Two-Gun Aaron and David Joshua. I'm afraid he's aligned himself with the Revenge Party. He has nothing to lose."

"Try to talk him out of that. I'd hate to see him in jail."

On his way out he met Dr. Swan, bound for Tsika's. "Ho Doc, what's new?"

"Nothing. Just the same old illnesses. Now I'm on the way to see little Leah."

"Good luck. I hope she's better today."

The doctor had been at the Wolf's home for only a few minutes when Aiku arrived. Elias was in the process of checking Leah's chest, but his adoring eyes were on Tsika. Neither was aware of Aiku until he was in the room.

Aiku scowled, but rallied to ask, "How's Leah?"

"Hello, Aiku. She's better today. It's a bronchial infection. I'm glad to see you after your prolonged trip. I hear you had many adventures and not all of them pleasant."

"That's right, but I'm here in one piece and busy already. I thought I'd drop in before I go back to Takattakah."

Doctor Swan rose to shake Aiku's hand. "I'm glad you made it back, Aiku. Your father told me of your miserable trek."

"It couldn't compare what some went through."

"We lost many people and I'm not proud of my record."

"No fault of yours, doctor. You had to combat exposure and illness along with inadequate food and medical supplies."

"The loss of Samantha during childbirth was frustrating. Under any other circumstances, she could have been saved."

"I know," said Tsika. "I felt so sorry for Rena, losing her daughter, but she's doing well now."

"Yes, and Fox has helped her, and that in turn has helped him." He smiled. "Also he's better since you're home, Aiku."

Aiku nodded, but was preoccupied. He was polite, but was concerned about the way Dr. Swan was looking at Tsika. Well, she was beautiful and they'd been together on the journey. Perhaps? No, Elias was at least forty years old. She couldn't be in love with him, could she?

"What did you think of the state of unrest when you arrived, Aiku? Dr. Swan asked, rousing Aiku from his turbulent thoughts.

"It's a mess. The Ross faction is still fighting the Ridge group and now the Western Cherokees have added another stumbling block to unity." Suddenly he stood. "Well, goodbye," he said abruptly. "I must be off for the meeting."

Tsika noticed that Aiku acted a bit testy in spite of his kind words. She smiled. He was jealous. How ridiculous! She shrugged. He'd get over it.

Dr. Swan dispensed the medication, saying, "Give Leah one pill every two hours and let me know if her temperature hasn't dropped within a few hours." Then he took her hand, "Tsika, I know now, I don't have a chance of winning you."

Evidently Elias had been very aware of Aiku's reaction. Had she heard right? "What?"

"I had hoped you—we—I see you're in love with Aiku."

She smiled dreamily. "Yes, I am. I don't believe I realized it myself because I've been thinking I should be true to Sean's memory and shouldn't fall in love again."

"You're a beautiful young woman. You can't hide yourself away. You must love and live again. I just wish it was Elias Swan you loved. Goodbye, my dear. I'll not speak of it again."

"I'm truly sorry Elias. I didn't mean to give you any false hopes." She kissed him on the cheek. "You are a wonderful person and I hope you find someone who appreciates you."

On June 21st, when Micha and Aiku returned to Fox's, they regretfully reported that no agreement had been reached.

"What's next?" asked Fox. "Another meeting?"

"That's what Reverend Bushyhead, who arrived recently, and Sequoyah have advised."

"And I've heard Sequoyah is a good mediator," said Fox.

"It's time to leave," Aiku announced.

Atta went with Aiku and Micha to the door and agreed to meet them in the morning.

As they departed the Fox home, Aiku remarked, "I don't like what I heard about James Barnes. He was the one involved in Walker's murder. He's bragging that the same could happen to others in the Treaty Party. While I don't like them or what they stand for, murder is not the answer."

"I don't believe he'd try anything until the results come in concerning the council meeting, Aiku."

"The former Treaty Party want to rule over the Western Cherokees since Chief Jolly died, but the West has elected three new chiefs to keep control."

"That's good, especially since the Ross Cherokees want to unite with the western Cherokees to form a combined government. That should discourage the Ridge Treaty Party group."

"The meetings were supposed to accomplish that, but Roper said someone got to the Western chiefs."

"Someone also got to General Abernathy at the fort with reports that the recent Eastern emigrants were murderers, arsonists and drunkards."

"I believe Ross settled that," said Micha. "He arrested the men bringing in the whiskey, disposed of it and set up guards."

"Going back to James Barnes and the Ross group he represents, they get more aggressive each day and Ross disapproves of it."

"They bear watching. Here we are. Come in for some corn."

"No whiskey thanks, but I'll speak to Tsika for a moment. I want to ask her about Nilla."

The welcome rain that day had turned into a drizzle, but probably would clear by tomorrow and bring good news.

"Shake off the raindrops and come in," Tsika called at the sound of footsteps on the threshold.

"Thank you. It's late, but I want to ask if you can let Nilla come to help us out."

"She probably could come, but not for long. She's getting married."

"To one of those young bucks from Ridge's plantation?"

"No," Tsika laughed. "They have been hounding her, but she's marrying Benji, who's arriving soon."

"Atta, the boys and I aren't very good at running a house, and now that Bernie is at Rena's and Nilla's here—"

"I'll see what I can do. I'll ask both of them to give you some time until Manda arrives. Then you'll have Nilla full time. How's that?"

"The best. I'll see you tomorrow."

Tsika arose at dawn, refreshed and ready for the day. It was clean and bright; rain-washed leaves glistened in the sunlight. It was a good day to gather eggs, tie grapes and pick berries for jam. The sweet fruity aroma was everywhere. She felt only good things could happen on a day like this. Perhaps Aiku would bring good news from the meeting, then would ask her to marry him.

She pumped water from the well, and starting to carry the

buckets to the house, she heard distant shouts, then the galloping of horse's hooves and finally screaming. The commotion
was coming from the west at the location of Boudinot's new
home. She deposited the buckets on the back porch and ran to
the front of the house. Horsemen were riding toward Park
Hill.

Riding by, Roper called to her, "Trouble at Boudinot's.
Some of Ross's men are violent, going against his orders."

There were several 100 acre farms between Honey Creek
on the Arkansas and the Oklahoma border. Park Hill lay to
the west. Aiku's, Okema's, Fox's Roper Chaim's, Wolf's,
Worcester's and Boudinot's were among those properties.

Elias Boudinot and his family were living temporarily at the
Worcester's until their home was completed.

At nine o'clock on June 22nd, Boudinot rode out to see
how his building was progressing. He was stopped by four men
who charged out of the woods and demanded he get them
medicine for their sick family members. Elias was in charge of
dispensing medication from the Worcestor Mission, so he
complied and he turned in that direction on foot. Two of the
men walked with him, the other two followed. Halfway there
one of the men in the rear plunged a knife into his back. Elias
cried out and fell to the ground. Then another hit his head
with a tomahawk splitting his skull. Carpenters working on his
building came running.

"Oh my God, we're too late, Amos. Run for help!' one
man called to a slave in the field. Go to Worcester's."

The murderers fled and the carpenters carried Boudinot to
the grassy field nearby. It was soon red with his life's blood.
The gifted publisher and lecturer, the good husband and father, and the mixed-blood, who thought he was doing the best
for his people, was gone.

Worcester told the slave to warn Stand Watie, close cousin
of Boudinot's that he could be next on their list, then he sat by
the window fearfully awaiting *his* turn.

Simultaneously, John Ridge was dragged from his home by

another incensed group of armed men to the field behind his
home where he was stabbed repeatedly, then thrown into the
air to fall upon the ground with a thud.

His wife, Sally and their children as well as a sister and
brother-in-law helplessly witnessed the horrible performance,
all screaming at the men.

"Stop, stop, oh, God, stop," and all were crying.

Left for dead, the men rode away and the slaves tenderly
carried their master's unconscious body into the house.

Distraught, Sally cried, "Oh my dear, what have they done
to you!" She clasped him to her and he died in her arms.

Major Ridge, the tall greying, dignified leader of the Treaty
Party was in Van Buren that morning visiting the sick slave of
a friend. On his return, his slave riding beside him, he was attacked in a wooded area where the road crossed Little Rock
Creek. Several shots came from the woods and Ridge's body
slumped in the saddle. The horse reared and the Major's body
slid to the ground. His slave raced to report the assassination
and to say he could identify two of the men.

Everyone in Cherokee country felt horror and sadness
concerning the three murders. No one would believe a negro
slave, and so many men were involved it was impossible to find
the perpetrators. The military at the fort tried to find the guilty
ones, but came up empty-handed. Fingers were pointed at
Ross because some of his sympathizers were suspected. Stand
Watie had not been attacked, but he blamed Ross for the
crimes and gathered together a band of men intent upon murdering him.

On June 23rd, although all was still in confusion and people were mourning, there were some who were thinking of the
future. The Ross Party now felt for the first time, there would
be no obstruction for the unification for the Eastern Chero-
kee-Western Cherokee government.

As Tsika awaited Aiku's visit, she started to make jam.

His enthusiastic greeting resounded, "This house smells so

good, I'll have jam and bread for breakfast."

Tsika smiled. "Join the group. Leah is proof that the jam is made. See her face?"

She was demanding, "More, more." Her blue eyes were dancing. Who could deny her?

"I'm so glad she's better."

"So are we, I assure you," said Missy. "It's no fun being up all night—that is, with a sick baby."

"Your blush is very becoming, Missy, and it reminds me of a certain someone else we know," Aiku grinned.

Fussed, Missy said, "Isn't she a darling?"

"Your mother or Leah?"

"Go on with you," said Tsika. "Missy, take Leah for her walk, and I'll finish pouring the jam into jars."

After they left, Tsika and Aiku walked to the grape arbor. Now, she thought, he'll ask me. Now.

"I see you've been busy," he said, when he noticed the neatly tied grape vines.

She nodded. Dressed in her doeskin tunic, beaded headband and moccasins, she felt that would move him.

"Shall we stroll by the river?" he asked.

She smiled. *It would be now.* But at that moment, Micha rode up to them. Hurriedly he dismounted. "Ride with me to Ross's, Aiku. We're tracking Stand Watie and his men. He's threatened to kill Ross and a group has volunteered to surround his property and to protect him."

Aiku ran for his horse, jumped on and they rode away. His expression as he turned to wave to her was one of regret and —what else—desire?

Tsika went back to the grape arbor, sat for twenty minutes thinking, and came to the conclusion that Aiku wasn't ready. Was she reading too much into his casual glances? She'd better stop mooning around and get back to work. Angrily she wiped the tears from her eyes with the back of her hand.

Damn it, she'd *show* him she didn't need him!

She rose, and there he was standing before her, arms outstretched. She went to him to be enfolded.

"I couldn't go, Tsika. I—I wanted to know if we could take up where we left off in 1824."

"No," she shook her head. "I can't do that, Aiku. Those years between 1824 and 1838 were special years. I can't forget them. They belong to Sean and the children."

Aiku frowned. "How can I convince—"

"But now I can leave them and start a future with you."

"Oh thank God, you had me worried." He held her closely as they kissed. "You're truly my woodland princess."

She smiled. "That sounds familiar."

"How will Owl and Missy take this?" he asked.

Tsika laughed. "They'll be delighted."

"Here comes Missy now. Let's tell her."

"You can't tell me something I already know," she grinned.

The three hugged one another. Caught in the middle, Leah screamed, "You're pinching me in this hug."

"For good reason, little one," Tsika exulted. "You're the beginning of our new family."

Characters

WOLF FAMILY

GREAT WOLF, a chief • Full-blooded Cherokee

STAR FLOWER, his wife • Full-blooded Cherokee
  Arapho, first son • Marries Becky McAllister, a white girl
  Juni, second son • Marries Ulah Fox
  Tsika, daughter • Born in 1806, marries Sean Dolan in
    1824; three children
  Micha, third son
  Greta, daughter • Marries Okema, a Shawnee

NIAHMI, Great Wolf's mother • Dies on trek to Oklahoma

FOX FAMILY

WHITE FOX • Full-blooded Cherokee

SWIFT WINGS, first wife • Dies in childbirth; two sons
  Aiku, first son • In love with Tsika
  Atta, second son

LAURA, second wife • Has three daughters; dies
  Uhla • Marries Juni
  Alda • Marries Roper Chaim, friend of Aiku's
  Mary

RENA, third wife

SEAN DOLAN • White lawyer
   Melissa • Born in 1825
   Beth • Born in 1826
   Danny • Born in 1828

AIKU FOX and *TANI* • Marry in 1824; two boys
   Owl • Interested in Melissa
   Rabbit

OTHER CHARACTERS

CHARLES BENTON • White farmer, friend of the
   Cherokees; dies

RENA BENTON • Has two children; later marries White Fox
   Samantha • Dies of childbirth on trek to Oklahoma
   Kim • Marries and has one child

COCHEE • Murderer and member of the Georgia
   harassment group

RON BULLOCK • Manager of Riverview; Tsika's and Sean's
   enemy

DOLANS • Sean's parents; North Carolina Congressman
   and wife

JAKE • Last manager of Riverview

HISTORICAL CHARACTERS

JOHN ROSS • White Bird, one-eighth Cherokee, a beloved
   spokesman for the Cherokee people and their head chief

MAJOR RIDGE • Council member friend of Ross's, later a
   member of the Treaty Party; mixed blood

JOHN RIDGE • The major's son; educated at Cornwall

ELIAS BOUDINOT • Lecturer, publisher, later member of Treaty Party; mixed blood

SAM WORCESTER • Missionary, teacher, translator; white

SOPHIA SAWYER • Peppery, opinionated spinster from Boston; teacher at the Brainard Missionary School

SEQUOYAH • George Guess; devised the Cherokee Syllabary in 1821; mixed blood

DANIEL BUTTRICK • Missionary teacher and friend

ELIZUR BUTLER • Doctor, missionary, teacher

GOVERNOR GILMORE • Aligned with Jackson to move the tribe

PRESIDENT JAMES MONROE and *PRESIDENT ANDREW JACKSON* • Both in favor of moving the Cherokees across the Mississippi